THE
BROKEN
BOW

A TRUSTY DAWSON, DEPUTY U.S. MARSHAL WESTERN

LARRY D. SWEAZY

THE BROKEN BOW

P

PINNACLE BOOKS
Kensington Publishing Corp.
www.kensingtonbooks.com

To Liz and Chris

Acknowledgments

Life goes on while a writer is writing any novel. The period during which this particular novel was written was especially challenging. We were deep in the middle of the COVID-19 pandemic and my wife, Rose, encountered some serious health issues, as well, making writing a little more difficult than usual. We are lucky to have great friends and family, Amber Reynolds, Matthew Clemens, Greg and Marybeth Maack, and Liz and Chris Hatton, along with many others, who helped us, checked on us, and dropped care packages at the door during our darkest times. We really couldn't have made it through that struggle without any of you, and we are eternally grateful for your love and continued support.

Rose continues to recover, and like with every book before this one, she has read, offered the use of her favorite red pen, and her forthright opinion. There were times when I thought that part of our life was over. I'm so glad it's not. She is my rock, and I love her more than I can say.

Thanks, too, to my longtime agent, Cherry Weiner, who was there for us along with our friends and family, and for me for my career every step of the way. Also, thanks to my editor, Gary Goldstein, and all of the staff at Kensington who have participated and helped put the Trusty Dawson books out onto the shelves. And finally, thank you, dear reader, who has ridden along with me on this latest adventure. I especially appreciate the emails I receive from readers who want to know more about Trusty and my westerns. It means a lot to hear from you. Especially on those dark days.

This one is a little more special because of all of you.

Chapter 1

Bismarck, Dakota Territory, December 1888

Trusty Dawson cinched the saddle as tight as he could without causing his durable strawberry roan gelding that he called Horse to object. He wanted to be ready to ride after seeing Marshal Delaney in his office. He'd had enough of the rickety and windblown capital city. Too many people to be concerned with, even this far north. Any happiness in this new place would be found alone on the trail. He hadn't come to terms with his new assignment any more than he'd adjusted to the frigid weather. The Dakota Territory looked and felt like hell had frozen over to him, and his skin and his mind didn't take well to the cold—or being sent somewhere to be kept out of sight. If that was the real reason he'd been sent to Bismarck in the first place.

Once Trusty was finished with the chore of preparing Horse, he remained inches from his ride, head down with the rim of his faded blue Cavalry Stetson campaign hat resting on the saddle. He was listening to the two men in the next stall talk amongst themselves. The pair had got his attention and made him want to know more about them. Caution and suspicion came easy to Trusty these days.

At first glance, the men seemed harmless enough, sewing machine salesmen making their way across the prairie, selling the marvel of the Singer Manufacturing Company to women in need of more time that the modern invention would afford them. It was the taller man of the two that especially bothered Trusty. There was a darkness about the man's choice of dirty gray clothes and his sidearms—a Colt .45 on each hip—that seemed out of place for a salesman. This man's hardened eyes suggested that he was more of a hired gunslinger, a protector, than a man who hocked wares for a living; his eyes were as black as the steel and cast-iron sewing machines that sat in crates loaded on a wagon outside the livery. The shorter of the two men was tending a lone horse, a sway-back black draft mare, with white stockings above her hooves, that Trusty supposed was set to lead them on their sales route.

"We've hit a vein of luck with this weather, Miles, but I fear it's not going to hold. I think we should head south instead of west." Miles was the one that Trusty was concerned about, dark and unamused by the shorter man's expression of fear. Names always helped—if they could be relied on to be true. The man speaking was short and thin in a fit way, not a hungry, sickly way. He was outfitted in natty clothes fresh off of a tailor's needle, a crisp blue linen shirt, clean white collar, and a brown tweed vest. He wore a thick suede overcoat with a rabbit fur collar, clean of any lint or dirt and open, not buttoned down for extreme temperatures. A struggling farmer would see the short man coming from a mile off and know he was a huckster of some kind, though at the moment, the sewing machines appeared to be a legitimate concern, not snake oil or other flights of fancy. A Singer could change the life of any woman who could afford and learn how to operate the mechanical contraption.

Miles shook his head, objected to the change in plans with a grunt, then said, "West is the route we agreed on, Mr. Carmichael, and that's the route we take. I got my reasons to go west, and you've got your prospects along the way. I say we go now like was planned."

Carmichael held fast, planted his feet firmly on the straw-strewn floor, acting as if he were the one in charge. "Do you know where you are?"

Trusty peered over the saddle as he began to fuss with his bedroll, a thick buffalo blanket, tightening it down again, giving himself a reason to stay inside the stall and listen. Horse snorted and kicked his rear leg hard enough to toss a bit of straw into the air. The roan had a restless streak in him that Trusty recognized and appreciated, but he wasn't going to be called off the two men by the beast. Both of the salesmen knew he was there but weren't paying any attention to him that he could tell.

Carmichael and Miles stood opposite each other, both of them looking like mules refusing to budge. The short man made the first move. "It was my friends and colleagues, Holland Freeman and Earl Lancaster who set out on a fine winter day much like this one that brung us here in the first place. They journeyed away from Bismarck enjoying a rare, warm January day with coats unbuttoned, immune to any icy touch, or so they thought, as they made their calls on one soddie to the next. Them and a whole lot of other folks who'd lived on this land for the ages thought they'd been allowed to breathe safely from the wrath of winter who should have knowed better. A whoosh of wind hurried straight down from the north with the force of a white four-footed monster, bringing with it a blizzard that no one was prepared for or had seen the likes of before. Them two fellas, the finest Singer salesmen as was ever seen in this territory, plum froze to death, just like more than two hundred other people, a lot of them children, lost in the blizzard, seekin' their way home with nary a coat or scarf around their necks. Just because the sky is clear right now don't mean it can't change on the turn of a bird's wing. This is the Dakota Territory. You can't trust what you see with your own eyes. I ain't ready to freeze to death, Miles, and I doubt you are neither. South is a safer bet for livin' another day. I'm certain of it."

Miles stiffened, looked down on Carmichael since he towered over him a good five inches, and shook his head again. "Don't matter if we go south or west. A wind like what you say shows up, ain't nobody gonna out run it. We go west, you hear?" It was then that Miles tore his attention away from Carmichael and made eye contact with Trusty. "You got a problem, stranger?" His voice was hard, and his jaw set forward as he took in the man he saw, assured now that he was being listened to.

"Not at all," Trusty said. "Just finishin' up with my horse and I'll be on my way. Your friend there is right, though. From what I've seen around here it's best not to trust the sky overhead. I heard tell of that Children's Blizzard that befell so many families back in January. Winter up this way seems to have an appetite for fools and the unattended."

"You callin' me a fool?"

"I'm not callin' you anything. Just makin' a statement is all."

"If I want to know what you think, I'll ask you."

Trusty forced a smile, patted Horse, and walked to the front of the stall the two men stood in and stopped, blocking any exit from it. Like Miles, he was outfitted to ward off trouble if it came his way. One holster was armed with a Colt .45 with carved ivory grips and a six-inch barrel. His belt was fully complemented with cartridges, and a Bowie knife hung opposite the pistol in a worn black leather sheath. A single gun was enough for him. If it wasn't, then his Winchester '73 was loaded and waiting to be called into action in the scabbard on Horse's right side. "Suit yourself, friend, but I'd heed your partner's warning. Blizzards are as common here as rattlesnakes in Texas."

Miles judged Trusty head to toe like he was an opponent of some kind. He let his gaze stop on the badge that was securely pinned on Trusty's chest. "Never been to Texas so I wouldn't know. Like I said, you need to mind your own business, Deputy. Ain't nothin' that concerns you here. We're honest, hardworkin' men, lookin' for our next sale is all."

"If you say so."

"I do."

"Now, now, Miles," Carmichael said, it ain't prudent to be rude to a Deputy U.S. Marshal. He didn't mean no disrespect, Marshal, we're just startin' out as a team. We've got a lot to learn about each other's ways."

Miles sneered at Carmichael, and for a second Trusty thought the tall man was going to smack his partner in the mouth, but that didn't happen. Miles unclenched his fist and smiled, offering the first bit of charisma since the conversation began.

"You gentlemen have a fine day, and be careful out there," Trusty said, holding Miles's stare, before he set one boot in front of the other and headed for the open door of the livery. "I hope you have good luck on your trip." He didn't wait for a response, just kept on walking until he was outside the wind-blasted gray barn, glad to be free of the tension, the smell of horse shit, and the uncertainty that men wearing guns on their hips always brought him. It was then, just beyond the door, that Trusty glanced over his shoulder and caught sight of Miles's gaze following him outside. Trusty nodded, then headed toward Delaney's office, allowing his hand to dangle as close to his Colt as it needed to be. It was better to be prepared than to be dead.

Marshal Michael Delaney remained sitting behind his simple oak desk when Trusty walked into the office. Delaney wore a perfectly trimmed horseshoe mustache, white as Dakota snow and thick as a drift alongside a barn. He wore gold-rimmed spectacles and was hunched over a stack of papers, mumbling to himself as he ran his long, narrow finger down an open ledger. "I've been expecting you, Sam. Sit down." Delaney didn't look up, didn't dare lose his place among the numbers. The order was firm enough launched as it was by his deep, gravelly voice, to be taken seriously.

Trusty appreciated the fact that Delaney called him by his given name, Sam. Most people called him Trusty whether he liked it or not. He did what he was told and took a seat in a solid chair that fronted the desk. The finish was starting to wear off the seat and arms of the chair, reflecting its time spent in Delaney's presence and maybe the Marshal before him. A curtainless window arched up behind the Marshal's desk with bright, golden light, penetrating the office making the room more hospitable than it would have been any other time of the day; the color tones were usually marked by cold, gray uninspired shadows. This wasn't Trusty's first visit to the Marshal's office, and it wouldn't be the last, but there was an institutional smell to the place and a sense of confinement that didn't appeal to any of his senses. He was always quick to leave after any necessary business had been conducted.

"I'm assuming you've already cashed out?" Delaney said, looking up as he settled back into his red leather chair.

"Yes, sir. I plan on stopping at the bank on my way out of town."

"In a hurry to leave Bismarck?"

"No more than usual. I had enough of city life as a boy."

"Saint Louis, if I recall."

"That'd be correct, sir. My father still owns a blacksmith shop there."

"Explains your build and demeanor a bit, doesn't it?"

Trusty didn't show the flinch on the outside that he felt on the inside. He'd given up the hammer and the anvil, and all of the work that came along with forging iron into something useful a long time ago, but the early days of his life, muscles to some extent, broad shoulders, and workingman hands gave away the experience and the forced occupation of his boyhood. He tried not to think too much about the past, those days when fire and smoke seemed to be his only kin. His father was a cold and distant man with a taste for whiskey and rage, especially after Trusty's mother had died when he was eight years old and left the two of them to survive each other's presence. At least there had been some comfort and predictability to be found in the iron and fire.

"I suppose so," Trusty said, with a glance to the toes of his well-worn boots.

"You get back to Saint Louis often? I'm partial to that city, myself. It's always buzzing with excitement. People coming and going every day."

"I try to avoid going home if I can. Especially now."

Delaney nodded; he understood Trusty's meaning without being explained to. "There's still no word on Marberry's location, if you were wondering. He's disappeared."

"I've been given to understand that Marberry isn't my problem or my assignment."

"You understand correctly." The Marshal drew in a deep breath and leaned forward. His attention to business had changed from numbers to Trusty. "It makes no difference why he has offered a bounty for your life, the fact is he has, and we will find him and hold him to account, while you continue on with your duties here. I will ask you again if you want to ride with another marshal to help look over your shoulder?"

"I prefer to ride alone."

"I figured that's what you would say. Have it your way, then, Dawson. I have a warrant I want you to collect on. I think you're the right man for the job. It will be your sole focus until the paper is served."

"Just one warrant, sir?"

"There'll be plenty of mileage to compensate you for the lack of multiple assignments."

"It's not that, sir. I'm not concerned about the money."

"What then?"

"Coming back to town so soon after I leave."

"This won't be an easy card to pocket if that's what you're thinking. You'll head south, then back north again if what I've been told proves to be true. I think you'll have a challenge with this one. The ride will be long, especially this time of the year. The weather will be as much a test to you as your collar. You won't be returning to Bismarck anytime soon."

"Okay, that suits me. What do you have?" Trusty hoped the warrant would take him farther south than the confines of Delaney's jurisdiction reached. He wanted to look for Theodore Marberry, the man who had put a bounty on his head. If that wasn't enough of a reason, Trusty needed to see the child who was in Marberry's care, at least at the last sighting of her. A baby girl, born to Marberry's daughter, Jessica, a woman Trusty had loved since he was a boy, and who, if it was to be believed, he was the father of. He had to find out. He had to know for sure if the baby was his blood, but he was trapped by the badge, the bounty, and the duty he'd swore to uphold. Being a Deputy U.S. Marshal was all he'd had until the moment he'd encountered the news, still unproven, that he had a daughter out in the world somewhere.

"A Yanktonai Sioux called Charlie Littlefoot," Delaney said. "His birth name was *Hadakah*, if that matters. Translates into something like 'the pitiful last,' which could account for some of his troubles. He is accused of raping a white woman in Fort Yates, a captain's wife who is now with child. Littlefoot escaped the jail and is thought to be heading north into Canada. On the run, dangerous and smart. Just the kind of challenge you like from what I can glean from your records. First thing I need you to do is head to Fort Yates and make sure the story is straight. Then if everything adds up, you'll need to track down Littlefoot."

"Is this captain still on duty?" Trusty was disappointed

at the thought of Canada. It was not the direction that he wanted to go.

"Yes. James Pierpoint Plumright. I would seek him out before speaking with anyone else. You'll need his favor, I would imagine, when it comes to speaking to his wife."

"And if the story doesn't add up?"

"You'll know what to do, but my guess is that it will. At least on the surface of things."

Trusty couldn't hide the frown on his face or the fear that the warrant would take him farther from his personal search for the baby girl. He didn't even know her name, had only seen her briefly disappearing in a crowd. He could be chasing a fairy that really didn't exist. "Canada's a little out of our jurisdiction, isn't it?"

"I've paved the way for you to meet up with a Mountie from Wascana, Henri Bisset, if it comes to that. That is if you have to cross the border. Bisset's a good man. You'll like him. We've had some dealings in our time since I've been here."

Trusty settled back in the chair and tried to think of a way to get out of the assignment. Canada in December was the last place he wanted to be. The only way he could go on his search alone to find the baby girl was to quit the Marshal service, but that wouldn't do. Not now. "Why me, Marshal? You have deputies who have more experience with the Yanktonai and that part of the country than I do. I don't have any knowledge of that corner of the world, especially Canada if I end up there."

"You'll be a fresh set of eyes. Besides that, I'm hoping nobody knows who you are that far north—including Charlie Littlefoot. He's faced trouble before and knows most of my badges by their first names."

"What kind of trouble?"

"Whiskey arrests. The usual. Nothing violent or mixed up with white folk from the fort, which is why I want you to poke around before you try to pick up his trail."

What Delaney said made sense to Trusty, but it still felt like more punishment for his unresolved troubles than a tried-and-true strategy. "And you think I'm the one to find out what smells?"

"I do. Your reputation and service as an Army scout, and then a marshal has been exemplary. I know that you think you were sent here as a punishment for losing Judge Hadesworth, but I have requested your presence in the Territory more than once over the years, and have always been denied," Marshal Delaney said, his eyes warmer and more personal than Trusty had seen them since he had arrived. "I think you're a damned good deputy, Dawson, and I think you have the makings of a Marshal appointment in the future if that's your desire. We all have our failures. It's what you do after that failure that matters. Finding Charlie Littlefoot is your chance to prove yourself all over again. I hope you see that is the case and not the punishment of it."

"I'm beginning to," Trusty said. "I appreciate your confidence in me."

In good weather the ride south to Fort Yates was a two-day journey. Luckily, the temperate day had held without turning into an unexpected blizzard like the natty Singer salesman in the livery had worried about. Not that it wasn't cold beyond Bismarck, out in the open, as Trusty was now. But the ride could have been a lot worse. Less than an inch of snow sat atop the frozen ground, and the wind was mild, a soft push out of the southwest instead of a constant, angry rage out of the north. With the right gear, and layers of clothes underneath his buffalo coat, Trusty had been comfortable as he rode. Glad to be free of Bismarck and all of its confinements, though he was wary as a mouse ducking a hawk's shadow every time he approached any kind of human traffic on the trail—which had been rare.

Starting as late in the day as he had, Trusty didn't get as far as he hoped he would. Darkness forced him off the trail miles from his first stop, a thick spot along the way called Cannonball, a trading post on the Standing Rock Reservation. If Charlie Littlefoot had headed north, it was likely he had gone through there.

Luck had accompanied Trusty on the trip so far, offering him a thin grove of cottonwoods that reached up a slight ravine that protected the campsite from the wind. To make things even easier, Trusty had spied a jackrabbit before the light faded away into the fullness of night, and a quick, accurate shot had allowed for a dinner of roasted meat instead of jerky and beans. Bedding down on frozen ground and staying warm, not freezing your fingers or toes off was a learned skill, and Trusty's time in the Dakota Territory had been short. Still, with his blankets, buffalo coat, and a decent fire, along with the luck of the weather, he had found some comfort. Sleep didn't come straight away. In the darkness of night, protected by the glow of the fire, happily alone out of Bismarck, back on the trail, he could breathe easier. His mind didn't turn toward what lay ahead, but what was behind him. He thought of Jessica Marberry and still had a hard time believing that she was dead. He had known her, loved her since he had seen her for the first time in his father's blacksmith shop. Happiness in the world seemed less possible without Jessica in it. But she had left a baby behind. The baby was the reason for the bounty. He hated living his life like a prey animal, men coming for him for the sport of it, for the money. If he was honest, he also hated riding alone. Somehow, some way he had to find his way to his daughter and claim what was rightfully his.

Trusty finally found sleep, hugging the pile of orange coals as close as he could, dressed in his riding clothes and coat, hunkered down under a buffalo blanket. The night was clear with thousands of silver stars pulsing overhead. The downfall of riding alone was the fear of sleeping too deep, but there had been no sign of riders on the trail for hours, so it had been easy enough to relax, which as it turned out, was a mistake.

The snap of a twig and a snort and rustle from Horse roused Trusty from his slumber straight to his feet, his hand reaching for the ivory grips of his Colt as he stood, half awake, half unsure if he was having a nightmare, or truly standing before a short man with a scattergun aimed straight at his belly. Trusty's finger found the trigger out of habit and preparedness.

"Well, well," Carmichael, the shorter of the two sewing machine salesmen said, smiling with the glint of the moon bouncing off his teeth. "We meet again, Trusty Dawson. Only now I know who you are and what you're worth. A thousand silvers can change a man's life. Especially a man like me who has to travel hundreds of miles in hopes of making a sale, riding with idiots, and freezing my ass off for pennies instead of dollars."

There was no sign of his partner, Miles, the one Trusty

had originally feared. Carmichael didn't demand that Trusty drop his gun or raise his hands in surrender. He didn't say anything else. The huckster just smiled wider and pulled the trigger of the scattergun he had aimed at Trusty's gut. But he was too late. Trusty pulled the trigger of the Colt first. The two explosions of gunfire joined together, rumbling across the frozen prairie like the thunder of a coming storm, followed by the thud of one body hitting the cold, frozen ground.

Chapter 2

Gladdy O'Connor stared up at the ceiling, spent, a slight smile on his gaunt, stubbly face. His stupor was interpreted by a plump girl with pale white skin and swirling red hair as she pulled a plain shift over her head. Her warmth lingered in the shape indented on the feather mattress; a turn and a tuck that had resembled a quick and playful wrestling match, with the girl surrendering just at the right time. The thought, pleasure, and relief lingered until Gladdy stirred from under the blanket, certain that the day was dying, and he had a chore to get on with, a life to live outside of the thin cathouse mattress. Leaving a rented girl was always easy, not that he would know anything about any other kind of girl. Love and the commitment of marriage didn't interest men like Gladdy O'Connor.

"You got time for another?" The girl had said her name was Rona, but Gladdy didn't care what she called herself. It was her sweet Irish lilt and coarse red hair that had caught his attention; he had been swept away to the past, to the green and rolling hills of the home country, innocent and wide-eyed as he was there, when anything was possible.

That and the first girl he'd bedded was a redheaded farm girl just as milky white and plump as this one. Her name had been Fiona, and she had sparked something deep inside Gladdy until she took a tumble in the hay with his best boyhood friend, Tommy Murphy. He hadn't thought about Fiona in years. Maybe it was the melancholy of losing his brother, Haden, and the harsh reality of being truly alone for the first time in his life that had brought on the memory. Or maybe it was just the red hair and warmth of a woman next to him. It had been a long time for that, too.

Gladdy sat up in the bed and felt the first shiver of cold air. There was a comfortable crack under the window set open wide enough for a mouse to squeeze through. The wind from the outside was anxious to invade new places and wash away memories of the old world. "I wish I did have time for ya again, fair Rona, but I best be gettin' on," he said. "It was fun while it lasted."

A smile flittered across the girl's cherub cheeks. "Maybe another day, then, mister. You'd be a right fine regular. You know how to treat a girl. You're not rough and take a minute to nuzzle me neck. I like that."

Gladdy smiled back, allowing the compliment to warm him. It almost washed away the need for a cigarette. Almost. He let the smile fade and set about rolling a fresh stick from his Bugler bag. "I'm not from around here."

Rona turned from the window; her best parts all covered now as her gentle face twisted from pleasure into disappointment. "Ain't nobody from around here. Passin' through just like you, headin' west in search of a far-off dream that likely ends with the tip of an Indian arrow piercin' their heart. I got no desire to see the other side of the Mississippi.

Nothin' there but danger and broken promises, if'n you ask me."

"I gave up dreamin' a long time ago." Gladdy went on with finishing the roll of the cigarette with a gentle lick to the seam to complete the mindless task. He looked the girl in the eye before he set a match to the thin Bugler. Rona was younger than he'd realized, at least ten years his junior, or maybe more. He hadn't cared before. She wasn't human then. Just a vessel to welcome his release and his overwhelming need for a touch of friendliness. He hadn't realized how starved he was for the personal rub and connection with another person until he'd landed square in the middle of St. Louis.

He sucked in the tobacco smoke, harsh, bitter, and comforting, exhaled, then jumped up to put his holey long johns on. Gladdy's mood had shifted from the past to the present. He needed to get out of there before he started liking the girl too much, fell for her in a way that shackled his ankles. This wasn't the time to become a regular or lose his heart to a working girl.

"You don't have to run off." Rona walked toward him with an intentional sashay and a glint in her pale green eyes. *Damn if she wasn't nearly perfect.*

"I do have to run off. I came here with a purpose in mind, a grudge to seal shut and repay a promise I made to my dead brother."

Rona slid up in front of Gladdy, pressing against him as he finished the buttons on his long johns. "Ain't nothin' meaner than a snake set on revenge my old pa used to say. Course he said a lot of things, liquored up as he was most of the time." She started a slow grind, smiling as she went. "You want me to help you with them buttons?"

Gladdy stepped back quick like he'd just took a whiff of

freshly made poison. "I done told you, I can't stay around here. I got things to do. Now, go on, get."

Rona wore disappointment like a pair of comfortable shoes. Her face looked set and dour in mood, plastered with a downward sneer as she backed away, heading for her dress with an outstretched hand and eyes hollow of any hope.

"I don't mean you no harm, girl. It's just that I have to leave." Gladdy was relieved by her surrender and tried to ignore the attraction that had started to grow again south of his belt buckle.

Fully dressed, if it could be called that, since she wore nothing more than a faded yellow housedress over her shift and a pair of shiny black shoes with no soles. Rona made her way to the door, grasped the handle, and stopped with a bit of shy hesitancy; her dourness had melted into sadness. She eyed Gladdy longingly, looking him up and down one last time. He thought the redheaded girl was gonna offer herself to him again. "I hope you don't die a painful death out there, but I know you will. Everyone does," she said without offering so much as a smile. Then she left as quietly as she had come in.

Gladdy had a bad feeling about what was next instead of a good one. He stood frozen, mouth agape, and more than a little unnerved. He knew Rona was right. His life of late had been awash in the spill of blood, and if he took the time to consider how close death had come to kissing him for the final time, he would have hightailed it to the first church and sought redemption and a new path of the righteous kind instead of staying on the killing path. But that wasn't Gladdy O'Connor's way, either. He wasn't a settling man of any kind, and though he had his fears, dying being among them, he wasn't about to give up on setting a wrong to right. He owed Haden that much. And he'd always enjoyed watching things burn that he'd set a match to. Fire made him feel more alive than anything else. Even tuckin' and rollin' with a whore called Rona. The thought of striking a match to flame made him feel a whole lot better, and he knew it was time to go do what had to be done.

Theodore Marberry's house was easy enough to find. The three-story Victorian house sat on a brick street lined with towering oaks, a picture of tranquility and wealth that Gladdy O'Connor could barely comprehend. The trees that had stood in front of the black wrought iron gates for a hundred years looked like durable and imposing soldiers set to guard a pile of gold, offering a bounty of shade in the summer, but only thin, skeletal shadows in the late winter day. Even in the fading gray December evening, the house looked perfect, well-kept, the windows glowing from the inside out, lit by captured fires in the six fire-places and the lamps flickering on tables set near the windows, proud of their glow. Marberry's house was a beacon of warmth and comfort, but more than that, even compared to the stately, but slightly smaller houses around it, some-how dimmer and less in a way Gladdy couldn't put into words, the house looked alive; like it had a heartbeat; like it had eyes watching him from afar; like it had skin and a will of its own. The hair on the back of Gladdy's neck snapped to attention at the thought. He looked all around him to make sure that he was alone, that he hadn't been singled out or spied on by one of Marberry's men com-manded to protect the house—if such a security force ex-isted. It would have been if Gladdy owned a house like the one he stared at in awe. He would have protected it to the death. A sudden sadness washed over him in a wave as he settled down, and exhaled, focusing his sight back on his quarry. It was gonna be a shame to burn such a beautiful house to the ground.

There was no rush to the task. Of all the things that Haden had taught Gladdy, and the lessons were many, patience and information were the most important tools that a man could attain. As a boy, just in his teens, the opportunity of war had served as his primary schooling. Taught by masters in the way of guns, explosives, surveillance, escape tactics, and most important of all, how to kill a man without losing yourself in a pool of grief and regret, Gladdy had quietly excelled in every course. He had stood back, watched and listened, and smiled deftly when most men judged him as a mindless Irish oaf, not worthy of most jobs, overlooked. He had been left behind sometimes or would have been if it had not been for Haden, forever his big brother. Haden had cut a path for him, always included Gladdy in every campaign, no matter the size or importance. It became apparent to him early on that if he was invisible or underestimated, then Gladdy most often found himself in the position of advantage, in a position of power.

He leaned on the base of a hundred-year-old oak tree, molding himself against the hard bark that looked more like stone than wood. The urge to roll and smoke another Bugler was strong, but Gladdy restrained himself, just like he had at taking another turn at Rona. Drawing any attention to himself would only threaten the relinquishment of the grudge. Now that he had arrived, the journey over, with his feet firmly planted on the ground where he would stake his claim honoring Haden's senseless death, he could take his time. There would be no fire set tonight. Maybe not even tomorrow. He was there to learn the ways of the house. And more important, if Theodore Marberry was in residence. It would be foolish to burn down a man's house if that man was not there to see what his own actions had brought. Gladdy wanted more than Marberry to see his house reduced to a pile of cinders. He wanted the man to be inside, fighting for a way out, trapped in the flames, his flesh melting off his bones. The deed would not be complete until the man who had facilitated Haden's death was dead himself after a good dose of suffering. The sight of the house had stirred the truth out of Gladdy: Fire alone would not be enough to heal the hurt he felt for the loss of his brother.

The street in front of Theodore Marberry's house was mostly quiet as the sky sucked the light out of the day. Gladdy felt like he was a world away from the countless cathouses, saloons, and general stores that populated St. Louis. He'd never been in a place as refined, as settled as this was. Any sight of such places had been seen from afar with nary a glance. Men like him only shoveled horse-shit on streets like Marberry's to keep it clean, from fouling the fragrant and rich air.

Gaslights flickered in front of all of the houses on the street. Every window started to glow with warmth and safety. The closeness of fire was a comfort. The wealth that surrounded Gladdy would provide him with more than a spark. Fire would be there for the taking when it was needed.

Gladdy stood as still as he could for an hour as soft, non-threatening gray light wrapped him up in a familiar and welcome blanket of darkness. A few carriages had come and gone. A lone horseman rode a proud black steed that snorted as it passed and looked straight at him, acknowledging his presence. The rider hadn't been paying any mind to his horse, had failed to follow the beast's gaze and alert. *It was a good thing horses couldn't talk,* Gladdy had thought. After the rider had passed, a dog barked in the distance. Then a stooped old woman, thin as a broom handle, tossed something out the kitchen door of the house closest to him; water from a bucket rained down on the cold ground in a loud splash. It would be cold enough to turn to ice overnight. But as he stood in wait doing his best to stay warm, hoping for a sign of Marberry, or life in his house, there had been nothing for Gladdy to see. Not one person had come or gone. Neither had a shadow danced past one of the many brightly lit windows. It seemed like the house was empty even though it was lit up like a party was about to start.

Time slipped away and the darkness grew even darker. Hurricane lamps were extinguished one by one as the tick of the clock continued in all of the houses except Marberry's. It stood aglow against a black, unmoving canvas. There was no wind or threatening weather to contend with. The promise of snow in December had failed to materialize, and Gladdy was happy about that. He fought off the cold by wrapping himself tighter in his duster, but always allowing his gloved hand to be close to the holster that held his Colt. Standing still became difficult, but he was frozen to the tree, intent to learn as much as he could about the house. So far it was nothing. Only puzzling. Why would someone keep the lights on so late into the night?

Boredom set in, and Gladdy's mind started venturing into the future, imagining the grand house as nothing but rubble and ash. Then just as quick, his thoughts would dive into the past. At one point, he thought he could feel Haden's breath on the back of his neck. Sensing the shadow that had always been at his side, Gladdy turned and expected to come face to face with a ghost. *He had hoped he would come face to face with a ghost*. But nothing was there. Just the empty street and more darkness.

When he finally had to pee and his knees and legs began to ache so bad he thought his feet were going to turn into noodles, Gladdy began to make a new set of plans. He wanted to get closer to the house, maybe knock on the kitchen door in the morning and see if there was any work to be had around the place. He had a fair amount of skill as a carpenter, could hammer a nail or whitewash a fence. He was handy enough to fake his way around the place, listen in and learn more, figure out where and when the best place was to strike a match and turn the house into a bonfire.

Satisfied with his plan, Gladdy sighed, gave thought to peeing right then and there, but thought better of it. He didn't want to get caught. There were enough outhouses along the way back to town to sneak into to do his business. That wasn't a worry. He was disappointed though. He had wasted the whole evening standing next to a tree when he could have been exploring the mattress with Rona. With pleasure in his mind again, he gave up the watch and loneliness, and headed back to town.

Gladdy hung his head low, disappointed that he had wasted time, didn't see anything or learn anything new other than it would be hard to sneak up on a place that was so well lit up at night. He wished Haden was with him to help him make sense of everything, tell him what to do next, but he wasn't. Haden was dead and Gladdy was truly alone in the world for the first time in his life. The realization almost made him puke, so he stopped now that he was half a block farther from Marberry's house to have a long-awaited for Bugler. He looked over his shoulder to take in the house one last time only to see the silhouette of two men, tall dark outlines against the glowing house, rushing toward him with rifles in their hands. Nobody needed to tell Gladdy to run. Not even Haden's ghost.

Chapter 3

Kosoma, Indian Territory, May 1888

Judge Gordon Hadesworth stood shoulder to shoulder with Trusty, staring at three men dangling from the gallows. The crowd was starting to move about, leave the spectacle, and get on with their lives. Trusty had escorted the judge more than once out of a town after a trial and a hanging. He was accustomed to his ways. It would be a fine meal, a good night's sleep, then a return to Muskogee the next day. At least that was how it had been in the past. This hanging had left Trusty on edge, and what he really wanted to do was to get out of Kosoma and away from the dead Darby Gang members as quickly as he could.

"Not one of the nicer places I've ever been," Trusty said.

The judge smiled, waiting for Trusty to lead him out of the crowd. "Not from the stories I've heard tell. There's a line of whorehouses and saloons from San Antonio to Abilene that tell of your exploits."

They had stood far enough from the gallows to make a quick escape if the need arose, but there was still a gathering of people milling about around them. More in front than behind. Main Street and arranged safety were just around the corner in an empty bank vault. Trusty didn't like that plan, but he was pretty certain that any threat would come from up close or from the rooftops overlooking the execution square. For now, everything was clear, but that didn't stop him from scanning the crowd like a scout expecting to find an ambush. His army training was never far away.

"You'd think a judge would be immune to embellishments and hearsay," Trusty said.

"We like rumor and gossip as much as any other man. Besides, you've a reputation to uphold. I am only endorsing your résumé and contributing to the myth that you are in the process of building, as well as living vicariously through your exploits. I am a bit jealous." The judge nudged Trusty with his elbow, then offered a smile to prove he was serious.

Trusty's face flushed red. There was no question that he had always liked the company of women and had a taste for good whiskey, but there was more to his past adventures than the judge knew, or that Trusty wanted to share. "We should be getting a move on, Judge. I think it's time to get us out of here. There'll be more time for you to ruminate about my travels when we're on the backs of our horses, bored by the landscape and my presence."

"You're never boring, Trusty. Though I will look forward to that conversation," the judge said with a step forward and the smile still on his face.

Sadly, that conversation never happened.

Dakota Territory, December 1888

Carmichael was dead. A single kill shot to the natty Singer salesman's forehead had ended any thoughts that had been brewing in his greedy little brain; exuberant plans divined from spending the bounty that came with ending Trusty Dawson's life. Weather, quotas, and the need for currency of any kind were no longer a worry for the short man as he lay flat on his back, arms spread out like a child's about to make a snow angel, dead eyes fixed on the sky. Blood pumped from the red circle in the middle of his forehead—a target not taken lightly—and fouled the ground next to his lifeless cheek in a growing pool. The frozen soil did not welcome the sustenance at first, until the warmth of the blood thawed the snow and escaped downward, tainting the dormant grass with an undeniable stain. A cloud of gun smoke drifted away on the breeze; a thin black murmuration of spent death twisting and fading away as quick as it had arrived.

The only worry Trusty had at the moment was where the other salesman was. Miles. A man who had looked like a gunslinger and a threat. Another validation that looks could be deceiving; a killer was never what he seemed to be.

A quick glance around proved there was no sight of Carmichael's partner. No wagon, no sound of horses echoing from nearby, no cock of a gun aimed at Trusty in retaliation, ready to finish what Carmichael had failed at. It was as if the salesman had dropped out of the sky, alone, unbidden, with only the intent to kill instead of selling a sewing machine, leaving his partner behind.

The two had seemed an odd, opposing, unmatched pair from the start. But that was far from the truth. Trusty knew, instinctively at least, that he had been tracked, followed, and hunted down with the sole purpose of being bagged and sold to the one and only high bidder, Theodore Marberry. The shadow of that man followed Trusty everywhere, from the thick of the crowded town to the solace of the windblown prairie. There was not one man who had tried to kill him, there were two or had been two when the journey had started. There seemed to be no escape no matter where he went or what he did. Theodore Marberry was determined to see Trusty dead. The dead man on the ground was proof of that. Sadly, it was the true existence of the baby girl that accompanied Marberry's bounty. A reminder of a life that existed beyond the gun smoke. The baby girl was hope. Marberry was death in a three-piece suit.

Trusty stood firm in his shooting spot, waking fully from the roused sleep—he hadn't even been given the chance to take a much-needed piss—fully expecting to be rushed, to be fired at from a sight unseen, attacked again. A normal man would have sought cover to protect himself, but being a target was becoming such a common occurrence that it was impossible to believe that there was any place to hide, to be safe. Every breath he took could be his last. That was his lot in this life, the life that he had chosen when he had bedded Jessica Marberry and enraged a protective father. Even with that, his life was still better than the familial servitude he had been forced to live and breathe in his own father's blacksmith shop in St. Louis. That was another kind of death that he had avoided, fled, but he still looked over his shoulder to see it chasing after him, too.

The weather, always a concern in the Dakota Territory, was mild and uninterested in brewing up a storm. The wind had taken a respite, had slowed to a crawl, allowing a cocked ear to listen deeply one last time for another man's presence. There was still nothing to hear, not even the echo of gunshots.

Satisfied for the moment that he wasn't a sitting duck, Trusty holstered his weapon, took that piss he'd been deprived of, and made his way over to the dead man. "You were right," he said, as he leaned down to close Carmichael's eyes, "a thousand silvers can change a man's life. You gave up your life without collecting a single coin for your troubles. Seems to me you would have been better off to have stayed the course and made your way door to door across the prairie hawkin' your wares and dreamin' happier dreams than collecting a bounty. You'd still be alive, and I wouldn't have to explain to the Marshal in Bismarck why you've been added to the list of men I've been forced to kill."

Trusty stood up then, shaking his head as he went, not offering a word of religious comfort to the dead man or the world around him. He'd held a grudge against God and the idea of Him ever since this unseen God had seen fit to inflict his mother with consumption, make her suffer endlessly, then take her away from him when he was nothing more than a boy. There was no settling a grudge like that. A man like Carmichael didn't deserve kind words anyway. Greed and desire had forced the salesman to pull a gun without just cause, and he had suffered the consequences of his action just like every thinking man should. It was a bad choice that had brought Carmichael to a quick end, but that didn't make the reality of killing him any easier to Trusty. Killing had never offered pleasantries or currency to Trusty's soul. He didn't keep a proud list of the lives he'd been forced to take, just an official list on his tarnished record. Wearing such a thing on his shoulder was against his grain. The faces of dead men showed up in his dreams sometimes, taunting him, smiling at him, condemning him.

That was enough of a burden to carry. He didn't need to be boastful about the blood he'd spilled. Being a black-smith would have been easier in that regard, though it would have meant living in another cage with its own hauntings and beatings.

Trusty made his way to Horse, who was standing stiff and uneasy, tied to a short picket line in the grove of cotton-woods. The strawberry roan, one ear red, the other white, blustered a little bit at the approach. A flip of the lip that Trusty knew was disregard for being bound too long and not allowed to forage for any green shoots of grass that might have been hidden in the frozen ground. He freed the horse and settled himself in the land of the living now that he was fully awake by pulling his Winchester from the scabbard, making sure that his rifle was ready to be fired. It was his turn to become the hunter instead of the hunted.

Carmichael's tracks were easy enough to follow. Each step the man had taken had been arrogant and heavy from the lack of worry of being caught or seen. The salesman had fully believed that he would kill Trusty; the imprints of the boots, hardly bigger than a child's, did not hesitate as they had hurried toward Trusty's sleeping body. Hunted men are light sleepers. The salesman had failed to calculate that quality into his assassination plan.

The stand of cottonwoods offered little cover for a man hiding amongst them. The sun wasn't hindered from any clouds, was bright as it climbed slowly to its apex, thrust-ing shadows forward with enough definition for the sil-houette of a human or animal to be easily seen. Miles, taller and thinner than Carmichael, might have tried to im-itate a tree if he was there, hugged it close, but he wasn't. The other tell was the sight of a few little birds flittering around at the top of a tree ten yards ahead. They lit on the breeze as Trusty continued his search, ears open as clear as his eyes, on alert for anything out of place.

It didn't take long to find the wagon full of Singer sewing machines. Two tall Springfield mules stood silent, latched to the lead, and bound together by a simple chain; there was no jerk line needed for just the two of them. A black tarp was tightened down over the crates full of wares, covered with a thin sheet of frost, magical machines manufactured to spin dresses, pants, and curtains out of cloth scavenged by the prairie squatters. But it wasn't the unattended wagon that had got Trusty's attention. It was the dead man on the ground next to it. Miles was face down; the back of his head caved in by a heavy object—which poked upward in the ground not far from him. It looked like Carmichael had hurled a sewing machine from atop the wagon down on Miles's unsuspecting head. It had been a quick, silent death. One that wouldn't have woken Trusty from his sleep or stirred Horse or any other animal like a gunshot would have.

There was no mistaking that the man was Miles, the other salesman. He wore two Colt .45's, one on each hip, and was still dressed in the same drab gray clothes that he'd worn in the Bismarck livery. Even with half of his head caved in and covered in blood, Trusty would have recognized the man; he'd committed both faces to memory in reaction to the ill feeling the men had given him.

Trusty stood at the side of the wagon, next to Miles, his Winchester in hand, though more relaxed now, studying the scene. It was easy to imagine Carmichael goading Miles into inspecting something on the ground, maybe the wheel of the wagon since it was close. He would have had one of the crates open, leaving nothing to do but pick up the sewing machine and toss it on Miles's head. If the throw missed, there would be trouble, and Carmichael most likely had a backup plan for that. Maybe he was planning on jumping his partner, wrestling him like he was a bear with a knife in his hand in hopes of slitting his throat. There could be no gunshot, nothing to stir the world or Trusty. It had to be a silent murder. One the greedy little bastard Carmichael had probably been devising since recognizing Trusty.

Trusty felt a moment of guilt as he stood over Miles's lifeless body. It was his actions that had caused the man's death. Had he known at the time—sleeping with the one and only woman he had ever loved, Jessica Marberry—would have such a high tide of ripples in his life and many others, he might have restrained himself. Might have, but probably not. He was sure that the sight of Miles would go on to live in the place where his dreams and nightmares visited him. Another ghostly face added to the roster of the dead that he carried with him everywhere he went.

On the trail to Cannonball, Dakota Territory, December 1888

Trusty rolled the dead men in blankets and loaded them in the back of the wagon. A helping hand would have come in handy, but there was no one but him to shoulder the load. His blacksmith muscles had melted into Deputy U.S. Marshal muscles; leaner, used more for lifting paper warrants than iron rods, but the heavy muscles were there when they were needed. Horse was not interested in Trusty's cleanup task. He stood and watched until it was time to be tied to the rear of the wagon. The beast complained about that, used to being in the lead; a lone rider like Trusty was accustomed to being. In return, Trusty paid the roan no mind, settled into the driver's seat of the wagon and headed south to his original destination, Cannonball. The campsite had been cleared of the notice of death except the blood that had soaked into the land.

As if to test Trusty even more, annoyed clouds started to stack up in the west, huffing and puffing full of another blow of hard, cold winter wind. The sky had transformed from clear to a darkening gray as Trusty had gone about the duty of loading up the two dead salesmen into the wagon. Like Horse's petulant attitude, Trusty hadn't been concerned about a turn in the weather until he had time to consider it sitting alone in the driver's seat. Trusty knew he should have been concerned about the weather. Dakota Decembers had as much empathy as a man set on collecting a bounty on some poor sap's head. A repeat of the Children's Blizzard was always a possibility, death from freezing one drop of blood at a time was more of a promise than an idle threat.

The wind turned sideways, and the temperature dropped a good twenty degrees as the gray clouds raced toward him. There was a familiar hiss in his ears, one that he had not known during his time in Indian Territory but had become well acquainted with upon his arrival in the purgatory of Bismarck. The constant wind that swept across the top of the open plains was no friend to any man or beast. Lack of trees, places to hide were as much an advantage as a disadvantage; Trusty could see and be seen from miles around. The crack of a rifle had the deadly ability to settle a score and close the gap in the blink of an eye. There was little or no thunder to consider in December, so if such a sound did erupt over the rage of the wind, all Trusty could do was hope that the unknown and unseen shooter failed in his attempt. He was tiring of having to worry if every breath he took was his last. Even the cargo in the bed of the wagon suggested that his concern would not end anytime soon, but he was determined to find a way to free himself of dying every two seconds.

He drove at a steady pace, pelted by unforgiving ice crystals, sharp and cold to his face, while the rest of him was protected as much as possible by his thick buffalo coat. The long robe of a thing still held the distant smell of life and sweat, especially when it was wet. His fingers tingled in the mittens, but he could still hold the reins tight enough to encourage the stoic Springfield mules that pulled him to Cannonball with enough enthusiasm for them not to rebel against an unknown driver. His toes tingled just the same as his fingers, and he feared frostbite was setting in, offering a nightmare of losing an appendage or something to the cold as much as he did dying. There was also the wonder and concern about the cold entering into his body, invading it, freezing him slowly to death, coursing through his body in search of his heart and turning it into a solid chunk of ice. There were advantages to a cold heart in a metaphorical sense, but that thought was better left to poets. At the moment, Trusty was focused on staying alive and nothing more.

Cannonball, Dakota Territory, December 1888

The Catholic mission stood as the tallest building in Cannonball. A steeple topped with a cross stood three stories tall, announcing the dominating Christian presence on the Standing Rock Reservation from a mile or more away. The practice of Indian religion, if it could have been called that, had been outlawed a few years before, and the missionaries had been encouraged to take up residence and spread their gospel without restraint; eternal life offered with a sip of wine instead of a bullet-proof shirt. Trusty, who had never been to Cannonball, was beset by the sight of the church. He'd ended up in the Dakota Territory because of a priest, his family, and their betrayals. Along with his grudge against the Almighty for taking his mother away, Trusty had a more recent wound to consider, one that was open, raw, and still bleeding if he was honest with himself when the thought of Michael Darby wandered through his mind or was put there by the sight and assault of a cross. The ex-priest had betrayed him, then died for him when they'd reigned in Judge Hadesworth's killer. He stiffened with distrust as he drove the wagon into Cannonball, unsure of where to go first, but aching to leave the place before he arrived.

The spot in the road was not a town like Trusty was accustomed to with homes, squalid and small, propping up a main street of false-fronted businesses. There were no dance halls, banks, or liveries to be seen, just the church standing dominant over a few smaller buildings; a trading post; a barn; a tool shed; an outhouse—shadowing them all with its presence. Residency was not the point of Cannonball. It was only concerned with salvation and commerce. And considering the weather, both looked to be in short supply. The place looked vacant. There were no people milling around, no horses tied to hitching posts in wait. Not even a stray dog was brave enough to conquer the wind and falling ice to announce his arrival. Trusty had to wonder if everyone had frozen to death regardless of the shelter they had built for themselves.

The mules were glad to face the small building that served as the trading post. A sign declaring the business swung back and forth, hung on a rusted wire, squeaking like a pond of frogs in spring announcing the arrival of a new season. Ice crusted the mules' foreheads, had gathered an inch deep between their ears. Horse was in no better shape with his strawberry coat layering to a distinct white as the ice turned to snow. The Dakota precipitation shot sideways one second, then dropped straight down the next, creating squalls in the sky that settled to the ground impatiently looking for a place to live the rest of their lives; there was no threat of the sun melting the ice and snow away anytime soon. Trusty worried his cold knees would shatter like glass when he jumped down from the wagon. Without any more direct regard for the three beasts who had accompanied him to Cannonball, he hurried inside seeking shelter for them all.

The inside of the trading post was well-lit and immediately warm. A fire worthy of melting iron roared in a fireplace that took up half the room. Trusty had half-expected to walk into a frozen tomb.

"Well, there you are Trusty Dawson," a white man with wiry long gray hair and plump cheeks flush with warmth said as he walked toward Trusty.

Trusty had been expecting a Sioux working as a trader. The man was short, his face covered with as much hair as on his head, with the rest of him covered in buckskin. Rabbit fur was sewn to his collar and sleeve and pant cuffs, a common fur found in Cannonball. Mukluks reached up to the trader's knees, tied tight with sinew laces. He was not familiar at all, but he knew who Trusty was. Recognition in the Indian Territory had been common. He had a reputation there, something he thought, and in a less than kind way had hoped that he had left behind. The day had proved that hope wrong from the start.

There was no one else in the room, which was the whole of the building from what Trusty could tell. The man must have slept somewhere else. "Do I know you?" He had stopped to get his bearings, surrounded, surprisingly, by a complement of well-stocked wares to serve the needs of travelers and residents alike.

The man headed straight toward Trusty, leading with a pot belly that jutted a respectable distance over his belt; the prairie obviously hadn't starved this man like it had so many before him. He wore no visible firearms but did nothing to conceal a thirteen-inch Bowie knife sheathed on his right hip. Fringe swished from the sheath as he walked. "I don't suppose you do. I'm Brazos Joe Moeker, entrepreneur and owner of this here establishment." He extended his stubby hand for a shake.

Trusty took the man's hand out of habit, surprised by the warmth and strength of it, and returned the handshake with suspicion. "How do you know me?"

Brazos Joe stood back and eyed Trusty warily, still hunkered under in his buffalo coat and outside garb, minus the mittens. "You think a Deputy U.S. Marshal carting two dead bodies and a load of sewing machines don't get no attention in these parts? Word of your arrival preceded your shadow by hours. Indians still be Indians, you know."

Trusty didn't say anything. There had been no sign of any living being from the time he had encountered Carmichael and Miles, but that didn't mean there weren't eyes on him. He was in Indian country, on a reservation, their land, not his. A shiver ran up his spine. Luck had served up a short meal to him from the looks of things at the moment. Maybe the Sioux didn't know about the bounty on his head. "I suppose I was just concerned about stayin' on the trail."

"A logical thing to do, but you had to know that we all knew you was coming this way before you left Bismarck, don't ya?"

Trusty stood firm, suddenly aware of how small the room he stood in was; it was packed with supplies of every kind; pots and pans; fabrics; even candy of a sort; you name it; from the floor to the ceiling. Warmth from the inside out attacked him all at once, and his coat felt like it was made of iron instead of buffalo hide and fur. Sweat poured out of his skin, and his lungs felt wet and heavy. "I'm lookin' for a man," he said.

Brazos Joe took a deep nod, looked to the floor, then backed his way to the counter from where he had come from in the first place. "Charlie Littlefoot. I know. We know. I suspect he knows, too, if he's still alive that you're on the trail after him."

"You don't know for sure if he's alive?"

"How could I?"

"Seems to me you know a lot of things."

"I 'spect I do, but that don't mean you should assume or expect me to know anything about Charlie Littlefoot's location or state of mind."

"So, he hasn't been through here?"

"I didn't say that." Brazos Joe planted himself behind the counter, his face lit by a lamp that burned on a crowded shelf behind him. A store of hairpins, some fancy and carved, others plain and straight, lined the shelf.

"When was he here?" There was no race in Trusty's heartbeat, no excitement at closing in on his quarry. Trusty had been wearing a badge long enough to know that a man like Charlie Littlefoot wasn't going to be easily caught. All he wanted to do was take off his damn coat. But he didn't move. Brazos Joe had just invited him to a dance.

"Ain't nothing around here that comes free," the trader said.

"I don't suppose it does. I got a wagon load of sewing machines, and some weapons that belong to two dead men. I figure that's a good place to start if a bargain is your aim."

"I hear you got more than that to offer a man in need of a silver or two," Brazos Joe said, reaching slowly under the counter with his right hand.

Before the trader could look Trusty in the eye and square his shoulders, Trusty had already torn into his coat and pulled his Colt from the holster. There was no escaping Theodore Marberry. Not even in Cannonball where the dead were equal to the living.

Chapter 4

"You move another inch and I'll blow your head off," Trusty said. He wasn't going to honor Brazos Joe with the pleasure of his good nature or the assumption that he was mistaking his intentions. The ivory handled 1880 Colt Single-Action was firm in his grip, and the six-inch barrel was steady in its aim and target. He'd kill two men in one day if he had to. "I'm in a foul mood, and I ain't ashamed to admit it. I got no patience for bounty seekers, mister."

"Now, now, friend, put the damn gun down. I don't mean you no harm," Brazos Joe said with a smile that held no menace. He looked like a mouse with a cockeyed grin.

"Raise your hands so I can see them in the light, then we'll finish this discussion."

"Sure, marshal. I can do that." Brazos Joe smiled and did as he was told, offering up a bottle of whiskey to the world and Trusty instead of a weapon intended to kill a man straight away. The amber liquid glowed from the flame that danced behind it, the bottle warm and half full of good times and comradery instead of a deadly threat.

Trusty sighed but didn't lower his Colt. "I ain't up to no tomfoolery at the moment, old man. I done told you that."

"If it was seeing you dead that I was interested in we wouldn't be standing here considering a drink of whiskey. I knowed you was coming, remember? If I was a bounty hunter, I'd be halfway to Saint Louis by now with you wrapped up like them two salesmen ready to collect on my good fortune. That bounty ain't worth the trouble it brings with it if you ask me, and I know you didn't, but I'm telling you so. I'm not risking the life I have here to spill the blood of a man I know nothing about." Brazos Joe continued to wear a jovial face as he sat the whiskey bottle down on the counter. Then he reached down and produced a pair of sparkling clean glasses without any fear at all that Trusty was going to shoot him. "You can put your gun away, marshal. You're as safe here as you are among your own."

Trusty didn't move a hair. He stood with the barrel still zeroed in on Brazos Joe's head. "I don't have a single reason to trust you."

"Looks to me like you don't have a reason to trust anyone except the man who gave you the job to go out in the world to track down Charlie Littlefoot. Good luck with that by the way. Charlie ain't gonna get caught unless he wants to or the fates offer up a chance and a dose of good fortune to you. From what I can see, luck don't favor you one bit, so that's not likely to happen." The trader matched Trusty's recent sigh, then went about pouring two whiskeys.

"You don't think that's brave, sharing a whiskey with a lawman on an Indian reservation?" The buffalo coat felt heavier than it had before; iron turned to lead by the alchemy of sweat. Perspiration ran down Trusty's forehead like he had just finished a foot race in summer. A healthy fire blazed in a wood stove to the right of the counter. Winter and its icy touch had retreated from memory but stood just outside the door with an axe made of ice and a kiss of wind so cold it could shatter a man's eyeballs.

Brazos Joe finished the pour and put the whiskey bottle back where it had come from. "You got bigger problems than the small offense you see before you, Dawson. Hospitality is hard to come by out here in this world, and if I'm guessing right about now, your toes and other parts of your body are still numbed to the bone. You're free to arrest the first kind man you've seen today, Marshal Dawson, but I don't think you will." He picked up a glass and offered it to Trusty.

"I'm warm enough to tell you the truth," Trusty said.

"Then put your gun away, take your coat off, and stay awhile," Brazos Joe said. "Don't be a fool and mistake this for anything other than what you see."

"How do I know that you're tellin' me the truth?"

"How can you not know?"

Trusty looked over his shoulder to the door he had walked in. Outside the wind still raged and the snow blew sideways, pelting the wood frame, trying to get inside. It was a white nightmare wrapped in ice with the tough grasp of frostbite hankering to nip away at any flesh it could touch. The trader was right. Trusty couldn't feel his toes. "I need to see to my horse and those two mules the Singer men drove."

Brazos Joe shook his head. "They done been tended to, just like I'm trying to do with you. Don't you worry none about your mount or them mules. They're all safe and warm as they can be in the barn by now. I got an Indian man that tends to the animals like they're his own."

Trusty didn't react, didn't move for another long second. He stood there silent and stiff as a lodgepole listening to the wind howl and the fire crackle, a mix of hot and cold, a man-made contradiction that offered him sanctuary or freezing to death. It didn't take much more thinking to decide where he wanted to be. The only other option he could choose was to walk out the door and trudge over to the church and beg the padre for a bit of warmth and comfort. That wasn't going to happen. At least not straight away. Trusty would take his chances with the trader.

He climbed out from under the buffalo coat and hung it on a peg on the wall. He was still dressed in layers, two pair of long-johns and his traveling clothes. Relieved of the weight, he was cooler, but not cold. He wiped the sweat away from his forehead and kept his hat on.

Brazos Joe stood waiting at the counter for Trusty to join him. Both glasses of whiskey were untouched, waiting according to manners for the guest to take the first drink. Trusty wasn't opposed to a taste of whiskey like some men were. He liked the burn of it on the back of his throat. Especially in Dakota Territory, though there had been few opportunities to let go and unwind since his transfer. His mind and heart were pulled tighter than a cat-gut string on a guitar, fearing the bounty and trying to figure out how to track the baby girl and still keep his badge. That didn't mean this was a moment to relax. It wasn't. He still wasn't sure what he thought about Brazos Joe.

"I see you've come to your senses." Brazos Joe smiled, showing a fair number of teeth in good shape, a rarity in older men this far north.

"Lack of opportunity forces a man to consider what's best in a hurry," Trusty said.

"Truer words have never been spoken. Help yourself." Brazos Joe nodded at the glasses.

"I appreciate it, but you first."

A smirk replaced Brazos Joe's smile. "You think I would poison you instead of shooting you?"

"Bounties don't come with instructions on how a man should die. Dead is dead. I've learned quick to be cautious if I'm gonna stay alive."

"You like living like a rabbit?"

"Not necessarily, but I like livin'. Mark my word, this threat ain't gonna last forever. I gotta outlive it is what I got to do. First whiskey is on you."

The expression on Brazos Joe's face was void of any emotion or feeling, blank as an undertaker attending a funeral. He took a quick slug of whiskey without breaking eye contact with Trusty. "Poison is hard to come by in these parts," he said as he set the empty glass on the counter.

"Seems to me you're a resourceful man, Mister Moeker." Trusty looked around the trading post again, making his point, noting the push of powdery snow making its way under the door—only to meet a quick end as it encountered the warmth and appetite of the stove. Even the rafters were hung with gear; reins, shovels hung on nails, more pots and pans. There wasn't a cobweb in sight. The place was as clean as it could be. "You got help here, too?" Trusty said turning his attention back to the man.

"Of course, I got help. You think an old man like me can keep up with a place like this. You went and got all formal on me, Marshal, callin' me mister. Offending you is not what I mean to do."

"Just tryin' to figure out where I'm standin' is all." Trusty grabbed the whiskey and downed it easily, not reacting to the burn. He'd had a better drink, but it added an unexpected flavor to the day. A welcome warmth stayed on his tongue and in his throat. "Now why don't you tell me how you know so much about my business."

Brazos Joe reached down and pulled the whiskey bottle back into view. Trusty put his hand up. "One's enough," he said.

"Suit yourself." The bottle disappeared back to where it had come from. "The answer to your question is simple if you think about it. All a man like me has to do is stand here and wait for the door to open and the news of the territory walks in with whoever comes with it. Don't matter if it's a Sioux or a white man, but I hear mostly Sioux, though the church over yonder brings in its own traffic, missionaries passing through on to a greater cause from out east and elsewhere. I see more and more folk every day, even here on the reservation. As far as I'm concerned, Cannonball is the center of the world, and all I have to do to know what's going on in it is stand here and listen to the words, to the silence, to the wind, and I know what's going on from here to Boston. I know what to fear and what to take advantage of if I need to. I have no motivation to lie to you, Deputy. I don't interfere with the law. Never have. I'm an honest businessman just trying to make a living."

If a man has to tell you he's honest, he's usually not, Trusty thought, but didn't say. "Makes sense, I suppose. Indian eyes and ears told you I was comin' with a wagonload of trouble."

"And the wind before that."

"Whisperin' about Charlie Littlefoot?"

"Once I heard he was on the run, I knew it was only a matter of time before a marshal came pokin' around, asking questions, thinking a white man on an Indian reservation knows more than the normal person would."

"Do you?"

"You know I ain't any more accepted in a place like this than you are. Can't say I ever expected to be nor wanted to be if I'm honest."

"That explains one thing, but not the other."

"The bounty." Brazos nodded as he said it. "Two hired men came in here a week ago asking if you'd been through in the last few months. They came up from the south, had Indian Territory dust on their horses' hooves. Both about equal height wearing a full complement of sidearms and worn trail clothes like you might expect. Long hair, bad teeth, eyes that had seen the war and liked what they saw. I picked up their names, if you care to know. Not that I trust the names to be true, but that's up to you to decide or find out. They didn't buy anything, either. Asked their questions about you and rode on once they were satisfied that I wasn't hiding you or lying to them. There's more than them two bumbling Singer salesmen out here looking for you, Trusty Dawson. You had some luck today you didn't know you had. Them two were preoccupied elsewhere—and no, I don't know where that somewhere else is, or where they went. All I know is, you need to ride like you're being hunted. You and Charlie Littlefoot are one in the same. Marked men. But I don't need to tell you that. I could tell you knew that death was stalking you when you walked in the door."

"You're not tellin' me nothin' I don't already know, mister," Trusty said, hankering for another swig of whiskey, even though he knew the best thing he could do was keep a clear and open mind. Last thing he needed to do was lose his wits at the end of a long day. "Except them names. That would be real helpful and much appreciated."

"What's it worth to you?"

"I done told you, I got a load of Singers outside your door."

"That ain't what I'm after."

"What's your price then?"

"Somethin' simple."

"Name it."

"When you come along Charlie Littlefoot, ask questions then shoot if you have to."

"Why would I do that?"

Brazos Joe smirked a bit, then reached down and pulled out the whiskey bottle and poured a shot in both glasses like he was about to seal a deal. "Because I figure Charlie's got a story, and if he was a white man, he'd have a chance to tell it."

"And because he's an Indian, he won't?"

"That's about right."

Trusty drew in a deep breath. It seemed like a fair trade, but one that wasn't likely to be a concern. "I can agree to that."

"Good, I hope I can rely on you to keep your word."

"You got a special place for Charlie?"

"I told you, I never met him. I just got a special place for what's right. Them two who aim to kill you call themselves Glo Timmons and Red Jack Lewis. Like I said, it's up to you to decide if that's their real names or not. That's all I can give you."

"Never heard of them," Trusty said. "But I appreciate the news. It might just help me to stay alive."

"I hope so," Brazos Joe said. "I sure hope so."

St. Louis, Missouri, July 1870

Twelve-year-old Samuel Dawson—he hadn't earned the moniker of Trusty yet—stood over the anvil beating a rod into a hook. His fortieth of the day. As part of the process of bending the iron to his will, Sam had to reheat the rod until it glowed red hot. A brick forge burned off to his right, the flames dancing on old wood, carnivorous as a dog eating a steak for the first time. He had to rebuild the fire every morning and keep it alive during the day, one of his many jobs in the shop. There was a well-worn path between his bench and the forge; the fire reached out for him every time he approached it.

The quench sat to his left, a small barrel filled with water at room temperature that tempered steel, set to harden before it was brushed and shined—if that was called for. He wore bib overalls without a shirt and hard toed boots that were black from the smoke and dirt in the shop. His arm muscles, as big as most boys four or five years older than him, glistened with sweat and were streaked black from soot. Each pound on the rod brought the metal closer to being what it was created for. His head had long since stopped hurting from the ping and sharp scream of the hammer's punch against the anvil, but his ears rang, and with the rage of the fire in the forge and his father banging around on one project or the other, he couldn't hear a thing beyond the shop's doors. Both doors stood open at the front and back to allow a draft to circulate fresh air through the large open room. Before it had been a blacksmith's shop, the building had been a livery. The stalls had been torn down long ago. The open doors did little to pacify the heat that had built overhead and come to stay in Sam's world, especially in the middle of a hot and humid summer. The sun was beating down on the metal roof of the place, making it even more of an oven than it already was; the only light inside came from the outside—and the fires that burned day and night. Some days, Sam thought he would melt, delirious from the heat, but fear of his father and the outcome of such a fall prevented him from giving in, giving up, even though he wanted to. Most days he felt half-drunk, his turn to the forge a stagger more than a rush.

Markum Dawson was a bigger version of his only son. Thick hair as black as coal, and his eyes, it seemed, had been transformed from blue by the ever-present soot—a magic that Sam was convinced came from his father's guts instead of his actions—were black, too. He believed his father had no heart and lead ran in his veins instead of blood. A sheen of sweat sat on Markum's body like an extra layer of skin. His father's father had been a blacksmith, too. But unlike Sam, who was an only child, due to his deceased mother's fragile health, Markum had nine brothers and three sisters. There had been plenty of hands to help carry the load—or a place to hide behind when rage and anger ruled the day. Sam had no brothers to hide behind. It was just him and Markum now, five years after his mother's death. They only spoke to each other when something needed to be said. They ate in silence, sat in silence, always cautious, giving each other leeway, keeping a safe distance between them, for fear of getting the sickness one or the other had.

"You need to finish up and load the last of those posts onto the wagon. We have a delivery to make after the day is done here," Markum yelled from ten feet away. He wore bibs like Sam, shirtless, only with a thick leather apron covering the front of him. He was puddling pig iron, creating a wrought iron gate. Sparks flew. Molten metal ran like a snake looking to add a bite to Markum's scarred forearms.

Sam heard most of what his father said but didn't acknowledge him. He kept hammering away at the rod. The last thing he wanted to do was make a delivery. Deliveries meant more beast of burden work. Carry this, put it there, sit down and don't say a word. The only joy was getting out of the shop, but that didn't carry much weight these days. The misery of summer made the heat impossible to escape.

"Did you hear me, boy?"

"Yes, Pa," Sam finally said with an angry swing of the hammer. Iron against iron. A crescendo that was lost among too many other crescendos to matter.

From there, the hours ticked away and as the sun dipped toward the horizon, Sam was convinced that it had fallen on top of the roof. He felt baked from the inside out. The reprieve came when the wrought iron fence sections had been loaded onto the wagon, and they were off, out in the street, the wind, thankfully, in his face. It wasn't cooler but it was a wash of some kind. By the time they got to where they were going, Sam's hair and skin were dry.

They pulled up in front of a two-story house, two blocks off the railroad tracks and a block from the shores of the river; Big Muddy; the Mighty Mississippi; Old Blue; The Gathering of Waters, depending on who was calling it one name or the other. It was easy to see that the house had taken on water from the springtime floods. A harsh brown line cut the clapboard siding from light to dark about four feet off the ground. There was a smell of rot in the air, dead fish, added with something cooking like rice and beans simmering on a stove. Smoke billowed out of the house's rickety brick fireplace. Most of the other

houses on the street were vacant, the tenants or occupants
run off by the threat of flooding, or by the anger of the
place; no one that Sam had seen looked happy or nice.
Ragged men scowled at the sight of them as they passed,
angry about the holes in their shoes, about having to walk
while Sam and his father rode. Wolf-sized dogs snarled
and chased the wagon, biting at the wheels. Children, bare-
foot and dirty from head to toe, looked away. So did the
women, of which there were few; most were skinny and
frail, tired from bringing one baby after the other into the
world. His father had nothing for any of them, even though
the price of the fence would have fed their families for a
month.

Sam was surprised by the stop. It wasn't the kind of
place they usually delivered to. Their customers at the
blacksmith shop ranged between the common man, horse
riders, farriers, mercantile men in need of iron skillets to
sell, all the way up to the richest of rich folks, who needed
their wagons and coaches repaired, like the high-society
Marberrys. Sam had befriended a girl named Jessica Marberry that he dreamed of at night and longed to see in the
day. She was a blond-haired angel who walked into the
pit of hell of the shop, without one complaint, always as
happy to see him as he was to see her. Even the fire re-
coiled in her presence, in awe of her willingness to stand
alongside it.

"Unload those sections and stack 'em by the kitchen
door," Markum said to Sam, nodding to the door next to
the chimney. Then his father reached under the seat of the
wagon and pulled out a wood box and jumped down without offering any explanation about the box, or what was
inside it. Sam had never seen it before. The finish on the box
was delicate and new, shining like a rare gem in the hot

light. The sky was white, like the sun had burned all of the color out of it.

Sam sighed and did as he was told, eyeing the box and his father, who walked up to the door and knocked on it. A tall woman with long brunette hair flowing over her shoulders came to the door, then stepped out of it into the pale evening. Her skin sparkled and her eyes, blue and soft, seemed to welcome his father like he was an old friend. She was dressed in a long linen gown of some kind, open in the front down to her navel in an embarrassing way, that offered a wide view to the deep cleavage of her ample breasts. Sam couldn't look away, especially when his father smiled at the woman, and opened the box to show her the contents, four silver knives that gleamed in the sun as bright as a star at night. The woman smiled, then looked over to Sam who was dumbfounded in a way he didn't understand. He lived in a man's world and knew little of women other than they were weak and died.

"Who is that?" Sam heard the woman say.

"My boy." Markum turned and glared at Sam, who had not unloaded one section of fence.

Sam stood unmoved by the glare.

"He's a miniature version of you," the woman said with a laugh. She looked younger than his father, maybe thirty, if that, and had an accent that sounded foreign to Sam, but he didn't know what it was. There were a lot of accents in St. Louis. "Come here, you, let me see you up close."

Sam expected his father to call him off, order him to unload the wagon, but he did nothing but stand there with the open box of knives in his hand. The woman had lost interest in the box as Sam walked toward her. He took in the sight of her, sure that he had never seen a beautiful woman like her before. "Hello," he said with a dry mouth, coming to a stop next to Markum.

The woman put out her hand, and Sam could only stare at her long, elegant fingers. Three of them were adorned with rings carrying stones he didn't know the names of— but they looked expensive and rare, like her. He would learn that the stones were opal, diamond, and pearl, and her accent was French, by way of New Orleans. But not that day. He didn't know what to do. *Shake it like a man's hand?*

"Kiss it," his father said.

And then Sam understood, so he did what he was told, kissed the top of her hand with a linger, his lips on the skin of a woman for the first time since his mother had died. She smelled of sweet spring flowers and tasted like rich cream, fresh from the udder. His mother had smelled of sickness and death; he thought every woman smelled like her. He was dazzled by this woman.

"I am Katherine Duchamp. I am pleased to meet you, son of Markum Dawson."

"I'm Sam," he said, looking past Katherine Duchamp, into the kitchen where he saw a Negro woman standing at the stove stirring a pot, and three women, younger than Katherine, sitting at a table, dressed scantily, too, eating together like a family.

It was Sam's first time to visit Katherine Duchamp's house of ill repute, but it wasn't the last.

Cannonball, Dakota Territory, December 1888

Trusty found Horse in a small barn that stood behind the trading post. Like Brazos Joe had said, his ride had been tended to, given a clean stall with fresh straw, a bucket full of oats, and was covered with a thick blanket easily identified as government issue; thick, gray in color, the quality still apparent. Horse was comfortable and the inside of the barn was warmer than he'd expected, just above freezing. There was no heat source to be seen, and no one around to see to Trusty's comforts. That was fine by him. The straw was deep enough to provide a decent bed. His own blankets and coat would protect him from the plunge of temperature. The trader had suggested Trusty seek shelter in the church for the night, but that wasn't an option worth considering. With that firm rejection, Brazos Joe had offered Trusty a place to sleep in the backroom of the trading post which he declined. A horse stall was warmth enough, safe enough, and provided an easy exit without putting anyone else at risk because of his presence.

Horse noted Trusty's arrival with a snort and stamp of his front right hoof. The exhale from the roan's long nose quickly formed into a visible cloud of tiny crystals, hanging in the air too exhausted to fall to the floor of the stall. The beast was no more accustomed to Dakota Territory than Trusty was.

Before bedding down, Trusty threw an extra blanket over Horse's back, then settled into the straw, feeding himself a bit of jerky, and checking the load in his Colt even though he knew it was full of cartridges. It was times like this that riding alone came with a cost and a coincidence that were evident whether the bill was to be paid or not: You never see a rabbit sleeping. It is always wary of the shadows dancing around its head or running from one place to the next.

Chapter 5

St. Louis, Missouri December 1888

Gladdy O'Connor was trapped by the darkness and the lack of familiarity with his surroundings. He didn't know which way to run, didn't have Haden to follow and lead him to safety like he always had. One of the two men, nothing more than a shadow with the dim gaslights stroking an unmistakable glint off the blue barrel of his gun, chased Gladdy from Theodore Marberry's house while another had appeared from the opposite direction, armed and as serious in his intention of capture. Stunted by his lack of sense and direction, Gladdy ran toward the most tenebrous section of the street. A clump of tall oak trees, their girth the size of sideway wagon wheels, loomed in the night generating long and deep shadows that seemed to make the black blacker. The choice seemed right for a second or two as Gladdy pumped his legs faster, but what he failed to consider was his eyesight was not that good, especially at night. He ran straight into a three-foot wrought-iron fence at full speed and somersaulted over it, landing face down on the cold, wet ground with a hard thud. His knee had caught one of the spikes, ripping his pant leg and skin. Nothing felt broken, but the air had been knocked out of his lungs on the landing. It took him a second to regain his breath and his touch with reality.

The two men rushed up on him. One stopped at his side, standing over him like an executioner. The cock of a gun got Gladdy's attention, and he did the only thing he knew to do: He played dead.

"What're you runnin' from?" the man said. His voice was deep, weathered, had a touch of Alabama or Mississippi in it. Gladdy couldn't tell which, but the tongue and the words were definitely Southern. That might work to his advantage. A fellow statesman, a fellow Reb. A reach back to home. If he strained hard enough, he could hear Haden's voice in his memory, the same pitch and turn through the red cedar forests they'd roamed wild in when they were just kids, not far off the teat.

"You deaf, boy?" The man tapped Gladdy in the side with the tip of his boot. It wasn't a kick; more of a notice that there was more to come if he didn't answer.

"I ain't no boy," Gladdy said, annoyed and offended by the word. He was unsure of what was going to happen next.

"You best stand up then and tell us why you been starin' at Mister Marberry's house all evenin'. Seems to us you're up to no good, and it's our job to find out who you are and what you're up to."

Gladdy made no effort to stand. He lifted his head, eyed the man, and, like he had expected, came face to face with a six-inch gun barrel. "You pull that gun away from me and I'll talk. Besides, it ain't against the law to stand on a street corner, is it?"

"Around here it is," the man said.

The other man joined the first one. Now there were two

gun barrels pointed at Gladdy's head. He was in no mood
to die. "What do I got to do to convince you that I ain't no
threat to anybody? I was just lookin' for a place to stay."

Whatever he said prompted the first man to kick him
again. Only this time it was harder, came an inch away
from cracking a rib. Gladdy cried out in pain and rolled
off to the side, out of striking distance of the man's boot.

"You lie to me again," the kicker said, "and it'll be the
last words you speak. You understand, boy?"

Pain reached through Gladdy's torso with long, spiky
fingers, refusing to go away as he cradled himself like a
baby. "I ain't no boy," he said through gritted teeth as tears
pushed down his muddy cheeks.

"Well, stand up and act like a man then," the man standing over him said.

Gladdy knew he couldn't stay on the ground forever,
that he'd have to get up, but he was trying to take as long
as he could and formulate an escape plan. At the moment
he didn't see one, and the last thing he wanted to do was
die on an unknown street in St. Louis. He had come too
far. Maybe the best thing he could do was play along. With
that thought, he pulled himself up from the ground slowly,
one knee at a time. His side still ached. He owed the devil
above him a punch or something worse in recompense for
the pain.

"Take his gun, Frank," the boot kicker said. He stood
back a few feet to give Gladdy sway and room to stand up.
There was no waver of the gun barrel pointed at Gladdy.
One foot the wrong way and the man was going to pull the
trigger.

Frank stood where he was, a gaslight behind him leaving his face darkened in a long shadow, but it was easy to
see that he was a tall man, wearing a thick duster to ward

off the cold winter air, a Stetson on his head, and a short beard on his face that showed white even in the night. The man was older just like the man who held the gun on him, now that Gladdy could see straight. "You get his gun, Clovis, I can smell his foulness from here."

"Seems to me he stepped in horse shit."

"Or failed to take a bath in the last month."

"You're one to talk."

Gladdy stood still, taking in the sights around him, not offering anything to the men, including his gun, which was still holstered. *Can I take them both in a draw?* He wondered. *Probably not. Am I gonna die if I do nothin' but stand here? Probably.* Any hope of bargaining with this fellow Reb had vanished.

While the two men, now known as Frank and Clovis were bantering back and forth, Gladdy summoned up what courage he could find, and, instead of reaching for his gun, he waited for the first man, Frank, to look away, then grabbed ahold of the barrel that had been pointing at him since he had been on the ground. In a quick second, he pulled the gun upward so the barrel was finally pointed away from him. If a shot was fired it would pierce the black canvas of the sky that hung overhead and shatter the silence of the night that had surrounded them since the initial confrontation. People in the fine houses on the street were tucking into bed. One by one the hurricane lamps in the windows were being extinguished. Any barking dogs had stopped their duty and joined their owners for a night of rest. Drawing attention might free him. Gladdy could only hope for a shot now. He had made another mistake, another miscalculation by not pulling a trigger. Maybe people were right about him. Maybe he was dumber than dumb.

Frank was shocked by Gladdy's surprising grab for

freedom. The gun almost slipped out of his hand. Instead of doing anything with it, he backhanded Gladdy with all of the might he could come up with.

The snap echoed and sounded like the first cymbal smashed together in the start of a complex musical performance; not nearly as loud as a gunshot, though. There was always more to come from men like Frank. Gladdy hadn't been expecting a blow of any kind. He stumbled backward, letting go of Frank's gun. When he came to grips with himself, still standing, he found himself staring down the barrel of the gun once again. The only difference this time compared to the last was in Frank's demeanor. He was angrier than a hornet who'd had a wing torn off him. "You move another inch and that'll be the last thing you ever do. You clear on that?"

Gladdy nodded and exhaled at the same time. There was nothing to do but surrender to these fellas. He hung his head in a familiar arch downward. He was angry with himself, not only for getting caught, but not completing the deed, not avenging Haden's death. Now he had to figure out how to stay alive so he could succeed, so he could finish what he had started. But doubt held a strong grasp inside his tortured mind. He wasn't sure that he could stay alive without his dead brother's help. Maybe it would be easier to join him in death.

"Put the hood on him, Clovis," Frank said. "We're takin' him to see the boss."

Gladdy didn't like the sound of that but didn't do anything to object. He was limp as a noodle. All of the energy he'd had was drained out of him by the defeat.

"You sure, Frank? Boss ain't gonna like to be disturbed this time of night," Clovis said.

"He'd be more disturbed to know some blackleg was pokin' around his house and we let him walk off."

Gladdy stiffened. "I ain't no swindler and I wasn't doing nothin' but standing on the street corner."

"You stand out like an elephant on an oar boat, you fool." Frank nodded at Clovis accompanied with an authoritative glare. "Go on, put the hood on him before he does somethin' stupid that'll cause me to pull this here trigger."

"He's still got his gun on him," Clovis said.

"Put the hood on him, then take his gun. He moves a muscle then I explain to the sheriff why he's got a bullet hole between his eyes. Shouldn't take much convincin' by the looks of this man that I had just cause to kill him."

Gladdy couldn't see a thing. There were two black burlap bags tied over his head to ensure his vision was completely denied; one on top of the other, tied separately around his neck tight enough for him to imagine what a hangman's noose felt like. His breath heated the bag, stank from the sourness in his mouth, while his fingers felt as if they had been licked by Jack Frost's tongue. Closed-in-misery pushed his fear to a limit he had never felt before, not even in the hard bevy of gunfire exchanges in the war and since, when he was sure he was going to die, but had somehow survived. At least there and then his death would have been instant and worthy of a cause—if he had been lucky enough to take a ball of lead in a killing place, the head or the heart. Those men, Clovis and Frank, didn't intend to kill him, but they wanted to make sure that Gladdy understood that they were in control, that his life was in their hands. He felt oddly relieved by the surrender.

Now he didn't have to think about what to do next. He couldn't move an inch without cutting off his breath.

He had been taken somewhere for a reason he couldn't divine. Big cities always made him feel lost and small, but this was different. He felt invisible, more alone than he'd ever felt. No one knew where he was at. No one cared.

Gladdy knew he was in a room underground, had been walked down steps, then tied to a chair by his two captors. They had retreated without words of comfort, instruction, or antagonism. At first, he was happy to be alone. Then time ticked off and his body settled down and his hunger began to sing from the inside of his flesh to the outside. The rope around his wrists remained tight, and he began to fear that he had been left to suffocate, to slowly die of hunger and solitude. Madness would take him before he wasted away. He was being tortured by his own mind, but there was nothing he could do to stop the demons from pooling around his head other than wish for Haden to come and rescue him. But he knew deep down that wasn't possible. His brother, his paladin, his hero was dead, never to be seen again. There was no escaping that truth any more than there was the chance that Gladdy O'Conner was going to walk out of the room unscathed, wherever it was, anytime soon. No one was going to help him. That's a hard truth to swallow when nothing else can go down your throat.

Water collected close by. Drip, drip, drip, like a bowl filling up. Or a room. *Was he going to drown?* Gladdy's imagination ran wild, high on anxiety, heavy with despair. All he could think about was the time when he was a boy, almost swept away in the current of a muddy brown river, hanging onto a tree root poking out of the soft bank, screaming his fool head off because his grip was loosening.

He didn't know how much longer he could hang on. Haden had saved him, of course, picked him straight up, deposited him on solid ground, and walked away silently. His brother didn't speak to him for two days; Haden had stayed distant and glum until he'd said, "I told you to stay away from the water." Gladdy had avoided rivers ever since, even if it meant missing a bath for weeks at a time.

Small places terrified Gladdy. He always swore he'd kill himself if he ever got sent to jail. That was one of the reasons he turned on Vance Calhoun and bought his freedom testifying against the man at his trial. He didn't care whether he was a snitch or rat, he had stayed out of jail. The other reasons were even simpler: Calhoun was mean to him, and he got what he deserved at the end of the rope.

It might have been minutes later, though it felt like hours, when a door opened, and someone walked down a set of steps in the room. The sound echoed with life and an immediate threat, pulling Gladdy's wanderings from the dark side of his mind back to the present. He girded himself, held his breath sure that he had taken his last one. If death would take him to Haden's side, he was ready to go—anything to free him of the closed in place he was in.

Light suddenly burned his tightly held eyelids as the hood was ripped off his head. Fresh air invaded his nose and filled his lungs. The foulness of his own making withered away, replaced by a moldy mildew smell. He had been in a cellar before and that's what it smelled like to him. He didn't open his eyes to see. He didn't want to look death in the eye. He just wanted his life to be over with quick. A swift slit to the throat, a bullet to the head. It didn't matter which. Just make it quick.

"Who are you?" a man asked. Not Frank or Clovis. Not a neighbor's voice with a hint of home, but an easterner's voice; a true Yankee who didn't fear showing who or what he was: tight and proper, demanding and proud without trying. "And who the hell are you working for?"

The question surprised Gladdy. He opened his eyes, blinking through the pain of newly found light, surrendering from death to what was before him instead. Two lamps burnt at full wick behind the tall, well-dressed man, who stood alone, six feet away, judging him. There were no weapons in sight, on the man's hip or otherwise.

"I don't work for no man no more," Gladdy said with a bit more spirit than he had intended. A shower of spit escaped his lips.

The Yankee veered to the right to miss the wet array. Disgust replaced the intensity of unfound knowledge in the man's coal black eyes. "What do you want?"

"A good bit of dinner and my flophouse bed would be a start, but by the looks of you, Mister Marberry, that ain't gonna happen anytime soon."

"You know me, but I don't know you."

"It was just a guess," Gladdy said.

"You're not from around here."

"How can you tell?"

"You talk like a carpetbagger."

"Frank called me a blackleg, now you call me a carpetbagger. Ain't neither, thank you very much. I'm just a man standing on a street corner one second, then the next your two thugs darned near kill me and capture me up, hogtie me, and leave me in the dark for hours. That ain't no kind of hospitality, if you ask me. You shouldn't go callin' a man names if you don't know nothin' of him and treat him like a roast chicken for dinner."

"I didn't ask you about that. I asked who you are. I'm not asking you again."

It was then that Gladdy saw the bulge of a derringer inside Marberry's coat pocket. The man was death himself, and there was a decision to make. Live or die. Which was funny, because it was an easy choice, even though minutes ago, Gladdy was ready for death, almost begged for it. All he had to do was look his fate in the eye and that had changed everything in a second. "My name is Gladdy O'Connor, but I doubt that name means a nickel to you."

"I can't say I have ever heard of you, Mister O'Connor." Theodore Marberry stood up and reached inside his coat, moving his age-spotted hand toward the derringer in his pocket.

"I worked for a man named Vance Calhoun. Does that name sound familiar, Mister?"

Marberry stopped moving, froze, and glared at Gladdy. Then his wrinkled face twisted and turned in pain, like he'd been stung by a thousand hornets. The old man, tall and rickety, but still proud across the shoulders, relaxed his hand then, took it away from the weapon, or the assumed weapon, and stood back a foot, reevaluating Gladdy as he went. "Vance Calhoun is dead from what I understand. Hanged. Convicted and tried of murder. An appropriate end to a life of a bully."

"I saw the hangin' myself," Gladdy said.

"My business with Calhoun, however brief and painful has come to a conclusion. If you are after anything of his, Mister O'Connor, you've made a grave mistake. I am a fair and decent man unless I am crossed, or members of my family are hurt and taken advantage of, then that is another story."

"My brother, Haden, is dead, too." Gladdy returned Marberry's stare. He had given up on burning the man's house down, at least for the moment, but he was doing his own bit of recalculating. There was still a chance for revenge. The man was standing in front of him, unattended by his thugs, armed with only a paltry woman's gun. He just needed to figure out a way to break free of the ropes that bound his hands.

"I'm sorry to hear that."

"You don't know how Haden died?"

"I don't see that it's any of my business."

"Your men did it. If I had to guess it was them two ugly sheep shearers you set after us in a double cross leavin' the Boss's ranch with that child he claimed was his. Shot and left for dead he was, my brother. A feast for the buzzards if it wasn't left for me to lay him under the ground and top his grave with a bed of rocks."

Marberry didn't budge an inch, didn't show a change of emotion, didn't flinch. "And you blame me for your brother's untimely exit from this life and not Vance Calhoun?"

"I do. I blame you as much as the man who set this tragedy in motion."

"And who would that be?"

"A Deputy U. S. Marshal that goes by the name of Trusty Dawson. I got a feelin' that you got a score to settle with him, too. Word is all over the territories about the bounty on the deputy's head, and I figure you're the one that put it there."

Marberry stepped forward this time. Close enough for Gladdy to grab him if his hands would have been free. "You're not getting one coin from me, O'Connor."

"If it was money I was after, I would have gone after Dawson myself instead of comin' here, wouldn't I?"

"You know where he's at?"

"I do."

"Then why didn't you say so."

"You didn't ask."

"Where is he?" It was a hard demand from Marberry. His straight teeth clenched together so tight that Gladdy thought the old man's brittle jaw was going to shatter. He had him now. "I've got my best two men scouring the wilds for Dawson. Every day I get a telegram that tells me of nothing but their failure to put an end to Dawson's life."

"Untie me," Gladdy said, "and me and you will make us a little business deal, Mister Marberry. Otherwise, I ain't tellin' you nothin' tied to a chair like a prisoner with nothin' to offer. If there's one thing I know how to do, it's where to find Trusty Dawson."

Chapter 6

Brazos Joe poured Trusty a cup of steaming coffee, then went back to his spot behind the trading post counter. The wood was worn smooth under his feet from holding his station day after day. "You didn't have to sleep in the barn."

"I wasn't sleepin' in the church."

"Father Kerry is a gentle man. He would have taken pity on you if you would have asked."

"I wasn't askin'. Thanks." Trusty took a long sip of the coffee and wished the man would shut up. "Pity from a collar is the last thing I'm seekin' at the moment."

"Must be a big beef with the church if you're willin' to spend the cold night covered in straw."

"My beef ain't none of your business, now, is it?" The response was curt, more so than Trusty usually offered. His words and the tone of his voice surprised him, didn't sound at all like he remembered. The memory of Michael Darby, ex-priest, and brother to the Kosoma Darby Gang, was a raw cut that had yet to scar over.

"I beg your pardon," Brazos Joe said. "I was just makin' conversation."

"Some men ain't convivial in the morning until they've had a taste of coffee. Not much need for conversation when it's me and my horse. I apologize for the appearance of being ungrateful for your fine hospitality."

"No offense taken. I didn't mean any harm."

"I know you didn't. What you need to tell me about is the two men that were askin' about me. I need to know what to look for."

"I done told you. They came up from the south, were of equal height wearing trusted sidearms. You know the kind of men. You've ridden with them yourself. The war still haunts them that they walked away from when they didn't want to."

"I suppose you're right." Trusty always regretted being born too late to fight in the war. Every man who had taught him how to be a soldier or a deputy had fought for their cause, one side or the other. Their skills came at a cost that he would never know or truly understand, even though he had fought in the Indian Wars himself. "I'll keep an eye out for 'em, but they sound like the rest, bounty hunters willing to trip over their own feet for a few silvers."

"More than a few, from what I hear."

"I know the man who put the bounty up. He'll try to get out of payin' if the day ever comes that someone shows up to collect. He can't be trusted." Trusty paused, didn't want to ruin his day with the poisonous thought of Theodore Marberry, and decided to change the subject. As always, the memory of the baby girl, faded, blurry, unsure, hung outside his grasp for an extra second. It would be easier to pretend that she didn't exist, but he couldn't do that. "How'd you end up here?"

"I ran home to Texas after the war," Brazos Joe said, looking a little relieved to talk about himself. "Started punchin' cattle north, which is how I got this far away from my own land. I scouted a new trail with Charles Goodnight, the Father of the Texas Panhandle, through the Trincheras Pass and ended up settling in Cheyenne for a time. One adventure led to another, and I decided this place was far away from everything that I was leavin' behind, that I'd be free. Of course, there was a woman involved in that decision, too. A woman can change the course of a river or history with the right kind of a smile."

"You're a little over five hundred miles north of Cheyenne," Trusty said, listening to the man, staring into his coffee, taking in the smell and the warmth that the trading post offered him. He was standing where he was because of a woman just like Brazos Joe, only his tale didn't look or feel as happy. A fire blazed in the stove to welcome hoped-for customers. "Must have been some kind of an adventure."

"A man migrates like the birds and the animals. That's a story for another day, Dawson. But I'll tell you this, runnin' never gets you nowhere. You have to stop eventually and look the bear square in the eye and then stab him in the belly, if you know what I mean." Brazos Joe took a breath, let silence linger for a long second, then said, "What are your plans?"

Trusty nodded, took a sip of the strong coffee, and stood up. His clothes, layered three deep, were starting to stick to his skin. "I'm off to Fort Yates. This stop and the trouble with Carmichael and his cohort slowed me down more than I anticipated. The weather looks fair at the moment so me and Horse need to ride with the wind at our backs while the opportunity to make up miles stays steady.

I've a duty to fulfill. The longer I diddle-daddle, the farther away Charlie Littlefoot gets."

"Don't overestimate Charlie's speed or will to disappear."

"What do you know of that?"

"Nothing other than I've lived among the Sioux for a time, come to know their ways as much as any white man can. I've laughed with them, fought with them, and shared a bed with more than one of them. If they don't want to be seen, they won't be. Charlie Littlefoot could be standing right before you and if he wanted to be invisible, he would be."

"Like an owl butted up against a tree trunk staring wide-eyed at you, blended so well even the yellow eyes look like leaves."

"Yes, something like that."

"Is he here in Cannonball, on the reservation?"

"Can't say for sure. I've heard the same thing you have. He's rushing north, out of reach of the law, and most likely deep into the forest, out of the sight and ways of white men for a while."

"And I'm heading south."

"He knows that, too. Seems counterproductive to me."

"I'm just following orders," Trusty said.

Brazos Joe took a deep breath and looked past Trusty to the door that led outside. "My wife was eyeing one of them machines in the wagon you rode in on." He stepped out from behind the counter, either to show Trusty to the door, or start a bargain.

Trusty headed for his buffalo coat, curious about Brazos Joe's wife. He hadn't seen hide nor hair of anyone else, more less a woman, in the post, but something told him she was the Sioux that Brazos Joe had spoke of. The coat was weighed down on a peg next to the stove. He still wasn't used to the heft of it, but knew the thing was necessary to stay alive. "I'll send the Singer company a wire once I get to Fort Yates to make them aware of the demise of their employees. I ain't taken no inventory of them machines, if you get my meanin', but I would imagine it would be a wise investment to make sure them mules are cared for and more than a few of the machines remain in their crates until somebody shows up to retrieve 'em. I don't imagine those two fellas were gonna make a stop in this part of the Territory or offer their wares to the Sioux. Women and children could benefit from the magic of a modern sewing machine or two if you get my drift."

"I sure think I do," Brazos Joe said with a smile growing on his chubby face.

Trusty didn't move. "But mind you, if I hear tell you're sellin' them machines out of this establishment, me and you is gonna have a problem. My blind eye is a gift to the womenfolk, not an offer to put a few extra coins in your pocket. I'll gladly pay for my keep overnight while we're at it."

Brazos Joe shook his head and allowed the smile to fade from his face. "No charge for you, deputy. But keep an ear out for the shadows that are trackin' your every move."

"Nothin' new about that, old man. That's the way I've ridden longer than I care to admit."

On the Trail to Fort Yates, Dakota Territory, December 1888

The sky reached up over the flat land like a thin cotton blanket had been pulled over the blueness of it. There was no anger or rage in the clouds, and no hard wind, either;

only a consistent breeze that blew up from the southwest. The trail was easy with wide vistas making it difficult to see where the sky ended and the soil of the good earth began. A light covering of snow was all that remained from an overnight squall, accumulating an inch at the most. The snow was deep enough to see jackrabbit tracks, or anything else living, animal or man, that had come across the trail before Trusty. So far, he had been alone, the only human being to be seen for miles on end. The ride was just the way he had hoped it would be, vacant of any apparent threats. It would be easy to see a man in the distance or for a man to see him; that was a given in Dakota Territory. There was no attempt to hide, to ride stealthily. That was impossible in this part of the world. Birds of prey flew high in the sky, and most everything else, rodents and snakes that made the prairie their home, lived underground, or close to it. Trusty wondered if gophers slept through the winter. The only shadow he saw was his own.

Fort Yates, Dakota Territory, December 1888

Fort Yates looked out of place, a city stacked upward on the prairie, built by unseen hands. Timber had been shipped in from Minnesota; a benign invasion of planks and poles that looked as out of place as the men who had brought them. The symmetrical frontier-inspired compound was in various stages of repair, disrepair, and new construction. Named for Captain George W. Yates, who was killed at the Battle of Little Big Horn, the fort had been occupied since 1873, when the Standing Rock Indian Agency had been moved from Grand River. Originally occupied by twelve men, the population had grown close to three thousand, with most men taking up residence after

Custer's massacre and other forts were consolidated. The government and most men in the army had had a hard time swallowing that defeat. A universal law, which Trusty had learned all too well in his father's blacksmith shop: a contraction always comes after an expansion. In both cases, in the shop and on the plains, fire always cooled, whether it was in a forge or a battle, and metal of any kind hardened, usually smaller than what it started out to be. Trusty was fully aware of the growth and the pall that hung over the fort. He was glad that he hadn't been assigned to Fort Yates during his time in the Cavalry.

Trusty's first line of business was to check in and establish a roof over his head; he was so cold and frosted he feared that parts of his body would never regain any warmth at all. The worry of spreading his seed and bringing another child into the world would never be a concern again. The second bit of business he had to attend to was wiring the Singer Manufacturing Company to make them aware of Carmichael's and Miles's fates. And the third, and most important business, was to find Captain James Pierpoint Plumright and start asking questions about Charlie Littlefoot and the incident that had brought Trusty to Fort Yates in the first place. He wanted to be fresh and warm before facing the captain. Any man whose wife has claimed rape by an Indian and is carrying a child—the parentage unknown to Trusty, or maybe anyone else at this point— would surely have an edge that would need to be dulled. Trusty hoped the captain would be helpful, but he wasn't counting on it. Marshal Delaney's take on the situation had been uncertain at best. Trusty figured Delaney was working with the Mounties, specifically with a man called Bisset, on that end. If there was one good thing about being among army men it would allow for a breath to be taken, a moment of relaxation to be held in his gut, to a point. The bounty never stopped following Trusty, but he was among men who had taken an oath to protect and defend, not profit off of the life of a fellow soldier, or marshal, which, depending on how it was looked at, was one in the same.

His presence had already garnered some attention as he and Horse strode through the gates of the fort. A couple of long-haired dogs, black and white, that looked more accustomed to herding than protecting, barked and danced around Horse's icy hooves. A few children had poked their heads out of heavy wood doors to see who had arrived, in hopes of news, candy, or something else that Trusty was unsure of. The children were Sioux, dressed like they had been remade in the image of a white mother and father; no braids, bowl cut shiny black hair, brown swarthy skin that could not be denied, hidden in clothes stitched together so they would look the same as all of the other children. Trusty smiled, waved in a muted, unexcited way, but he mostly ignored the children and the dogs. He had little experience with both and found them as unpredictable as the Dakota clouds that came and went with fury and then calmness; the weather was always changing just like the black and white dogs' course of direction, darting around Horse, barking and nipping. Horse, to his credit, followed Trusty's lead, ignoring the mild attack until one of the dogs got too close with a nip. Horse stopped without warning, exhaled deeply, offering a burst of steam from his nostrils that looked like it was boiling out of a sitting locomotive. Horse kicked with his hind leg, then stiffened into a fighting stance. The roan's deep brown eyes bore the fire responsible for the steam as he looked back to see if the kick landed where it was intended. It didn't.

"Come on, boy, let's go," Trusty said. Horse hesitated until Trusty yelled at the dogs. "Go on get. The both of you. Go home." To his surprise, the dogs stood back, which probably had more to do with the quick dump Horse let go of to add his two cents to his rider's command, than anything else. The annoyance of his arrival was expected, but Trusty was past ready to be out of the weather. He ached to be next to a warm fire. But first he needed to make his presence and arrival formally known by visiting the commander's office.

Colonel Edwin Franklin Townsend sat behind his desk, arms crossed, a scowl on his bearded face, with hard blue eyes focused on Trusty. Townsend had a no-nonsense reputation and still wore the air of West Point on his shoulders. At a glance, the colonel resembled Ulysses S. Grant, which endeared him to some men and provoked bile in the throats of others. "You're late, Deputy Dawson," Townsend said. His voice was gravelly in an unnatural way, like he was at the start of a sickness of some kind. The two men had never crossed paths before, but it was supposed by Trusty that their reputations had. From the looks of things, all that mattered to Townsend were Trusty's failures that had preceded him.

Trusty held back a few extra feet, standing rigid, not quite at attention, but close. He was not past resisting the urge and compulsion to salute a higher-ranking officer even though they served in two different organizations. "I ran into a little trouble outside of Cannonball, sir." Respect knew no boundaries. "But that trouble resolved itself." The air in the room was stale, like all commander's offices seemed to be. Being dressed down by men bestowed with power, medals, rank, and a higher level of education was an old routine to Trusty. He longed to be out in the air, comfortable on Horse's back, even in the brutal reality of the Dakota Territory. He'd prefer to freeze his balls off instead of answering to a West Point man any day of the week. The longing he'd had for the warmth of a fire vanished as soon as Townsend had opened his mouth.

"It ended with the deaths of two men," the colonel said. Not an ounce of flesh moved when Townsend spoke, other than his mouth, which on closer inspection, looked smaller than it should have compared to the size of his head. The man almost looked like he had been carved of granite, a soldier of great regard astride a just-as-proud mount, situated in the middle of a busy city square. There were no pigeons to be seen, but Trusty expected a flock to descend from the ceiling at any second.

"One man was already dead, sir," Trusty said. "The other drew on me as I waked into the mornin', buried under a thick coat as I was."

"So, the shooting was a mistake? An error of sleepiness?"

"No, sir. The threat woke me completely. The man, Carmichael, meant to kill me. There's a . . ."

"Bounty," Townsend said, cutting Trusty off with a tinge of annoyance. "Delaney transmitted all of your troubles, past and present, so I would know what to expect when you arrived. All things considered, I am not as certain as the Marshal that you're the best man for the job, but that is not my decision or charge to make. But I will tell you what my charge is, Deputy Dawson. Every inch of this fort and what happens upon its soil is my responsibility. This business with Captain Plumright threatens to stain an otherwise bright record of peace and prosperity in Fort Yates, and while you are here, you are to do everything in your power to clean this mess up and not stir up any more trouble."

"And how do you expect me to do that, sir, when Charlie Littlefoot is on the run, headin' north, while I'm here?"

"Do you believe everything you hear?"

"I suppose not. Are you sayin' Littlefoot is still close by?" Trusty said. He was reminded of what Brazos Joe had said, that if Charlie Littlefoot didn't want to be seen, he wouldn't be.

"I didn't say that at all," the colonel said. The color in his face was slowly changing from pale white to slight pink, the burgeoning of a fire set ready to turn to a quick blaze. "You should keep your eyes and ears open is all."

"Anything elsc, sir?" Trusty wanted to get out of the office before the man erupted into a full tirade.

"Yes, bear in mind that Captain Plumright carries with him a stellar record. He is a good man and should be treated as such."

Chapter 7

Fort Yates, Dakota Territory, December 1888

Fort Yates bore a familiarity to Trusty not only in its military ambiance and rigidness, but also by the rules of life that were dictated by its location on an Indian reservation. There was no saloon, no joyful tinkering of piano keys to be followed on a moonlit night, no women to be bought for the hour—at least, out in the open. Alcohol was not allowed on the confines of government land, the fort or the reservation. But that was on the surface, the lie that every white man agreed to hold tight and perpetuate until the sun slinked below the horizon. Where there was a gathering of men, a gathering of soldiers, there was always whiskey to be found—and most likely a woman or two to be had. Trusty wasn't interested in either at the moment, drink nor woman, but he wanted a place to gain his footing, to listen to stories and murmurs of the regimented men before he went looking for Captain Plumright in earnest.

It didn't take long, after getting Horse settled in the stable, and taking a bunk in the guardhouse, a long wood frame whitewashed building, for Trusty to start poking around. All forts had their gathering places, officer's clubs of sorts, separated from the enlisted men, where they relaxed, cajoled, and commiserated like any other normal man, out of earshot of their assigned troops; human frailties were only allowed to show among their own, if then.

Fort Yates wasn't any different from any other fort Trusty had been in. A collection of small rooms had been set aside for such use on the bottom floor of the officer's winter quarters.

He had no idea what to expect when he walked in uninvited. The room was warm, stuffy, and loud. A woodstove burned heartily in the corner, battering down the cold wind that followed Trusty everywhere he went. There were no windows to be seen. And every table, six of them, were full of men, some in uniform, others not, dressed in warm civilian clothes. All of them were in the middle of a card game, poker from the looks of it, and there were no women to be seen. The volume of conversation dipped as Trusty closed the door behind him. Loud voices quickly returned to their previous level once the badge on his chest was seen—and given approval of entry silently, no secret password required. It was like they all had been expecting Trusty to join them, had known he was coming, which was probably true. A new arrival on a mission was known by all. Fort Yates was an isolated island on a frozen sea of grass. Everybody knew everybody's business—and everyone knew of Captain Plumright's troubles and Charlie Littlefoot's alleged crime.

Along with the stuffiness in the small room, the air was thick with smoke. Cigars, cigarillos, and Buglers were common at every table. As was a water pitcher and glasses to match. Any amber liquid resembling whiskey was nowhere to be seen, which didn't surprise Trusty at all. Colonel Townsend looked like the kind of commander who followed the rules to a T and wouldn't allow such untoward and illegal behavior from his officers. There was, however, a bar of sorts, at the back of the room. A place where the water, cards, and other sundries were kept. A man stood in wait to attend the officers' every need. The man was a Sioux, tall, hair shorn short, shaved around the ears, blocked on the back of the neck without the possibility of a braid. Trusty knew that defining a man as a Sioux was a broad term, used by him and most every other white man, formed from what one Indian tribe had named another; the Ojibwa called the Lakota and Dakota tribes *Nadouwesou,* which meant adders. Early French traders cut off the end of *Nadouwesou* to sou and the tribes became known as the Sioux to most every white man thereafter. No Sioux that Trusty knew called the other a Sioux. There was no way to know if the man in wait was Lakota or Dakota without talking to him. Trusty's friend, Woman's Clothes, a scout for the army, and an Apache, had taught him what little he knew of the tribes and the Indian ways. Her gift of skills had saved his life more than once. Fighting in the Indian Wars had been a duty for Trusty, not an act of revenge or hate. But he was lost among the Sioux, and he was on the flat winter landscape that he had skated in on.

Trusty made his way to the bar, if it could have been called that, ignoring some of the looks shot his way from the officers playing cards.

"Hello, Marshal," the Sioux man said. He smiled and sat a fresh glass of water on the wood top bar.

"You can call me . . ."

"Trusty Dawson," the Indian interjected. His English was smooth. His voice was educated just like his hair cut.

I was going to say Sam Dawson, Trusty thought but didn't say. Instead, he nodded his approval, and said, "I'm a deputy, not a marshal. You don't have anything stronger, do you?"

"Only coffee."

"And what should I call you?"

The question looked like it surprised the man. "Oliver," he answered. "Oliver Heightsmith."

"That's your white man's name. What's your given name?" Trusty was insistent regardless of the volume that dropped behind him. He wanted to gain the man's trust as much as that was possible in the environment he was in. His back was to the tables, but he could feel a good number of eyes on him.

"We do not speak of that here. It is a life gone from the bottom of my feet."

"But not your heart?"

Oliver forced a quick smile, but his eyes were familiar with a sheen of ice. "You will take a coffee then?"

"Yes, I'll have a coffee." The Dakota wind howled outside the door, complementing Trusty on his choice. He still couldn't feel his toes even though the room seemed close and nearly as warm as a smithy shop. Whiskey would have been a preferrable drink.

"I'll have to boil it for you," Oliver said, then turned and hurried through a door beyond the bar, leaving Trusty standing by himself, readying himself to push for the Sioux man's true name even further. Surely, Oliver knew Charlie Littlefoot. They may have been of the same band, there was no way to know. Littlefoot was Yanktonai, or Dakota Sioux to most white men. Oliver could have been Teton, or Lakota, the other band of Sioux. Sam sat and watched the Indian go, settling himself into the place, trying not to stand out. *Good luck with that,* he thought.

St. Louis, Missouri, March 1873

At fifteen, Sam Dawson was as tall as his father and just as big and strong in the arms and legs. Maybe stronger. There were times when he felt like rushing his pa like a bull defending his territory, but he never did. Somehow, he restrained himself, walked away when there was an argument to lose, or just quit listening, just stared at the old man like he wasn't there. Of course, the older, stronger, and smarter that Sam got, the more responsibilities his father loaded on him. Not only was the forge and all of the water-bearing tasks his to maintain, along with the simple hooks and iron pickets, but now hauling, stacking, and tracking the inventory was his to watch over, as well. The only good thing about keeping the shop stocked in rods, wood, and tools, was the need to go out into the world leaving the darkness of the smithy and his father behind, at least for a little while. Many of those trips took Sam past Katherine Duchamp's house, where he always had an open invitation to stop and socialize or see if there was anything the madame needed. Springtime always brought a high demand for goods and services in St. Louis, as winter began to subside and thaw, and the western trails began to open up. The traffic in the city multiplied by tenfold, and so did men with needs outside of wagon wheel repairs or kettles to cook with on their journeys. Sam ran errands for Madame Duchamp when he had extra time, and that, too, allowed him time away from the shop.

After a long day of bending rods, Sam hurried across town to the riverside, anxious to see what the madame needed from him. His father never objected when Sam told him he was doing work for the woman. Sometimes, Sam lied, and rendezvoused with Jessica Marberry, spending time with her out of sight from everyone, instead of earning pennies from the madame. It was an innocent time, and Jessica couldn't sneak away often without a chaperone. They usually met behind the Methodist Church down the street from her father's house where they would hold hands and talk about the future, when they were both grown up. But on this night, Sam had told the truth to his father. He went straight to Madame Duchamp's house. Like usual, he walked in through the kitchen door without a knock.

"There you are, Mister Sam," Kabbie Mae Brown, the Negro cook said, turning to him from her permanent station at the stove. A pan of biscuits sat proofing on the dry sink next to the stove. It smelled like there was a batch in the wood-fired oven. Kabbie Mae was hovering over the top plates, using her nose to tell her when the biscuits were done. "The missus says for you to wait here. It's a busy night upstairs, you know. But she has a special job for you."

The request wasn't out of the ordinary, so Sam nodded and started to sniff the air and inspect the raw biscuits.

"You leave them biscuits be, boy," Kabbie Mae said, "I'll tan your hide if'n you touch them. Don't you laugh, neither. I got childs as big as you and when I get the switch they still run and hide."

Sam pulled back, resisting the temptation to stick his finger into the small pillow of dough. He smiled at Kabbie Mae, then rushed toward her as quick as he could, reached around her and stole a biscuit that was cooling on a rack on the other side of her. Before she could even think to slap him away, he had gulped down half of the biscuit. She chased him across the room, and stopped midway, laughing. "Lawd, have mercy, you ain't got no manners at all, Samuel Dawson. Some women are gonna have they hands full with you."

Sam finished the biscuit and smiled. Kabbie Mae was the only woman in the world who called him Samuel like his mother had. It made him feel warm and comfortable, like being in the kitchen did. "Can I have another?"

"No, you cannot. Now, you sits your butt down there and wait for the missus. I got some lemonade for you. Brought up from Florida by a man with ugly teeth and a fat wallet tryin' to curry favor with us all. Didn't work none, but I sure did like those lemons."

"I'll have some, thank you."

"See. You does have manners."

"Only for you."

Kabbie Mae smiled and went about getting Sam a glass of lemonade. "You're an ornery little devil, aren't you?" she said.

Sam relaxed into the high back chair, comfortable at the long table that sat ten. Some days, he felt like he belonged there, but deep down, he knew that wasn't true. He knew he didn't belong in a cathouse any more than he belonged in a blacksmith's shop. He was welcome there, and there was a difference. He had to make sure and not get the two confused.

Katherine Duchamp waltzed into the kitchen done up from head to toe; her brunette hair was piled up so high a bird might take notice and build a nest in it; her eyelids were painted blue to match her satin dress that hugged every curve; her feet were balanced in high heel shoes with sparkly gems on them and propelled her higher into the air. She was so beautiful she took Sam's breath away every time he saw her. There was a difference between her and the girls who worked for her. Madame Duchamp was a woman through and through, while the others were younger, still growing into themselves—like Jessica, only not that young. Sam knew the difference between women and girls, too, thanks to Katherine Duchamp.

"There's my Sam." She rushed to him and kissed the top of his head. The only way to ignore the sight of her large breasts inside the dress was to close his eyes. He didn't. "I need you to drive my carriage down to the train station and pick up a girl. She's coming in from the east, Boston, if you could imagine, to work for me. Can you do that?"

"Yes, ma'am," Sam said, standing up. He was as tall as Katherine Duchamp. "Is there anything else?"

"Yes," she said. "Keep your eyes in your head and your hands to yourself."

Kabbie Mae busted up laughing. Katherine and Sam both turned to her. Sam said, "What's so funny?"

"You ever see a dog chase after a wagon?"

"Yes," Sam said.

"You ever see a dog catch a wagon?" Kabbie Mae said. "No."

"That's right. Poor old dog wouldn't know what to do with that wagon once he caught it. Neither would you." The Negro woman laughed again, filling the kitchen with the glee of her own joke.

Sam stared at Kabbie Mae, not sure what she was talking about. He looked at Madame Duchamp for clarification, for help.

"Don't you pay any attention to her," Katherine said. She dug into a hidden pocket and pulled out a few silver coins. "The girl's name is Natalie Lynn Jenkins. Brown hair, carrying a white hat box on the eight o'clock. You'll know her when you see her." She handed Sam the coins. "Go on, you'll be late. It's not every day I get a new girl from Boston."

Sam took the money and hurried out the door. His feet barely hit the ground. He was as happy as he'd ever been doing something he was told to do. It was a rare feeling, and, of course, it wouldn't last.

Fort Yates, Dakota Territory, December 1888

A man roared with laughter behind him, and the room became more familiar. He thought about chasing after Oliver but thought better of it. He needed to make an Indian connection to Charlie Littlefoot, find a way to get an Indian to tell him the story—but he was stuck on names. People might have called him Trusty, but he knew better than anyone that it wasn't his own true name. Just a moniker given him in a previous life. He hadn't been so reliable of late, getting a federal judge killed and garnering a bounty that followed him wherever he went. His own name was Sam. Samuel. A gift from his mother who was more biblical than he was. She had hoped her son would counsel kings like Samuel in the Bible. So far, that hope had not come true. It was Trusty who answered to men of higher rank, looked at the toes of his boots as duties were assigned to him. Marshals and commanders did not care to seek his wisdom.

Trusty felt a presence settle next to him, but he continued to stare forward at the door, waiting for Oliver's return. He was uncomfortably warm, starting to sweat in the layers of clothes that he wore.

"I hear you're looking for me."

Trusty turned to face a man about the same age as him, weary with red eyes, with a hint of whiskey on his breath. This man, white inside and out, wore a square jaw, a thin mustache over his thick top lip, and the unmistakable glare of a man accustomed to being in charge. "I'm not looking for anyone at the moment. I'm waiting on a cup of coffee."

"I'm James Pierpoint Plumright."

"I figured as much."

"I'd kill that redskin if I was allowed to leave the fort."

"I'm not lookin' to talk with you right now, mister." Trusty's voice was dry and calm, his heartbeat steady. The sound around him disappeared as his focus zeroed in on Plumright. Some men got ramped up when they felt a confrontation coming on. Trusty, on the other hand, pulled back like a snail, in no hurry to force what was coming toward him.

"It's now or never," Plumright said. "I'm resigning my commission in the morning, packing my bags and my wife, and heading south, where it's warmer and more hospitable, within the week. Colonel Townsend has been kind enough to allow my presence on the fort to continue until we are packed and ready."

Plumright's departure was news to Trusty. He wondered why Colonel Townsend hadn't made him aware of the man's decision to leave the fort.

"It'll have to be in the morning, then, that we talk," Trusty answered. "I got a warm mug of coffee comin' and I'm settling down for the night. I came here to relax not to inquire about your troubles, Captain Plumright."

"You know nothing about my troubles." Plumright said the words with a spit on the end of the sentence.

Trusty waited for the twist on Plumright's face to relax

before he said anything else. All eyes were on him, and he knew it even though he still had his back to the crowded room. "My apologies, Captain Plumright. I don't think I'll be havin' that mug of coffee just now." With that said, Trusty turned to leave. He knew the feeling in the air all too well. He was talking with a man who had already lost face, his good name, by somehow allowing an Indian man to touch his wife. Plain and simple, James Pierpoint Plumright had nothing to lose.

The captain followed after Trusty, grabbed his arm, and stopped him mid-stride to the door. "I didn't dismiss you," Plumright scowled.

Trusty stopped and relaxed his arm and grip as much as possible. The last thing he wanted for himself or Plumright was a confrontation in front of a collection of the officers of the fort. "I beg your pardon, sir, but I'm leaving. I am not a member of your corp. I answer to the U.S. Marshal in Bismarck, and him to President Cleveland until the new man is sworn in next year. I don't want to discuss my reason for being here with anyone but you. I'm assumin' you don't wish for that to truly happen, neither. Now, why don't you unhand me, and I'll be on my way until we meet again."

Trusty watched Plumright's eyes to see if he had touched a commonsense nerve or if he should have been expecting a punch and a fight to come his way. He would not retaliate. He would subdue the captain, tainted by whiskey as he was, and try to do as little harm to him as possible. The room was quiet as a funeral. No one was weeping discretely. It didn't look like Plumright had any comrades in arms in the room that cared about him.

Plumright loosened his grip on Trusty's arm, allowing him to go free. Trusty didn't say another word. He headed straight for the door and walked out as calmly as he had walked in, leaving the captain to his own fate.

Trusty was two steps out the door when he heard the rustle of another man's footsteps coming around the building. He turned expecting a confrontation, expecting an angry captain pursuing a fight, or an unknown man filled with greed and hate, aiming for a bounty. Either way, without thinking, Trusty reached for his ivory-handled Colt. Such an act came as natural as taking a breath. All he wanted to do was stay alive and do his job. What he found in the darkness of night, offset by the glow of the secret club inside the non-descript building, was Oliver, coatless, hatless, without a weapon of any kind, cradling a bundle of wood like it was a newborn child, with purpose glazed in his deep brown, Indian eyes.

Oliver stopped, and a skiff of dry snow powdered up around his feet. The wind was more of a breeze, taking a break under the cover of darkness from the rage of the day. "You are leaving, Trusty Dawson? I'll have your coffee in a few minutes."

Trusty eased his hand away from the Colt and slid it to his side as quickly as he could. Oliver noticed, watched the slow-motion retreat with the realization that he had been a perceived threat.

"That'll have to wait for another day," Trusty said. "The day has been long for me, and as I could see, the captain, too."

Oliver nodded. "There is another room beyond this one."

"I figured as much. I smelled the whiskey on him. He wore it like a familiar coat."

Oliver shook his head. "I have never seen him until recently. The captain was not a man who blew off steam with the other men." A shiver ran visibly up Oliver's back to his shoulders. The night air felt twice as cold as it had in the day, yet Trusty could not bring himself to break off the conversation and let the man retreat inside. "He was pure in his ambition, from what I know, what I heard and saw, which was very little," Oliver continued.

This was not the assumption that Trusty had made about Plumright. He'd colored him as a hothead, a man enraged by the circumstances of his life, and while that might have been a correct assessment, there was more to consider, according to Oliver. Trusty knew the restraint of ambition, had seen it carried in the commanders and captains he had served with and admired.

"That's good to know, Oliver. I appreciate you telling me this. I'm here to find out the truth and nothing more."

"It wasn't until word came that you were coming that I saw the captain venture to the backroom," Oliver said. The shiver had dissipated, but his discomfort remained; eyes fluttering from one side to the next like a wary mouse scouting for shadows. Oliver feared being seen. Trusty knew the feeling.

"You didn't tell me your Sioux name?" Trusty said, ignoring the report of the captain's action. It was enough to know from what he'd heard and seen, knowing now that Plumright was separating from the army and sweated an outsider's arrival that Marshal Delaney's suspicion and direction in sending him to Fort Yates had been warranted. But he needed an ally who wore red skin instead of epaulets on his shoulders. He needed to know why Charlie Littlefoot ran, and more to the point where he would run to.

"My Lakota name is unspeakable here," Oliver said, tenser than he was before. He squeezed the firewood tighter to him.

"It is just you and me. There are no other ears here."

"Says you."

"Because I'm a white man?"

"With a badge on your chest."

"I'm a federal officer of the law."

"Who wears his past on his head for all of the world to see."

And there it was. A reason of distrust and disdain. Trusty had not considered his stripped-down Stetson to be anything other than a comfort, a broke-in piece of felt that kept his head warm and mostly dry. He hadn't considered the story the hat told to those who saw him coming. He had fought in the Indian Wars, and should have known better, especially on a reservation where he had hoped to gain a bundle of inside information just by asking.

"I'm sorry, you're right, Oliver. You should go inside. I'm cold with this coat on. You must be freezin'. You've told me enough, taken enough of a risk by talkin' to me. I appreciate it." Trusty turned to walk away then, but Oliver didn't move.

Trusty was about five feet away when Oliver said, "Otaktay. My name is Otaktay."

The words stopped Trusty, and he turned to see Oliver standing where he had left him, rigid, a little prouder, his eyes no longer wandering to the side in fear of what any white man thought. He was free, if only for a second.

"It is Kills Many in your tongue," Oliver continued. "My name is not something a captain wants to say when he is ordering an Indian to fetch him a whiskey."

Chapter 8

St. Louis, Missouri, December 1888

Gladdy O'Connor rubbed his free wrists, not losing sight of the ropes that had bound him or the man that had ordered them removed. Theodore Marberry stood a respectable distance from Gladdy. Frank and Clovis, Marberry's two thugs, had come running down into the cellar at the first beckoning. Gladdy figured there was a slew of thugs upstairs, waiting to be dispatched at Marberry's command. Which was just fine. He had figured out that if he was gonna escape, it had to be with his mind and mouth, not his legs. He stayed sitting in the chair, waiting for the order to stand to come from Marberry.

"You know what to do with him, boys," Marberry said, then walked to the stairs and ascended into the world above without saying another word. Each step echoed like a hammer on a coffin nail.

Gladdy's mouth went dry, just as he thought he was free to make a deal. He knew what was next, what the intent was; death had spoken and demanded his execution off-hand like he was ordering a drink in a saloon. There was no mistaking the look in both men's eyes. They were going to force Trusty Dawson's location out of him at any cost. Which was going to be difficult, if not impossible. Gladdy O'Connor had no idea where the Deputy Marshal was. He had made up the words, figured it was the only bargaining chip he had. Gladdy had thought he could ride out with one or two of Marberry's men to find Dawson and make an escape along the way. It had been a good plan, and he had thought it had been working, until now. Haden usually finished out the plan, or someone told him to go find out more information. Gladdy had been good about listening to people and reporting back what he had heard, but bad at talking and thinking. He sure did hate being alone. Especially right then.

"You best come clean, O'Connor," Frank said. He was the taller and older of the two. The obvious leader, the one in charge. He had a steel rod in his back kind of like Haden had had. Neither man wore a sidearm nor carried sheathed knives that could be seen. The only obvious weapons were their fists, which had yet to be formed.

"Last I heard," Gladdy said, eyeing Frank, noting the white in his beard, calculating whether he could take him in a good fight or not, "Dawson was headin' north."

"We know that." Frank flexed his hand then curled it into a fist. "Glo Timmons and Red Jack Lewis are in the Dakota Territory freezin' their asses off, trackin' Dawson with no luck like the boss said. You lied about making a deal, didn't you? Thought you were buying time. You made a big mistake, O'Connor. No one knows where you're at, and if I was to guess, I don't imagine they would care if they did know."

Haden would care, Gladdy thought but didn't say. He gripped the chair on both sides as tight as he could. Frank drew closer. Before the man could order him to stand and fight, Gladdy launched himself into Frank's midsection as soon as he was close enough. Gladdy O'Connor wasn't gonna wait for no beatin', no sirree. He *was* alone. There wasn't no one to save him. He had to fight his own way out of the cellar. He knew that for sure, that and he wasn't gonna take no beating without fighting back. He wasn't ready to die.

Frank, tall, and with more than twenty years on Gladdy obviously hadn't fully weighed the nerve of a trapped man with nothing to lose. The air erupted out of his mouth in surprise as Gladdy tackled him, driving him backward on unstable and unprepared legs. Clovis, who had been standing next to the stairs, fell out of sight. He hadn't thought it odd that the men weren't armed, just hopeful. If there was one thing Gladdy knew how to do, it was how to throw a punch.

The force of Gladdy's attack pushed Frank all the way to the moist wall of the cellar, where he finally lost balance and fell to the ground. Gladdy followed, landing a weak hook to the side of the man's face. It wasn't a direct hit. The punch lacked power and force, but the hit, along with the tackle, was more than enough to get Frank's attention. Clovis's, too. Before Gladdy could recoil and prepare to take another punch at Frank, Clovis knocked Gladdy upside the head with something, a bat, a broomstick, a slat thick enough to hurt like hell and send him rolling off of Frank; it felt like a thousand hornets had jabbed his cheek all at once. Clovis was on Gladdy like a hawk on a mouse, fast and furious, striking him repeatedly, driving him to the cellar floor. All Gladdy could do was roll up in a ball and protect his head, wiggle away as best he could. Like every other time in his life when he was in trouble, Gladdy came face to face with a solid wall with nowhere to go. He had to take the beating or find a way to stand up and fight.

"What were you thinkin' you idiot Mick?" Clovis yelled as he continued to strike Gladdy. "We was gonna talk is all." He stopped the beating for a second, then said to Frank, "You all right?"

Frank pulled himself up from the floor, and Gladdy took advantage of the break, unfurled himself, jumped to his knees, then leapt at Clovis like a maniacal frog, screaming as he leapt, rage and pain all mixed together. All he lacked was the long tongue to reel the man in, but his fist caught Clovis on the wrist sending the long slat flying. They were even, fist to fist, except the odds were still in the thugs' favor. It was two against one in a cellar, a death fight with no way to escape, and no one to come to the rescue. Gladdy tackled Clovis, unconcerned about Frank. The air stank of sweat, blood, and the kind of anger that led one man to kill another. His heart pumped with the rage of a gladiator. The sound of the quick beats was like the roar of a crowd, urging him on. All Gladdy had done was stand on a street corner. The two men didn't know of his plans, of his desire to burn down Marberry's house, but they had known he was up to something. There was no turning back time. Clovis fought back, pummeling Gladdy with repeated strikes that were less than punches and more like slaps; Clovis needed a weapon to fight with. He still employed those hornets, but Gladdy didn't feel any pain. He just wanted Clovis to stop. Stop hitting him. Stop breathing. Just stop. Gladdy wanted everything to stop. He wanted to go home, but he had no home to return to. It had been lost in a jumble of war, famine, and gunfire on a lonely road in pursuit of revenge. He was lost, never to be found again. He was alone. All alone. He bit

Clovis, opened his mouth and bared down on the man's shirt like he was tearing into a steak after not having eaten in a month. Gladdy grunted and snarled, transformed for a second from a fighting man to something akin to a wolf or a lion on a weakening kill. Frank pulled Gladdy off Clovis before he could grip any skin between his teeth. The sound of ripping cloth joined the chorus of his heartbeat, Clovis's screams, and Frank's demands, "Stop it!" If words could have lit a fire, the cellar would have exploded right then and there.

Frank hurled Gladdy across the room, and for a moment Gladdy felt like he had wings, was flying on the pure desire to kill a man. He had bit his lip in his attempt to bite Clovis, tasted the sweet, metallic liquid that had pumped up from his heart to his mouth. The flight was short and Gladdy crashed into a table bare of any plates or tools. He crumbled to the ground; the air knocked from his lungs with the sound of a fight on pause falling all around him. Silence engulfed him with the exception of his own body operating at full capacity, producing adrenaline with an out-of-control oil pump. Normally, Gladdy would have jumped to his feet and charged the two men, searching for a weapon of some kind as he went, a hammer, something heavy enough to crack a skull, but he remained on the floor, allowing the coolness of it to touch his skin and soothe him, if only for a moment. It was then that he heard a baby cry in the distance.

The growing wail of the child pierced through the thin walls and the dusty floor overhead, slaying the defense and violence of three men with a primal question: Is the baby in danger? Hurried footsteps thundered across the floor, loosened the cobwebs and dust from the exposed joists, showering the trio with ancient precipitation; dirt set free from concern. Gladdy panted like a prizefighter ordered to a corner, while Frank helped Clovis to his feet. All were bloodied and sore, physically and emotionally, but there seemed to be an understanding, an unspoken truce as the distant child raged for food or care or its mother's touch. It was not the bell that Gladdy had been expecting to end the fight. He was sure that death's door had been opened, and that at least one man, and maybe he, was about to be shoved through it. But instead, new life had shushed them all, death included, and sent them scurrying into silence, lacking resolve or a way forward.

Another pair of footsteps crossed overhead, heavier, manly, in a hurry, either frustrated by the noise of a child or concerned for its welfare. The cellar floor was littered with a new skiff of dust, as was the top of Gladdy's head. Then, to break the silence, Clovis screamed and danced like he had touched fire, slapping the top of his head to rid something off it. A spider as big as a gold piece fell to his shoulder, then to the floor, where Clovis proceeded to smash it with the whole of his weight under his boot. The crunch echoed past Gladdy's ear, and he laughed.

"Shut up," Frank said to Clovis, casting his eyes upward. "The boss." His gaze followed the footsteps into the distance, toward the muffled cries, chugging like a locomotive gaining speed after departing a water tower. The look in Frank's eyes was fearful, like Gladdy had seen of faithful men in a storm, fearing God himself would pierce their hearts with a lightning bolt.

"I hate spiders." Clovis stopped grinding the insect with his boot. A steam of blood flowed from a small wound on his hand, dropping to the dusty floor, pooling next to the crushed spider. He didn't complain about being in any pain. Terror held in his eyes as he focused on the eight-legged creature, making sure it was really dead.

"You won't have to be afraid of spiders, you keep up that noise," Frank said. "And you need to shut the hell up, O'Connor. One more laugh out of you, and I'll slit your throat."

Gladdy stopped the next laugh in his throat, glared at Frank, and flexed his fingers into a new fist. "Like to see you try. The two of you couldn't bring me down." He stepped forward, readying to renew the fight for his life.

"This fight is done," Frank said. "If the boss wanted you dead, he would have shot you himself or ordered us to do it, but if you keep talking, I'll tell him things got out of hand, that you said you didn't want to ride with us, and I'll kill you anyway."

"Boss don't like killin'," Clovis said. "Ain't got the taste for it. At least in sight of it. You'll see. He's again' things uncivilized. He's just filled with grief and hate is all."

The dust in the room settled to the floor, and the air seemed to cool a degree or two. "Why in the hell would I want to ride with the likes of you two?" Gladdy said.

"Beats bein' dead," Clovis answered, wiping his mouth with the back of his sleeve.

"Look," Frank said, "If there's one thing the Boss knows, it's getting even with a man that wronged him. He wants Dawson dead and buried in a bad way, and so far that hasn't happened. He trusts me and Clovis to do the job that nobody else seems able to."

"That ain't got nothin' to do with me." Gladdy stretched upward and cocked an ear toward the ceiling. The baby's cry had simmered to a whimper instead of a howl. "None of this hasn't got anything to do with me."

"You rode with Calhoun."

"I rode with my brother. I rode wherever Haden rode," Gladdy said.

All three men were standing in a semi-circle facing the stairs. Escape wasn't on Gladdy's mind now. He couldn't figure out what the two men were up to. He'd always had trouble with things like that, understanding why other people did the things they did, or said the things they said.

"That's in heaven or hell." Clovis eyed Gladdy with a glare.

"Don't you speak ill of my brother," Gladdy said.

"Stop it before it starts." Frank moved in between Clovis and Gladdy. "Look, here, the Boss knows revenge when he sees it. You came here to settle a score with Mister Marberry, but Mister Marberry believes you're blaming the wrong person for your brother's death."

"Really, and how's that?" Gladdy said.

"The reason why Marberry and Calhoun got all tangled up and your brother got killed in the crossfire was because of one man."

"I ain't followin' you," Gladdy said.

"If Trusty Dawson would have left the Boss's daughter alone, stayed out of her life like he was ordered to, none of this would have ever happened. You wouldn't be standing here, and your brother would still be alive, riding next to you on the trail, leading you on to one adventure or another."

"I guess I ain't never thought of it that way," Gladdy said. "So, you're sayin' that I ought to burn down Trusty Dawson's house 'cause Haden's killin' is all his fault?"

Frank nodded and allowed a slow smile to slide across his face. "I'm saying you should have a burning desire to kill Trusty Dawson is what I'm saying. He might as well have put that bullet in your brother's heart himself."

"Huh, maybe you're right. And Mister Marberry, he's gonna pay me if I do the deed like he's offerin' to pay everybody else?"

"He's offering you something better," Frank said.

"What's that?"

"He's offering you a job for as long as you want to keep it." The smile was settled on Frank's face. His eyes looked unnatural in the dim light of the cellar. *Take the bait,* Frank's whole body demanded.

Gladdy took a deep breath, looked up the stairs, found a bit of silence with his ears since the baby had ceased its wailing, and said, "When do we ride?"

Chapter 9

Fort Yates, Dakota Territory, December 1888

Trusty knocked on the door, stood back, and waited as patiently as he could. The sky was a casual gray, pocked with growing puffy, wind-filled, clouds. Dry snowflakes swirled around his boots, and the cold air that punched at his bare face felt like a hammer taken to glass. It wasn't the first time since he'd been in the Dakota Territory that Trusty had considered growing a beard to help keep himself warm. Only an age-old hurt and resentment had kept him from it. If he grew a beard, then his reflection would be that of his father and not his own. Anything that reminded him of St. Louis, or his past never set well with Trusty no matter the miles or the time away from the city.

Heavy footsteps beyond the door made their way toward the knock. The house was built like the guardhouse where Trusty was bunking but was divided into five individual quarters for the officers who served under Colonel Townsend. There was no grandeur to Army residences, especially in the Dakota Territory. The long house was plain and wind-battered, the exposed wood as gray as the sky.

James Pierpoint Plumright swung the door open and

said, "What?" He was dressed in his riding boots, uniform pants, with suspenders over a bleached white undershirt. He looked thinner and younger than he had the night before. His hair, a mop of brown straw on the top, had yet to be combed for the morning. "Oh, it's you."

Ice and small snow crystals accumulated on Trusty's shoulders as he stood in wait. Wind continued to snake around him and found a new doorway to invade. Plumright stood back a bit, assaulted by the cold and the interruption, but didn't give the weather or the coldness of it any acknowledgement.

"Good morning, captain," Trusty said.

"What do you want, Marshal?"

Trusty could see past Plumright. The interior of the front room was sparse. A fancy Chesterfield sofa, light wheat in color, covered in brocade fabric, sat among a collection of crates, some open, some sealed shut with Boston, Massachusetts, stamped on them in fresh black ink. "It's Deputy, sir. Marshal Delaney resides in Bismarck."

"So be it, Deputy. What do you want at this early hour?" Plumright had red streams crisscrossing his eyes along with the drooped eyelids from a whiskey hangover.

"I can come back later." Trusty didn't want to poke the bear any more than he already had.

"You're here. I repeat, what do you want?"

"I would like to speak with your wife if she is available," Trusty said. "And then I will be on my way. I won't bother you anymore, Captain Plumright."

"She's not going to talk to you." Plumright reached up, grabbed the door, and started to close it.

Trusty slid his boot inside to block the captain from shutting the door on him. Along with the cold biting at his face, and the encounter with the captain the night before, a change of mind came to Trusty, and he decided that the bear needed to be poked to consider the seriousness of his presence. "I would like to remind you, sir," he said, "that I was sent here by Marshal Delaney and endorsed by Colonel Townsend on a federal investigation. As part of that investigation, I need to talk with your wife, who, as is no secret is in the middle of the resulting troubles. I can come back later," Trusty said, holding eye contact with Plumright, "if she is indisposed, but I will talk to her one way or the other."

"She will not be speaking to you, Deputy. I have attained legal counsel and have been advised not to make Amanda available to you."

"You don't think that's a mistake?"

"I think I will do anything I can to protect my wife. I will also remind you that I am taking leave of Fort Yates in a matter of days."

"I can see that. Has Colonel Townsend been made aware of your counsel's advice?"

"No, and it doesn't matter if he has. I've made my statement. Amanda's made her statement. You'll find all you need there. We are done here, Deputy, so if you please, remove your boot from my door."

Trusty didn't move, remained calm, took a deep breath, and looked past Captain Plumright. He could see the shadow of a woman, standing still, just out of sight. Amanda Plumright was listening to the confrontation. Trusty didn't want to upset her. He pulled his boot away, and said, "As you wish, Captain. But I'll be back."

"I won't be here." Plumright glared at Trusty, then slammed the door in his face.

Trusty stood there for a moment, allowing the wind, snow, and the sound of rattling wood to settle around him.

This wasn't the first time he'd had a door slammed in his face, and Trusty didn't suppose it would be the last. But he knew one thing. No matter what, he was going to talk to Amanda Plumright one on one no matter what it took. Even if he had to wire Marshal Delaney to ask him to have the president himself make it happen.

Trusty stood at the door and listened to the captain's feet stomp in the direction that they had come from the first time. But he didn't go far. A rising tide of voices clashing together—a man's and a woman's—reached through the wooden door and encouraged Trusty not to move an inch. Snow piled on his shoulders, promising him a quick burial if he stood there too long, but it didn't matter. Instinct demanded that he stay, and his instinct turned out to be right. The argument quickly ceased, followed by familiar footsteps pounding back to the door, only this time the sound was more like a man walking on ice instead of beating on war drums.

The door flung open and James Pierpoint Plumright stood before Trusty red-faced and tense as a bow string pulled back ready to fire. "My wife demands that I invite you inside, Deputy." The captain stood aside then, offering entry into his home. The bow misfired, was broken, and there was no mistaking the defeat in Plumright's downcast blue eyes. He didn't appear to be a man accustomed to losing an argument.

"Thank you." Trusty brushed the snow off his shoulders, kicked the ice off his boots, and accepted the invitation.

Plumright closed the door behind Trusty and glared. "I am opposed to this."

"You've made that clear." Trusty could smell a hint of bacon coming from another room, the kitchen in the back.

He had yet to eat, but his appetite was for information, not food.

Amanda Plumright walked into the room, and any sense of noise, smell, or cold discomfort vanished from Trusty's body and mind. She was taller than her husband, but her hair, long and flowing over her shoulders, was nearly the same color of brown. Her eyes were cornflower blue and just as penetrating as any girl in a Vermeer painting. The obviously pregnant Mrs. Plumright wore a maroon morning robe, heavy in fabric with white fur cuffs and collar, hiding her feet, which Trusty assumed were covered in fur of some kind, too. Her belly was as round as a ball, almost ready to pop. She was probably close to her time to birthing the child—not that Trusty knew much about such womanly things. And that was the problem, the reason why he froze at the sight of Amanda Plumright. He couldn't help but think about Jessica Marberry. Jessica had died in childbirth, and a bit of sadness and melancholy rolled over Trusty as he considered all that he had lost by not being with Jessica, and what lay ahead in Amanda's path, considering the charge of rape and the state of her marriage, as obviously fragile as the sign that she was truly pregnant.

"Ma'am," Trusty said, doffing his hat, scattering snow onto the bare wood floor.

"I must apologize for my husband's behavior, Deputy. He has been under a lot of strain of late." Amanda spoke with a measured, educated voice, eastern, Yankee to those in the south and to some in the north, too. She looked like a woman who was accustomed to having fine things in her life and married a military man in hopes of rising through the ranks with him—or that was Trusty's perception based on his own relationship with a woman who came from a higher station in life than he had. His problem was that he didn't share Captain Plumright's ambition or background. He had never been good enough for Jessica's family being a blacksmith's son, an Army scout, or a deputy marshal.

"I'm sorry to barge in on you," Trusty said, fighting off the suddenness of the warmth that he felt inside and out. "I was hoping to set a time when we could speak, but the captain told me last night of your impending move, so I figured the need was urgent, which is why I showed up here unannounced." The buffalo coat felt heavy. There was more than one fire burning in the section house, most likely one in the kitchen and one in the small parlor that angled off the even smaller entry room where the three of them stood. Crates littered the way for as far as he could see. The outside weather had all but disappeared. If the wind and snow had riled up, Trusty couldn't hear it, didn't much care about what was going on outside the Plumrights' residence at the moment. His full attention was on Amanda, and a growing feeling that there was nothing he could do to help her.

"I told you," James Pierpoint Plumright said, "everything you need to know has already been documented in our statements."

Before Trusty could say anything, Amanda sneezed, drawing both men's attention to her.

The hardness on Captain Plumright's face fell away, and a new wave of concern focused on his wife. Trusty was glad to see that, had been worried about the woman's welfare since he'd heard of the crime from Marshal Delaney. He wondered if Amanda Plumright had been shunned, cast aside, or blamed because she had been taken by an Indian. That didn't seem to be the case.

Amanda dug into a pocket, pulled out an empty hand, and sneezed again. "I've left my handkerchief on the bureau, James. Could you get it for me?"

Plumright stood his ground, looked to Trusty then back to his wife. She sneezed again, her eyes pleading, horrified at the lack of manners. Trusty remained still, out of the fray. The captain seemed hesitant to leave the room, to leave them together, but if he were a gentleman of any sort, he was going to have no choice at all but to leave the room. "If you insist," he said.

"I do," Amanda answered. "I fear I'm catching a cold." She rested her hand casually on top of the ball that was her belly, her baby, and sniffled loudly but as delicately as she could.

"As you wish." Plumright glared at Trusty as he hurried away but didn't say a word to him.

As soon as he was out of sight, Amanda reached into her other pocket and pulled out a piece of neatly folded paper. She offered it to Trusty, all the while holding her index finger up to her lips, begging him to remain quiet.

Trusty understood, took a stealth step, reached out, took the note, and stuffed it in his pocket. As he settled back to his original place, Plumright hurried back into the room with a white handkerchief in hand. The exchange had taken seconds and was successful. The captain didn't seem to have seen anything. He handed Amanda a handkerchief, and she turned away before saying a word. After wiping her face, she rejoined the two men in good form and smiled.

"That's better," she said.

"I'm sorry I have bothered you'all this morning." Trusty stiffened and stared at the captain. "Is there a time I can come back?"

"There is no better time," Plumright said. "But if you must, then before dinner would be our request. Amanda?"

Amanda nodded. "That's fine, James."

Relieved, Trusty relaxed and made his way to the door. "I'm sorry to have bothered you." He opened the door, confronted the cold, and continued to walk outside the house. He felt like a thief robbing a bank in broad daylight.

James Pierpoint Plumright followed Trusty to the door and stopped, eyeing him with suspicion. "Please show my wife the respect she deserves, Deputy. This is her first child."

Trusty was down the stoop and a few steps away from the door. He turned to face the captain, a little surprised that the man had said, "her first child," instead of "our first child." It was a hint about his state of mind, that perhaps Captain Plumright held a concern that Charlie Littlefoot was the baby's father and not him. The two men had more in common than the captain knew. "I am not here to hurt anyone, sir. I just need to find the truth."

"What you need to do, Deputy, is find that Indian and bring him back here for trial. Every second that we stand here, he is farther away, aided no doubt by his own kind who celebrate his actions instead of condemn them," Plumright said.

"Marshal Delaney has eyes on the border, and a man on the other side if Littlefoot crosses into Canada."

"The Mounties always get their man."

"That's what they say."

"Unless the Indian went south instead of north."

"Why would you say that?"

"Because the Indian isn't stupid."

Trusty found it interesting that Plumright wouldn't say

the man's name. It was understandable, especially if Charlie Littlefoot was guilty of the crime he was accused of. "We have it on good authority that he is heading north."

"I hope you're right, Deputy. You've already wasted a lot of time. The Indian has a long head start in any direction he went."

The wind and snow had not slowed down while Trusty had been inside the captain's quarters. Just the opposite. The sky was hateful with wind sending dry snow spiraling in all directions as it fell to the earth. The temperature had plummeted to a bitter cold that promised to freeze anything it touched. Frostbite was a real danger. Trusty could feel the cold all the way to his bones. "I'll return later, Captain. I'm sorry to have bothered you."

"You are wasting your time, Deputy," Plumright said, then slammed the door. A boom echoed toward Trusty and was pushed back by the wind and snow. The precipitation didn't tinkle softly as it hit the ground and everything else, it stabbed, promising to cut with all of the serrated edges of the flakes.

Trusty hurried off, not stopping until he found sanctuary in the guardhouse where he was bunking. Once inside, he stopped to warm himself before going any farther. Once he stopped shivering, he dropped his hand into his pocket and pulled out the note that Amanda Plumright had slipped him. He was safe to read it:

> *Please find him before they do.*
> *Otaktay will help you.*

The note wasn't signed, but there was no mistaking that it was written in a woman's hand. Trusty read it again to make sure he understood what it said, and what he had to do next. He had to find the Indian who called himself Oliver, and then get on Charlie Littlefoot's trail. It seemed it wasn't only the U.S. Marshals, and the Canadian Mounties who were after Charlie. *They* were. Whoever *they* were.

Chapter 10

Trusty wasn't surprised to find the room empty. It was mid-morning and a weekday to boot. He wasn't looking for an officer blowing off steam or taking a sip of whiskey in the backroom. He was looking for Oliver Heightsmith. Otaktay. Kills Many. According to Amanda Plumright, Oliver could help him find Charlie Littlefoot. Trusty had reservations about that, but he didn't want to intrude on Amanda any more than he had to. The situation with her husband and life in general seemed as fragile as an ice-covered pond in springtime. He was about to turn around and leave, begin asking around for Oliver, but he heard a door close beyond the makeshift bar.

Oliver entered the room and stopped when he spied Trusty. "Deputy Dawson," he said with a little bit of a jump in his voice. "I wasn't expecting anyone to be here." He was carrying a box that seemed a little heavy and sat it down on the bar with some effort.

"I was looking for you." A spike of cold air scratched

Trusty's face as it pushed past him. The room smelled musty and old.

"Is there anything wrong?"

"Are we alone?"

"No one is here but us. The drinking room is as empty as this room."

"I spoke with Amanda Plumright."

"I am surprised to hear that."

Trusty nodded. "The captain was hesitant to let me speak to her."

"I believe that." Oliver was dressed almost the same as he was the night before, dark trousers, a clean, pressed white collarless shirt, starched with sharp creases. The two of them were about the same height, taller than a lot of men, able to look each in the eye easily. Trusty hadn't met many Sioux men, or didn't know if he had, and he wondered if they were all as tall as Oliver.

"It wasn't much of a conversation," Trusty said, digging into his pocket, pulling out the note that Amanda had passed to him. "She gave me this." He held up the note. "It says for me to find him before they do and that Otaktay, you, will help me. Who are they? Is Charlie Littlefoot in danger?"

Oliver lowered his head, then looked back up to Trusty with a sigh. "I have heard grumblings about a posse of men going after Charlie, but I saw no one leave, no one of stature take out after him. I thought it was a rumor, but Miss Amanda must know something more than I do and cannot tell anyone. She is a prisoner of her husband. We all are prisoners of the walls that surround us."

"I assumed as much," Trusty said, stuffing the note in

his pocket. "Captain Plumright isn't going to be a captain much longer."

"And he will be able to go wherever he wants to," Oliver said.

"You think he is gatherin' up a group of men to go after Charlie? Is that it?"

"Now that you've shown up, yes, I do think that. Your presence makes the investigation real."

"Why not just wait until the child is born?"

"And see if the skin is brown or white? That proves nothing."

"I'm sorry, you're right to point that out to me. I beg your pardon," Trusty said.

"If the baby is an *iyeska,* what you would call a half-breed, that doesn't mean Charlie is guilty of any crime. If a man and woman wish to lay with each other that is not a crime, is it?"

"Depends on who you ask, I suppose," Trusty said. "If the woman is married, that is a crime in her church, maybe even in her territory. I don't know, but I understand what you're sayin', I think. Charlie and Amanda had more than a friendship."

"Yes," Oliver said. "We all warned him off it, but there was no stopping him. Or her. The captain. He did not treat his wife very nice at all, Deputy. If you know what I mean."

"I think I do. You can call me Trusty. Everybody does."

Oliver smiled. "I will ask you the same thing you asked me. What is your real name?"

"Sam. Samuel."

"From the Bible?"

"Yes. My mother had high hopes for me. She wanted me to be a counselor to kings." Trusty allowed a brief, soft smile to cross his face as the memory of his mother passed across his mind's eye. The image of her was fading, and he longed to hear her voice, but the sight of her calmed him a bit, rooted his feet on the floor that he stood on. He understood more about women in difficult marriages with angry men than he cared to admit.

"It seems that her wish has come true," Oliver said. He had remained standing behind the bar, stiff as a board, which might have been his normal stance for all Trusty knew, but not uncomfortable. The more Oliver talked, the more Trusty liked him.

"You wear a badge. Your counsel frees some men and jails others. You speak with men of power regularly. They listen to you closely, trust you to come all of this way in search of the truth. Your mother, she was wise, saw that in you as soon as you were born."

"I suppose you're right. I never thought about my badge like that." The notion comforted Trusty even more, considering he had pondered the desire to remain a deputy instead of throwing it all away to search for the baby Marberry girl. "I think Amanda is concerned about this posse, about what they will do to Charlie."

"They will kill him if they find him. They will hang him and leave him swinging as one more example of what they will do to a man who even thinks about violating their women."

"I know that. At least, I think I know that. If you can help me to stop that, if you can help me find Charlie before they do, I would be much obliged. My aim is to head north from here. The thinkin' is that Charlie's headin' to Canada to disappear there for a while."

Oliver nodded and walked out from behind the bar. "If I tell you where Charlie is going, I will betray my people.

They will never trust me again. Not that many of them trust me anyway since I work here, picking up after white men, serving their every need, or finding someone who can. They say I am white on the inside and brown on the outside, lost to the ways of the Lakota. But that is not true. I know who I am, where I come from, and where I belong. I can protect my people with the words that touch my ears in this room. I am so invisible, so little of a threat, that these officers, these powerful white men talk freely as if I do not exist. That is how I know as much as I do. But I cannot tell you where Charlie Littlefoot is going. I cannot help you or Miss Amanda in that way."

Trusty eyed Oliver and considered what the man had said. He knew enough about the ways of the Indian to know what Oliver had said was true. He also knew there was another way to get what he wanted, what he needed, and he thought he understood what Oliver was saying. "What if you show me? What if I force you to show me?"

"Are you arresting me, Deputy Dawson?" Oliver said with another nod and half a smile.

"I will if I have to."

St. Louis, Missouri, April 1875

The night was bright with a full moon overhead. Seventeen-year-old Sam Dawson had heard once that the April full moon was called the Pink Moon. It didn't look pink to him. It looked red. Everything looked red. He was as angry as a fire ant, its nest kicked by a stupid human being.

The cool limestone wall of the monolithic Methodist Church in St. Louis proper held him up. His back was plastered to the wall as he stared out into the night, rubbing the side of his cheek, doing his best not to let the feeling of Jessica Marberry's kiss go. But it withered quickly and there was nothing he could do about it. She was gone. Most likely forever. Shipped off to England, as far away from him as possible. Her maid had found her diary, read all about Jessica's feelings for Sam, and told Theodore Marberry about it. Marberry had already come to the blacksmith shop and warned Sam off her, told him not to see her ever again—but they hadn't listened. Sam and Jessica snuck out to see each other as often as they could. She had begged Sam to run away with her, but he knew in his heart of hearts that he couldn't take care of Jessica, not how she was accustomed, and he was afraid of Marberry, was sure he would come looking for them if they did run away. Sam stood alone. The last place he wanted to go was home and be more miserable. So, he went to the only place he thought he might have half a chance of finding some comfort.

Madame Duchamp's house was lit up like there was a Saturday night party going on even though it was the middle of the week. What had once been a depressing and rundown street had transformed since the arrival of Madame Duchamp and her girls. Determined not to be looked down on any more than possible, the madame started to funnel some of her profits directly into the house she did business in. She had the roof repaired, and the clapboard siding replaced and painted. A nice wrought-iron fence made by Sam and his father surrounded the property. Flowers and bushes were planted in gardens, and lush grass had replaced the dirt that had made up the yard. Madame Duchamp was not worried about floods destroying her work. Her attitude allowed for her to see past the risk of her location—she was willing to repair whatever was broken or damaged. That went for her girls, too. She provided medical care for them, insisted that they were clean, and schooled them if they didn't have an education. The neighborhood benefited most from the woman's presence and hard work. Success breeds success. Most of the houses that stood on the street had been repaired or were in various states of reconstruction, some with Madame Duchamp's financial help. She insisted on contributing to the world around her.

Sam zig-zagged through various buggies, wagons, and horses that were parked in front of the house. More than one steamer had arrived earlier in the day, and word was Madame Duchamp's house was the place to be. By now, Sam could come and go from the house as he pleased. There was only one rule: He keep his hands off the girls, and the girls keep their hands off him. The latter was the hardest. It seemed one of the girls was always trying to tempt him into a dark corner. But Sam's heart belonged to Jessica Marberry. Until now. That heart was just beginning to break.

Sam staggered into the kitchen out of breath. He had run all the way to the riverside. Kabbie Mae was usually standing at the stove, but she wasn't there. No one was. The kitchen was empty. So were the pots, pans, and dishes. There was no sign of any food at all. The place looked like it had been attacked by a swarm of rats who hadn't left one crumb of bread behind.

The house was full. Loud. Piano music tinkered away at a fast pace, but the sound of it was distant over the roar of the crowd. There was laughter and men talking in full-throated voices. Girls giggling. Sam was accustomed to a party-like atmosphere in the house, but this was bigger than anything since the Mardi Gras carnival Madame Duchamp hosted earlier in the year. He leaned against the interior wall of the kitchen, gaining his breath and composure. The wall throbbed with a vibration of people and music that Sam had never felt before. Once he got control of himself, he went to the door to peer out into the large dining room that sat adjacent to the kitchen. Beyond the kitchen was a grand entryway with a staircase that spiraled up into the rooms of debauchery, pleasures, and secrets Sam was yet to understand. He had learned a lot by being around the house, but he lacked practical experience. He wasn't going to dare break Madame Duchamp's one rule.

The house was packed with people. Men mostly. Sam spied the madame standing in the center of the entryway, welcoming guests, directing traffic, looking beautiful as ever in a green velvet dress that looked like it had been painted on her. There was little left to the imagination. Sam had to force himself to look away from her every time she was dressed for a night's work. Madame Duchamp saw Sam from across the room and shot him a smile.

He smiled back, then looked away to see a familiar face. His father was descending from the upstairs with a girl on his arm. Natalie Lynn Jenkins, the girl from Boston who Sam had ferried to the house the first night she'd arrived in St. Louis. Long brown hair, a little plump, but curvy, too, in a pretty way, especially how she stuffed herself in a dress. Natalie was only a few years older than Sam, and she never failed to grab his attention. She was a temptress, one of the girls who was always trying to steal away with him, promising to teach him how to French kiss and more. He always resisted.

Anger raged inside Sam at the sight of his father. He nearly bit his tongue off. His ears throbbed and he felt hot, couldn't breathe. He had to get out of the house, so he bounced off a few walls and ended up outside, where he lost the will to run, because he didn't have anywhere to go. He sat down on the stoop, a mix of sweat and tears.

A long moment later, the door opened, and Katherine Duchamp walked outside. "I was hoping I would find you out here."

Sam looked up at her, all glassy-eyed. "How long has he been coming here?"

"You're going to have to learn that a man's business is his own. Your father's presence here has nothing to do with you." She sat down next to Sam. She smelled of tobacco and sandalwood; fresh but tainted in a way that she never had been before.

"Did he come here while my mother was alive?"

"I wasn't here then. You know that."

"You know more than you are saying."

"Maybe. Maybe not. You will understand the desire to be with a woman one of these days. Soon, I think. Yes?"

He shook his head. "I already know that desire. The girl I want to be with is on her way to England. I'll never love anyone like her. I'll wait for her. She'll come back, and I'll be here."

Katherine smiled and edged closer to Sam. "You are a romantic. How nice. I did not know that about you, Sam Dawson. Do not ever let that go. Do not change no matter how much it hurts."

"Jessica is the only girl for me."

"I suppose she is. Now, you need to wipe this anger and sadness off your face and come inside. Dance with the girls. I will allow it tonight. But no visits upstairs. Not now. Not ever. You must find you way out there, not here. Understand?"

Sam nodded, then said, "I won't go in if he is still inside."

"You father is gone. But if I were you, I would forget

you ever saw him here. You are here with your own life. You must understand he has his own life, too." Madame Duchamp stood up and reached her hand out for Sam's. "Come, you need to smile on this night. There will be time for the sadness of a broken heart some other time."

Fort Yates, Dakota Territory December 1888

As much as Trusty was happy to settle into Horse's saddle again, he wasn't looking forward to the long ride north. He hadn't counted on riding with a traveling companion, but it had occurred to him that if he was going to ride with anyone, riding with a Lakota Indian made the most sense. There was no one who knew the land and how to survive on it better than someone like Oliver. He hoped Oliver would feel the same way. Trusty knew that riding with him came with its own set of concerns.

There had been little to tidy up other than checking in with Colonel Townsend and telling him what he had learned. Trusty also implored the colonel to keep James Pierpoint Plumright at the fort, but Townsend made it clear that he had no jurisdiction over Plumright's actions after he separated from the Army. That gave Trusty and Oliver a two-day head-start if the assumption that Plumright was riding out in search of Charlie was true. Trusty hoped that was enough of a lead, but it also created another problem as they rode north: traveling in a land covered in ice and snow. They could be easily tracked.

His gear was packed. Trusty was dressed in his riding clothes, back in the buffalo coat, but he had traded out his Cavalry Stetson for a hat made of beaver hide and fur that kept his head and ears warmer than the Stetson. He looked like a mountain man from the past, readying to quest over the Yellowstone Mountains instead of riding north into Canada. Horse didn't seem to mind the extra weight. Trusty nickered him out of the fort's livery once he was fully settled into the saddle. The Sioux kept their horses in a different barn, closer to their section of the fort. He hoped Oliver would be waiting for him. There was always the chance that the Indian wasn't going to meet up with Trusty, ride with him like he had agreed to after the threat of arrest, but Trusty had taken Oliver at his word. There was no time to waste as far as he was concerned.

It was a relief to find Oliver waiting for him. His horse, a tall chestnut gelding, was packed and ready to go as they stood outside of a small hut-like building. There was no one to see the man off. Oliver was alone, dressed in his own set of furs. It wasn't snowing at the moment, but the cold wind was unrelenting. It pushed and bit and attacked anything in its path without remorse.

"I'm glad to see you," Trusty said, bringing Horse to a stop. A cloud of ice crystals exited the horse's long nose as he exhaled. Trusty could see his own breath linger as a small cloud for a second before it dissipated.

"It is a long ride north," Oliver said.

"It is. I've been thinkin' about this. There's somethin' I should tell you before we set out."

"What is that?" A look of concern fell across Oliver's chiseled stone face. Ice had already started to collect on his eyebrows.

"There's a bounty on my life. A man has put out a thousand silvers as the price to see me dead. Whatever danger comes from the elements and Captain Plumright and his gang, if there is one, there are other dangers to consider that you should know about. I'm not going to force you to come along with me, but if you decide not to ride alongside me, I hope you'll tell me what you know about Charlie's whereabouts.

"I was attacked by a man north of Cannonball on my trek here from Bismarck seekin' to collect on that bounty. I had to kill him to save myself, and he in turn had killed a man he rode with to claim the bounty all for himself. I can't guarantee that's not going to happen again, considerin' this man, Marberry, has a set of his own men out here in the Territory searchin' for me, too."

"You speak of those Singer salesmen," Oliver said.

"Then you already knew."

"Of course, I did."

"And you're ready to go anyway?"

"Charlie Littlefoot is my friend and my brother. Miss Amanda is in as much trouble as Charlie, if not more. I have no choice but to ride with you, Trusty Dawson. But"—Oliver paused and allowed his face a hard look—"you must also know that you and I will not be friends or partners or the boss of one or the other. As a Lakota I have many enemies, and the white man more than any others remain so. You must always remember that I am Kills Many here, away from the fort, where I am able to breathe the air and the freedom it promises. And you are a warrior, a veteran of a war who fought against my brothers and sisters for no other reason than to take our land and our way of life because you and your people think they need it more than we do. I am only here because Amanda Plumright is a gentle woman and Charlie Littlefoot does not deserve to die because of who he loves and a mistake he made.

"All right, then, Oliver. Let's go find Charlie."

Chapter 11

Frank rode ahead of Gladdy and Clovis, solidifying his position as the man in charge. Gladdy wasn't about to call the man Boss. Marberry, either, as far as that went. But he was happy to have somebody to rely on when it came to getting through the day. The plan was to ride to a place called Aberdeen in the Dakota Territory and meet up with Glo Timmons and Red Jack Lewis, if the two hadn't put an end to Trusty Dawson yet. There were a million other places that Gladdy would have rather ridden to. Somewhere warm like Arizona instead of north, riding straight into winter's wide open cold mouth, but he felt lucky to be alive, that Marberry hadn't just had Frank and Clovis kill him. Marberry didn't come across like he was the killing kind, not like Vance Calhoun, Gladdy's old, and now deceased, boss. Calhoun would slit a man's throat or beat him senseless just for looking at him cross-eyed. Marberry seemed uppity and desperate to Gladdy, like he had his hands in a mess he didn't want to be in. Well, that made two of them.

The weather in St. Louis was mild in comparison to what lay ahead. Gladdy wore a regular canvas duster and his dirty old felt cowboy hat. The rest of his gear was on a pack horse, loaded down with all sorts of doodads and blankets that offered to slow them down. But he wasn't going to say so out loud. He was happy to have the prospect of a warm bedroll and a bowl full of beans when he needed one. The opportunity of a ride with a mission to kill, fully packed, almost made Gladdy feel like his life was normal again. Except it wasn't. Life would never be normal.

Frank pulled his horse's impatient head back, a black gelding he called Burt, and said, "Won't be gettin' many more chances to blow off steam once we get out of the city." He nodded at a saloon, bright lights, music pulsing from the inside like it was a Saturday night instead of a Tuesday.

Gladdy was surprised at the offer to stop at the saloon. Frank had come across as a strict man on the job. Something told him he had a lot to learn about the two he was riding with. They were an odd pair, opposites that seemed to fit together because of time and circumstance. Gladdy wasn't sure whether the two men liked each other or not.

Clovis looked over to Gladdy with a wry smile on his face. "Frank's got a girl there he wants to see 'fore leavin' town is what it is, ain't it, Frank? You want to take a quick poke at Clarice before you leave the confines of Saint Louis, don't you?"

"She ain't my girl."

Gladdy kept his mouth quiet now that the stop made sense. He wouldn't mind participating in the same kind of feminine acquisition, though he was leery of such things, all things considered. That Rona girl with the cherub cheeks he'd taken a roll with upon arriving in the city had done her best to get her hooks into him. He wondered if this Clarice was the same kind of girl. Didn't matter much once he thought about it. All three of them had a job to get to. No woman was gonna tie any of them down for a long stay. He might as well have some fun while there was fun to be had if the man in charge was gonna do the same thing. Marberry had paid for the trip half in advance, so not only did Gladdy have the prospect of a decent bedroll, but he also had a few coins in his pocket.

"If you say she ain't your girl, Frank, that's fine with me. You sure do seem sweet on her." Clovis let the smile stay on his face. Most of his teeth were good, but his dog tooth was starting to rot. It had a pin hole in it that was spreading brown, like a rash had taken hold that wouldn't let go.

"I'm stopping. You two do whatever the hell you want to." Frank hurried off then, stopping at the hitching post outside of the saloon. He tied up Burt and stalked inside.

"Don't pay him no mind," Clovis said to Gladdy. "He'll be in a good mood for a couple of days after he leaves Clarice. She puts a magic spell on him like no other girl ever has."

"What about you? You got a girl in there, too?" Gladdy stared at the saloon, starting to salivate at the thought of the taste of beer and a girl calf jumpin' on his lap.

"Nope. I like my whiskey and money in my pocket. Women don't like you to have neither. At least that's been my experience."

"Don't you get lonely?"

"Nope. Do you?"

"Not lately."

The two men silently agreed to move on, following after Frank, who was on his own mission of obvious pleasure.

Both men tied up their horses next to Burt. When they pushed through the batwings, Gladdy spied Frank heading straight for a plump blonde, fancied up in a tight, sparkly red dress, that he assumed was Clarice.

The air was filled with smoke, laughter, and a quick piano song, mixed all together with the smell of yeasty beer. It seemed every night in St. Louis was a celebration; someone was either coming or going somewhere. Gladdy'd never seen anything like it, never been in a city that felt like the ground was always movin' under your boot heels.

Gladdy and Clovis hung back, giving Frank sway with his intentions.

Frank tapped the blonde on the shoulder, who was talking with a cowboy at the bar. The blonde, this Clarice if Gladdy was right in his thinking, didn't look none too happy about being interrupted. She glared at Frank and said loud enough for anyone within twenty feet to hear, "What are you doin' here?"

Frank stepped back like he had been slapped. The man had been a take-charge kind of man since Gladdy had encountered him, but now he looked like a pup snapped at by its teat-sore mother.

Clovis swallowed, and said, "Oh," as soft as his surprise by the greeting would allow him. "That ain't good."

"We need to talk, Clarice," Frank said as he grabbed her hand and started to pull her away.

Clarice was having none of it. She put the brakes on her feet like a train coming into the station too fast. She pulled back and broke free of Frank's grasp, her face red as a ripe radish and just as hot.

The cowboy was on his feet before Clarice broke free and tumbled back into him. It looked like there had been a transaction about to take place and Frank had horned in when he shouldn't have. That was how Gladdy saw it all play out. He stood halfway between the bar and the batwings as his hope of finding a good time girl for himself faded quickly. He'd spied a brunette stuffed in a red dress made like Clarice's and just as tight, as soon as he'd walked in the door of the saloon. The brunette looked mighty tasty.

"You best leave this girl alone, mister," the cowboy said. He was tall as a windmill and just as skinny. He wore a big hat and a mustache that was so thick he could have swept the floor with it. Both he and Frank looked to be about the same age, and Gladdy was already sizing the two up against each other trying to figure out which one could take the other in a fist fight. It was even odds at the moment, but heavy tension rippled through the saloon, and every sound in the big open room dropped noticeably. Everything but the piano. The player, a short, bald man wearing a white shirt and black string tie, played faster than he had before the disagreement had started.

"This ain't none of your business," Frank said. "Come on, Clarice," he begged. "I'm ridin' out of town. I just need a minute with you."

"You best get, then." Clarice planted her feet and anchored her hands on her broad hips, leaning back into the cowboy, who looked like he was holding her up.

"You heard what Clarice said. Now go on, there's the door," the cowboy said. "Come on darlin', let's me and you go somewhere quiet so we can finish our conversation."

Frank grabbed Clarice again. This time harder, by the wrist, his face turning red to match hers. "You stay here until I'm done talkin' with you."

The cowboy took quick offense to the intrusion and pulled Clarice away from Frank, breaking the grasp. Then he set himself between the two of them with a fist rising into an upper cut as he finished the move. The quick punch caught Frank under the chin, unprepared, sending him sprawling backward as a spray of blood escaped his mouth. He'd bit his tongue.

Gladdy stepped forward, willing to jump into the melee, but Clovis pulled him back, deciding that Frank was out-matched. "This ain't our fight." He nodded toward two bouncers, both big as bulls, heading toward the trouble with fixed eyes and hands made into fists of their own.

The room went quiet except the piano. The player ignored the situation. Or acted like he was ignoring the situation and played faster and faster. Gladdy didn't know the song, but it sounded like a rope getting pulled too quick to a yank back.

The cowboy rushed Frank who had stumbled off a table, sending pitchers and mugs shattering to the floor. A crowd of standing men, with a few girls mixed in, quickly created a wall resembling a ring around the two men.

Frank bounced back up, persistent and enraged, and met the cowboy with swinging fists of his own, landing a solid punch directly to the tall man's nose. That hit offered an-other spray of blood to the floor and added the sound of crushing bone to the tinkling piano keys.

The cowboy stumbled back with a surprised look on his face caused by the pain that came at him from such an undesirable foe. He regained his footing, wiping the blood from his face, slinging it to the floor, and bounced his head as he reevaluated Frank and his abilities. "You want to end this now, mister, all you have to do is walk out the same way you came in."

Music tried to drown them out, but it was no use.

"I ain't leavin' until I speak with Clarice," Frank said.

Then he went at the cowboy again dodging and darting, swinging and flailing, doing his best to make himself an unpredictable target.

Gladdy was becoming uncomfortable. The air inside the saloon was closing in on him, and smelled of blood, sweat, and the anticipation of escalating violence, that in Gladdy's experience, had always turned out bad. "Frank's in trouble," he whispered to Clovis, unsnapping his holster at the same time.

"That fella's got more men rooting for him than Frank does. You keep your hands where everybody can see them. You don't need to draw no more attention to us than there already is."

The two bouncers pushed through the fight circle and went straight for Frank. They grabbed him, but not before he got in another punch at the cowboy. It was more graze than a hit, but the crack of skin echoed through the saloon like a lone clap after a bad performance.

Frank was riled beyond restraint. He was a mad animal, determined to stay free and have his way. He was loose and slippery with his own sweat; his strength seemed to have multiplied in a way that made him stronger than before. He broke free of the biggest bouncer, swinging as he went. His nose flared, foam bubbled off his lips, and his face had transformed from a mild man on his way out of town to a red-faced devil bent on revenge no matter the cost. He swung at the other bouncer, missing as he went. The bouncer had been ready for him and threw his own punch, landing it directly against the side of Frank's cheek. The hit was no clap. It was the cringing sound of a jawbone snapping in two. More blood expelled itself from Frank's mouth as he stumbled backward, groaning as he went. The men behind him parted, allowing room for the falling man to crash to the floor without being touched. But the fall was not graceful or soft. Frank struck his head, right at the temple, on the corner of a table as he made his way to the floor. Another thud, then a thump as his body caught up with the rest of him. He landed on the floor like a pigeon shot from the sky, falling straight to the earth, dead before it hit the ground. All Gladdy and Clovis could do was watch in horror.

The piano stopped playing and silence proceeded to overtake the room.

"Somebody better send for the doc," a man said.

Gladdy couldn't see Frank on the floor from where he stood, but he could see the cowboy who was staring down with a concerned look on his face. Clarice was standing on the opposite side of the ring, and after a few seconds, she waved her hand in front of her face and fainted, drawing a collective gasp of concern from the crowd. A man caught her mid-fall and eased her to the floor. Another man pushed by Gladdy and ran out the door, leaving him to wonder if he should do the same thing. With Frank hurt, or worse, the ride to Aberdeen to find Trusty Dawson looked to be in serious jeopardy. Anything he owed or was given by Theodore Marberry was null and void. He could have just slipped out of the saloon and disappeared, but he didn't. Clovis stopped him by saying, "We best leave and get on with what we're doin'."

Another man, standing close enough to see Frank said as loud as he could, "It looks like you best get the undertaker not the doc. This man ain't breathin'."

"It was self-defense," the cowboy hollered. "You'all seen it, right. That feller came in swingin', puttin' his hands all over Clarice. I didn't have no choice but to defend her."

Every man, and the women, nodded, agreeing with the cowboy.

"We best go now, before they turn on us," Clovis whispered.

"What about Frank?" Gladdy said.

"You heard what the man said. He's dead. Now, come on, let's go. I ain't ready to die by association just yet. Are you?"

Chapter 12

North, on the trail out of Fort Yates,
December 1888

A thick wall of steadily falling snow met Trusty and Oliver as they rode north; it was an unwelcome white flag, from sky to earth, with no promise of surrender. The blank color of the sky was hard on the eyes. The ground before them was just as white and just as bright, but more precarious than the sky. Rocks had turned to icebergs with only their sharp, slippery tips showing above the frozen sea of bent and dried grasses. Snakes made of snow squiggled from the northwest to the northeast; fanged vipers with skin made of diamonds that glittered briefly in the fading light. Each step Horse took was a challenge in staying upright, planted on four hooves, but the strawberry roan did not hesitate. He paced along, head down without hesitation as he pierced the wind and complied with his rider's command.

Trusty shielded his vision by pulling the hood of his buffalo coat as far down as it would go. Both of their horses had transformed from roan and chestnut to albino white as they collected an easy half inch of snowflakes and pellets on their manes, withers, and rumps. There was no escaping the snow. It was wet instead of dry as the temperature hovered just under freezing. Which seemed odd. It felt like it was warm instead of cold, especially in the layers of clothes with the durable, heavy buffalo coat.

Trusty hadn't come to a complete understanding to the moods of the Dakota weather, his time there had been too short. He was sweating and cold at the same time and starting to think that Arizona sounded like a better place to be, except that would take him farther away from the baby girl. He would never find her west. His gut told him that she was in St. Louis, under lock and key with Theodore Marberry. If she were his, of his blood, she would need rescued. But brought home to where? On the trail, hunting down criminals or escorting judges from one hanging to the next? What kind of life would that be for a girl? Or him, if he had to give up the badge. Trusty had no idea what he would do, or how he would live, if he was left to raise a baby on his own. Being lost in a snowstorm seemed to offer a better prospect at living. But he longed to know the truth. Was the baby girl, born to Jessica in another man's bed, really his own?

Horse continued his steady pace, eyeing the ground with a frozen face as he went. The only reason they could keep going and not get lost was the lay of the land. The rise that edged north along the Missouri River was easy to follow. But slow going. Snow was falling fast, an inch or two an hour, and the horses and their riders rode with caution. There was a good thing about the weather, though. If there was a place where a man with a bounty on his head could feel safe, or as safe as possible, it was riding on a narrow trail in a snowstorm, covered in white, melding into the landscape like he was a part of it, not outside of it, an easy target. Worries of sudden death had been left behind in the fair weather south of them, though Trusty still held a concern about Oliver's welfare. The Indian's disappearance from the fort would be noticed by white men and Indians alike. Would they come after him, too? Would Captain Plumright and his alleged posse of men follow them north in hopes that Oliver and Trusty would lead them straight to Charlie Littlefoot? It was something to consider and to be wary of, along with the bounty hunters that Brazos Joe had warned him of. For now, he felt safe, protected by the weather instead of attacked by it.

There was no conversation between Trusty and Oliver as they edged along the river, no joy or comradery to be shared as they settled into the journey north. Tracking a man to bring him to justice was nothing to celebrate. Oliver had made it clear that he was there only because he had been asked to ride with Trusty by Amanda Plumright. Trusty had to wonder about their relationship, how deep it was, and why Oliver would drop everything to ride into the weather and danger by a simple request from a white woman. There was more that he didn't know about the pregnant woman and her Indian friends, and that made Trusty just as wary as a clear day would have, making him an easy shot.

Trusty stayed in the lead and planned on remaining that way until Oliver gave him the word that they needed to go off the trail, take an Indian route instead of the normal way a white man would venture. Trusty looked over his shoulder every once in a while to make sure that Oliver was still behind him. The Indian was a white blur, barely visible, his own head down, covered by his own buffalo hat and coat. Oliver looked like a white bear sitting on a white stallion; any color had been covered up, stricken, erased from the Indian and his horse.

It wasn't long before Trusty stopped Horse and waited for Oliver to join him. He had to admit to himself that he couldn't see the way forward. The wind had picked up, and even though the snowflakes were heavy with moisture, the wind whipped them around in a frenzy that made the sky look like the ground, and the ground look like the sky. "I've lost the trail," he said as Oliver pulled up alongside him.

"It is easy to do if you have not spent much time in this part of the world in the winter. The river will take us far," Oliver said. He cocked his head downward. "But that might not keep the windigos away."

"Windigos?"

"Giants who like the taste of human flesh. They like this kind of weather. They can walk freely in the world without worry of being seen."

It was good to know that Oliver had fears of his own. Trusty didn't know much about windigos, but they were among the last things he was worried about even though they sounded a lot like bounty hunters. Freezing to death or tumbling into a ravine ranked high above flesh-eating giants at the moment. "Can you see the way?"

"No, but my horse can."

"And you trust him not to walk us in circles?" The falling snow suddenly abated for a second or two, allowing Trusty to see a white ribbon of frozen water, covered with more snow, arching north; a curvy path to Canada awaiting them both. He had forded many a river, but he had never used one directly as a trail. Thoughts of falling through the ice and freezing to death crossed his mind. No matter what, bounty or no bounty, Plumright and posse, if there was one, risk of injury, and the possibility of death were never far away. But he would have preferred that kind of death than meeting up with one of Oliver's windigos or Marberry's hired killers. "You lead," he finally said.

Oliver agreed by nickering his horse around Trusty, trailing down the slight ravine that led to the river. Trusty held back and watched until the Indian and his ride were firmly planted on the frozen river. He joined them, tracing their route step by step as closely as possible. Horse didn't seem to have any trouble navigating the way down, but stiffened as Trusty did, responding to the tension held in the reins.

Once they were on flat ground, there was plenty of room to spare. The two men rode abreast, silent again, facing the north wind with their heads down and ears open. If there were any enemies about, they would remain hidden, buried in the snow like the rest of the world, doing all they could to survive. Killing of any kind would have to come on another day or if the current blast of snow relented. That didn't look like it was going to happen anytime soon.

Horse, it seemed, was glad to have a companion to ride along with. The two horses rode side by side, their breaths and exhales mingling into a single cloud, disappearing almost as quickly as it had appeared. Horse had always been amenable with other horses, enjoying company when it came, but never objecting to the loneliness of a single rider, at least as far as Trusty could tell. Though, most of the time, Trusty didn't pay all that much attention to Horse's social life. He viewed the beast as a mode of transportation and little more. That didn't mean that Trusty didn't take care of Horse. Just the opposite. He knew that he had to take care of the horse so the horse could take care of him.

Trusty was surprised when Oliver started a conversation by asking, "Why don't you have a name for your horse?" The wind had calmed or had been shunted by the ravines on both sides of the Missouri River. Snow still fell at a steady rate, accumulating on everything around them like it had one purpose and one purpose only: Bury the entire world in a white blanket, covering everything it touched with icy fingers. From every perspective, the snow had been successful in that quest.

"I don't know that it's a name really," Trusty said, "He's a horse. Simple as that. What do you call your horse? I haven't heard you name him."

"Because you have not been listening."

"The wind roars in my ears and this hat muffles your words, even now."

"This is *Takoda*. Friend of Everyone." Oliver patted the chestnut gelding, sending an avalanche of snow to the ground, exposing a sweaty brown neck. Snow began to collect on the smooth horsehair immediately with a ravenous appetite to cover it again. Oliver and Takoda would be hard to see, invisible as they traveled. That was a plus even with the windigos walking about freely. A single plus that didn't stop Trusty's teeth from chattering and his bones from aching from the cold.

The surface of the river was flat, easy riding. The snow was wet, making the way a little less slippery than Trusty had expected. He tried not to think about the ice under Horse's hooves. He just hoped it was thick enough to hold their weight.

"Takoda seems like a good name, I suppose," Trusty said.

"I have known Takoda since he was a colt. He bounced

and ran through the field from one friend to the other, never making any other horse angry or feel threatened. I liked him right away, and he liked me. I have been lucky to have him as my friend for ten years. A horse will name itself if you pay close enough attention, tell you what he wants to be called if you listen. Horse is not your friend?"

Trusty sighed and looked away, then turned his gaze across the frozen river to the white, unknowable world on the other side of it. There was nothing to see but a rise covered in snow. All of the scrub had been covered. There were no trees, no birds, no sign of life, just a blank world that didn't seem to end or begin. He hadn't seen a living creature other than Horse, Oliver, and Takoda, since they had left Fort Yates. "I never thought about such a thing, whether I was friends with Horse. I didn't grow up around animals other than when they came into my father's blacksmith shop or I had to deliver shoes to the farrier. I learned to ride in the city on livery horses that were let to me when my father needed to send me on an errand or a delivery. I rarely rode the same horse twice. We had no dogs, though there was a wily old, orange-coated tom cat that hung around the shop. He was good at keeping the mice and rats at bay. My pa didn't pay the cat any mind because he served a purpose and had said so more than once. He never called the cat by name and neither did I."

Oliver didn't say anything, just kept riding Takoda nose to nose with Trusty and Horse. Snow continued to fall, and the wind danced up and down the river, tossing snow around like it was nothing, making the world ahead of them even whiter and denser, if that were possible.

Trusty continued talking, not concerned that the volume of his voice would attract a bullet or a chase. If anything, the weather, beyond the physical discomfort of it, was liberating. "I didn't have a mount that was my own until I joined the Army, and then it was a government issue horse, a big beefy black gelding with a solid white blaze on his nose. Stood a little over sixteen hands when he was full of himself. I was told he had a war horse lineage that reached into the past at least a hundred years. I was surprised that I was assigned to him. He looked fit for a general, and trotted like it, too. Easiest horse I ever had the pleasure of riding."

"Someone knew what they were doing. You are not a small man, Trusty Dawson," Oliver said.

"I suppose so. Our temperament matched close enough, and I got to tell you that I got on with that horse better than any other."

"Did he have a name?"

"Jasper."

"What?" Oliver said, cocking his thick fur hat toward Trusty. Oliver's bronze Indian face was peppered with snowflakes. They melted as they hit his skin but collected on his thick black eyebrows. "I didn't hear you."

Trusty had spoken so softly that the horse's name had been whisked away on the wind. "Jasper," he said, as loud as he could without shouting. "He came with the name. I didn't give it to him."

"What happened to him?"

Trusty didn't answer, didn't want to, but he had already replayed Jasper's demise in his head and his heart at the mere mention of the horse. He had never talked about Jasper's death with anyone, and he didn't want to talk about it now with a stranger. He urged Horse on, leaving Oliver and Takoda behind him several lengths.

The air temperature had dropped, and the snow began to fall harder, hitting Trusty in the face and turning to ice as the flakes slid down his face. The sky had grayed with anger, and the wind whipped around him with pin-prick pokes at every thrust. His eyes watered, and if a man had looked him square in the face at that moment, he would have sworn that Trusty Dawson was crying.

Oliver caught up with Trusty, and yelled, "We have to stop. We can't go on. I can't see the river's edge. If we continue, we could become lost and lose the trail north. We need to make camp."

"It's too soon to stop," Trusty yelled back. He didn't have the sun to judge the time of day, but it only felt like they were a few miles outside of Fort Yates.

"If we keep on, we will die," Oliver said. "Or injure our horses. That would even be worse. They are in need of a break and the warmth of a fire as much as we are."

Trusty couldn't argue with that and gave way to Oliver, allowing him to ride ahead and find a place to camp. His watery eyes were nearly blind with whiteness, and he knew the Indian had a better sense of where they were and what to do than he did.

It wasn't long before Oliver stopped at a thin copse of skinny cottonwoods, twenty feet tall, no bigger around than a normal-sized man, that had taken root next to the river's edge. The tree limbs were bare, heavy with snow, causing some of the weaker branches to fall to the ground. Sticks and bark poked up out of the snow for the taking, and it wasn't long before Oliver had a fire lit and alive. Trusty struck a canvas shelter before the fire. The horses stood together, tethered, the snow knocked off their backs, and covered with wool blankets. There was nothing to do but wait out the storm and settle in for the coming night—which promised to be colder than it had been, if that were possible.

A pot of coffee sat simmering on the fire, the aroma of it mixing with the burning wood. There was a bit of unexpected comfort to be found in the middle of the snowstorm, and Trusty was glad that he had taken Oliver's urging and got off the trail.

"I didn't mean to bring up a bad subject earlier, about Jasper," Oliver said. He sat shoulder to shoulder with Trusty, much like the horses, sharing the warmth of companionship.

Trusty didn't mind. He usually rode alone, but sharing company, especially in such miserable conditions was a change of pace. If he had been alone on the ride, he probably would have kept going, pushing his way north or thinking he was riding north. Somebody would have likely found him in the spring when the world thawed out, dead from stubbornness and stupidity instead of a bullet.

"I haven't thought about that horse in ages, is all. He was a good horse, and it was my inexperience that got him killed. That's not something a man wants to admit or talk about, especially when they're in the situation we are. I ain't never been really good at admitting failure or defeat. If I'm bein' honest, I think both have been rarities in my life once I got out on my own. But my failings have been big ones, cost lives. That's not easy to live with some days."

Oliver nodded, reached for the coffee pot and poured two mugs worth. Even in the middle of nowhere he was a barkeep. "The sun rises in the east every day. It is the only thing that does not fail us." He handed Trusty a mug.

The coffee smelled like the inside of a house, warm

and cozy, and tasted just as good. After swallowing the first drink, Trusty relaxed his shoulders and stared into the mug. "I was at Fort Robinson when I rode Jasper. One summer day meant for takin' it easy after a long campaign, I rode out into the countryside, and took a snooze under a shady oak tree. I let Jasper graze in the grass, not thinkin' a thing that there would be snakes about, something that could harm Jasper. Mind you, I always worried about snake holes when we was on the run. But Jasper, just like Horse, seemed to have a sense about where to put his hooves. Anyways, I woke up, and there was Jasper chewing his way through the nicest stretch of Nebraska grass you ever laid eyes on. All of a sudden, the horse reared back and screamed with a small rattlesnake attached to his nose."

Oliver did not look at Trusty, and for a moment, the wind relented. It was as if the wind and the world beyond the camp wanted to listen, too. "A massasauga. My people believe the snake is sacred, and we ask it for protection."

"I killed it, is what I did," Trusty said with a pause. "Then it killed Jasper. His nose swelled up and he couldn't breathe. There was nothing I knew to do for him other than to sit there in that perfect meadow on that perfect summer day and watch him die."

"You had never lost a friend before?"

Trusty turned to Oliver, eyes red with the pain of the past, the burr of the cold air still stabbing at him, and said, "I've lost my fair share. My mother died when I was just a boy of eight. I wasn't with her. She died alone. But my father blames me for her death."

"Why's that?"

"Because I left her. She sent me on an errand and when I came back, she was dead. No matter what happened, my father was always going to be angry with me. It's just the way he was. If he could have traded me with her, he would have. I should have never left her."

"You didn't leave Jasper."

"No," Trusty said. "I didn't."

Chapter 13

***North, on the trail out of Fort Yates,
December 1888***

The ferocity of the wind and snow did not die down. Just the opposite. In a matter of minutes, the world around Trusty turned whiter and deadlier than he had ever seen it. His eyes hurt from the brightness that reached deep inside his skull; it was like the roots and branches that held his eyeballs in place were permanently frozen, threatening to snap at any second. He had never felt pain inside his body that intense before.

The cold wind felt like it had a grudge to settle with him. It targeted his bare skin on his face, chiseling with more force than he could believe existed. Tears, not from pain, emotional or physical, but from an uncontrollable reaction from inside his body, froze as they escaped his eyelids. His mind begged for warmth and an escape route to the desert.

Oliver's face suddenly appeared inches from his own. Two worried eyes buried underneath a cascade of ice trailing down from his hat and eyebrows. "You need to hold onto the tree as tight as you can. This *iwoblu* is at its fiercest. The blizzard will kill us without remorse or reason, other than we are here, in its way." There were only slivers of Oliver's brown Indian skin to be seen. Every movement he made was stiff, and his words carried on the unrelenting wind as soon as they escaped his mouth. His breath turned to ice clouds and shattered in hard puffs, falling to the ground, adding to the depth of the frozen world at their feet. His words were debris, and his actions were honest. Oliver wanted them all to survive.

"Like everything else," Trusty yelled over the wind. It seemed like the whole world was out to get them; him. He could see the shadow of two trees just beyond Oliver and made his way to the closest one without hesitation. When he blinked again, Oliver was gone, and Trusty found himself lost in the violent vortex of snow, ice, and wind that sought to dominate him in every way. His lungs protested the taking of every breath, and his heart resisted every beat, promising to freeze the blood that flowed through it mid-beat. There was no choice but to close his eyes and hang on to the tree with every ounce of energy he had left.

Oliver was gone. Horse was gone. There was nothing Trusty could do to save them, to help them survive. There was nothing he could do to help himself but refuse to give in to the wind and cold. He wasn't sure if he had it in him to live another second in the freezing cold, in the whiteout that had erased all of the colorful, waking world he had known. While he had become accustomed to death riding sidesaddle on his shadow, the threat of the bounty always following him, peering around the next corner with a rifle barrel aimed at his head, he had never felt the invasion of a natural force so severely before, attacking him inside and out with a deadly persistence. The wind and cold hurt as much as the bullet had when he'd tried to save Judge Hadesworth in Indian Territory. He was surprised that death had come to him dressed in white instead of black.

It would have been easy to have given in to the attack, to the storm, and surrendered. There were few people left in the world who would have missed his presence. His father, while still alive and toiling away in his blacksmith shop in St. Louis, had cut ties with Trusty, with a boy named Sam, long ago—if there ever had been a true tie to begin with. The vine that held father and son together was his long-dead mother and the demand of parenting, the responsibility of bringing a child into the world. When Trusty was old enough to leave home, he did. There was no good riddance or goodbye from his father. There was nothing but a side glance, then the swing of a hammer as Trusty said he was leaving. The ping of that blow still reverberated in his ears.

He had no wife, no girl to return to or hope that he could win her heart someday. Jessica Marberry, a girl he had known and loved since they were children was dead. Leaving him with a bounty on his head, purchased and pursued by her angry father, and the largest question in his life: Was the baby girl his daughter. Vance Calhoun, Jessica's husband, had convinced Trusty of the truth. He had, himself, pursued Trusty with his own grudge to settle.

Would he ever know the baby girl?

Did she need rescued?

Did she need him?

How could *he* raise a child on his own and remain a marshal?

Would she be better off if he was dead?

Trusty didn't know the answer to any of those questions, but standing there, hugging that cottonwood tree, holding on for dear life, fighting with every ounce of himself that he could muster, he knew the answer to his own question. Maybe it was his grief and regret about losing Jasper, not being able to do anything to save the beast, that made him realize what he had to do. Maybe it was about losing himself and Jessica, and any hope of a future with her in it. Or maybe it wasn't that at all. Maybe it was just life and where he had found himself: Facing death one more time when he wasn't ready for it to take him.

Trusty knew right then and there that he had to find out for sure if the baby girl was his blood, his responsibility, deserving of all that he could give her, no matter the cost or the consequence to his life. And for that to happen, he had to stay alive. He had to live and survive whatever came at him, no matter who or what that whatever was. He had to find that baby girl. Whether she knew it or not, she needed him, and he needed her. He owed the baby the truth just as much as he owed it to himself—and to Jessica, too.

As he faced his own mortality, lost in the middle of the storm, Trusty came upon a way to do just that. Brazos Joe had warned him about the two bounty hunters in the territory looking for him. Trusty had to assume that somehow, someway, those two men had a tie to Theodore Marberry. And he had to assume that if he found those two men or those two men found him, he could find his way back to Marberry. Then he would find the girl or be able to find out where she was. It was a simple plan. All he had to do was make himself easy to find, make himself a target. That wouldn't be hard. The hard part, other than staying alive at the moment, would be keeping Oliver safe and completing his charge, fulfilling his marshal's pledge to bring Charlie Littlefoot to justice. The downside of the plan was that he would be directly violating an order to let the Marshal service handle Marberry and the bounty. He knew he couldn't do that now. The storm had made clear the precariousness of life. It had made the bounty and the cause of it personal to Trusty. He had to live for the baby girl so she would have the chance to know who she was, where she came from, and who her mother and father really were. Every child deserved that much in their life. It seemed so little, but so much.

Somehow, Trusty needed to find a way to do everything and remain in one piece, so that he could have a future, so that he could have a life. If he was a father, then he swore that he wouldn't be anything like his own father, distant, angry, and detached, not hardly a father at all. Trusty would be the father he had always wished he'd had for himself. Having death smack you in the face with icicles as sharp as daggers sure did help bring purpose into focus.

The feeling in Trusty's fingers was gone. He feared frostbite, losing all of his digits from the winter attack, leaving him unable to fulfill his missions, both professional and personal. His toes were just as numb, and it hurt even more to blink his eyes.

Trusty's embrace of the cottonwood tree remained tight, and the wind continued its relentless determination to loosen his grip and toss him as far as it could. He had not regained sight of the horses or Oliver. He was still encased in the frozen cocoon of the blizzard.

A freight train full of wind rushed by him at top speed every few seconds, making it impossible to hear anything but his own thoughts—and those were screams demanding that he hold on and stay alive.

And almost as quick as the blizzard had come, it ceased. The wind pulled back with sudden, willful restraint, almost like it had read Trusty's mind, or known the fragile condition of his body, pushed to the edge of freezing, shutting every vital organ down with the touch of ice and dagger-shards. Snow flittered straight down from the changing sky, the flakes shrinking in size and construction from large, wet, and fluffy, to small pebble-like flakes that looked more like sleet than snow. He stood there for a long moment, not trusting his eyes or ears. He waited for another blast of wind and an attack of ice to rage behind the storm's turn to relief. It didn't come.

The light changed, too. It went from bright and painful to gray and unbearably comfortable, like someone had pulled a thin blanket across the sun and told it to rest. Trusty didn't know if that was a good thing or not, and it took him a minute for his vision to adjust, so he could make out his surroundings. With everything being white and snow-covered, it was hard to make out anything right away. His immediate concern was for Horse. The beast, thankfully, stood shoulder to shoulder with Takoda. Covered in snow as they were, they looked like conjoined twins, two horses glued together out of common sense and the need to stay warm and survive. Steam modulated out of both horse's noses; steady, measured, like a locomotive sitting at the station in no hurry to leave. The steam was life, survival, and patience all wrapped in one that relieved Trusty's concern about Horse's welfare.

Oliver stood beyond the two horses, stiff and unmoving, transformed into something nearly as unidentifiable as the two mounts. If Trusty hadn't known it was a man standing there, it would have been easy to assume and fear that what he was staring at was a human-sized bear standing on two legs, formulating an attack.

"Are you all right?" Trusty called out. His voice carried

on the wind, but he didn't care, wasn't concerned about giving away his location any longer.

"Yes. You?" Oliver was more subdued, his voice fragile, chattering.

Trusty broke away from the tree, certain now that he would live to see another day and made his way through the snow toward Oliver.

The snow had drifted in deep swirls created by the wind and its flare for sculpture. The ground looked like it had been made by an artist, mad with inspiration. "We need to get a fire going," Trusty said, ignoring the frozen cloud that came out of his mouth.

"The sky is clearing to the north." Oliver gazed over his shoulder and dusted a handful of snow off himself as he did. "If we set a fire the coming night will reflect it and show our position to those that hunt you and Charlie Littlefoot."

"Good. Let them come." Trusty shook his entire body from head to toe, sending a small avalanche of snow to the ground. He was still worried about losing his fingers.

"Are you crazy? We cannot take on Captain Plumright's campaign of men from the fort if they are following us. Or the bounty hunters who seek to kill you. I'm sure you are a good shot, Deputy Dawson, but I am not loaded with unlimited ammunition. I am not a particularly good aim, if I'm being honest with you."

"Good to know." Trusty felt a few pounds lighter with the snow off his shoulders and sleeves. He went to the horses and started knocking the snow off them.

Oliver stood in his spot, unmoved, incredulous. "That is not why I am here."

"What do you mean?"

"I am not an extra gun to protect you or enforce your

laws. I am here because Charlie is a brother, and Miss Amanda is a kind friend. I am here to make sure that Charlie isn't hurt and receives fair treatment by the white men who pursue him. My presence is the only way I know to ensure that Charlie isn't killed, and then I cannot be too sure of that. White men kill Indians and don't bother to ask questions later."

"Killed by me? It's not my intention or my orders to kill Charlie. It's my duty to escort him to the trial and nothin' more. But, if I am put in a corner and it's my life or Charlie's, then I'm gonna do everythin' I have to do, to save myself. You had to know that was part of the deal, Oliver. I am here to bring Charlie in and protect myself."

"Charlie Littlefoot is not a violent man."

Trusty finished wiping the snow off of Horse's back, then pulled the blanket off that had been covering the roan. The saddles to both horses had been removed when the horses had been tethered. He shook the blanket with vigor, snapping the material, shattering the ice that had built up on it. The crystals and snow fell to the ground, joining the rest of the ice in a slight pile. Horse shook just like Trusty had when he'd had the chance, sending even more of the white stuff to the ground.

"You really want to build a fire?" Oliver said.

"Yes," Trusty answered, "as big a fire as we can build."

Oliver shook his head, sending a storm of snowflakes into the air, then stalked off, mumbling something to himself in the Lakota language that Trusty didn't understand, but knew if he tried hard enough, could translate. Oliver thought that Trusty was a crazy white man, and he might have been right about that. There was nothing crazier than a man with a reason to live, or a reason to die.

Chapter 14

Gladdy rode as hard as his horse and the packhorse he towed would allow, leaving the saloon and Frank's dead body behind him. Clovis had pushed his horse into the lead, and Gladdy was happy he didn't have to think about which direction to run, even though he wasn't sure that runnin' had been the right choice to be made. Clovis had made the decision not to stand up for Frank, or high tail it back to Mister Marberry and tell him what had happened. Gladdy had followed along without offering much of a complaint. That was what he had been hired to do. Not make decisions. Not be in charge. He was the odd man out, the new kid, the unknown rider, and he liked being in that position. He had always liked riding in the back to low expectations. Except now, there wasn't no one ahead of him except Clovis. The only decision that Gladdy had made was to empty Frank's belongings, panniers, satchels, and rifle scabbard, and load them onto the packhorse. There was no leavin' that stuff behind for those fellas in the saloon.

The packhorse, as loaded down as it was, kept Gladdy

from riding away in a cloud of dust. The streets were wet anyway, and the sky promised more rain or snow; the wind in his face was as cold as the tip of an icicle. They got away fast enough only because nobody was giving them chase.

Clovis stayed just far enough ahead for Gladdy to follow. This sure wasn't how Gladdy had expected things to go as they took off out of St. Louis, but he had been riding long enough, fighting one kind of battle or another since he'd been in the saddle, always in some kind of dangerous and unpredictable situation to know that anything could happen. Look what had happened to his brother, Haden. There one minute, then shot dead the next. Still, he hadn't expected a man like Frank to meet his end because of a woman. A saloon woman, to boot. But that's what had happened, him and Clovis were still gonna head west to meet up with Marberry's two hired men in Aberdeen and bring him back news of a dead marshal. The plan and the job were the same, only the man in charge was different. In the end, it didn't matter to Gladdy. Without Frank, it would be easier to wander off and get his freedom back if that's what he wanted to do. Or he could keep on riding with Clovis, maybe cash in on Trusty Dawson's head, and collect a decent payday . . . then ride off on his own again or not. He wasn't too keen on killin' a marshal, but nobody said he had to pull the trigger. Either way, Gladdy was sure that ridin' with Clovis was better than sittin' in some cellar, bound up like a pig about to be taken to slaughter, or out on his own, scrambling for his own eggs every second of the day.

A cold rain started to sprinkle down from the night sky. Darkness and clouds hid the stars and moon, and if it wasn't for following Clovis riding ahead of him, Gladdy wouldn't have known which way to go. His sense of direction had gotten all turned around after Haden had been killed. It was a wonder that he'd made it to St. Louis at all.

The city fell behind them and once they crossed The Big Muddy, farms and homesteads started to dot the land. Most of them were dark, and it was the proximity of the houses close to the road that allowed Gladdy to see them at all. Others still had a candle burning in the window. As they rode, though, the sight of any human residence was becoming slimmer and slimmer, giving Gladdy reason to relax a bit. An occasional look over his shoulder told him that they weren't being followed, at least as far as he could tell. The packhorse struggled to keep up.

Clovis pulled back so that he was head-to-head with Gladdy, which allowed him to slow his horse and the horse behind him to catch a breath and take a steadier pace.

"I think we're safe now." Clovis took a glance over his shoulder just to make sure he was right about what he'd said.

Gladdy kept his eyes forward, relying on his ears more than his eyes for any pursuers that were there. "Ain't no reason for anyone to come after us, Clovis. We didn't steal nothin' from them or hurt any of their like. What are you so worried about?"

"Weren't you payin' attention? That wasn't the first time we was in that saloon. Frank stopped in there every chance he got, and I was with him. They know me as much as they know'd Frank."

"Yeah, so what's that got to do with us?"

"Me, you fool. I owed some of them fellers money."

"You cheat 'em, Clovis?"

"Don't matter, do it? Frank's dead and they know I ride with him. They could gang up on me just like they did Frank and send me up the river to be rid of me, settle their debts with a bullet instead of a demand that I pay them back."

Gladdy pulled on his chin, then looked behind him in the dark. He didn't see nothing but an endless sky and a road that disappeared into the black of night. "You think I'm a bit dense don't you? That's why we took off west, are stayin' the course. You need the money."

"Tell me a man that don't need the money?"

"I ain't dense."

"I know you showed up at a man like Marberry's house intent on settin' it on fire. Lord knows what your reason was, but it was a foolish move. You stood out like a sore thumb. Brought trouble upon yourself is what you did."

"I done told you that Marberry set up a trap that got my brother kilt. An eye for an eye is what I was after. That's all. You'd do the same if you had a brother like Haden."

"Don't matter. Look, I don't know if any of them boys from the saloon is comin' after me or not. They got Frank, and I 'spect they'll have a mess to clean up since he's dead. We just need to be cautious is all I'm tellin' you."

"I didn't do nothin'," Gladdy said.

"You was with us. A gang of three, and one of them got pushy with a woman and the fight started from there."

"I ain't worried about hangin' for somethin' I didn't do. I've done a lot worse than walk into a saloon with two other fellers to worry about that."

"Have it your way."

"We still ridin' to Aberdeen then?"

"You got somewhere else you want to go?" Clovis said, tightening his grip on the reins of his horse.

"Nope, I done decided I was stayin' on the job we took from Marberry. I could use a payday just like you to see me through for a while. We both agree on that. It ain't like I got any prospects on my own."

"Just as long as you know who's in charge."

Gladdy looked over to Clovis and saw a hardness in his face and eyes that he hadn't seen before. Maybe there was more to the second-in-charge man than he'd originally thought. Didn't matter really. There wasn't no place to go, and he'd been honest when he'd said he hoped for a payday. He'd been scrounging to make do since Haden had died. This ride with Marberry's two men had been the first thing that had come along that offered him any sight of relief and with an opportunity to put some real money in his pocket. As long as Clovis did the killing. Hanging for shooting a marshal was a sure thing, and that was the last way Gladdy wanted to die. He'd watched Vance Calhoun twitch and gag like a moth caught between two fingers until the life finally went out of him. Pissed his pants, too, in front of God and the whole town. Nope. That was no way to die. Gladdy had to figure out how to get Clovis to pull the trigger, kill Trusty Dawson for him, and then if that happened, he could shoot and kill Clovis and collect all of the money from Mister Marberry. Simple as that. Gladdy was proud of himself for thinkin' the plan through to the end. He figured Haden would have been proud of him, too.

"You're in charge, Clovis," Gladdy said. "No question about that. Whatever you say goes."

"That's a wise choice, O'Connor. Frank never took to my ideas and now look at him. Dead is what he is, and I'm still ridin' west. He'd have done himself a favor to have not gone into that saloon. I warned him that it would lead to trouble, and I was right, wasn't I? You pay attention to what I have to say and me and you'll get along just fine."

"We split the bounty on Trusty Dawson fifty-fifty, and you got a deal and a partner."

"Sixty-forty. I have to do the thinkin' for both of us."

Gladdy smiled, then nodded. "I guess you're right about that. Okay, it's me and you, Clovis. Sixty-forty."

"I'm glad you see it my way. Now, let's find us a place to camp before this rain gets worse. And keep an eye open behind you." Clovis spurred his horse then, hurrying along on the road ahead of them.

"Sure thing, Boss," Gladdy said, nickering his horse to keep up with Clovis.

There didn't need to be a moon in the sky. Clovis's smile was so wide there might as well have been two moons instead of one. Gladdy felt pretty good about what he had done. Now all he had to do was keep Clovis thinkin' he was in charge and the two of them would be all right. Until the time came to end it all and collect on Marberry's promise of more riches than one man had a right to for killin' another man.

Chapter 15

South of Cannonball, Dakota Territory, December 1888

Oliver quickly set about splitting found wood at exact lengths to make a lean-to. "The cold air of winter brings its gifts," he said to Trusty as he split in two a large cottonwood branch that had snapped off the tree tethering the horses.

"I don't see no gifts in this kind of weather. All of my appendages feel like they're about to fall off, if I can feel them at all," Trusty snarled. He took a piece of wood from Oliver, stomped off, and placed it on the back of the lean-to carefully, restraining his dissatisfaction as best as he could.

The sun was dropping fast to the horizon, and the remaining light of the day was gray and murky without any threatening change to be seen in the sky. They had little time to complete the lean-to and get settled in before the coldest part of night came after them. Just because the blizzard had twisted and turned southwest didn't mean the weather was anywhere near livable. The air was still biting cold, and the wind, even though subdued, sought to get inside a man's clothes like the invisible snake that it was.

Trusty hurried back to Oliver with a shiver and a wish that he was soaking in a hot bath in a whorehouse somewhere south of the Mexican border that welcomed warm breezes instead of freezing-ass cold. His mood was moving from sour to testy as quick as the wind had moved the snowstorm from over their heads.

"You see how easy this wood splits?" Oliver raised his short-handled axe and drove it down the center of a branch with ease, exerting little effort. His breath formed a small cloud that disappeared almost as quickly as it had appeared. The branch snapped in two almost instantly as the blade ran down the center of the tree limb. "It is much harder to cut when the wood is warm. The winter gives us opportunity and ease. We made quick time on the frozen river, unobstructed, flat as it was. You do not see what this frozen world gives us, Trusty Dawson. You only see that it tries to harm you. It is a wonder any of your people can survive here."

"I'm freezin' my balls off is what I know."

"Not for long." Oliver smiled, then grabbed up another long branch and split it with ease.

Trusty quit his grumbling because the cold air hurt his teeth when he opened his mouth. He walked away from the Indian with a couple more branches and set about working on the lean-to. It wasn't long before the shelter was complete, packed with snow so the wood didn't show. It looked like a snow cave, big enough for one man to sleep set in the middle of the cottonwoods. Trusty was a little sweaty inside all of the winter garb he wore to stay warm. He wondered if the sweat would freeze.

All that was left to do was make a fire. Oliver insisted

on digging into the snow and finding fist-sized rocks before the first flame was lit. Trusty stood back and watched. The Lakota seemed to know what he was doing, where to look, where the right kind of rocks he needed would be. Trusty's observation of Oliver's ways wasn't a matter of learning. He was more interested in staying warm, with his back against the wind, instead of acting like it didn't exist, tramping around the riverside hunting for rocks. Though he couldn't help but to notice and see that there was much more to the Indian than he had originally seen at the fort, quiet, in service to officers of the army that saw him as the enemy, if they saw him at all. This man, hunting rocks to stay warm and survive looked different, taller, more assured, more himself, in a way Trusty couldn't quite figure out how to reason, other than Oliver looked like the Indian he was instead of the white man he tried to be at the fort. Both were ways of survival, but this one seemed to fit the Indian just right.

Oliver made quick business of placing the rocks on the ground in an order that made sense to him. Satisfied with his project, the Indian began to build the fire. Once the flame had taken hold, Trusty set a larger piece of wood on the pit along with some brown grasses.

"You are sending a bright signal farther than you realize," Oliver said. Concern settled on his face as he looked past Trusty, into the distance, to the south. The snow had stopped, but with the light as dim as it was, it was still hard to tell where the ground ended, and the sky started. There was nothing on the horizon except flat land that tumbled into an occasional bump, all covered in the same snowy whiteness that surrounded them. Snow-covered buttes glazed the horizon in the distance. The ground underneath them would give way to a sea of grass in the summer and fall, but it was hard to imagine anything alive at the moment.

"We're outfitted to fight whatever comes along," Trusty said.

"Ten men to two?"

"You think Plumright will round up that many men to ride north to hunt down Charlie Littlefoot? Even the most fragile rabbit will hear them coming."

"I think Captain Plumright will do whatever he needs to do to stop Charlie from returning to the fort."

"So, Charlie can have his say in court?" Trusty was ambiguous to the idea of an Indian speaking in a court of law.

"That won't happen, and you know it." Oliver was more annoyed than Trusty. "No Lakota man is going to have his words heard in the white man's court of law. But there is always the chance that justice will be served regardless. I have to hope that Charlie could go free. But what would happen then? That does not mean he would ever be safe. Not here. In the only home he has ever known."

"You think that he is innocent?"

"Of the crime he is charged with? Yes, of course," Oliver said. "But I only know the people involved, and I know Charlie would not hurt a woman like the captain's wife. That is the captain's way, not Charlie's."

"The captain seems like a complicated and angry man."

"He has been from the day he arrived. I know little of his life, and I do not wish to," Oliver said, "but he is not a gentle man and I believe he has committed crimes of his own. Crimes that may not be worked out in the white man's court of law, but crimes just the same."

Trusty looked away from Oliver to the log struggling to catch fire, then glanced out into the world, and wondered if his plan was a smart one. Plumright might be more dangerous than he had given thought to. He couldn't afford to make another mistake. He could get himself and Oliver killed. He'd feel worse if something happened to Oliver than to him, but if he was dead, then the baby girl would be left on her own, in the care of Theodore Marberry, raised just like Jessica had been, in the prison of wealth and expectations, without ever knowing her true father. There were worse things, but the thought of the girl on her own in the world made Trusty cringe. But he knew he couldn't just sit there and wait for trouble to come to him. "If there are men other than Plumright close by, then we need to know, need to draw them to us, out in the open. This is the only way I know to do that. We can sleep in shifts, then get back on the trail in the morning."

"It will be colder without the heat of another," Oliver said.

Trusty ignored the comment, knew that Oliver was right, that two bodies inside the lean-to were better than one, but that wasn't going to change his mind. "I'll take the deep part of the night. If they come at us, I think it will be then."

"I don't like this."

"I know. But we're targets either way you look at it, from Plumright, or them bounty hunters that Brazos Joe told me about. I'd rather take my chances in this camp with the rise of the hill behind us and some trees to protect us instead of riding on the river out in the open in daylight, waiting for my head to explode."

"You make a valid point," Oliver said. "We need to finish before nightfall so you can get some sleep."

"I hope I can get warm enough to get some shut-eye."

"You will. I have all that you need." Oliver smiled, then stalked off toward the horses, carrying a Henry rifle with him, cocked and loaded, ready to respond to anything that came his way. It wasn't that long ago that Trusty wouldn't have trusted an Indian with a rifle so close to him, but there was something about Oliver that made him feel comfortable and at ease. It was an unusual and welcome feeling. The Indian Wars were over, at least for Trusty, but the memory of them remained buried just below the surface of his thin skin.

The lean-to was enclosed, and protected from the wind as it was, much warmer than Trusty had thought it would be. Oliver had made a bed of buffalo blankets with rocks pulled out of the fire, wrapped in leather, and placed in between the warm fur of the buffalo. Trusty snuggled into the bed, fully dressed, still in his layers, but with his boots off. His toes felt like they were melting, perched against the hardness of the hot rock underneath the blanket, but it was a great relief to feel them. Oliver remained outside, taking his turn at watch, staying close to the fire. It didn't take long for Trusty to fall asleep, to drift off into a comfortable rest. The long ride and the struggle to stay warm throughout the day had drained him more than he had given it credit for.

Fully realized dreams rarely came to Trusty. Sometimes there were snippets of visions, a person from the past, or even those in the waking world, that would haunt him when he first awoke, but by the time he had washed his face and had his first pee, the dream was gone. Trusty always had somewhere to go, another place to ride to. Mileage rates paid his way as a marshal, but it was more than that. Trusty never wanted to stay in one place too long. Setting down roots had never been a desire or a dream.

Until now, at least in this sleep. He found himself in a dream, in a green world, sitting on the front porch of a cabin made of freshly cut wood, staring out over a calm parcel of land, rich with green summertime grass, the seed tassels yet to ripen, swaying with the rhythm of the wind as it breathed across the field. Birds chattered. Insects buzzed. The sun sat halfway in the sky, wary of nothing, not even a cloud. If there was ever a more comfortable place, Trusty had never seen it, and he most certainly had never been there.

A casual movement at his feet took his attention away from the view in front of him. Trusty looked down to find an unknown dog at his ankle. Short brown hair, happy and smart amber eyes just like Horse's, and a flip of the tail at the moment of recognition. It was a boy dog, about the size of a first-year sheep; a guard for the farm as well as, from the look of it, a loyal friend. It was something felt and understood in the eye-to-eye exchange. Trusty wondered if he had named the dog like he had named his horse in the waking world he had left behind. This place was most definitely a dream. He had never owned a dog before.

The wind touched his nose, bringing with it the smell of baking bread, that warm comfortable smell of home that engaged Trusty's memory of his own boyhood when his mother had been alive with the energy to work in the kitchen. She had loved to make the daily bread, and Trusty, Samuel to his mother, had loved to eat it. Bread had never tasted the same after she had died. But this bread, this smell, it smelled just like what his mother had made.

Footsteps approached from inside the cabin. The floor vibrated with every step, and Trusty half expected his mother to walk out onto the porch. He begged for it to be her, hoped more than anything it would be her. He had never dreamed of her after she had died. He could barely remember what her face looked like and what her voice sounded like. The footsteps, not heavy, just normal, like the day was uninterrupted by any tension kept coming, until the screen door pushed open. Trusty felt his eyes watering up with hope. It wasn't his mother who walked toward him, though he wasn't disappointed.

"Do you want some coffee," Jessica Marberry said.

She looked like she had when he had last seen her in Oklahoma Territory, when the baby girl had been made—unknown to him—and they had gone their separate ways. She wore a flowing emerald-green dress that reached to the ground. A high collar made of rabbit fur was turned up to ward off wind that didn't exist, covering the back of a matching green hat that only allowed Trusty a peak of Jessica's golden hair. Her profile was regal, straight nose, high cheeks, rosy from the chill, with a thinker's forehead. She had the smooth gait of a woman full of confidence and good breeding. If she were a horse, there would have been no mistaking her for a thoroughbred. She didn't look dressed to be where she was, and she wasn't. Jessica was dressed just like she had been in Muskogee when fate had intervened in their lives one last time and made sure they crossed paths.

The dog stood up and went straight to Jessica. "There you are, Buddy. I wondered where you were. But I should have known you were here with Sam. You're his shadow, aren't you?"

"Buddy?" Trusty said standing up. Three feet and a dog separated him from Jessica. His mind knew that she was dead, that this was a dream, but his heart didn't care. If he had a choice, he would have signed a piece of paper right then and there to stay inside this dream forever.

"You named him; don't you remember?" Jessica said with concern. "Are you all right, Sam?"

"I must have dozed off is all." Trusty wanted to rush to Jessica and take her into his arms, but he was afraid she would disappear if he did.

"I'll get you that coffee." Jessica turned to leave, but Trusty reached out and stopped her from leaving. Her skin was warm, as real as the smell of baking bread. He couldn't resist and pulled her to him and gave her a deep and loving kiss. To his relief, she responded in kind. When he finally pulled away, Jessica's face was flushed. A curl of fine straw-colored hair fell across her forehead. "You must have been dreaming."

"I think I am," Trusty said.

"I'll get you that coffee." Jessica hurried to the door. "But we don't have too much time to dilly-dally. She'll be here anytime."

"She?"

"Yes, she. Her. Ours. You know?"

"No, I didn't know. Why didn't you tell me?"

It wasn't until then that Trusty saw the change in Jessica, moody, uncertain, bound to her father and her wealthy way of life in a way that a blacksmith's son could never understand. A cold wind blew between them and rustled Jessica's dress. "I didn't know until it was too late. I had no choice but to marry that horrible man."

"Vance Calhoun?"

Jessica nodded. "Father insisted. Said he would cut me off, not pay a dime for any of my living expenses if I didn't marry him. He wanted that ranch, he wanted to move into the cattle business and Calhoun was the deal he had been looking for. And what was I? A widow, once married, childless, on the verge of becoming an old maid. He wasn't going to have it."

"So, he sold you to the highest bidder."

"The only bidder." Jessica stared at Trusty with tears forming in her eyes. "I'll get that coffee. She'll be here any minute." And then she disappeared inside the door. Buddy followed, but was prevented from going inside, from being with her. He whined and looked to Trusty for help.

Trusty's throat was dry, and he couldn't feel the tingle in his fingers. He could see them shaking, but that was all. He was cold all over his body even though the sun was beating down on his face.

"Buddy." The dog turned to face Trusty, knew its name, which surprised him. "You could have told me."

The dog wagged its tail and sat down by the door. Pots and pans clattered from inside, but not loud enough to overcome the sound of a wagon racing up the drive. Trusty turned to see it, hoping upon hope, just like he had been expecting to see his mother instead of Jessica, to see the baby girl all grown up. But he didn't see her. What he saw surprised him and frightened him in a way he wasn't sure he understood.

He recognized the wagon right away. It was loaded with Singer sewing machines. A dead man was driving. Carmichael. The natty little salesman who had killed his partner so he could keep all of the Marberry bounty for himself. Miles, with the left side of his head caved in, sat next to Carmichael smiling like he had just won a big faro game. Two lathered Springfield mules pulled the wagon toward the cabin faster than mules ought to have been able to run. The sky behind the wagon swirled into a black web, with lightning being born inside it.

Jessica stepped outside the door with a cup of coffee in

her hand, but she stopped solid at the sight coming for them. "I'm too late. I've always been too late to help." Buddy slipped inside the door and disappeared.

Thunder cracked and the coffee cup shattered into a thousand tiny pieces, raining down to the floor of the porch like salt poured on a wound. Trusty reached for his gun, but it wasn't there. He had no weapons, nothing to protect himself with. All he knew to do was push Jessica inside the cabin to protect her, but she wasn't there. She was gone. He was about to turn and run inside to look for her, to find a gun. If it was his cabin, there had to be a gun, a knife, something to protect himself with, but the sight of the wagon and Carmichael stopped Trusty in his tracks.

The salesman was standing up with a rifle aimed straight at Trusty's chest, his heart the target. The mules ran on their own. And Miles, smiling with his half face and half mouth, still dripping blood, sitting calmly on the seat of the wagon holding a pristine white bassinette. When Carmichael pulled the trigger of the rifle it didn't erupt, or clap thunder. Instead, the air was filled with a baby's cry, penetrating, deep, longing, hungry, and still alive.

Trusty heaved as something heavy hit his chest, gasped for air to fill his lungs. He blinked and rolled his eyes, and when he did, the wagon, Carmichael, Miles, and the bassinette, were gone, and he was awake, back inside the lean-to.

The crying baby still rang in his ears, and it took him a long second to realize that sound was the wind screaming outside and nothing more. He had never felt so alone in his life.

Chapter 16

**South of Cannonball, Dakota Territory,
December 1888**

Darkness ruled the world when Trusty rushed outside of the snow-covered lean-to. As far as he could tell, it was the middle of the night. Stars, pinpricks of molten silver, throbbed and pulsed clearly overhead, but there was no sign of the new moon. No blankets of clouds to be seen, either, no angry swirl of weather dumping its bounty of frozen water onto the earth; the air and everything in it was vacant of any moisture at all. The blizzard had been pushed east, exiled into another territory, leaving dry air in its wake. All that was left was the wind, the power that had, thankfully, vanquished the storm to parts unknown.

A wall of wind smacked Trusty in the face with a cold punch, doing its best to push him back where he had come from. The protection of the lean-to had been solid. That was no surprise. But the cold was a bone-chilling cold, invading his body through every open pore of skin; he ached to return to the warmth of the buffalo blankets and the hot rocks in between them, but he knew he had to escape into the real world, no matter the rage of the storm. The dream had left him shaken and uncertain. He was half in this world and half in the sleep world he'd been ripped from. The sight of Jessica and the baby drifted away like a dandelion seed on a spring wind. No matter how hard he tried to grab at the baby, to touch her, to see her face, those parts of the dream slipped through his fingers, his mind, and were gone; dust sparkles that had never really existed. "Jessica," he whispered as he wiped his eyes. The wind answered back with the scream of a child torn from its mother too soon.

The fire was dead. There wasn't a single orange coal to be seen. The wind had conquered the flame, returned it to the nothingness it had come from, and Oliver had let the fire die for some reason.

There was no warmth or comfort to be found outside of the lean-to, but Trusty had not expected to find any.

He searched for Oliver and the horses, but the only horse he saw was his own, still tethered, covered with snow and ice atop his blankets, standing just beyond the pit of dead fire. There was a shiver to Horse's stance that concerned Trusty, a weakness that wasn't there before he had gone to sleep. And then there was the sense of aloneness in the camp. There was no sign of Takoda or Oliver. It looked like they had been sent along with the fire and snow to somewhere else, unseen, perhaps against their will. *Or had they fled while Trusty slept?*

Trusty was not dressed to be outside. He had left his buffalo coat and hat inside the lean-to. But he didn't move. He focused his eyes and ears, watching and listening for anything that moved. All he heard was the wind pushing around him, angry that he was in the way. Finally, he surrendered to the cold and made his way to Horse. "You all right?" he said as he knocked the snow and ice off the blanket that covered Horse's back.

Horse shook, sending even more snow and ice to the ground. In the gloom of the night, the gelding looked more purple than roan. Trusty ran his hand down Horse's long nose, his memory feeling the dream dog, Buddy, instead of the horse. He pushed away the emotional attachment that had ridden into the waking world with him as best he could. In reality, he had left the dog behind, a dog he really didn't know, but loved somehow in a way that was even more unfamiliar to him. He was replacing that feeling with more affection for Horse than he usually felt.

Trusty was happy to see Horse, that his ride was still there, alive, okay, but in need of some warmth. "Where's your friend?" he said as he untied the tether line. "Where's Oliver and Takoda?" He looked around the camp, out into the darkness as far as he could see. There was nothing there. No sign of life at all.

Horse didn't answer, but a sound rolling toward him on the wind caught Trusty's attention. Horses riding hard. The unmistakable sound of hooves hitting the snow at a faster than normal rate of speed carried on the wind like a dish breaking in a small kitchen. Multiple horses. Not one. Trusty rushed back to the lean-to to get his Colt and rifle. He had left the weapons behind along with his coat.

When Trusty hurried back out of the snow cave, fully armed, he found himself surrounded by four men atop their horses, all with their rifles aimed right at him. He had hoped it was Oliver with Indian friends. Now he had to worry about facing the bounty alone. His plan of setting a bright fire seemed to have worked better and quicker than he thought it would. He had also counted on Oliver being there with him, but the Indian obviously had his own ideas about that.

The exhaust of the breaths from all four of the horses joined together and created a thin, see-through cloud that made all of the men look like they were standing behind frosted glass; obscured, unclear, their faces dark under the brims of their hats. With no direct light to define the riders, Trusty had to wonder if he was awake or dreaming, if Carmichael was lurking in the shadows, ready to have another go at killing him. The Colt in his hand felt real. The cold felt real. And the rifles pointed at him looked real. He wasn't taking any chances.

"You better just put that gun down, Deputy."

Trusty recognized the voice right away. It belonged to Captain James Pierpoint Plumright. He didn't move. "I expected to see you sooner or later," he said.

"Did you hear my order, sir," Plumright said.

"My guess is that if you've lit out of the fort, you're not a captain any longer. Not that I would obey your command anyways. I think we already established that chain of command at Fort Yates. I didn't answer to you then and I won't answer to you now."

"What you established after leaving the fort, Deputy Dawson, is that you associate with the enemy and are not to be trusted whether you wear a badge or not. Where is your Indian friend anyway? I don't see a sign of him." Plumright edged up and grabbed the saddle horn with his left hand; a Henry repeating rifle was balanced against his shoulder, held by his right hand. His horse was only a couple of feet in front of Trusty. The other three riders, who Trusty didn't recognize, held back, their rifles unwavering in their aim just like Plumright's.

"I have no idea where Oliver is at," Trusty said. "He stood watch and when I woke up, he was gone."

"Sounds about right. Led you up the river while word was sent out to Charlie to head down out of Canada."

"You know that for sure?"

"Why would I tell you?"

"Why don't you shoot me if you're going to."

"Are you in a hurry to die, Deputy?"

"No more than any other man is ready to die. But if you're not gonna shoot me, then the respectable thing you should do when you ride into a man's camp is to tell your toughs here to take down their aim. I've got enough coffee for us all."

"We have our own pack, thank you."

"I was just offerin'."

"I ordered you to drop your weapon," Plumright said.

"Nah, I don't think so."

"Looks like we're at an impasse."

"Looks that way. You can kill me and bury me in the snow, but sooner or later somebody, the Guardsmen, Bill Tilghman, Heck Thomas, or other U.S. Marshals, will come lookin' for me. Might even be both, or the army since they'll know it's you they're lookin' for. Now, the way I see it, Plumright, you got enough problems to deal with right now, includin' the ones you're creatin' for yourself by bein' out here looking for Charlie Littlefoot when you should be back at the fort, still in uniform, tendin' to your wife's delicate condition. The last thing you need is Bill Tilghman on your tail or spendin' the rest of your livin' days in a jail cell for the act of murderin' a U.S. Marshal, wonderin' what the heck your child looks like."

"What are you suggesting?" There was a hard edge to Plumright's question.

"I'm not suggestin' anything. Just sayin' there's no way to see a child grow up behind prison walls is all."

"You need to leave my wife out of this."

"I suppose you're right about that, Plumright, but she's square in the middle of this journey I'm takin' north. You've got a lot to lose. Even more now."

"And what do you suggest?" the captain asked.

"Honestly?" Trusty said. "You all help me make a fire, tend to your horses, then come first light, you take out of here and head back to the fort where you belong. Forget about this quest of revenge you've set yourself on and let me bring in Charlie alive. Unless, of course, there's a reason why you want him brought in dead."

"You'd do the same thing as me if it was your wife who was plundered and left to wonder if the baby that she's carryin' is a half-blood or not," Plumright said.

"I got to admit that's a hard road to travel, Plumright. I guess a man wouldn't know how he would react until he was in that situation himself."

"You'd kill the son of a bitch. That's what you'd do."

"No, I wouldn't."

"Then you're a fool."

"You're wrong. I understand how this world works. The cards are stacked in my favor. Charlie Littlefoot hasn't got a chance in hell of goin' free no matter what anybody says. I know that. You know that. And more than anyone, Charlie knows that. You kill him, you'll face your own kind in a court of law, and if you ain't been payin' attention there's been white men convicted and hung for killin' Indians when there wasn't no cause to. Murder is murder."

"We just want to have a little talk with Charlie."

"Sure, you do. And then you want to make him disappear. All you have to do is say he tried to escape, and you shot him dead. You know how many times that excuse has been used?"

"That line works if it can't be proved otherwise, can't it? You think you're smart, don't you, Deputy?"

"I think I'm cold and I want some coffee. Either shoot me or get down off your horses and help me get a fire a goin'." Trusty held Plumright's gaze for a long second, then headed over to the wood pile that he and Oliver had built, ignoring the four riders, tempting them, all the while to shoot him—almost certain they wouldn't—wondering where in the hell Oliver was.

St. Louis, Missouri, September 1877

Kabbie Mae Brown sat on the kitchen stoop smoking a pipe. It was after lunch, midday, with a perfect blue sky to gaze at. A skein of geese flew overhead, drawing her attention to it. She watched the vee of flapping wings until they disappeared over the southern horizon. The tips of the maple trees were turning red, and the air was cool, promising to get colder as the autumn months began to step forward. The change of seasons was at hand, allowing the world to slow down a bit and take a breath. There were no buggies in front of the house, no horses tied to the hitching post. If a man didn't know the place was a cathouse, he would have walked right on by it without offering it a glance or a moment of judgment.

"You's the last person I expected to see today, Samuel Dawson," Kabbie Mae said to Sam as he walked up to her.

"Thought I'd better come by to tell you goodbye," he said, stopping before her.

"Where you gonna go, Mister Sam? This be your home."

"Army. Joined up. I head out to Fort Robinson in the

morning. If I never come back to this place, it'll be too soon." His clothes still smelled of soot and ash. He wondered if he would ever get the smell of the blacksmith shop out of his skin.

"This place ain't so bad." Kabbie Mae took a long draw on the pipe then exhaled wistfully. "Shore ain't gonna be the same around here without ya. You come to tell the missus you leavin'?"

Sam nodded. "She here?"

"In the parlor last I knowed. She's gonna be sad at the news. Me, too." Kabbie Mae looked up to the sky where the geese were a few minutes before but were gone now. A cloud had taken their place. "You best come see me in the kitchen before you leave the house. I'll hurry up a tin of biscuits for you to take on your travels."

"Thanks, Kabbie Mae, I'd like that." Sam edged his way past the Negro woman, walking through a puff of skunky sweet smoke as he went. He found Madame Duchamp where he expected to, curled up on her favorite French carved and gilt sofa, staring out the window of the turret it was situated in.

"You startled me," she said, sitting up. She wore a long robe like she had just stepped out of a warm bath. She pulled it a little tighter. "I wasn't expecting to see you today, Sam. Why the serious look on your face?" There was no sign of any other of the girls, seven of them at the moment as far as Sam knew. The house was quiet as a saloon on a Monday morning.

"I thought I'd better come and tell you goodbye," Sam said. "I'll be leavin' out in the morning."

Katherine Duchamp stiffened, her deep blue eyes searching Sam's face, trying to understand what was going on. "Did you get into it with your father again?"

Sam looked down at the hard toes of his boots. "Yes. No. We're always at it with each other. He doesn't know that I'm leavin'. I'm not gonna tell him that I joined the army. I'm just gonna go and be done with it."

Katherine exhaled and nodded. "I see," she said.

"I have to get out of here. I don't want to wake up in twenty years and still be tied to that forge and quench. I want to live a life of my own. I don't want to be a blacksmith. I don't want to be like my father. I don't want to live in that hell anymore."

"It's about more than that, isn't it?" Katherine stood up so she could look Sam in the eye. "It's about Jessica Marberry. I'm sure of it."

Sam nodded again. "I got a letter. She's stayin' in England for good. Getting married. Never returning to Saint Louis unless it's for a visit."

"That's it, then. You have no reason to stay here."

"There's nothing for me to hope for now is there?" Sam said.

"I suppose not." The robe loosened a little bit, pulling away from her perfect navel, revealing it in the dimly lit room. "I always knew you were a romantic. So, you're off out into the world on your own. Maybe that's not a bad thing. Get away from here. Have an adventure or two. Are you ready?"

"I have to be."

"Maybe. Maybe not. I'll tell you what. I'll break my rule. You can have any girl in the house as a going away gift. My treat. Natalie has always had a liking for you. Do you want her?"

"No," Sam said, as soon as he heard the name. "Never."

"I suppose not, now that I think about it."

"Who then? Gloria? That new little mulatto. Is that what you like, Sam? Or do you even know?"

Sam shook his head, then said something that surprised him, but it didn't, not really. "You. How about you?"

Katherine Duchamp laughed uncomfortably. "Me? I'm not one of the girls."

"You're the prettiest woman in the house, and the one that's been the most kind to me. I figure if there's someone who could show me what I need to know, it's you."

"I'm nearly twice your age."

"What difference does that make?"

Katherine sighed and looked Sam up and down, like she was trying to see him with a different set of eyes. "You really think you could handle me?"

Sam grinned. "You really think you can handle *me*?"

"Oh, aren't you sly." Madame Duchamp exhaled, then smiled. "Just this one time, you understand?"

"Yes," Sam said. "I understand."

"Only because you're leaving." She reached out for his hand, but he didn't take it right away. He looked at her long, elegant fingers with the three rings on it, opal, diamond, and pearl, then took her hand into his, raised it to his lips and kissed it, lingering longer than he should have, allowing his tongue to get a full taste of her soft, inviting skin.

South of Cannonball, Dakota Territory, December 1888

The fire crackled heartily with flames rising almost a foot in the air. Heat cut into the cold air like a warm knife taken to butter. Oliver had chosen a productive spot to pitch the camp in. The cottonwoods offered a plentiful array of firewood, allowing for the four men and Trusty to take relief in the heat. Horse, too, benefited, after being pulled close to the fire by Trusty. The shiver and concern about Horse's health faded away quickly. The beast had been freezing. Trusty had to wonder how long the fire had been out, how soon after he had gone to sleep in the lean-to that Oliver had left the camp. Why was another question. One he didn't have the answer for.

Captain Plumright's posse, if it could be called that, was made up of former soldiers, loyal to him for whatever their reasons, who had stayed close to Fort Yates, were ready for the call to ride when it came. None of them were overly forthright in the associations with Trusty, and one of the men, a tall, bearded fellow with eyes made of black diamonds, had yet to speak a word in Trusty's presence. Plumright himself was none too pleasant, sitting across the fire from Trusty who was waiting for the flames to calm down enough to put the coffee to a boil. Black Diamond Eyes sat next to the captain—or ex-captain, depending on how you looked at it. The other men, one short, a less severe-looking man, named Reed, who had worked as a stable-man, sat next to Trusty, while the fourth, a middle-aged "two-gun" man, sat on the other side of Reed. He wore matching Peacemakers on each hip, the holsters unsnapped and greased for a quick pull. Trusty assumed Two Gun was an ex-soldier based on his army boots and holsters. All of the men and their horses seemed calmed by the warmth of the fire. Trusty wasn't comfortable, all things considered. Not only was he outgunned, but he was also surrounded by strangers whose intentions ran opposite of his. And they had no one to answer to other than their own conscience. He had to wonder if they knew of

Marberry's bounty. Most likely not. Otherwise, he would have been dead, and most likely in the land where Jessica kept a cabin and the Singer salesman ached for revenge.

The wind had died down, but it wasn't completely silent. Sparks reached high into the air, creating an orange cone spiraling into the dark of night with cracks and pops as it went. Fire had almost instantly created a protective circle in the camp to keep the night and the frigidness of it at bay. Dawn would break soon, and the light would show the way forward, and hopefully offer Trusty a clue at what happened to Oliver.

Reed, who had warm blue eyes and a gray wiry beard that poked downward like a short bib, began working the fire to tame it. Trusty stared across the fire at Plumright, who returned the look. The situation was tense, and Trusty knew one wrong move, or one wrong word could set the posse against him. While he had played a bluffer's hand daring Plumright to shoot him or join him for coffee, and won, there was no guarantee that the bluff would hold. Trusty knew he had little power in the situation he had found himself in other than the badge that he wore on his chest. His use of the "shoot me and get it over with" bluff was risky, and he knew he couldn't keep using it, especially when there was a bounty on his head. He really wasn't ready to die anytime soon—but the ploy had, thankfully, worked with Plumright.

The fire cowered to Reed's will, and it wasn't long before there was a grate over the subservient flames and the coffee pot was set to its duty. A full helping of snow had been placed inside the pot to melt and supply water.

The aroma of coffee soon joined with the burning wood sending an air of familiarity around the camp, cutting the tension but not eliminating it. Trusty kept a look out for

Oliver, but he knew if the Indian was close by, he wouldn't venture into the camp with Plumright and his men there. It was probably best that Oliver wasn't there. *Had he known Captain Plumright and his men were coming? Is that why he left?*

Plumright walked over to Trusty and said, "What are your plans, Dawson?"

"Ride north at first light. I'm not makin' any changes to my route or my cause unless I'm forced to."

"I'm not going to get in your way, if that's what you're suggesting."

"Are you following me?"

"We're not abandoning our mission to capture the Indian, either. I plan to return Charlie Littlefoot to Fort Yates for a trial."

"I can't stop you from that," Trusty said, watching Reed check the coffee. The older man held the action of a care-taker in his every move, quiet without opinion, bound by an invisible tie of some kind. Trusty could only imagine what the tie to Plumright was. "Unless you do somethin' to break the law, then we'll have a problem. You know that don't you?"

"I'm no fool," Plumright said. The captain was about to say something else, but an out-of-nowhere crack of a gunshot stopped him and drowned out his words. Trusty wasn't sure which.

Reed, who had stood up to fetch the coffee pot off the grate and start filling mugs, stopped like he had run into an invisible wall, mumbled something, then swatted weakly at his head, like he was trying to shoo away a swarm of hornets that had appeared out of thin air, set on an attack. A bright red dot of blood appeared in Reed's forehead as his skull collapsed inward. More bone and blood blew out the back of his head as a bullet exited his skull. Before Reed even teetered backward on his boot heels, another shot rang out, hitting the man in the forehead again, just an inch to the left of the first shot. The short man tipped over backward without any resistance, hit the ground with a thud, encasing himself in six inches of snow all around his short, rotund body. Reed didn't know what hit him, didn't even get a chance to call out for help or say goodbye.

Black Diamond Eyes jumped up out of instinct, reaching for the Colt on his side. Another shot came and caught him in the shoulder. The tall, bearded man, swayed to the side like he had been punched or hit in the arm by a battering ram. He groaned as he tried to stay on his feet, still reaching for his gun, still trying to fight the good fight and shoot back into the darkness. It was a noble effort, but a stupid one, realizing quickly what was happening. Another shot came, and the first intended target—Black Diamond Eye's chest—was hit square on this time. He stumbled backward, fighting as he went down, instead of collapsing like Reed had. His Colt slid out of his weak grasp and hit the snow before he did.

"Put the fire out," Trusty said as he rolled to the ground. He started shoveling snow onto the coals that had been host to a small, comfortable fire before the shooting had started. "He's using the light to target us."

"I knew I should have killed that Indian when I had the chance," Plumright said.

"You don't know who's out there," Trusty said. It could have been Oliver. Or a bounty hunter. Or Charlie Littlefoot himself. There was no way to know for sure, and Trusty didn't have time to make assumptions. He just needed to kill the fire and stay alive.

Plumright was pretty quick when it came to saving his own life. He was prone on the ground before another shot fired, not interested in helping Trusty extinguish the light. He scampered toward the safety of darkness beyond the fire.

Two Guns was on the ground, too, opposite of Trusty, with his feet toward the fire, kicking as much snow as he could onto the pulsing coals. At least Trusty had some help.

Another shot came. This one hit the rise of the hill behind the fire, thudding into the snow just above Two Guns's head. Six inches closer and the man would have been as dead and useless as the other two riders.

Once out of the touch and danger of the light, Plumright righted himself, pulled his sidearm out and fired off three quick rounds in the direction the shots had come from.

Trusty held off to see what happened. He continued to douse the fire with the help of Two Guns. Darkness returned to the camp once the coals were extinguished and covered. A plume of steam rose into the night air, carried to the east, toward the breaking of dawn on the far horizon. Daylight would expose them all over again.

He joined Plumright and took aim with his Colt in the same direction that the shots had come from. Reed and Black Diamond Eyes were dead. There was no saving them. Two Guns took shelter behind the lean-to, drawing his aim into the darkness.

Each of the three men expected another volley of shots fired their way, but none came. Horse hooves hit the ice running, the sound echoing freely up from the river. An unseen man riding off, in a hurry to flee, heading north into the darkness. All Trusty could do was hope that there was only one man, and that that man wasn't Oliver. If it was, his guide had transformed from a mild mannered Indian, set on satisfying the bidding of a pregnant woman, into a cold-blooded killer on the run.

Chapter 17

Gladdy O'Connor had never been to Kansas City. They skirted the West Bottoms, the center of the world when it came to shipping and butchering cattle from all over the west. Most of the cows had come from Texas. Gladdy had ridden drag a few times on cow punches from Vance Calhoun's ranch in Paris, Texas, but he admittedly wasn't a good cowboy. He never had a good enough relationship with a horse to trust it when it came time to cut a sick cow out of the herd or tie down a wayward calf if it got separated from its momma. Haden, on the other hand, had loved the life on the ranch and took to cattle drives. The cowboy work was a long way from the kinds of things they'd done together in the war. Gladdy preferred riding along on protection duty, more capable with a gun than a brand. But here they were, him and Clovis in the West Bottoms, and the smell from the stockyards, packing houses, and warehouses was foul enough to knock a buzzard off a shitwagon and remind Gladdy of days gone by that he didn't miss as much as he thought he did. He missed riding with Haden more than anything. Clovis was no Haden.

Once they made their way into Kansas City proper it was easy to see the prosperity that the cattle industry had injected into the city. Tall limestone and brick buildings jutted into the sky, reaching up twelve and thirteen stories. They rode by a department store that took up a whole city block, and there were more people than horses in the streets, on the boardwalks, everywhere Gladdy looked. Traffic was eight horses wide on the street, and he nearly lost the pack horse to a wagon collision more than once. He followed Clovis dutifully after makin' the promise that Clovis was the man in charge, but Gladdy was nervous in the city—just like his horse—and more than a little annoyed about riding without knowing where in the heck they were going.

"Can we stop, Clovis?" Gladdy said, pulling back on the reins of his horse. Wagons, people on foot, both men and women, dressed like it was Sunday, and horseback threaded around him, miffed that he was impeding their way forward. Gladdy was developing a quick hatred of cities and the city folk that lived in them. He longed to be back on the trail, out and away from people. It had been a nice ride from Saint Louis once they'd calmed down and gave up the worry that they were bein' chased by a posse of some kind.

"We're almost there," Clovis said, edging his horse backward and coming to a stop even with Gladdy.

"Where is almost there?"

"We have to get rid of the pack and the horses."

"Why in the heck do we need to do that?"

"Well, Frank had it in his fool head that we was gonna ride from Saint Louis to Aberdeen on horseback. I thought that was foolish, ridin' eight hundred miles in the winter straight into the north country. I said as much more than once, but Frank had his mind made up. Well, Frank's dead, and I think that way of travelin' is a fool's road to hell frozen over. I don't like winter weather much myself. Do you, O'Connor?"

"Can't say that I do."

"Well, then, here's what we're gonna do. I'm wirin' Mister Marberry and tellin' him of the change of plans. I figure we got enough money to get to Aberdeen on the train, but not enough to return. I'm gonna ask Mister Marberry for a way back for the both of us once we catch up with Trusty Dawson and finish that assignment."

"We got to meet with them two fellas."

"Glo Timmons and Red Jack Lewis."

"Yup, them."

"Between me and you, once this job's over with, I'm thinkin' of headin' back south. I was raised outside of Atlanta, and I think winters there spoilt me some, if you know what I mean. I didn't see no real snow 'til I came north after the war was over."

"War ain't over accordin' to some fellas."

"Good for them. It is for me. Should be for you, too."

"A train ride sounds nice. Better than spendin' a week of Sundays outside in the cold. I like how you think, Clovis. I sure am glad you're in charge. Not that I didn't like Frank and all. I know he was your friend, but he's dead. I'd rather ride in a train any day. That's all I'm sayin'. I didn't mean to speak ill of the dead. My momma raised us up to be respectful of such things."

"Frank dug his own grave as far as I'm concerned," Clovis said. "He had funny ideas about a lot of things. I never did know how he got to be so tight with Mister Marberry, but he did. He was sly like that, gettin' people to like him. Don't go worryin' about how tight Frank and

I was. We got throwed together, and our partnership lasted longer than I thought it would. I'm just glad I walked away from it still alive."

"I've slipped out of a few scrapes myself lately. I hope this plan of yours works."

"Don't you worry none," Clovis said. "I got my thinkin' cap on seven days a week. I got us here, didn't I?"

"Because of that saloon girl, I'd say."

"Well, there is that ain't it? Come on let's go. Daylight's fadin' and I want to get to the livery closest to the train station to see if we got any chance at unloadin' these horses."

Gladdy smiled and kneed his horse forward, taking after Clovis at a steady pace, looking forward to the comfort of the train and getting out of the busy street. Kansas City was the noisiest, smelliest place he been in since he'd left Indian Territory. Kosoma. Now that place was really stinky. He hoped Aberdeen was a better place to land than where he was at or where he'd been.

Clovis was right proud of himself, flush with cash and nothing more than a traveling bag to his name as he settled in on the train. Gladdy followed along with his head up, shoulders square, and his chest stuck out like he was the cock of the walk. All told, Clovis had got sixty dollars for the horses and gear from the livery man. And he'd sent off a wire to Mister Marberry, tellin' him—not askin' him—of the plan to take the train to Aberdeen. The plan had been expedited, Clovis had said in the wire. That had been Clovis's big word, not Gladdy's. He'd never heard that word before in his life. There was a lot about Clovis he didn't know, but he was learnin' awful quick that the man thought highly of himself. Gladdy didn't know much, but he knew that kind of attitude was dangerous. He'd seen head men, captains in the army and crew bosses alike who had got men killed by underthinking their plans and bettin' too high on their confidence. He knew he needed to give Clovis a wide berth and question everything that the man said or did, even though at the moment, they were comfortable inside the train, waitin' on it to head north instead of on the back of a horse, riding straight into a snowstorm. Gladdy kind of wished he'd got a new hat. All Clovis had done for him was to treat him to a steak dinner at Delmonico's. He had to admit it had been a fine meal.

They settled into their seats and stowed their bags underneath. Neither man wore their sidearms or showed any weapons at all. Gladdy always wore a knife inside his boot. He figured Clovis did, too, but didn't ask.

Clovis took the window seat and exhaled deeply as he snuggled into it. "Now that was the best steak I ever ate. I think I'll sleep away some time once we get rollin'."

It was afternoon with the sun peaked at its apex in the clear sky. There was no concern for weather, snowy or otherwise. The temperature had been mild, above freezing, making the inside of the train car comfortable, almost too warm once all of the people came in and got themselves situated. Every seat was full, with a wide variety of passengers sitting shoulder to shoulder. Single men. Families. A woman traveling with two little girls. A priest, and a whole load of other people that Gladdy hadn't taken much notice of.

"I get antsy in closed in places," Gladdy said. "I was about to go a little mad when you and Frank left me down in that cellar."

"We didn't know what to do with you. Frank never liked to kill someone without reason."

"What about you?"

"I didn't have a say. We was in Mister Marberry's house, and he's funny about blood bein' spilt under his roof. He's worried about how he looks to the world."

"You know I still carry an uneven grudge against that man, don't you? His man killed my brother."

"I know you done told us more than once." Clovis hesitated and looked Gladdy up and down in the seat next to him. "What about you? You ever kill a man without a good reason?"

"I do what I'm told, just like you. Don't you worry none. I'm not gonna slit your throat while you sleep. You're in charge, remember? You're the lead man. And you done bought me that nice steak dinner. Who's gonna kill a man who feeds him well and keeps him warm?"

"It *was* a fine meal."

"Yes, I'd say it was."

The train lurched forward and started to move. Gladdy and Clovis both retreated to the comfort of their seats, relaxing back into the soft red brocade material. It took Clovis longer to fall asleep than Gladdy thought it would.

Gladdy didn't wake up until after the first water stop. He found the seat next to him empty. Clovis was gone, had squeezed in front of him without waking him. The train rocked and swayed as it gained speed, and Gladdy took a minute before he did anything. He was slow to wake.

An older man sat in the seat across the aisle from him, staring into the ceiling of the train car, bored, daydreaming, not paying any attention to anything. A woman with gray hair and a plump face stared out the window, ignoring the man. They might have been traveling together, or maybe not. It was hard for Gladdy to tell. "Excuse me," he said to the man, "did you see where the man next to me went?"

The older man looked surprised by the question, almost like he had been woken up himself. "Gentleman's car is two up. If I were to guess, he opted for a cigar and card game. Looked the type to me."

Gladdy knew men like this one. Nose in the air, thought they were better than him, went to church on Sundays, and thought they belonged in Heaven because they dropped pennies in the offering basket. Truth was, if it wasn't for the woman next to the old man holding him back, he'd be smokin' a cigar and throwin' back a whiskey or two himself.

"Thank you, kindly," Gladdy said, standing up, steadying himself on the seat in front of him, getting his train-legs as quickly as he could. He staggered forward, anxious to leave the judgmental man behind.

The old man was right. Gladdy found Clovis sitting at a poker table in the smoke-filled train car. There was no cigar in front of Clovis, but there was a highball of amber water that Gladdy knew to be whiskey. He stood inside the door, taking in what he saw.

The car was paneled with dark wood, maybe walnut, with sconces topped with green shades attached to the walls above the tables. There were eight settings to play cards that Gladdy could see. Most of the blinds were pulled tight on the windows, and the sconces flickered right and left as the train wobbled and swayed down the track. The sound from the wheels underneath was constant, iron rolling on iron. It was a hard hum that his ears got used to after a while. A long bar, ornate, carved of a different wood, maybe mahogany, with male lion heads on the corner posts frozen in a growl, took up half the car on the right side. A bartender, short, skinny, and bald, wore a white shirt with a black sleeve garter on his left arm, looked a little overwhelmed. There were no empty seats at the bar. Nine or ten men, some in business suits, others in everyday clothes, clung to the bar, waiting for a drink or were in the process of taking one. Along with the grind of the wheels were the loud conversations that had nowhere to go but to circulate inside the train car. Gladdy could hardly hear himself think. He was glad there wasn't a piano playing. He had never been comfortable in saloons of any kind. Get in, get out was his philosophy. Down a drink, poke a girl, and get on your way before some kind of trouble stirred up . . . or a girl tried to sink her hooks into you. The last thing Gladdy wanted to do was end up like Frank.

Three men that Gladdy hadn't ever seen before sat at the poker table with Clovis, who was focused on the game and hadn't realized that Gladdy had come into the car. A tall pile of chips sat in front of Clovis. Same with the other three men. It looked like the game was just getting started.

The sight worried Gladdy a bit. They had pocketed a fair bit of money for all of their gear in Kansas City, but Clovis hadn't parsed any of it out to Gladdy, claiming that he was the man in charge, and it was his role to look after the finances on the trip. Gladdy being Gladdy didn't argue, but he hadn't known that Clovis was a gambler any more than he knew Frank was heart sick and in love with a saloon girl. That hadn't turned out too good for any of them. All Gladdy could do was sit back and watch and hope that Clovis had more of a level head than Frank did. Otherwise, from the looks of things, they could lose everything. At least they were on a train where it was warm and comfortable. If there was trouble to come, it would be their last stop in Aberdeen. He hoped the two men they were meeting up with weren't hard fellas to read or ride with. He was thinking this trip was a mistake. He should have high-tailed it on his own when Frank had gone to meet his maker.

Gladdy watched the dealer at Clovis's table, a tall thin man with a horseshoe mustache and a hand-rolled cigarette dangling from his mouth, shuffle the cards and deal four cards up and one down. Five Card Stud.

Clovis showed a ten of hearts, a seven of spades, a queen of hearts, and two of clubs. Not much to go on, depending on what his down card was. Clovis kept the ten and the queen. When the dealer tossed the cards across the table, Clovis angled his elbow and caught the top card just right and sent it skittering to the floor. He leaned down real quick, before any of the other men could object, and flipped the card back up on the table, then wagged both of his hands, silently showing and saying that he hadn't cheated. But he had, and Gladdy had seen him. Clovis had slipped a card out of his sleeve and replaced it with the one that had fallen on the floor.

Gladdy's throat went dry, and he scoped out the rest of the men around the bar and in the room to see if anyone had seen what he had. It didn't look like anyone did, which allowed a deep breath of relief to escape his lips. Clovis went on to win the hand, collecting a nice pile of chips from the dealer and the two other men. One looked like a cowboy and the other one looked like a banker with a bad eye. One eye went up and the other eye went down. Gladdy didn't know if he could sit at the table with a man who had such an affliction. He'd get caught starin' and lose his place in the game.

Clovis got right full of himself as the chips in front of him began to pile up. The cheat had set him on a winning streak. The three men looked beat, downtrodden every time Clovis pulled out a winning hand, which was more often than not. Gladdy watched close, if Clovis was cheatin' on every hand, he couldn't see it. Only that once, but that had been enough to know that Clovis was up to something he shouldn't have been. All Gladdy could do was stand there and watch Clovis get cockier and cockier, betting the big pile on hands that didn't make no sense. An over-confident man was dangerous according to Gladdy's way of thinking, and his gut told him to leave the car and go back to his seat. But he couldn't take his eyes off Clovis, or the pile of chips that represented his own future. He should have run when he'd had the chance.

Clovis elbowed a card to the floor. This time, the cowboy watched as close as Gladdy had, and saw the stupid trick Clovis was tryin' to pull.

"He's cheatin'." The cowboy jumped up, and pulled his gun, a New Model Remington '75, that looked a lot like the '73 Colt Gladdy carried, and pointed it Clovis's head— that had popped up from leaning over to retrieve the card and swap it out with the card up his sleeve. "Stand up, man," he ordered.

The color drained out of Clovis's face. He sat frozen in his chair as silence settled around him. The only sound that could be heard was the roll of the wheels of the train. Every eye in the place was on Clovis. Gladdy hadn't spoken to him since he'd come into the car, so as far as he knew nobody had any idea that they were traveling together.

"Somebody send for the railroad detective," the banker-looking man with the bad eye said. He was on his feet, too.

Gladdy started backing to the door as discretely as he could.

"I said stand up," the cowboy shouted. "You done took all of our money. But not no more. We're takin' it back, and you're in a heap of trouble. Stand up."

Clovis had no choice but to do what he was told, starin' down the end of the barrel like he was. At that second, it looked like his luck had run out—but the next second, not so much. For some reason the train came to a screeching stop, sending everyone forward, back, then sideways if they lost their balance. Clovis held his own, but the cowboy and the banker tumbled forward.

Clovis made eye contact with Gladdy and yelled, "Run!"

Nobody had to tell Gladdy O'Connor twice that if he didn't run, he was in deep shit, especially since Clovis had just identified him as an associate. That made Gladdy a cheater, too, whether it was true or not. Gladdy didn't have nothin' to do with the card game, but every man in that gentleman's car was going to judge him as a thief because he was riding with Clovis.

Gladdy ran out the door of the car, hustled into the next one, picking up speed as he went. Clovis had managed to catch up and was on his heels.

More luck. The train started moving again.

More trouble. The cowboy, and another man, maybe the railroad detective, were close behind them.

Gladdy hurried through another car with Clovis close behind him. "We're gonna have to jump at the next coupling," he said.

Damn it. Gladdy didn't want to jump, but he knew he didn't have a choice. The last thing he wanted was to be locked up in a small compartment on the train and turned over to the sheriff in the next town. That wouldn't work in his favor no matter how much he pleaded innocence and stupidity. He didn't know Clovis was a cheater.

Gladdy pushed out of the door of the passenger car and didn't stop to think about what he was doing. He just kept going, sliding down the steps, and dove into a roll off the train. He hit the ground just right, and tumbled into a soft peat bog, cushioning the landing. More of Clovis's luck.

Clovis did the same thing; hit the ground a little wobbly, then rolled out of sight from Gladdy.

The train was moving at full speed again. The engineer was unaware of the tussle and crime that had occurred in the gentleman's car. But the cowboy got off a shot. It didn't hit anywhere near Gladdy. For the moment, he was safe, intact, and hoped Clovis was, too. Though there was gonna be a reckoning once they got on their feet. If this was the way it was gonna be, then Gladdy wasn't takin' orders from no one. Especially from a cheater like Clovis.

Chapter 18

Darkness settled around Trusty as the smell of the extinguished fire filled his nose and smoke burned his eyes. The wind had shifted and pushed the smoke straight at him and Two Guns. He couldn't see clearly, but there was nothing wrong with his ears. All he heard was the ever-present wind. "You all right over there, Two Guns?" Trusty said.

"Two Guns? Name's Jonah Farley if you don't mind."

"I beg your pardon."

"I'm fine. It's a shame about Reed and Smoot, though. You got any idea who that was doin' the shootin'?"

Black Diamond Eyes must have been Smoot. He was frozen stiff staring up at the cloudless sky in a forever gaze that wasn't going away anytime soon. Dawn was breaking in the east. Gray light cutting into the blackness with slow and steady restraint. Trusty would be glad to see daylight again. "Can't say for sure who it was."

"Wasn't that Indian that was ridin' with you that the captain was trackin', was it?"

"I thought he was after Charlie Littlefoot?"

"You find one, there's always more."

"If you say so." Trusty hesitated, then looked over his shoulder and called out for the captain. "You all right, Plumright?" Only the wind answered him back. No other human presence responded. The silence got Trusty's attention. He stood up with his Winchester in hand, ready to answer back to the next shot if it came. His eyes had adjusted enough to the darkness to see his way forward. Jonah Farley stood up and followed after him. Both men stopped at the tether line to find the captain's horse missing. They stared out in the distance, before saying anything.

"I didn't hear him leave," Farley finally said.

"He crawled off into the darkness after the shooting stopped." Trusty continued to look into the darkness, surprised that Plumright had managed to sneak away. "I heard the shooter ride off, but I didn't hear the captain take out after him. Did you?"

"Nope," Farley said. He hitched up his pants, resettling his government-issue holsters on each hip, reminding Trusty that Farley was a military man, too. Or an ex-military man. He hadn't had the chance to get that familiar with the man. Just because he wore a military holster and boots didn't make him ex-army. "I didn't hear nothin' but the wind. You figure the captain took out on his own after that shooter?"

"He thought it was Oliver who was shootin' at us. I suppose he did," Trusty answered. "Oliver had enough of a relationship with the captain's wife to cause some consternation between him and the captain, I suppose."

"If you ask me, James Pierpoint Plumright should have

kept the fires warm in his own home, so another man didn't have to."

The remark surprised Trusty. He cocked his head toward Farley, and looked him up and down again, casting aside any judgment he might have held against the man. Dawn was breaking harder in the east, allowing a little more light to fall on the camp and Farley's face. Maybe he wasn't the faithful lieutenant that Trusty thought he was. "What do you mean by that?"

"Just what I said. Look, Marshal, I ain't got no beef with you. You were shootin' into the dark to protect yourself and us just the same as I was. I appreciate that. But I'm standin' here wonderin' where the hell Plumright ran off to now, all the while I'm freezin' my ass off and expecting the shooting to start again at any second."

"Welcome to my life."

"I'm sure you're gettin' paid more for this than I am. I'm here at Colonel Townsend's behest. It was his order for me and Smith to ride with Plumright. Keep an eye out for trouble, and make sure that Charlie Littlefoot came back to the fort alive. That simple. Plumright might have figured that out for himself and planned on taking off on his own the first chance he got. Just a guess, but it makes sense to me. Reed was the only one of us that held any loyalty to the captain, had served with him for several years, always buffeted trouble away from him when he could. Now look at Reed. Dead and frozen. Plumright don't care about that. He's bloodthirsty. Wants that Indian, or any Indian that was sympathetic to Charlie Littlefoot, dead and silenced for good."

"So, he knew of Plumright's intention?"

"Of course, he did. Anybody with half a brain knows

Plumright will kill Charlie Littlefoot if he gets within a hundred feet of him."

"You know more about all of this than you're sayin'," Trusty said.

"I know Reed and Smith are dead. They need a proper burial in ground that's frozen solid as rock. I have to go after the captain and do my best to keep an Indian alive even though I don't want to. How's that for irony for you? I've spent the last ten years of my life fightin' Indians, doin' my best to stay alive, now I have to keep a West Point officer from killin' one in cold blood."

"We have to go after the captain," Trusty said. "I figure he's tracking Oliver like he was tracking us."

"Reed was trackin' you. You think Plumright has those kinds of skills?"

"I don't know what skills he has; all I know is that he's gone."

"We need to find Charlie Littlefoot first. That's all I'm sayin'."

"I agree with you." Trusty was a little relieved to hear the man was on his side of things. That is if he was telling the truth. There was no way to know that for sure, other than to pay attention to his instincts, keep his eyes and ears open more than normal.

"You gonna help me bury those two?"

"I suppose so."

"Well," Farley said, "if we can't dig a grave, we can always light a big fire."

"If the ground is too hard, we won't have a choice."

"We better get to work."

"I suppose," Trusty said, looking out over the frozen prairie again, hoping to see Oliver or the captain riding back to camp. Instead, he saw the vastness of the land opening up as the new day's light reached and touched the ground, promising to shine on it, but not warm it. There was nothing alive in sight. Trusty wondered how anything stayed alive on the cold, barren ground before him.

Rapid City, Dakota Territory, April 1878

The city was only three years old, called the Gateway to the Black Hills, but that didn't matter to Sam Dawson or his two friends, and fellow soldiers, Luke Elijah and Joe Rawls. They were there for fun after a long hard winter at Fort Robinson, and not interested in much else. All about the same age, Elijah hailed from Illinois, and Rawls was a born and bred Nebraska boy, aching to join the army as soon as he was able. Rawls had lost an aunt and uncle to the Cheyenne when he was a boy, and he wanted to pay them back the only way he knew how: with a rifle and an army of like-minded men at his side. Elijah always said he had nothing else to do other than be a farmer, and he wasn't any good at that. Both reasons were good enough for Sam to become friends with the two. For the first time in his life, he was never alone. The Army had given him brothers he'd never had. Now they were on leave, with nothing but time on their hands and a little money in their pockets.

"I hear there's another new town north of here that might be more fun," Elijah said. They all stood surveying the city from its edge. From where they stood, it didn't look like anything special, were a little disappointed by the few buildings they saw along the stream the place was named after. "Deadwood, I think it's called. About another forty miles."

Sam shook his head, while Rawls stood quietly between them. Rawls was the shortest of the trio. Sam was the biggest, most muscular. And Elijah was tall and wide-eyed. "We'd lose four days."

"Three at the most, the way we ride," Elijah said. All three of them had their government mounts. Jasper for Trusty, and two no name horses with numbers, that were more valuable than anything else the Army had trusted them with.

"I don't think it's worth it." Sam had his feet firmly planted. "We should just find us a house here and stay for a little while. That way you get to know what's what and who's who."

Rawls stirred into the conversation, confused. "House? What kind of house?"

Sam chuckled. "A whorehouse. A cathouse. Whatever you want to call it. There's usually a flophouse nearby and a saloon or two."

"I think we'd have better luck in Deadwood," Elijah said. "I got a hankerin' to play some cards and win me some money."

Sam sighed a bit. As much as he liked being part of a crowd, he wasn't used to it. He had come and gone where and when he wanted to for a long time. The only person he had to please was his father, and then if his errands had something to do with the shop or Madame Duchamp, he had free reign. "Look," he said, "let's go into this town and see what we can find. If it's boring, then we still got time to make it to Deadwood. It'll be tight makin' it back to the fort before our leave runs out, but we can do it if we don't run into trouble."

"What kind of trouble?" Rawls said.

"Don't you worry about that," Sam answered. "Come on, let's go."

The house they found in Rapid City was nothing like Madame Duchamp's house in Saint Louis. It was drab, dull, and lacked the taste of a refined woman who had been reared in New Orleans. But that didn't matter to Sam as he eyed the girls in the dim parlor. Rawls and Elijah stood behind him, not sure what to do, pulled in by Sam's encouragement and the confidence the half bottle of whiskey the three of them had shared gave them. Rawls had developed a noticeable nervous tick in his cheek as soon as they had walked into the house.

There was no madame, but a man named Hiram who saw to the business transactions. Hiram looked like his previous line of work was as an undertaker. The girls, unfortunately, reflected the grayness of the place, and didn't hold a candle to the class of women Sam was accustomed to. There were six of them, a little scrawny, dull-eyed, uninteresting except a pair of twins about Sam's age on the end. It was the tale of those that had brought the trio to this house in the first place. The twins were blond, buxom, with their faces painted and their clothes clean and colorful. One wore purple and the other pink. Besides that difference, they were identical.

Sam walked over to the girls, stopped in front of the twins, and said, "I'll take them both."

"That's extra," Hiram responded with a monotone voice that held no expectations other than a man saying no.

"That's fine with me." Sam had saved his errand money

from Madame Duchamp, and along with his Army stipend, money was the least of his worries.

The girls stood up, and Sam walked right by Rawls and Elijah with a girl on each arm, who it seemed, could not believe what they were seeing. "Don't do anything I wouldn't do, fellas," he said, then disappeared up the staircase.

The tales that Luke Elijah and Joe Rawls told about Sam once they returned to the fort were half-true with more embellishments from all three, but one thing was true. The girls liked Sam, and Sam liked the girls. Especially girls with blond hair that reminded him of Jessica Marberry.

South of Cannonball, Dakota Territory, December 1888

Trusty and Jonah Farley rode north with the fire still smoldering behind them. Each man towed a riderless horse. Farley pulled Reed's stout black gelding while Trusty held the responsibility for Smith's horse, a smaller paint mare. All of the animals seemed agreeable to the situation. Even Horse, who usually objected to being tied to anything, didn't mind the paint mare pacing after him. Something about the horse's attitude had changed once Oliver and Takoda had come along. Or maybe it was how Trusty had looked at the horse for himself. They had been lost to each other in the blizzard, and when that storm had subsided, was finally over, Trusty had never been so glad to see a horse still standing in all of his life. Horse had been with him in all of his travels as a Deputy U.S. Marshal. They had ridden from one end of Indian Territory and back again, through good weather and bad, in troubled times, like the loss of Judge Hadesworth, and easy times, when the riding was soft, and the delivery of a warrant was effortless. Then on the ride to Dakota Territory where the world was cold and inhospitable, doing its best to make them uncomfortable and kill them with its touch. Horse had been an agreeable mount who asked for nothing more than to be treated decently, fed, and warmed when it was possible. The truth was, Horse was the only consistent creature in Trusty's life, and the animal had never betrayed him, just looked to him with understanding eyes, willing to bear the weight of him, and take him wherever he wanted to go. The thought of losing Horse had made Trusty reconsider his need for him, his use for him, and his affection for him, too. He patted Horse's firm roan neck and nickered him forward as gently as he could.

The ground had been too hard to dig, so Trusty and Farley had no choice but to build a makeshift pyre. The funeral fire had been easy enough to build with the wood that Oliver had collected, and what other wood lay scattered around the stand of cottonwoods. The smoke billowed upward, then shifted south as the wind pushed it away. Trusty and Farley were heading north toward Canada, doing their best to track the two horses that had fled the camp: Oliver's and Plumright's. Both men remained quiet, their eyes to the ground as they trudged through the snow, following the tracks left behind. The wind skirted across the ground, sending white ribbons sliding across the prairie, erasing the shallower tracks, but leaving the deeper ones. A stronger wind would make the tracking even harder. With little brush, and the grasses knocked down by previous snow and ice, finding a break to point the way north was going to be harder and harder. In the beginning, Trusty had relied on Oliver to lead them north because his own tracking skills in the winter were not that good. All he knew now was that he had to keep going. With more than one man to track, that, at least, made the task a little easier.

The day before them promised to be mild. The wind was more of a breeze than a constant gust, and the temperature had climbed upward with the sun in the clear sky to a temperate and tolerable level. Without any clouds to dim the sun, it warmed Trusty's face as he trudged forward with Farley at his side. Just as he topped the crest of a rise, he looked back one more time to the spot where the two men had lost their lives. The smoke was thin, a cloud itself reaching from the ground to the sky, nothing more than a sad monument to what had happened there. Once the fire died and time and the weather covered up the ashes, or distributed them far and wide, the lives of the two men would be lost to the wind forever. It was a shame, but that was the way of the world, especially in the middle of a frozen nowhere.

They had ridden for almost two hours, quiet, without seeing anyone or anything alive, still edging north along the Missouri River.

"It's another day's ride to Canada," Trusty said. "You don't have to go that far with me if you don't want to."

"I figure Canada will look a lot like this," Farley answered. "I gave my word to Colonel Townsend that I would ride with Plumright. I plan on seein' this through, if you don't mind. What are you gonna do in Canada?"

"I've planned on riding there from the start. I've got orders to meet up with a Mountie who has knowledge of the land and the way of the Indians. If anyone is hiding Charlie, he'll know where to look. I hadn't counted on

Oliver coming along with me. That complicated my plans, and then you and the captain showed up, so there's that, too. I should have been to Canada by now."

"Them fellas deserved a decent burial, if the fire could be called that."

"Depends on what you believe, I guess. Our Indian friends believe the fire sets the spirit free. Maybe they're right. Who knows? I don't take much to religion, and I try not to think too much about dyin' and what comes after if anything. I rode with an ex-priest not too long ago. A good man who struggled with the bad inside of him. I think he might have complicated my view of such things."

Jonah Farley didn't say anything right away, just kept his eyes forward, and chewed on his lip a bit. "You know that Indian's innocent, don't you? He didn't do nothin' with that woman that she didn't want him to."

Trusty stopped Horse, and Farley followed suit. They were atop the rise with a clear view of the white, frozen world around them. There were no threats anywhere to be seen, and two sets of horse tracks easy enough to follow. "My gut has said that from the beginning. Marshal Delaney had his doubts, which is why I came to Fort Yates in the first place instead of heading straight to Canada. I think the real problem here is Plumright himself."

"A man who doesn't get his way or is made to look bad is always dangerous. Plumright has always had airs to wear that showed a thin-skinned, quick-tempered man. I always felt sorry for his wife. No one knows what goes on behind closed doors, but he must have crossed her in an awful way."

"Why do you say that?"

"Why else would a white woman take up with an Indian?"

Trusty didn't know how to answer Farley's question. All he could do was look out over the land before him and hope like hell that he found Charlie Littlefoot before Captain Plumright did. There was a baby coming into the world that would need its father. Just like his own. Wherever she was.

Chapter 19

White Earth River, Dakota Territory, December 1888

Trusty and Horse paced forward, head to the wind, with more snow and ice accumulating on them than Trusty thought they could tolerate. He longed to feel the warm sun of spring, see the world transform to green, hear the birds singing happily, and smell the bloom of the wild-flowers. He had never felt so disconnected from the living, breathing world as he had been since riding in the Dakota Territory. He wondered if the snow was going to make him blind to color forever. All he could see before him was a blank landscape void of any interest or distinction. The ride had made him reconsider his plan to bring in Charlie Littlefoot, then go after Theodore Marberry on his own. He should have headed southeast when he left Fort Yates, headed to Saint Louis, instead of trekking north into the barren, icy land that he now found himself in. Duty and regrets had kept him going, but the sooner he was able to leave the Dakota Territory, the better.

Stopping now was not an option. Trusty could barely see ten feet in front of Horse's nose. They were heading due north, straight into the wind, certain that if they stood still for even a moment they would be buried in the snow, suffocated, sent straight to a hell that bore no fire, was not warm, but forever white, painfully cold, leaving them both entombed in eternal ice, a statue of dedication and lack of sense.

"I think we're being followed, but I can't tell for sure," Trusty said to Farley. He had seen shadows dancing in the periphery of his vision, on the edge of the whiteness where he thought the ground met the sky but couldn't be certain. The world could have been turned upside down and he wouldn't have known the difference.

"I thought the same thing. I can't tell if it's an animal or a man, or if I have been imagining things," Farley answered. His words turned to ice crystals and shattered to the ground as soon as he spoke. "Might be both, but I've heard tell of wolves packing in the forests that reach down from Canada. It might be one of them scoutin' us for dinner. If you've never seen a pack of 'em take down a proud, antlered elk, you should. It would scare the bejesus out of you. A man with no gun has no chance at defendin' himself from an attack from them unholy monsters."

"We've got plenty of arms."

"But not the instincts that they do. Keep an eye out is all I'm sayin'. There are more than men out in the world intent on doin' us harm. Some animals have to eat, and a man's flesh ain't no different to them than a mule deer, other than it might be a little rarer—which would make it even more tasty if you know what I mean. I don't cotton to no wolves. I fear them more than anything else."

Trusty nodded but said nothing. He just stared at the trail before him, searching for moving shadows and the sound of man or beast. All he knew to look for was something that resembled a dog. He'd never seen a wolf in his life.

There were more trees now, pines and firs hugging the edge of the trail; ravines that reached down to the river. They had left the Missouri and tracked upward into the Dakota Territory as far as it reached, taking the tributary, the White Earth River, north toward Canada. Once the river disappeared into its headwaters, they would be on their own with no frozen river to follow, only instinct and the stars to lead them to their final destination. There had been no sign of Oliver, Plumright, or Charlie Littlefoot. There had been no sign of any other humans, and that made Jonah Farley's presence on the ride even more pleasant and surprising. Trusty liked having the man along. Though he didn't trust him completely, he seemed a genuine man, loyal to the orders given to him by Colonel Townsend, and capable of surviving in the territory, comparable to Oliver and his Indian skills. There was no question that Farley had spent time among the Lakota, but Trusty didn't know the details. Farley had been reasonably tight lipped about his past.

"Can't say that I've ever seen a wolf," Trusty said. "Where'd you see yours?" It helped to talk, to move parts of his face so it didn't freeze. It also helped keep his mind off the cold, the desolation, and the fear that the being, animal or man, that was following them meant them harm. The best thing to do was act normal and keep a hand close to his gun if it was a wolf sizing them up to attack.

The two men rode side by side with their voices low. There was a constant roar of the wind that ruled out any other sound in the world.

"I was out Yellowstone way when I was a tadpole. Went west on the Oregon Trail in a wagon train with my folks.

We hailed from Pennsylvania, and my pa got the urge to start over out west after his brother, my uncle, made the trip and found some success in California. By the time we got to the end of the world, my ma and two younger sisters had died of the fevers and pox that spread through the population. It left me to be raised by my pa, who by that time wasn't much in the mood to do anything but drink whiskey and rage at the world for his misfortune. My uncle took us in for a while, but my pa wore out his welcome there, and we ended up comin' back east, made it as far as Kansas City before he gave up and died on me. I was fourteen. Saw those wolves on the way back. I thought for sure my pa was gonna feed me to them to be rid of me, too. But he didn't try. It was the god-awfulest thing I ever did see, six wolves nipping, pushing, jumping on the back of a grand bull elk, biting into it in a way it couldn't fight back with that big rack of antlers. I cried when it gave up with a swoon and call and fell to the ground. Sometimes when I have nightmares, I see that elk and what's left of him after the wolves and the ravens had their way with it. We watched it all, couldn't take our eyes off the tragedy of it."

Trusty's mouth was dry, and his teeth were so cold he thought they would shatter when they chattered together. His eyes were dry, too, surprisingly. Farley's story sounded a lot like his own: raised by a father who didn't want to be a father after his mother had died. If they had been in a saloon, Trusty would have bought the man a beer. But they weren't. All he could do was nod and keep riding. Snow danced in front of him and cut a vee around him and Horse. Farley trudged along, his head down, his eyes diverted to another time and place. They rode silent for a long time, both of them listening for the wolf without hearing any living thing. The wind deafened them. The snow blinded them. And the past rode alongside both men, tormenting them with its fangs and lack of compassion.

An hour later, Trusty thought he saw another shadow, only this one wasn't of a four-legged creature or a man. It was the shape of a cabin, standing alongside the ravine, overlooking the river. The cabin was foggy at first, and then plank by plank, with a decent roof and all, the shelter became clear, and Trusty was certain that it wasn't his imagination or a mirage toying with him. "You see that, Farley?" he said.

"I do. And whatever it was that was trailin' us, fell off us, but that don't mean it's gone. Let's hope the place offers a decent camp where we can warm up. I ain't felt my toes since we left Fort Yates."

The cabin was empty, abandoned long enough for squirrels and other creatures to take advantage of the cracks and crevices to come and go as they pleased so they could make a home of it for themselves. There were cobwebs everywhere, and the smell of urine and scat was so thick it slowed Trusty's momentum from bursting completely inside, desperate to leave the wind and snow behind. He stuffed the sleeve of the buffalo coat against his nose, but it didn't help much; the smell had been closed in for God knew how long.

The place looked like a hunting cabin of some kind, not a regular stop or stay for anyone. There was a rickety table made of thin maple in the center of the open room. A curtain that had been used for privacy at one time hung in shreds from the ceiling. The material had been used for nesting material and sat like a pillow in the center of what remained of an old sleeping cot. A stone fireplace dominated one wall, and there was enough scrap wood and dried leaves that had made their way inside for kindling to start a flame, but nothing that would sustain a long fire. One of them was going to have to go back outside and hunt down some firewood.

Farley walked into the cabin behind Trusty and stopped inside the door. "Lord have mercy it smells like somethin' up and died in here." Somehow there was still glass in two window frames that let light into the interior.

"Keep the door open," Trusty said. "I'm going to round up some wood for a fire, and make sure the horses are settled." He wore his Colt on his hip, had the coat open so he could get to it if it was needed, but had left his rifle in the scabbard, along with the rest of his gear on Horse. Warmth was the first order of business. Then he would see if the cabin would afford them comfortable lodging.

Trusty made his way outside, glad to be free of the horrid smell, and made his way along the side of the cabin, keeping an eye to the ground and an ear open against the wind for anything that moved. He was on alert for a wolf, bounty hunter, or Plumright himself, to appear out of the nothingness and try to kill him. The wind was not as fierce as it had been riding along the river. The cabin sat back in a thick of tall pine trees, almost hidden from view; he would have missed it if he hadn't been looking for wolf shadows. The fall of the snow had slowed, offering a reprieve from precipitation, but still granted him a blank sky overhead. There was four or five inches of white fluff accumulated on the ground. Deep enough to hide any kind of older tracks, human or animal, from sight.

To Trusty's surprise there was a small two-stall barn behind the cabin, big enough for both horses to shelter out of the weather while they were there. Trusty was sure both horses needed as much relief from the wind and snow as he did. The constant cold was making him angry.

His bones protested every move and his blood threatened to freeze. No wonder Indians didn't travel in the winter unless they had to.

He abandoned his quest for firewood and saw to the horses, moving them into the barn, clearing them of snow and ice with gentle pats and wipes, feeding them some oats from the pack once they were comfortable. "I'll bring you some water once I get it melted, buddy," Trusty said to Horse with a pat on the neck. It was the first time he had ever used any kind of nickname or term of affection with the horse. He was surprised by the words that came out of his mouth. Horse didn't seem to notice. He was too interested in the oats.

Satisfied that the horses would be safe in the little barn, Trusty set about scavenging for firewood. He edged his way around to the back of the barn and found himself in a thick clump of hardwoods, oak, hickories, and some softer birch. He realized he didn't have his hatchet with him, a tool that would make splitting frozen wood a little easier. When he turned to go back into the barn where his gear was, he saw movement out of the corner of his eye again. He froze in place, caught his breath deep in his chest. Trusty was certain of what he saw; a man not an animal on two legs, scurrying to hide behind a tree. He pulled his Colt out of the holster and gripped the ice-cold trigger with his index finger. He hadn't lost that feeling, not like in his toes. "You, there," he said, "come out with your hands up."

A cloud of icy breath appeared from behind the tree Trusty had aimed for. Resignation. Hiding was impossible. "Don't shoot, Dawson, it's me, Oliver," the Indian said, as he stepped into view with his hands up.

"You alone?" Trusty said.

"Yes. On foot. Takoda stepped in a hole and broke his

leg a day ago. I had to shoot him to end his suffering." Oliver looked cold and defeated in a way Trusty hadn't seen him before. His trousers had a hole in the knee and a fresh scrape dashed across his sad brown face. The Lakota had seemed confident in the elements beyond the fort at the start of the journey. Now he looked like a beggar asking for a handout, his eyes pleading for Trusty to take him in.

"You're sure you're alone?"

"I spied a wolf tracking me and you and the man you're riding with. There's no one but me. The wolf is watching us, I'm sure, tracking our patterns, waiting to tell others when we are out in the open, on our own. Vulnerable. They wait until we are vulnerable."

Trusty didn't move, still held Oliver's chest in his bead. "You left me out there on my own."

"I knew Plumright and his men were coming."

"Two of those men are dead. We were attacked not long after they rode in."

"I was north by then. I rode as hard and as fast as I could to get away from the camp. Plumright would have killed me."

"I wouldn't have let him."

"He doesn't take orders from you or anyone."

"Why should I believe you?" Trusty said.

"I have never lied to you, Trusty Dawson. I feared for my life. I knew they wouldn't harm you. The captain is not that stupid."

"Who was shooting?"

"I don't know."

"Plumright disappeared, too. Took out after the shooter that I thought was you. There were only two sets of horse tracks. Yours and the captain's so I got good reason to be suspicious of you."

"I swear to you that I was not the person who fired those shots into the camp. I could have killed you, and I am not that stupid, either. The last person I want to be accused of killing is a U.S. Marshal. All I wanted to do was to find Charlie Littlefoot with you so he would get a fair chance. That is why I came back to you, to ride with you again."

"With me?"

"Yes, I have struggled to catch up with you after losing Takoda. What else would I do?"

Trusty sighed and lowered his weapon. "So, I am to take you at your word?"

"It is all I have to offer."

Trusty nodded then, as satisfied as he could be that Oliver was being honest and genuine with him. But before he could say anything else, or welcome Oliver back into his fold, a shot rang out from the distance, speeding across the frozen white land, echoing like thunder, as the bullet crashed into the tree next to Oliver's head.

"Get down!" Trusty shouted, just as another shot rang out.

Oliver did as he was told, but Trusty couldn't tell if he had chosen to fall or if he had been shot. He didn't know if Oliver was dead or alive.

Chapter 20

Gladdy O'Connor skidded across the cold ground like a lump of rancid lard thrown out to be finally rid of it. Bits and pieces of flesh and pride were left on the ground behind in torn, bloody spots. Rocks, pebbles, jagged ice, and bushes tore at Gladdy's clothes, ripping at his skin and clothes wherever they could find an opening. It felt like he had been hit straight in the face with buckshot, or salt pellets—he had felt both before but never like this. He'd never had reason to jump off a perfectly functional train to save his own hide. He never thought he would stop tumbling, falling, and rolling. He wondered if this was how he was going to die; running like a scared pig trying to escape being slaughtered.

It was dark, nighttime, and the jump from the train had been a leap of faith, a dive onto the hard ground that had promised pain, uncertainty, and freedom from his pursuers. Gladdy feared breaking a bone, a leg, more than anything. That would leave him stranded out in the middle of nowhere, lame, and more dependent on Clovis than he already was.

He came to a stop inside the grassy edge of a flat Nebraska field. Maybe a wheatfield of some kind, or a prairie; Gladdy didn't know the difference, didn't care. The grass was dried and dead, bent over, frozen in retreat. There was a thin layer of ice on everything, and some powdery snow scattered over the frozen ground. The dirt felt like stone underneath his body, hard, unrelenting, offering no give at all.

Pain traveled up and down Gladdy's body from one end to the other. He could taste salty blood in his mouth, but he could wiggle his toes and flex his fingers without any trouble at all. Ten and ten, everything still worked, everything moved. Nothing felt broken. He sucked in some cold air and was finally able to regulate his breathing. The pain in his chest started to fade away. His lungs were working, hadn't been poked by a stick and deflated. Stopped, motionless, lying on his back, with his eyes struggling to stay open, the world quit bouncing around; he stared at the sky overhead. It was a cloudless and moonless night. Cold. Made him shiver for the first time since landing on the ground. Distant stars twinkled but offered little light. There was no town, sod houses, or nearby pond to reflect anything but black ink pocked with pulsing silver dots. The roar of the train rolled north with the wheels, cargo, and angry men who had chased him and Clovis to the end, echoed across the flat ground and faded away into nothingness. Steam lingered long after the train had disappeared, the narrow cloud of it dissipating in the air without the power of the wind to make it vanish right away. Once the train was out of sight, an empty silence filled his ears, reminding Gladdy that he didn't know where he was at. He only knew that he was lost, somewhere north of Kansas City. And for a moment, at that very moment, he felt like he was all alone in the world even though he had seen

Clovis jump, too. He had lost sight of the cheater in the middle of the rolls and tumbles they'd both had to take.

As far as Gladdy could tell, he was just scraped up a little, bleeding from skinned knees, torn palms, and his scratched-up face. He wiped a piece of gravel from his cheek. It had been slightly embedded next to his nose and was covered with blood. There were more small rocks on the other side of his face, easily pushed away, didn't have to be dug out. From there, he worked up some strength and sat up, wiping his face again, only this time with the back of his sleeve. He wondered where Clovis was. There was no sound, no sign of the man. Gladdy had a few things to say to the boss, which now that he came to think about it, sitting there in the dark, a little beat up, blood trailing down his lip with no prospect of a warm bed or decent meal, he was regretting putting his fate in Clovis's hands in the first place. Some boss he was. The man was a cheater, and as far as Gladdy could tell, a liar to boot. That wasn't the kind of man who should be a boss, though that's exactly what his old boss, Vance Calhoun, was. A bad man not to be trusted with moods, money, or women, from how things had turned out. Haden, on the other hand, had been his true boss, his North Star, the only man in his life who never led him into bad trouble. Not like this. *Maybe,* Gladdy thought, *it's time I become my own boss. Maybe it's time to leave this nonsense and get on with my own life. Marberry could come after me if he wanted to. So what?*

Gladdy pulled himself up and limped his way back to the railroad tracks. He looked up and down them and saw nothing other than the rails disappearing into the dark. Then he retraced his steps, tried to recall the path he tumbled from the train on. "Where you at, Clovis? You all right, Clovis?"

Silence answered him back. There were no crickets to chirp, no other night bugs to mock him or laugh at him, though Gladdy wished they would have. The silence was unsettling. He walked a little to the right, then half-staggered ten feet up the tracks. He stumbled over a lump of something on the ground. It was Clovis, prone, face down, not moving.

Gladdy leaned down and poked at the man's shoulder. "Hey, Clovis, come on, get up. Let's go."

There was no response, and no movement from the man. It was too dark to tell if Clovis was breathing or not. A bad feeling came over Gladdy then, just like the one he'd had when he figured out that Haden had got shot. "Don't you be dead, too, Clovis. I don't know where I am or what I am going to do without you. You got all our money and was supposed to get me to Aberdeen." He rolled Clovis over, leaned in close to the man's face, close enough to see if he was breathing, close enough to see that he had slammed headfirst into a rock the size of a steer's head and caved in his forehead. The rock had stopped his tumble quick and hard. "Ah, damn it, Clovis, you're dead, too, ain't you?"

Clovis's eyes were fixed on the stars overhead, staring into space without a blink or show of pain of any kind. To make sure that he was dead, Gladdy felt through Clovis's coat, searching for a heartbeat, searching for something moving that would prove him wrong. "I can't get you no help out here." He pulled his hand off Clovis's chest, looked around him again, hoping to see a cabin, or a sod house with a lamp burning in the distance, or hear a dog bark, alerting him to the location of a farm somewhere nearby. There was nothing, not the slightest sound. Just Gladdy's own heartbeat racing with nowhere to go. His breath made a thin cloud of steam like the departing train. He screamed as loud as he could, let out all of the primal anger and fear that had built up inside of him for a long time, then jumped up and down and stomped his feet. Before he knew it, tears were streaming down his face. Sad tears for Haden. Angry tears for Frank and Clovis. Sad tears for himself. He screamed again, then collapsed to the ground next to Clovis. "Damn, you, Clovis. Why'd you have to go and leave me out here. Now what the hell am I going to do?"

Gladdy didn't do anything for a long time. He sat on the cold ground, his arms clung to his chest to help keep himself warm, doing nothing but staring at his boots. His mind wandered in and out of his childhood, nothing more than Haden's shadow, where he remained on the trip across the ocean, through the war, and after, right up until the day Haden had died. Then, lost, and set on revenge, he had stumbled in with Frank and Clovis, and now here he was, alone again, not so long after losing Haden. He knew he should just stay that way, alone, on his own, by himself. "But I don't know how," he said aloud to no one in particular. And no one answered him back. Clovis was stiff, starting to freeze, unable to urge him on or give him the confidence to get moving on his own. Not that he would have anyway. Clovis hadn't thought about anything but himself. Now it was Gladdy's turn. He took another deep breath, stood up, and steadied himself as he stood over his dead boss.

Gladdy had thought he would trick Clovis into thinkin' he was in charge then leave when the gettin' was good.

Except that was a lie to himself and he knew it now. He was never gonna leave Clovis. He would have followed him to Aberdeen and done whatever Clovis wanted him to. Go after Trusty Dawson, then ride all the way back to St. Louis to collect the bounty because that's what he did. He followed other men because he couldn't lead himself. "Look where that got you, Gladdy O'Connor. Just look at yourself now." He was disgusted with himself and the situation he had put himself in. He stomped the ground again and nearly slipped on the ice and fell. He could have hit his head on the same rock that had killed Clovis. Then where would he be? Dead. That's where. In hell, heaven, or somewhere in between. But he didn't fall. He caught himself, steadied himself again, and stood flatfooted on the frozen ground. He exhaled and gritted his teeth. "I can't stay here and die," he said. This time, the wind answered him back, pushing a breeze across his face, bringing with it the sound of something new into the world: the distant roll of another train heading his way.

Gladdy looked down at Clovis knowing he had to decide what to do. Staying in the spot, giving the man a decent burial, then leaving seemed the right thing to do. Except the ground was frozen and he didn't have a shovel. He didn't have anything to dig a hole with. It was December, he reasoned, with the worst of winter yct to come to these parts. More snow and ice. That would cover Clovis up, or a coyote would wander by and help himself to a meal of a toe or a finger. Gladdy shivered at the thought, but there was nothing he could do about it. The train whistled again; the blast riding more confident on the night air as the locomotive chugged closer. Gladdy looked down at Clovis again, sad at the situation that he had found himself in, knowing he had to go. He leaned down and rummaged through Clovis's coat and pulled out his wallet. There was twenty dollars in it and a piece of paper stuffed in between the bills. He pulled out the paper and held it close to his face so he could read it: *Meet Glo Timmons and Red Jack Lewis at the Ward Hotel. Room 313.*

Gladdy slid the paper back into the wallet, stuffed the wallet inside the pocket of his own coat, then helped himself to Clovis's sidearm, a '73 Colt Army. He would have taken the gun belt and accompaniment of cartridges, but Gladdy wasn't a two-gun belt kind of man. One gun had always been enough for him. But he wasn't gonna leave a gun out in the middle of nowhere to rust away. He might need it.

"I'm sorry it turned out this way for you, Clovis," Gladdy said, as he stowed away the Colt. "You had a run of luck that went from bad to worse. Your head was in the wrong place at the wrong time. What happened to you could have happened to me, and I know it. If there's a life after this one, I hope you get what you deserve, good or bad. That's the only prayer I know to say for you."

The train drew closer and Gladdy hurried to the tracks, hoping like hell there was a car he could hop into if the train wasn't moving too fast. If he didn't continue his own dose of bad luck and fall off as he was trying to get on. But what choice did he have? None. He couldn't stay there, and he knew it. He had to leave out on his own, and by God, he swore to himself, it was gonna stay that way. No more bosses for him.

The train came along pretty quick, and it was a long one, an ore train pulling four-wheeled, open-top jimmies. Lots of them. They went on for as far as the eye could see, disappearing into the dark. There weren't any other kind of railcars, none that would offer Gladdy shelter from the weather and the wind. It was either stand there and watch the train roll by, then walk to Aberdeen or pick a car and stay as warm as he could. He decided that walking was a bad idea, so he started a slow jog, eyed a car with a handle that didn't seem to have anything sticking out of the top, then chased after it until he caught the handle and pulled himself up off the ground. It would have been a harder jump and climb if he had been loaded down, but as it was, he was able to climb inside the empty car and settle into a corner. He didn't look back. Didn't give Clovis or Frank another thought. Not right then. He had to figure out how to make himself comfortable.

Aberdeen, South Dakota, December 1888

It was a longer ride to Aberdeen than Gladdy thought it would be. There were all sorts of annoying starts and stops that had to be made along the way. He was cold, stiff, thirsty, and near starved for something to eat by the time he realized he was in the right town. The train yard, like most train yards was on the outskirts of town, and he had to be careful not to get caught coming out of the car. Train police didn't care much for free riders.

It was early in the morning, just after the rise of the sun. The air was cold, but not so cold it hurt your face when the air touched it. He might have just got used to winter. There wasn't a lot of snow on the ground, and to Gladdy's relief, there weren't too many people around, either. Peering up over the lip of the jimmy, he saw a man standing at the back of the locomotive, his head up, talking to an engineer leaning out the window. He went to the other side of the car and slid out as quietly as he could. Once on the ground, he sneaked his way out of the train yard without alerting anyone to his presence. Gladdy was proud of himself. He squared his shoulders, held his head up high, then stepped up on the boardwalk, looking for the closest place to grab up some breakfast. He was so hungry he could eat two cows. Once he had his stomach satisfied, he figured he might treat himself to a bath and a shave. He had twenty whole dollars in his pocket thanks to Clovis. Then after that, he might just find him a girl or two, before wanderin' over to the Ward Hotel, wherever that was. He wasn't in too big of a hurry to put himself back in Theodore Marberry's services. Heck, he might not. He might just make his own way. Aberdeen looked like a hustling, bustling place. Surely a man like him could make a respectable life for himself there without answerin' to no one or trailin' after a card cheater or a womanizer.

Gladdy felt pretty good about himself and his prospects right then, but if he would have thought back over his life, he would have seen that those good feelings never stayed around too long, and for some reason, bad luck or whatever, he always found himself staring face to face with some kind of trouble he couldn't figure a way out of on his own.

Chapter 21

Oliver rolled onto the ground, then scurried behind a thick oak tree, doing his best to make himself a difficult target. He couldn't hide his breath, small immutable puffs that pulsed once or twice, then rode the wind, vanishing into the sterile whiteness. The Indian said nothing, tried to melt into the tree bark like one of his brother owls, but he was too tall, wearing dark clothes in bright sunlight, unable to disappear or fly away on silent wings.

Trusty wasn't sure where the shot had come from, just knew the direction. He had his Colt aimed at the blank nothingness, waiting for another shot to erupt, to attempt to silence Oliver. He didn't have to wait too long. A bullet hit the tree in front of the Indian, shattering bark like it was made of glass. Shards of black ice exploded, flying in every direction. The shot echoed outward, bouncing off the flat, frozen ground with nothing to stop it. The blast went on and on like it would never end; thunder looking for a storm to join and celebrate. Oliver stood fast, wasn't hit, was well protected from the shooter at the moment, but Trusty wasn't sure he was safe at the corner of the barn. If he could catch sight of who was shooting, he would have a better idea of what to do next.

Jonah Farley opened the cabin door, alerted by the gunshots. He stood back, out of sight, so he wasn't a target himself, and shouted, "You all right out there, Dawson?"

"Stay inside, Farley," Trusty answered. He could see a rifle barrel sticking out of the door.

Oliver was shivering, waiting like a halted rabbit for a shadow to pass over him. Silence followed Trusty's order to Farley. Only the wind had anything to say. It picked up a howl, carried some snow, piled it into the substantial drifts on the side of the barn, and screamed past the small encampment, chasing the thunder of the gunshot. There would be no storms anytime soon; the sky was clear and cold without any clouds in sight.

The shooter followed up with another shot.

This time cold hard wood shattered just above Trusty's fur hat. Splinters rained down onto him, but he didn't flinch. He was focused on the ridge where the shot had come from. A puff of hot gun smoke blew to the north on the wind, showing the shooter's location for the first time, if only for a brief second. Long enough. Trusty fired back even though he knew he couldn't penetrate the rise in the ground that the shooter was hiding behind. He fired again, motioning with his free hand for Oliver to join him.

Oliver understood that he was being covered and darted from one tree to the next, making his way toward Trusty.

The shooter fired again, followed Oliver's path, hitting the next tree dead in the center. More bark chips scattered into the air, then fell to the ground, falling like icicles from an eave, spiking upward in the ground when they landed. Trusty responded with another shot even though he was starting to worry whether he had enough cartridges to cover Oliver. Farley must have seen his breath and fired a shot from his rifle toward the ridge. A small explosion of snow jumped from the ground. Oliver hurried to the next tree.

With only three shots left, Trusty motioned for Farley to keep shooting. He wanted to see if he could get a better line of sight at the shooter, take a real shot at him. With his Colt pulled back, Trusty started to edge to the other side of the barn. Once there, he scurried to a tree, sure that the angle he was at protected him from being shot—if there was only one shooter. He zigzagged his way up a hill that would allow him a clear shot behind the ridge.

Trusty was certain that he was in the clear until he heard a twig snap behind him. *Please let it be a wolf,* he thought, freezing, not taking another step.

"Drop the gun," a deep male voice said.

Damn, not a wolf.

Trusty hesitated for a moment. He had a knife sheathed inside the buffalo coat, but that was the only weapon he had on him besides the Colt. He had just gone after firewood. He didn't think he'd need an armory to protect himself.

"You heard what I said, Marshal. Drop the gun."

The shooting stopped. Wind pushed between him and the man behind him. There was no other noise than the beat of Trusty's heart in his ears. "You know me, but I don't know you." It wasn't Plumright. The voice was distinct, different. Not a West Point, east coast military man with a grudge to settle.

"Drop the gun. I'm not telling you again. Then turn around slowly."

Trusty drew in a deep breath, then did as he was told,

letting the Colt slip from his hand, hoping that Oliver and Farley were okay, that they would come for him, back him up, and get him out of the jam he'd found himself in. The Colt landed on top of the snow and sunk in a few inches.

Trusty turned around to face the man who had him in his gun sights.

An Indian stared back at Trusty, ten good feet from him, holding a Henry rifle aimed at his chest. "You look surprised," the Indian said.

"I expected you to be a white man."

"I am the man you have been looking for."

"Charlie Littlefoot?"

"That's what I am called at Fort Yates. Out here I have no name. I am only a lonely runner sliding along on top of the Mother trying to stay alive and outrun the men who wish to see me to the Great Beyond."

"I understood your Indian was *Hadakah*."

"Some names fit a boy, but not the man he grows to be."

"The pitiful last ain't the kind of moniker anyone would like," Trusty said. "I know a thing or two about that myself."

Charlie Littlefoot scowled and said nothing. He was a big man with big feet. Another expectation that Trusty was wrong about—he had expected a small man with small feet. Charlie looked to be about six feet tall, two hundred and fifty pounds, with long wild black hair tumbling out from underneath a thick beaver fur hat. He wore a buffalo coat, mukluks, and there were no other weapons showing on his outside dress. His face was free of a beard, but it looked red, burnt by the ice and snow, frost bit. Little beads of ice had made themselves at home in his thick eyebrows.

"That man doin' the shooting with you?" Trusty said. He cocked his head toward the ridge where the shots had come from.

"No," Charlie said, shaking his head, "there are three men. Plumright and two others that joined up with him from the east. I know nothing of them other than they are well-armed and look like they know what they are doing. One of them is circling around behind the cabin. The other is taking up another spot a hundred yards or more to the right of Plumright. The captain is doing the shooting while they get in position. They have more ammunition than you and your partner do."

"He's not my partner." Trusty stared at Charlie, not breaking eye contact with him, trying to judge his intentions. Indians were hard to read. "You seem to know a lot."

"They were tracking Oliver. I tracked them. I knew of this cabin, have slept in the barn on more than one night. Death has visited the inside of that cabin one time too many. The walls are coated in blood and look to be coated in more. The barn has been my home until I decided what to do. But now I have been found."

"It smells pretty bad in there."

"That is the least of your problems."

"My problem, at the moment, is that I am unable to defend the men who are with me while you hold me at gunpoint."

"What do you expect me to do? You have been sent to apprehend me and take me back to the fort for trial, for something I did not do. I will hang for a crime I did not commit. Am I supposed to walk up to you and turn myself in? No, I don't think so. I . . ."

A gunshot interrupted Charlie's words. He stopped, froze, became still as a tree. Charlie and Trusty both looked in the direction where the shot had come from. It was the other man, a hundred yards away from Plumright. Trusty could only hope that Oliver was safe in the barn, or in the cabin with Farley by now—who at that second, fired off a shot in retaliation.

"I don't know what kind of man you are, Marshal," Charlie continued. "Are you a fair man? A man of his word? Or are you a man like I have come to know in my time at the fort? A man who carries a gun, and wears a badge on the outside to make up for what he is not on the inside? Are you a coward or a man of honor? I do not know. Oliver fled your company, but yet you protect his life with your own. You confuse me, Trusty Dawson."

"Amanda asked me to help. She asked me to find you before Plumright found you. Marshal Delaney, the U.S. Marshal sent me to the fort, and then out here not only to find you, but to find the truth. Even that man in there, Jonah Farley, thinks you are innocent. I don't know about that, but Plumright seems determined to silence you. That gives me cause to question him more than I question you. Amanda Plumright was seriously concerned about your welfare."

Charlie didn't flinch at the mention of Amanda Plumright, the reason why they were all there in the first place. "I kept a lookout for Plumright. I knew he would come looking for me. It is better to be behind your enemy instead of ahead of him."

"We all thought you were in Canada," Trusty said.

"I am here. That's all that matters."

"Seems to me you have a choice to make."

"I know what my choices are. I know who my enemies are," Charlie answered. "I just don't know who this man standing before me is, a man who wears his name like a badge but speaks with his heart."

"My name is Sam. I never asked to be called Trusty any

more than you asked to be called *Hadakah*. It came with the job."

Another shot. Another answer back from Farley.

Charlie bristled. "The other man will be behind the cabin soon. Our time is running out. Oliver and your friend will be caught in a crossfire, if Oliver is still alive. What am I to do about you, Trusty Dawson? Trust you? Stand with you against these men who wish to see me dead? Or kill you, too? I know I can kill them. Outwit them. Especially out here where the ravens and the wolves tell me their secrets in a scurry and silence, where loud men trudge forward, focused only on their prey, not the noise they make or the trail they leave behind. I am not worried about them, but you, I am unsure of you. You have some ways of the earth, of the People. You know how to become one with the land more than most."

"I have ridden with Apache scouts and done my best to learn from all of your people that I have encountered."

"After you went to war with us."

Another shot rang out, echoed upward past them, the sound spiraling through the bare trees, escaping into the sky. Farley answered back with three shots in a row. He must have seen something.

"My duty is to return you to the fort. It is not to judge you or harm you in any way. If you say you are innocent, then you are innocent until proven guilty. That is how our laws work."

"For white men."

"You have to decide. I will not bind your hands or your spirit," Trusty said, unless you give me reason to. "You can ride to the fort with me, or flee to Canada, but I think you've already decided not to do that. Seems to me you don't want to live the rest of your life lookin' over your shoulder or jumpin' at every shadow that falls on you. I give you my word that I will give my life to see to it that you are safely delivered back to the fort. You have more champions there than you know."

"I need no shields, but you are right, I cannot run any longer." Charlie lowered the barrel of the Henry, then exhaled, and looked away. "Oliver is my friend, my brother. I cannot stand here and let any harm come to him. I will not give up my rifle or my weapons."

"I'm not askin' you, to," Trusty said, allowing himself to relax a little bit.

"I have an idea," Charlie said.

"For some reason, that doesn't surprise me," Trusty answered. "You seem like a man who has a plan for everything."

Trusty and Charlie split up. Trusty edged around to face off against the shooter who was going to set up behind the cabin, while Charlie went after the other one. Farley was already going one on one with Captain Plumright. Once Trusty and Charlie took out the two shooters, they would meet back at the cabin and then go after the captain, four against one. Trusty liked the odds, but like all gambles, it didn't work out the way he thought it would. He was able to get a shot off and surprise the man behind the cabin, but he had only wounded him, didn't kill him, shot him above the heart, not in it.

Trusty rushed down a hill, with the cabin in sight, dodging in and out of trees, unsure if he was a target or not. The man was laying on his back, in full winter gunfighter regalia, his clothes, pants, duster, and hat, were made of fur-lined black leather. His gun, a Winchester like Trusty carried, was inches from his right hand.

"Who are you?" Trusty said, with the barrel of his gun pointed at the man's forehead.

"What's it matter to you?" He had a wooly face, covered with a thick black beard that matched his clothes, beady eyes, and a little stream of blood trailing out of the corner of his mouth.

"I like to know who is tryin' to kill me."

"Every man in the Territory who wants to collect a thousand silvers." The man's breathing was labored, and he held his chest, putting pressure on the wound. Blood seeped through his fingers and dropped to the ground cutting through the snow like acid burning through metal.

"So, you're one of them, joined up with Plumright to make a gang," Trusty said.

"He joined up with us." The man coughed, and his voice grew weaker. He leaned over and spit more blood into the snow.

"What's your name, mister?" Trusty said.

"Timmons. Glo Timmons. I guess you got a right to know. Me and Red Jack Lewis came from Saint Louis way to find you, but you've eluded us at every turn."

"You were through Cannonball?"

"That trader fella told you, huh?"

Trusty nodded. The shooting had stopped completely. No shots from the cabin, Plumright, or from Charlie's direction. Silence returned to the icy land, but like before, there were no birdsongs, no animal scratches, no sound of any living thing. If anything living was around, they stood in watch, perhaps, if they were a crow, a raven, or a wolf, waiting on some meat to scavenge. "Were you hired in Saint Louis, or did you come on your own?"

"Why's it matter?"

"I figure I got a right to know who wants me dead."

"I think you know the answer to your own question."

Trusty nodded again. *Marberry. They were Marberry's men all the way out here. There was no escaping the man.* "I need to end this," he said aloud but not to Timmons.

Glo Timmons grabbed his chest even harder, then started to gurgle and shake. Death had come to take the man, and all Trusty could do was stand there and watch the dreaded darkness do its job.

Chapter 22

Aberdeen, South Dakota, December 1888

Gladdy was so happy he could have skipped his way into the town of Aberdeen, but he didn't. He didn't want to draw any undue attention to himself. The last thing he needed was more trouble. He was pretty certain he had left all that nonsense behind him now that Frank and Clovis weren't pulling him one way or the other, making stupid decisions for themselves, and getting themselves into a fix, before they even had a chance to finish Marberry's bidding. Now, all Gladdy had to do was decide whether or not he was gonna disappear, take Clovis's wallet full of twenty dollars, and get on with his life, or find his way to this Ward Hotel, and hook up with two more of Marberry's men, Glo Timmons and Red Jack Lewis. Who knew how that would turn out? Gladdy didn't like the sound of those two men, but there were a thousand silvers at the end of that rainbow, if he fell in with them. Besides, he knew Marberry, and maybe if Gladdy did what Frank and Clovis couldn't, then maybe Marberry wouldn't let those two fellas cheat him out of what was rightfully his. He liked the sound of that. What was rightly his. Nothing in his life had ever been his own, not even the chance to make a simple decision for himself like where to live or what to work at. Haden used him for an extra set of ears 'cause everyone who passed him thought he was an imbecile and talked like he wasn't there. Somebody was always makin' decisions for him. Until now.

Aberdeen wasn't a very old town, and a lot of people called it The Town in the Frog Pond because it flooded a lot of times in the spring. There were ditches and wells dug to help alleviate that problem. Since it was winter, flooding wasn't so much of a problem. Everything was covered in about an inch of snow. He had just about forgot what green grass or green trees looked like. He was tired of being cold.

The main street that ran through downtown looked like a lot of places Gladdy had been, but there were more brick-fronted buildings in this town than others. More real fronts on two- and three-story buildings than false fronts. There seemed to be a lot more shops, too, which might have been the result of the four railroads that serviced Aberdeen, ferrying goods and folks north and west to start a new life—or back east where they'd come from, in failure or resign. Gladdy shook his head at the thought. If it was him, he would have got on a train and gone somewhere warm, but he had heard that some people came from countries with long and brutal winters, and the Dakota Territory reminded them of the place they'd come from, made them less homesick. Good for them. He could barely remember winters in Eire. He had been too young to care, or notice. He'd never had much of a home to be sick for.

The twenty dollars Gladdy had lifted from Clovis's wallet was burning a hole in his pocket. He couldn't wait to spend it. That wasn't going to be a problem in a town like Aberdeen. The first thing Gladdy did was find him a bathhouse. It had been a good stretch since he'd had a dip in a hot tub. He almost couldn't stand the smell of his own stink. Good thing it was winter and not summer.

The place Gladdy found was run by two Chinese men, which didn't matter to Gladdy none. He made his way to the tub and eased down into the hot water, not sure if all of his parts were all the way thawed out. The water surrounded him, and the head Chinese man gave him a good scrubbing, then asked if Gladdy wanted a haircut and shave, to which Gladdy said, "Why, yes, I think I do. Could you see to it my clothes is washed, too?"

The Chinese man shook his head no. "No time for them to dry." He was short, had shiny black hair with a pigtail, and wore a beige tunic over his pants. He smelled of bleach, burnt tobacco, and a food smell Gladdy didn't know.

"Oh, I guess not. That's all right. I think it's about time for a new shirt and britches anyways."

"There's a dry goods store next door; you tell them Mister Ho sent you. They give you a good discount, I guarantee it. You like Chinese food? My sister, she run a restaurant two doors down from the dry good store. It's called Mrs. Ho's."

"Nah, I'm more of a steak and potatoes kind of man."

"That's okay with me." Then the Chinese man went about scrubbing Gladdy's back while Gladdy fell silent and enjoyed the warmth of the water, and the dirt coming off his body. The Chinese man whistled a happy song that Gladdy didn't know, either, but he didn't really care. It was good not to worry about anything at the moment. It had been a long time since he'd heard a happy song.

Once he was dried and dressed, he decided to get himself some breakfast. It had been a while since he'd had a good meal, too. He might just have to indulge himself in three squares a day for a while. There looked to be enough restaurants in Aberdeen where a man could eat at a different place every day of the month and not go to the same one. He found a little café and had a helping of bacon, eggs, and two cups of coffee. The waitress was a nice-looking girl who said her name was Mabel. He gave Mabel a nickel tip for smiling at him and keeping his coffee mug filled to the brim.

From there, Gladdy decided he still had plenty of money in his pocket, and headed into the nearest mercantile, more interested in buying pants and a shirt from the shelf than going to a tailor. He didn't have that kind of time. A smile was fixed on his face, and his step was light, especially now that he didn't have to smell himself, even though his clothes were still a little stinky. There wasn't a mournful thought in his happy, contented head about the fate Clovis had suffered jumping out of the train or the bad luck Frank had created for himself. No, sirree. Not one thought about them two dead fellas crossed Gladdy's mind. He was free as a bird to fly where and when he wanted, and he had some money in his pocket to get him there, wherever there was.

"May I help you, sir," a bespectacled bald man said to him. There was an accent on the man's tongue that Gladdy didn't recognize. He'd heard Germans and Frenchmen before, but this was different. Maybe a mix of the two, or something all of its own. People came from all over in places like Aberdeen.

"Where you come from?" Gladdy said, coming to a full stop, just inside the doorway.

"Amsterdam, Holland. You know where that's at?" The

man looked Gladdy up and down, his nose twisted to the side a bit. "You sound Irish."

"That a problem?"

"It doesn't have to be if you're a paying customer."

"Where's Holland?"

"On the other side of the world." The man's eyes fell to the gun that Gladdy wore on the side of his hip. He had unbuttoned his coat. The shop was warm. Warmer than he'd thought it would be. "This is a no-carry town," the man said.

"I ain't gonna be here long."

"Doesn't matter. You best check in with the sheriff, then check out when you leave."

"Sure, I'll do that." Gladdy drew in a deep breath with no intention of checking his gun, then looked around the shop. It was neat, everything stacked by size, the floors swept, nothing out of place. He didn't necessarily like the shopkeeper, but he figured the place would do as well as any other. It was good to know that Aberdeen was a no-carry town. He'd have to be careful. Didn't want to get in any undue trouble. "You gonna sell me some pants and a shirt, or what?" he said.

"Yes, sir, I can do that. Wintertime gets a little slow. Not many travelers coming through to take up stakes out yonder. Where are you heading? You said you was passing through."

"I didn't say that, did I? I said I wasn't gonna be here long."

"Same thing, isn't it?"

"Why do you need to know where I'm goin'?"

"If you're going north, you'll need something a little

thicker to keep you warmer. Depending on how far south you're going, then maybe not so much."

"North for a while, I suppose. Then maybe east. I'm not sure exactly where I'll hire out next." Gladdy smiled and puffed his chest out, proud of himself, trying to make himself more important than he was. The shopkeeper already looked down his nose at him because he was Irish.

"Okay, this way. Let's look at some wool pants and a heavier shirt for you." The man headed off, and Gladdy followed.

By the time Gladdy was done shopping at the mercantile, he had spent five dollars and fifty-three cents—that morning. On breakfast, a bath, haircut, and on a new shirt, Levi pants, and a pair of long johns that the man guaranteed would keep his privates warm in below-zero temperatures. Gladdy didn't like the idea of freezing his balls off. He wanted to use them first and headed out of the mercantile to find himself a girl. He left his old clothes for the shopkeeper to do with what he wanted to. He could burn 'em for all Gladdy cared. It was best to get while the gettin' was good. He didn't know if Marberry's men were the type of fellas who would allow a stop for a poke or not.

Fellas down in Deadwood had brothels run by Dirty Em and Madame Mustachio to satisfy their needs. Both women had migrated to Deadwood from California and Nevada respectively, professionals who learned their trade on the outskirts of the western mining towns. From what Gladdy saw, Aberdeen was no Deadwood, but he didn't have far to look for the saloon district. Where there was whiskey and wine, there were women to be found.

The first place Gladdy found himself, was a hurdy-gurdy house where a man could buy himself a dance with a woman for a dollar and a beer for a dollar, too. Most of the women were older, wider in the hips, and Gladdy had more in mind than a dance, though he wasn't in the mood for a dalliance like he'd had in Saint Louis with that red-headed girl who had tried to sink her hooks into him. Good luck with that. Three or four dances and he'd be down to a little money and have no pleasure to show for it. Gladdy was all left feet and elbows when it came to dancing. He left out of the hurdy gurdy place and found himself a real saloon with real working girls on the floor. He spied one, a tall blonde with a pair of mountains for cleavage in a purple satin dress, approached her, and found out she charged twenty dollars for a roll. That was what most women got for the night. When Gladdy objected, the blonde said, "You're in the wrong place, cowboy. If you want a cheap time you need to head down the street to the Red Dog Saloon. The girls down there will suit the likes of you."

"I was tryin' to negotiate. You don't have to get all huffy, lady."

The blonde spun around and walked away without saying another word. Gladdy headed to the door, dejected and losing his patience. Maybe he would just call it a day and look for a woman the next day.

Instead of finding his way to the cheaper saloon, Gladdy made his way through town and found himself standing in front of the Ward Hotel.

The Ward Hotel was a giant building, taking up a whole city block, reaching six stories into the air. It was faced with red brick all the way around and looked mighty fancy to Gladdy, but he supposed Mister Marberry was a man of certain wealth and put his men up in nice places. It was just the look of the place that made Gladdy go inside to seek out the two men, Glo Timmons and Red Jack Lewis, to see for himself if he wanted to ride with them. The ride, going after Trusty Dawson, was the only real prospect he had, unless of course he wanted to strike out on his own, but that didn't seem prudent. He'd already spent half of the money he'd pulled from Clovis's wallet, and the sun hadn't even set on the first day he'd spent in Aberdeen. If Marberry put his men up in the hotels like the Ward for the whole trip, that would provide a softer bed than he could provide for himself.

The lobby inside the Ward was just as fancy as the building was outside. The floor was laid with a shiny oak floor, with sofas and high-back chairs situated around a fireplace with a hand-carved mantel . Lions stood at the ends of the mantle, guarding the fire and offering a hunter's gaze to anyone who sat in front of them. Wool rugs dotted the floor in somber colors, deep reds and browns, spun in a circular pattern working its way from the inside out. A clerk's cage, carved like the mantel, stood against the back wall of the lobby, with a tall young man with black hair standing behind it. He wore a crisp white shirt with a black string tie dangling from his neck. The place smelled clean like soap and fresh linens had been spread on the floor, not smoky and dirty like the hurdy-gurdy place and the saloon he'd just left.

"May I help you?" the clerk said. He had a thin mustache on his lip and curious blue eyes that judged Gladdy from head to toe. He sure didn't like how people looked at him in this town.

"I'm meetin' a couple of friends in room 313."

"Friends, you say?"

"I didn't stutter." Gladdy eyed the hallway that opened up past the clerk's cage and kept walking.

"You can't go up there, sir." The clerk leaned over the counter. "That's for guests only."

"I'm a guest of my friends," Gladdy said over his shoulder.

The clerk was out of the cage and hurrying after Gladdy. For a second Gladdy thought about running, but that wouldn't do him no good. He'd already told the clerk where he was going. He stopped and faced the oncoming man. "I done told you, I was invited to room 313." He took the note out of his pocket, the one he'd taken out of Clovis's wallet, along with the twenty dollars. He handed it to the exasperated clerk.

The note had been written on Theodore Marberry's stationery. Gladdy hadn't noticed that before. It didn't matter to him, but it obviously mattered to the clerk. "So you work for Mister Marberry?"

The question surprised Gladdy, until the clerk pointed to Marberry's name on the paper.

"Why yes, yes, I do. Me and them fellas, there."

"Why didn't you say so?"

"I didn't know I had to."

The clerk handed the paper back to Gladdy and walked off without saying so much as have a good day. City folks were rude. Gladdy stuffed the note in his pocket, then found a set of stairs and made the climb to the third floor. Room 313 was located in the north corner of the building. Gladdy stopped at the door, took a deep breath, adjusted his gun inside his coat, and knocked on the door with as much confidence as he could find within himself.

Nothing happened at first, then he heard feet shuffling

on the other side of the thick wood and the door swung open. "What?" Theodore Marberry demanded to know. He was tall, thin, dressed in blue suit pants, a white shirt buttoned to the neck without a tie, and a vest that matched his pants. He had short-cut white hair and didn't wear any facial hair at all. The man was all business down to the ice inside his hard eyes.

Gladdy staggered backward. He had been expecting a gunfighter-type, someone who lived up to the name Red Jack Lewis or Glo Timmons. Blood drained from Gladdy's face. He was not expecting to see the Big Boss Man.

Marberry poked his head out the door and looked up and down the hallway, all the while pulling the door to. "Where are the others?" he asked in a low voice, just above a whisper.

"Frank and Clovis is dead," Gladdy said.

"Dead?"

"Yes, sir. Frank was killed outside of Saint Louis, got into a fight and lost, and Clovis, he died when we had to jump off a train. Hit his head on a rock."

"Why in God's name did you have to jump off a train?" Marberry looked at Gladdy like everybody else had looked at him, like he was dumber than dumb and the words he'd strung together didn't make an ounce of sense. "Oh, never mind. What about Timmons and Lewis? Where are they?"

"I don't know what you're talkin' about. I thought we was supposed to meet them here. That's what this here note says." Gladdy pulled the paper out of his pocket and thrust it toward Marberry.

"I know what it said, you idiot, I wrote it." Before Marberry could say another word, the sound of a baby whimpering, working itself up to the first cry after it woke up, shattered the silence of the room behind Marberry. "Now look what you've done. You woke it up."

"I didn't mean to. I didn't know you had a baby in there."

Marberry sighed and lowered his head, stood back and opened the door. "You'll have to do if the rest of them aren't here. Get in here before it starts screaming."

Gladdy did what he was told. He walked inside the room, which was more like a suite, though he wouldn't have known about such things. There was a fireplace, a sofa, and a smoking chair, in a small room. An open door led into a bedroom, and Gladdy got his first look at the baby, a blond-haired girl dressed in a simple cotton gown, held by an older woman, white-haired like Marberry. She was bouncing the baby, trying to pacify her. It wasn't working. The cries were full-throated now.

On closer inspection, Marberry looked like a man who hadn't had much sleep lately. His eyes were red, and he had bulbous pillow sacks under them. Agitation sat on his face like a common visitor had come to stay for a long spell.

Marberry sat down in the chair and motioned for Gladdy to sit on the sofa. He waited until the woman shut the door before saying anything at all. The baby's cries were muffled, but they set Gladdy's teeth on edge.

"This is going to be the end of me, I'm sure of it," Marberry said. He reached over to the table that sat next to the smoking chair and grabbed a bottle of whiskey. He poured himself a couple of fingers and drank it down in one gulp. He didn't offer Gladdy a drink.

Gladdy sat down on the sofa cautiously, like he was sitting in a bed of poison ivy. "I don't know what you mean, sir."

"You wouldn't. Are you sure you haven't seen Timmons and Lewis?"

"I wouldn't know them if I bumped into them at the bank."

"And Frank and Clovis are dead?"

"Yes."

"Why am I not surprised." Marberry looked at Gladdy again with judgment in his eyes. "You're all that's left. You know why you're here, don't you?"

"Clovis said it was because I know what Trusty Dawson looks like, that I was on his trail with Calhoun."

Marberry jumped up like he had been bit by a snake. "Don't you ever speak of that man in my presence again, you understand?"

"Calhoun or Trusty Dawson?"

"Calhoun, you fool."

"I didn't mean no harm." Gladdy stayed sitting. He cast his eyes to the ground, beaten like a dog.

Marberry began to pace. "I don't know what happened to Lewis and Timmons, but I can't stay here any longer. You'll have to escort me and Matilda to Bismarck. You'll have to do. I have no choice but to leave out of here as soon as possible."

"Why are you going to Bismarck?"

Marberry stopped in the center of the room and looked Gladdy in the eye. "We're going to Bismarck because sooner or later, Trusty Dawson will show up there. He won't be expecting you in his own backyard. He won't be expecting you at all, come to think of it." He looked like he liked the idea he had just stumbled on.

"I don't get your meanin', sir."

"You're going to Bismarck to kill Trusty Dawson. Does that and a thousand silvers make sense to you now?"

Gladdy stood up, nodding. "Yes, sir, I suppose it does. And I don't have to share them silvers with no one?"

Marberry shook his head. "Not as long as you're the one who kills Trusty Dawson. All of that money is yours. All yours."

Chapter 23

Trusty stood over Glo Timmons's body and wondered how many more men were going to have to die because of the one stupid, intimate moment he had spent with Jessica Marberry. A tryst in a far-away hotel after a happenstance meeting well over a year before. A long-held dream, finally able to be with the woman he had always loved, had turned into an unending nightmare. Not only for Trusty, but for countless other men, certain that their life would be richer, better, if he was dead. "This has to end," he said again, louder as the anger grew deep inside of him. Glo Timmons had no response. The wind ate Trusty's words and spit them out, carrying them south with every sound and word that he had spoken.

Trusty looked across the open plain as it reached up, bleached white, frozen hard as rock, into the ridge that gave protection to at least one more of the errant shooters. Plumright and the Lewis fella were still out there. But the two were, Trusty assumed, outnumbered. Oliver and Farley were in the cabin, and Charlie Littlefoot was stalking his prey—both men—somewhere unseen. Four against two unless Plumright and Lewis had backup that he didn't know about. Trusty liked the odds, but he didn't want anyone else to have to die, to pay with their life for his lapse of judgement—including himself.

He had known that nothing good could come from spending the night in Jessica Marberry's bed, but he had not been able to contain his desire. She didn't have to drag him into her bed; he jumped at the chance. Her father, Theodore Marberry, had sent Jessica to England at the first sign that feelings were developing between them. Jessica had stayed in England for her education, then got married, but her husband died before they could have any children. She returned to the states, back to the home where she had grown up in Saint Louis, where after a few years of rightful mourning, she encountered Trusty while traveling with her father on a business trip in Indian Territory. What happened after Trusty left Jessica's hotel, knowing they could have no future together, was only speculation on his part, but he assumed Jessica had told her father of their encounter, or did once she figured out she was pregnant, sending Marberry into a rage of embarrassment. A marriage between a business associate, Vance Calhoun, a landowner with his own aspirations and brutal tendencies, was quickly arranged, and Jessica went to live on his ranch in Texas. She and her father had duped Calhoun into thinking the child was his own to save face, but somewhere along the line Calhoun figured out the lie, that Jessica was already pregnant when they married. Most likely after the baby girl was born. Jessica died not long after as a result of the child's birth. Calhoun went on a tirade, found out that Marberry had set a bounty on Trusty's head for a thousand silvers and went after that money for himself—Calhoun had been the one to tell Trusty that he was the father of Jessica Marberry's baby. Calhoun killed a few men along the way and met his own sad end at the end of a rope. He was one of the first men to pay the ultimate price for Trusty's ill-fated dalliance, even though Trusty figured Calhoun would have ended up dangling from the gallows anyway after meeting him. He shuddered at the thought of Jessica being anywhere near that man. Desperation had ruled the day..

Theodore Marberry was still out there somewhere, enticing men with his silver to kill Trusty. And the baby girl, a baby Trusty was more and more convinced was his own flesh and blood, was still out there, too. He needed more than Calhoun's word and a quick glimpse of the baby to know for certain that she belonged to him. He knew in his heart he had to find the baby. He had to see her.

Trusty slid along the barn, leaving Timmons's dead body where it had landed, and made his way back to the cabin. Silence followed him, left him unsettled, but there was nothing he could do about that. He tapped on the cabin door before entering. "It's me," he whispered. The last thing he wanted to do was surprise Farley, and take a shotgun blast to the gut and die for no reason at all.

"Where the hell you been?" Farley shouted from inside the cabin.

Trusty was hit with the stench of death and rot immediately, that had taken up residence in the pores of the interior as he made his way inside. He almost lost what little food had settled in his stomach.

Oliver was laying on the floor. Blood was everywhere. Farley was on his knees, hovering over Oliver, his back to the door. Trusty couldn't tell what was going on, whether Farley was helping Oliver or putting an end to his life.

Trusty closed the door, and said, "Farley, what are you doing?"

Farley turned around with both of his hands covered in blood. "I'm tryin' to stop the bleedin', you oaf. He's been shot in the leg. Can't you see that?"

That's what Trusty had hoped for, that Farley was trying to save Oliver. Not that he'd been shot in the leg. That must have happened when Trusty had encountered Timmons.

Oliver's eyelids were flickering like candleflames in the wind trying to stay lit. His mouth was open, gasping for air, and his chest was heaving up and down. One more man down. One more man in pain for something Trusty had done. Rage touched the tips of his fingers just as shooting outside the cabin resumed.

"I can't make the bleedin' stop," Farley said.

Trusty looked at Oliver closer and saw his fate clear as Glo Timmons's had been. Death had come to stay in the small camp by the river, and by the look of things, it didn't look like it was going anywhere until every man there was under its black wing. With a long sigh, Trusty made his way to the window, and peered outside to see if he could tell who was doing the shooting, or where it was coming from. Behind him, Oliver heaved and rattled, doing his best to fight off the inevitable. Trusty saw two puffs of gun smoke rise into the air over the ridge, and another, an answer back from the thick woods where he had first encountered Oliver. Plumright and Lewis were shooting at Charlie Littlefoot. Charlie needed his help.

"You stay with him," Trusty said, heading for the door.

"He ain't gonna be here too much longer," Farley answered back.

Trusty stopped at the door. "I'm sorry, Oliver, you're a good man. You didn't deserve to die like this."

Oliver lifted his head and struggled to hold his eyes open, then said something that Trusty couldn't hear. The shooting volleys continued outside. Farley leaned down to try and understand what Oliver was saying. Once he was done speaking, Oliver laid his head back on the floor, his eyes glazed, staring at the ceiling. His right leg twitched.

"He said to tell Amanda he was sorry he couldn't bring Charlie home. You have to do that now. A baby needs his father," Farley said, then paused with a sad exhale. "That make sense to you?"

"Charlie needs my help," Trusty said. "I was hopin' no other men would have to die today for a mistake I made, but if that's what it takes to get Charlie Littlefoot back to the fort, then so be it." Trusty reached for the door. Just as he did, Oliver gurgled one last time, then fixed his gaze permanently on whatever it was he had been staring at above him. Farley took his hat off in respect. Trusty made his way out the door, doing his best not to be seen or allow his grief and anger to lead him brazenly out into the open. He wanted to burst out with blazing bullets, but he knew that would be a mistake.

Trusty went from one tree to the next, hoping that Farley would back him up, but he hadn't asked for that.

Charlie shot at the ridge with little hope of hitting anything. Nobody was moving. It was a standoff. One that puzzled Trusty as he did his best to join up with Charlie. He thought that Lewis was going to take a tack around the camp and catch Charlie in a crossfire. As it was now, the two men were stationed behind the ridge. He assumed that it was Plumright and Lewis, but he could have been mistaken. He hoped not. One more misjudgment might be his last.

The stand of trees that Charlie had chosen to hide in

was thinner, with the trees being farther apart, but the trunks of the trees were wider, making it easier for Charlie to be protected—but harder for Trusty to get to him. When he finally made it, running from one tree to the next, Charlie was loading his Winchester, set for another volley of gunfire. "This is your plan?" Trusty said.

"The other one circled back like something had called him off. Maybe when you shot his partner, he got scared and decided to give it up."

"There's two men shooting."

"I don't think so. I heard the rear of a horse, then a run. I think Plumright is trying to make us think there are two men there. Deception is as common to him as breathing."

"Where'd Lewis go?"

"You know him?"

"The man I shot told me his name. They're bounty hunters."

"Looking for their thousand silvers?"

"You know about that?"

"Everybody knows about that, Trusty Dawson. I am surprised you have lived as long as you have. You have my respect for that."

Another shot came from Plumright and hit the ground three feet in front of the tree Charlie and Trusty were hiding behind. Then silence. A minute later another shot came from a different place, twenty yards to the left of the first.

"See," Charlie said, "he had long enough to get from one spot to the next. It's a ruse. That man Lewis has fled. The captain had nothing to keep him here other than the promise of your head and the money that comes along with it, but then he would have had to split it, or kill Plumright. I think the captain has something else up his sleeve. If you walk away from here alive you should be wary of the hawk's shadow."

"I've been living like a mouse for a long time." Trusty aimed his Colt and fired at the ridge, the bullet hitting just shy of where the last shot came from. "We need to give Plumright a choice. Give up or die."

"You mean that?" Charlie said.

"I'm hopin' he sees no way out of this and surrenders, allows me to do my job and escort you back to the fort alive."

"I'll go around to the side, then we'll move up together," Charlie said.

"I want him to return to the fort with us," Trusty said, grabbing hold of Charlie's arm, stopping him in his tracks. "We're not executioners."

"You may not be, but Captain Plumright would have put his revolver to my head the first chance he got. I plan on staying alive and returning with Oliver at my side."

Trusty blinked, lowered his head. He hadn't told Charlie that Oliver was dead. It didn't take words for Charlie to understand. He pulled away from Trusty and slinked from one tree to the next.

Plumright resumed firing into the woods but missed Charlie every time. Trusty shook off the bad feeling he had and got moving. He had to be able to talk to Plumright before Charlie got to him. Luckily, that's exactly what happened. Trusty was able to position himself behind a tree over the ridge, about ten yards from Plumright. He had a clear shot of the man. And it was just Plumright. Charlie had been right about that. Lewis had fled, ridden off for whatever the reason.

"It's over Captain Plumright," Trusty yelled out.

Plumright spun on his knee and fired from a gun that looked like a Colt with a twelve inch barrel from a distance. The heavy, long barrel bounced upward when the bullet took to the air. It wasn't until then that Trusty saw that Plumright had been wounded. His left shoulder was soaked in blood.

Trusty didn't fire back. "You need to stop this now. We can all ride back to the fort and settle this where it matters."

"Where it matters?" Plumright answered back, his words riding on the wind without fear of being heard. "Don't you understand the shame and embarrassment I feel with the whispers, people, men and women, pointing at me, judging me because of their rumors and gossip. I am never returning to the fort, and neither is Charlie Littlefoot."

"I wish you'd reconsider," Trusty said. He spied Charlie's shadow first, creeping up the ridge ahead of him, casting grayness onto the pristine snow, silent as an owl's wing, confident as a wolf stalking a wounded elk.

Plumright saw Charlie before Charlie saw Plumright. The captain raised his gun in an instant, sighted his target, and took a deep breath. A deep breath that gave Trusty the time he needed to intercede. His body took over from his mind. His own hand raised, and his finger pulled the trigger a whisker before Plumright pulled his. Dueling thunder echoed across the snow-covered prairie, followed by the thump of one man falling to the ground with a bullet lodged in his chest.

Trusty stood behind the smoke with the taste of gunpowder full in his mouth, already resorting to regret. Though he knew he had no choice if he wanted to try and save

Charlie's life. He had killed James Pierpoint Plumright, not the Indian.

Charlie Littlefoot stood behind a tree, bark shattered off its trunk, alive but obviously aware of how close he had come to dying. Silence returned. The wind died down, and the threat of dying with the next breath receded like clouds parting after a storm. The last thing Trusty had wanted to do was kill another man, add another name to the list of men whose lives had been taken from them by his gun, but the way he saw it, he didn't have a choice. One more time, he didn't have a choice.

Abilene, Kansas, October 1882

Sam Dawson had spent his last day in the Army a week prior and was left with the decision of what to do with his life. He had time on his hands and money in his pocket, so he was in no hurry. He always had the option of returning to Saint Louis. As far as he knew his father was still toiling away in the blacksmith shop. Sam supposed all he had to do was walk in and take over the forge and quench and he could pick up where he had left off before joining the Army. *When hell freezes over,* he thought, staring into a half-empty mug of beer. The last place he wanted to go was Saint Louis. There'd only be two reasons he would ever do that. If Jessica Marberry returned or Katherine Duchamp needed him for something. Neither seemed likely anytime soon. He'd received sporadic letters from both women, but nothing that suggested he should return home. The other option, the one that had brought him to Abilene was the chance to join the U.S. Marshal's Service. He had an appointment the following day with the Marshal, Tom Holland, at the Kansas District office. Sam was ambiguous about the job, though it would allow him to ride in an organization with rules that paralleled the Army. He liked the idea of riding alone more than he thought he would. While the Army had given him comradery, he had spent most all of his life on his own and that was where he had found his comfort.

Sam sat in the Bull's Head Tavern, a place full of conflict and history, whiling away the afternoon. Phil Coe, the original owner of the place had painted a bull with an erect penis on the side of the building. Wild Bill Hickok, the marshal in Abilene at the time, had been so outraged by the painting, he had threatened to burn the tavern down. When Coe ignored Hickok's order to paint over the bull, Hickok hired some men to do the painting himself. That act set off a feud between Coe and Hickok that eventually ended with Wild Bill killing Coe. Hickok met his own death in Deadwood at the hands of a man out to avenge the death of his brother sometime later. It was difficult not to be aware of those events as Sam sipped his beer and contemplated his own future. He had no gun on his hip, no reason to carry one since he wasn't in the military or wearing a badge. But he wondered if maybe he ought to leave that kind of life, and start fresh, head west, and learn a new trade.

Instead, he did nothing but sit there, taking in the ambiance of the place, until one of the working girls, a blonde with long legs and a skinny waist asked him if there was anything she could do for him.

"As a matter of fact, you can. Are you free for the rest of the night?"

The girl took his hand, and said, "I'm not free, but the night's yours if you think you can afford it." She grinned at the challenge.

Sam stood up, smiling himself. "I think I can manage. Lead the way."

White Earth River, Dakota Territory, December 1888

For the second time on this trip, a fire served as a burial and a final tribute. Charlie Littlefoot was able to give Oliver a proper sendoff, a release of his spirit to the Great Beyond with words and actions that Trusty would never understand; a mournful Indian song and dance joined the wind and offered a sad respite from the constant onslaught of angry air.

The fire smoldered, and three men rode away from the cabin and funeral pyre, abreast, quiet, heads down with the wind at their backs. Trusty rode on the left, Farley on the right, and Charlie Littlefoot in the middle. Their destination was set, and their course was to return south, to Fort Yates. Another horse trailed behind Trusty, riderless, with the body of Captain Plumright rolled in a blanket and bound over the saddle.

They were all leery of hawks, shadows, and men who sought to do them harm, but that did not stop them, or hold them back. Duty for Trusty was done all except the escort home, and that was something he'd had plenty of experience with, though the outcome and the consequences had been uneven and harmful as much as they had been successful. He could only hope that there would be no trouble this time. But hope, like warmth and comfort, had been hard to come by of late.

Chapter 24

The three men moved slowly down the river with the
wind finally at their backs. Some parts of the Missouri were
bare ice, offering little traction for the horses, while other
sections of the river looked like giant waves frozen in mid-
thought, two-feet high snow drifts curved and crested with
a spate of diamonds, a sculpture that looked more like the
sea than the Dakota flatland. The wind swirled some loose
snow off the surface in places; threatless white tornados
spiraling into the sky for the fun of it or to join the snow
falling to the ground. Gray clouds suffering from the same
boredom as the wind came and went in the shape of waves,
too, full of snow at times, ice in others, then a mix with rain
added in for spite. What was consistent, what did not ever
change, was the bite of the ever-present cold, always tearing
at open flesh with its sharp-knife touch. There was never
any silence, at least that would allow a man to have a long
think. The wind screamed and yelled and threw a temper
tantrum because it could, because it was unstoppable without
anything to do but to push forward. Trusty had decided long

ago that the weather in the Dakota Territory acted like an unruly child but was more dangerous than all of the bounty hunters in his wake. He knew more about bounty hunters than children, and up to this point in his life, that had made complete sense to him.

None of the three men, Trusty, Charlie Littlefoot, or Jonah Farley, talked much as they rode south toward Fort Yates. There was no sense in opening your mouth to allow in more cold air, and besides, what could be said already had been said before they'd left out of the cabin. Their route was certain, and the intention of the ride was clear. Escort the dead body of Captain James Pierpoint Plumright back to Fort Yates for a proper burial by his wife and family, if there were any, and deliver Charlie Littlefoot to be jailed until he faced trial. Whether or not the Indian was guilty of the rape he had been charged with was not Trusty's concern, duty, or judgment—he didn't plan on staying for the legal proceedings that Charlie faced—that was left to the army and its judicial processes. But what Trusty didn't know, and took him a hundred miles to question, was who had accused Charlie of rape in the first place. Amanda Plumright? Or her husband, James Pierpoint? He had been tempted to ask Charlie the first night at the campfire but had decided to honor the silence that both men seemed to have relegated themselves to. Trusty and Farley traded off watch. Charlie, while not bound or shackled, remained at the camp with one man or the other. Trusty had given Charlie his word that he wouldn't treat him like a prisoner unless he had to on the ride back—which Farley had objected to. So far, Trusty had no reason to suspect that the Indian would flee. Charlie seemed resigned to his fate, eager almost, to return to the fort, and get on with what the future had in store for him. After all,

Trusty had not found Charlie. Charlie had found him. And Plumright, obviously, dead as he was, tied to the back of a horse was no threat to him, but there was still a threat to them all. Red Jack Lewis was still out there. And who knew who else, eager to cash in on Theodore Marberry's pile of silver. Bounties died as easily as roaches; lighting a candle scattered them and stepping on them only stunned them.

The next day was the same as the first. One hoof in front of the other. Cold eyes watered from the assault of the wind and the frozen white world they made their way in. The day after that was the same. Each man rode silent, head down, wind at their back, fighting off frostbite, all of them praying that the horses that carried them had the fortitude and will to deliver them safely to the fort.

The only moment of concern Trusty had was the sighting of a lone wolf, tracking the three of them, following along high atop the ravine of the riverside, curious, but wise enough not to offer a clear shot. The wolf, gray and thin from the trials of winter, never took his yellow eyes off the trio, always looking for an opportunity to alert the pack of a weakness, of a time to attack. At night, they heard it call to the others, who answered back one by one with warnings and instructions: *Stay the course. Don't let them out of your sight. They are killers.*

It seemed as if all of the men in the world who had wished them harm had retreated to somewhere warm, waiting like the wolves for the right time to show themselves and resume their quest and desire to kill when the trio was at their weakest and most tired. Trusty was glad for the silence and the return south, but he had long tired of shadow-checking over his shoulder. The encounter with Timmons and Lewis at the cabin had unsettled him more than he cared to admit, and the wolf was just a reminder of being stalked for nothing more than being human.

The long ride gave Trusty time to consider what he would do after surrendering Charlie Littlefoot to Colonel Townsend. His options seemed limited. Continue riding as a U.S. Marshal, or break free, lay down the badge, put no one else at risk, and ride east, back to Saint Louis, knock on Theodore Marberry's front door and settle the bounty once and for all—then demand to see the baby girl. If there was a reason not to do that, Trusty couldn't think of one. At least it would be a little warmer in the city than it was on the prairie.

Fort Yates, Dakota Territory, December 1888

A change had taken place in the fort since Trusty and Oliver had left it. The wide expanse of buildings was still snow-covered, and the promise of a long, dark winter hung over every aspect of life like a thick gray pall, even as life in the fort continued to move forward, horses coming and going, regiments moving about, preparing for one thing or another. Supplies came and went on wagons, crates with tarps over them, all covered in the sheen of the latest drop of precipitation, snow, ice, or rain. The commerce of the place and the weather was not going to change, but the people about on the street seemed to be more cheerful, lighter in their step, their mood more festive, arbitrated with the arrival of pine garlands strung along the fronts of buildings, wreaths attached to doors, and candles lit in windows. Somewhere a choir practiced age-old carols; the songs filled the air with the certainty that Christmastime had arrived in Fort Yates. The church, made of wood, with a steeple pointed to the heavens, was white as the virgin snow that topped it, and looked like it had been scrubbed and washed while everything around it was drab and worn. Trusty looked away from the church, reminded of his ride with Michael Darby in Indian Territory, and the certainty that any of the questions he held in his mind or heart wouldn't be answered there. Not even in the season of light and love.

The festiveness vanished from all the faces of the passersby as soon as they saw Trusty riding side by side with Charlie Littlefoot. Charlie rode with his head down, ashamed, not willing to look anyone in the eye. Jonah Farley had the worst duty of pulling Plumright's funeral horse behind him. It didn't take much deduction by anyone in the fort to figure out who the dead man was. The only speculation left to the onlooker was how the captain had died and by whose hand. The assumption was most likely that Charlie was the killer, but they would have been wrong about that.

Like all small towns and forts, word of their arrival rolled out ahead of them like the first gray clouds of a storm. By the time Trusty got to the building where Colonel Townsend's office was housed, the colonel and his cadre of men were already outside waiting for them. Townsend, plump as a holiday turkey, stood in full uniform, in front of six men, all with rifles in their arms, at ease for the moment, in case trouble had come calling. Trusty didn't blame them for their show of force. He would have done the same thing if he had been in charge.

"Whoa," Trusty said to Horse, who stopped on a dime, ready, it looked, to be housed in a warm barn. The roan gelding had been amenable on the ride back to the fort, comforted by the company of other horses, but the cold air and the trials of the long trip were weighing on Horse.

His eyes were glassy, and the tips of his ears had lost their hair and were fading toward black with frostbite.

Once Horse was settled, Trusty dismounted and made his way to Colonel Townsend. He resisted the urge to salute when he came to a stop in front of the commander. "Colonel," he said.

Townsend eyed Trusty with an expression that was hard to read; contempt, pride, or a mix of that made something completely new. "I see you have lived to see another day, Deputy Dawson." The colonel looked past Trusty to Charlie who was having a staring contest with the ground. "But you have brought death with you."

"Captain Plumright, I'm afraid," Trusty said.

"The Indian?" Townsend said, with a nod toward Charlie.

"By my weapon, sir. Plumright was intent on killing my charge, and I had to get between that if I was gonna fulfill my duty. I pulled the trigger with regret, but Littlefoot is here, alive, and ready to stand trial."

"You could have saved me the circus."

"Justice is never my assignment, sir," Trusty said. "I would appreciate it if you would take possession of the prisoner, and have your men take the captain to the undertaker. I am in need of a warm bath and a night's rest before I resume my journey."

"You're not staying for the trial?" Townsend said, not budging on Trusty's request. It looked like the next move had to be the colonel's idea, not some lowly deputy's idea.

"No, sir, I'll be headed north, back to the office of Marshal Delaney."

"For another assignment? Why not just wire the man?"

Trusty didn't move, stood frozen before the fort commander on equal footing and felt no need to explain himself any further. "My horse is in need of a rest, too. Once I take him to the livery, I'll assume my accommodations will be the same as they were before I left out of here."

Townsend stepped down off the boardwalk, holding eye contact with Trusty. "Take the Indian into custody men and see to the captain. I believe it should be the Marshal who delivers the widow the bad news."

"You want me to tell Amanda Plumright that her husband is dead?" Trusty said.

Behind him, Jonah Farley slid off his horse and planted his feet on the ground. "I'll be happy to escort the captain to the undertaker."

Townsend nodded. "Thank you for your service, Farley. I expected a different outcome with you involved in this mess."

"Sorry to disappoint you, Colonel Townsend." Farley tipped his hat, then began to untie Plumright's horse from his own.

"I'm sure you did your best." Townsend turned his attention back to Trusty. "You know where the Plumrights' residence is located, don't you, Deputy?"

It was Trusty's turn to nod. "I'm sure she'll be aware of the bad news before I knock on the door."

Townsend smirked, watched four men lead Charlie Littlefoot away, and said, "You can make it official."

With Horse fully secured and relieved of the weather in the livery, Trusty made his way to the officer's quarters where the Plumrights had resided. He knocked on the door, which held no wreath or air of festiveness that had permeated the rest of the fort. An older woman, wide waisted, with brittle gray hair and a flabby neck, answered the door. "Hello. What do you want?" she said. Her tongue struggled to speak English over the German it had been born to speak, and she spoke just above a whisper. The woman seemed annoyed, kept looking over her shoulder.

"I need to speak to the lady of the house."

"Missus can't come to the door." The German woman started to close the door, but Trusty stubbed his boot between the jamb and the door.

"I am here on official business, ma'am. I'll only be a bother for a short time."

A red curtain worked its way up the woman's face, not stopping until it reached her puffy forehead. "I know who you are and what you want. You are a bearer of bad news. Everybody knows who you are. Now go away, Trusty Dawson. Missus knows her husband is dead. She knew he would not return alive when he left." Her final words had a little bit of spit on them.

Trusty thought about turning around and leaving, knowing he would have to face Colonel Townsend without fulfilling his command—but that didn't matter. Trusty didn't answer to Townsend. But he stood staring at the old German woman, not willing to leave after hearing a shuffle of feet behind her.

"Let him in, Marta," Amanda Plumright said. Trusty recognized her voice right away even though it was weak and distant.

Marta scowled at Trusty. "She should be in bed." Then she opened the door to let him inside.

"Thank you, ma'am," he said, as he walked into the captain's quarters. The room was warm. A fire blazed in the fireplace in the front room that was decorated with heavy furniture covered in velvets and brocades.

Amanda Plumright stood next to the fireplace wearing a long red robe, thick, and cuffed with white fur on the sleeves and the bottom hem. Her long brown hair was down, draped over her shoulders, and her face was more sunk in than the last time Trusty had seen her. Her belly, too, which had protruded in front of her was less in size, too, deflated, missing the baby that had been there. She had given birth since he'd left, and he didn't know the outcome. The only sound he heard was the tick of the mantel clock.

"It's good to see you, Deputy Dawson," Amanda said.

He suddenly felt self-conscious, a rare event. He was fresh off the trail, in dire need of a shave, a bath, and a change of clothes, standing before a refined woman in a nice house, dripping on the carpets like a man of bad manners, or worse, the killer of her husband. "I'm sorry I don't have good news for you, Mrs. Plumright."

"Amanda, please." She had penetrating blue eyes that would not be refused.

"I'm sorry to tell you that your husband is dead, Amanda."

She didn't falter with grief or feign surprise. Amanda Plumright stood rigid, facing Trusty, taking the news with knowing eyes and sad cheeks. "James was hellbent on dying. It is a shame he missed the opportunity to see his son come into this world. I knew he, and everyone else, expected otherwise. The baby is white if you are wondering, Deputy."

"That's really none of my business, ma'am."

"I suppose not." She cocked her ear toward the doorway that led out of the room, then turned her attention back to where she was. "Could you check on the baby, Marta. I'll only be a minute."

"Are you sure, Missus?" Marta said.

"I'll be fine Marta."

A distant whimper hurried Marta out of the room. The look of disapproval on her face didn't disappear until she did.

"Marta is very protective of me, Deputy. I apologize if she was rude."

"I'm fine. Is there anything you would like to know?" Trusty said.

A slight smile crossed Amanda's face, then it faded as quickly as it had come. "I can imagine what happened. I don't need the details. I only know the outcome and what lies ahead for Charlie, no matter what I have to say about the incident. You must think I am without morals and fortitude."

"I am only sorry for your loss, ma'am."

"I suppose you are." She paused, was still standing by the fireplace. Her face was lit with a warm glow now. "Do you have children, Deputy Dawson?"

Trusty didn't know how to answer that question. No one had asked him such a thing since he'd come into the knowledge of the baby girl's existence. He stuttered and shrugged a half attempt at the word, "No, I don't think so."

The response brought a slight chuckle from Amanda. "At least you're honest." She stopped again, looked to the ceiling, searching for a way to say what she wanted to. "There's more to a marriage than bringing children into the world. Our marriage, James's and mine, was broken long before we arrived at this fort. I was lonely and I made a mistake, an attempt to make up for what I had done, I had to seduce my own husband. You must think I was relieved when the baby was born and it was a Plumright, but that wouldn't have mattered to me. The child, Deputy, and I would have left out of here, where we would have lived our lives the best we could. Blame shouldn't be placed on a child for the actions of their parents. But you and I both know that is not how the real world works. A half-breed child would have never had a day's peace. As it is, my son will never know his father, and that is a tragedy. But his father was an angry man, a man who would have never put the child before himself. The child, Deputy, is the most important thing and his innocence must be cherished for as long as that is possible. Wouldn't you agree?"

"Yes, ma'am," Trusty said. "I would."

Chapter 25

Gladdy O'Connor had a few dollars left in his pocket and couldn't imagine all of the fun he could have with a thousand silvers. He'd never have to sleep on cold, hard ground again. Or alone. He could buy a different girl for every night of the week. His horse would be fine, maybe a race winner, fast and sleek, full of spirit and speed. Not like that swayback mare he rode out of Saint Louis on. The possibilities of what he could buy were endless. He could have his clothes tailored by the finest tailors—and then maybe bein' dressed head to toe like a dandy, he could take a steamer back home to Eire, and walk around the old place with a cane and a derby, showing everybody what he'd become. Even in Eire no one ever thought he'd amount to much. Gladdy liked that idea, was proud of himself for comin' up with it. He went on with that daydream, eyeing a red-headed girl in a make-believe pub in Dublin, exciting himself with all the things he would do to her and with what . . . until the baby started crying again in the other room, bringing him back to reality, planting his feet firmly in Aberdeen, South Dakota.

Matilda, the old woman whom Gladdy assumed was Marberry's wife, burst out of the room first, carrying the screaming baby. That's all the baby did was cry and sleep, cry and sleep, all hours of the day and night. It was enough to make a sane man crazy.

"I am not leaving this hotel, Theodore," Matilda said, walking like a sergeant leading a parade of cadets, patting the baby on the back, not being deterred by Marberry. He followed her out of the room with less enthusiasm. "It is Christmastime. Look out the window. The rest of the world is going about the business of enjoying a holiday, and here we are holed up like we are prisoners. We should be home, in Saint Louis, the house all decorated, and our lives back to normal." She stopped, patted the baby a little harder, who let out a loud burp, then stopped crying right away. A look of sadness crossed Matilda's face. "This is the first year without my Jessica, and it's almost too much to bear. Do you understand, Theodore? I miss our daughter."

Marberry had stopped in the middle of the room.

Gladdy sat in the chair, easing back, doing his best to become one with the fabric and disappear from sight. Matilda already acted like he didn't exist, but he didn't want to change that, or draw himself into their feud. Marberry might notice the level of whiskey was a little less than it was before he had left the room.

"That is why we're here, Matilda," Marberry said. "To repay that Dawson boy for what he has brought upon us. Your grief is not unnoticed. If we were at home, the reminders of our Jessica would be everywhere. You would remember every Christmas you ever spent with her."

Matilda had had her back to Marberry until that moment. She spun around like she had swivels tacked to the heels of her hi-top shoes. "How can I forget even a second of time that I spent with our daughter, Theodore?" She stepped closer to him with a cross look on her face that looked just as comfortable there as the agitation on Marberry's. "This is your fault, too. Not just that boy's, though I'll gladly tell him so if I ever see him. I've wanted to say that to you for a while, but I haven't had the courage or the strength until now. I was afraid for the baby. If you wouldn't have interfered and sent Jessica to England, where she suffered from homesickness and tragedy, then come home to find even more lovesickness, tragedy, and dare I say abuse from that thug of a man you cajoled her into marrying, things would have turned out different."

Marberry stiffened, not backing off from the fight. He ignored Gladdy, too, who was starting to become more than a little entertained by the whole spectacle. He never imagined rich people disagreed and fought like cats and dogs, but they sure did. By God, they sure did.

"She thought she was in love with that blacksmith's boy. Dirty and slow-minded as he was, that Sam Dawson. She had to do better than that. She needed to see the world. She needed to find a man who was worthy of being with her. I was not going to let her think that she could love a man like that Trusty Dawson character for one more second."

"She would still be alive!" Matilda screamed, which, of course, set the baby on another crying jag. The cries pierced Gladdy's eardrums, and he put his hands over his ears to muffle the sound.

Tears rolled down Matilda's face.

Marberry's face turned red with rage.

Matilda stomped straight toward Marberry, shoved the crying baby into his hands, then stormed into the bedroom and slammed the door. The baby girl screamed even louder. Marberry held the baby out away from him, horrified, with the look of a man holding a puppy for the first time, afraid it was going to pee on him, replacing the anger and agitation on his face. He hurried over to Gladdy and thrust the baby girl out to him. "Take it," he demanded, then hurried off after Matilda.

Gladdy had been around children when he was a lad in Eire; his house welcomed a new baby every nine months and his poor old mum had to resort to whatever way she could to find a little peace and quiet in the tiny cottage they all called home. He knew exactly what to do for the poor little girl. He quickly settled the screaming, red-faced baby into the crook of his arm, and went for the whiskey bottle with his free hand. He opened it, took a deep swig for himself, then took another drink, held the whiskey in his mouth, then stuck his finger in his mouth and soaked it with the whiskey. Then he stuck his finger in the baby's mouth and started to massage her gums with his whiskey-drenched finger. A couple more dips and rubs, and the baby quieted right down. It wasn't long before she fell fast asleep in his arms.

Marberry and Matilda screamed at each other long into the night, but it didn't matter. Gladdy and the baby slept in their own stupor, oblivious to the arguments or the reasons for them.

The whiskey bottle sat empty on the table.

The next morning, a knock came at the door stirring Gladdy awake. He looked at the cradle he'd made in his arm the night before and the baby was gone. He licked his lips, tried to wet his dry mouth with a gulp of air, but it didn't help. His head hurt a little, and for a second, he wondered if he was dreaming. Another knock came. This time it was more forceful than the first, convincing Gladdy that he was indeed in the real world. He wondered what had happened to the baby as he hurried to the door and pulled it open.

A tall man with the face of a bull, hair as red as any Irish girl Gladdy had ever crushed on, stared at him. He nearly took up all of the doorway. "Who are you?"

"Gladdy O'Connor. What's it to you?"

"You work for Marberry?" The man's breath smelled foul, and on closer inspection, his clothes were soiled and dirty, like he had been rolling in a pigpen or hadn't taken a change of clothes in a week of Sundays.

"Maybe. What do you want?"

The man started to push his way inside the hotel suite, but the sudden scream of the baby from the bedroom stopped him in his tracks. "What's that?"

"A baby. What'd you think it was?"

"Don't get wise with me, you scrawny little fool."

"You don't know me well enough to call me scrawny."

Gladdy's response unsettled the man. He hadn't been expecting it. He chuckled even though it looked like he didn't want to. "Where's Mister Marberry?"

Before Gladdy could say another word, Theodore Marberry stalked out of the bedroom, annoyed as usual. "What in the name of Sam Hill is going on out here?"

"Somebody lookin' for you, Mister Marberry," Gladdy said, stepping back to give Marberry a full view of the bull-sized man standing in the door.

"I thought that was you, Lewis." Marberry tried to look past the man. "Where's Timmons?"

"Dead," Lewis said.

Ah, Gladdy thought, *this is the man who was supposed to be here in the first place.* Red Jack Lewis. Now it made sense.

"Dead? How?"

"Trusty Dawson killed him."

If a pin would have dropped out of the sky, it would have sounded like a gong when it hit the floor. The room went that quiet. Even the baby sucked in a breath and joined in the moment of silence.

"And you didn't kill him?" Marberry yelled.

"I was outnumbered, Boss. There were four of them."

"That doesn't matter. You're supposed to be the best man for the job, and here you are looking like a defeated ragamuffin, coming to my door for a handout."

"I'm not lookin' for no handout," Lewis said. "I didn't know where else to come but here."

The baby started crying again.

"You, fool," Marberry said. "You could have led them straight here."

Lewis shook his head. "They headed back south. The three of them, totin' a dead man home. A Captain Plumright who joined up with us intent on killin' 'em all, but they kilt him instead. Don't know why they didn't burn him up like the Indian that we kilt, but they didn't. Dawson ain't got no idea where I went, and it didn't look like he was too interested in knowin', neither."

Marberry stiffened and continued to ignore Gladdy. "You could have followed him and shot him when he wasn't expecting it. Then we'd be done with this whole affair, and we could return home. That would solve my problems with Matilda, and my life would return to normal."

"I'm sorry, Boss. Without Timmons, I didn't know what to do. Bein' out in the open like we were in the snow and cold, it's the worst kind of hell I've ever knowed. I was in a hurry to come back to civilization, if that's what this can be called."

Gladdy nodded. He knew that feeling well. He'd been lost after losing Haden. He was still lost without his brother, but he wasn't gonna tell that to no one.

"Well," Marberry said. "You're here and there's nothing that can be done about that now. You need to go get yourself cleaned up. We're leaving out of here as soon as we can."

"Where are we going?" Red Jack Lewis asked, exasperated.

"Bismarck," Marberry answered. "We're going to wait for Trusty Dawson to return there, and then one of the two of you is going to kill him, if someone doesn't beat you to it. Do I make myself clear?"

"Yes, Boss," Gladdy and Lewis said in unison.

The baby cried louder than she ever had before. Gladdy swore the baby girl's cries rattled the windows.

For the second time in a month, Gladdy was happy to settle into the seat of a train car. Only this time, he had the comfort of knowing his way was paid for by Theodore Marberry instead of a gambling man like Clovis. If there was a reason to jump from the train in the middle of the night, it would have come as a surprise. Lewis sat across from Gladdy, while Marberry, his wife, and the fitful baby occupied a sleeper compartment just beyond the seats. Gladdy and Lewis could see who came and went from the sleeper with ease. Their job was to guard all of the Marberrys on the two-hundred-mile trek to Bismarck.

The train was full of Christmastime travelers, happy, relaxed, and warm—which Gladdy appreciated. He was relieved to be in a train car away from the elements. He could get used to looking after a rich man, bein' told what to do and how to think, if it meant ridin' in the comforts of a train all of the time—especially in the Dakota Territory.

"Why are you wearin' such a silly smile?" Lewis said. He had changed into a fresh set of traveling clothes, had taken a bath, but had forgone a shave and a haircut. Gladdy was sure there was something living under all of the red hair, but he wasn't sure what.

Gladdy looked away from Lewis, out the window to the barren white landscape rolling by. "Just happy to be sittin' here instead of out there is all. It's Christmas, too. Ain't that something to be warm about?"

"You ever met this Trusty Dawson fella?"

Gladdy nodded. "Had a run in with him in Oklahoma Territory."

"How'd that turn out?"

"I barely got away. He had backup from The Guardsmen. I'm lucky I'm still here talkin' to you if I'm honest. Vance Calhoun, the man I hired on with, was no slouch, had the temper of a badger and liked causin' pain and sufferin'. I never thought anybody would take him down."

"But Dawson did."

"Yeah, he did. That was somethin' I wasn't expectin'."

Lewis leaned forward and looked around to make sure no one could hear him. "The only reason I'm here is 'cause I ran like a rabbit. Once Dawson kilt Timmons I knew I was next. That man don't miss much when he shoots at you. That fool Plumright wouldn't listen, thought he had a plan to trick Trusty Dawson, but he's a wily one, that Marshal. Plumright ended up like your old boss, just like a lot of fellas taken by greed with silver in their eyes." Lewis took a breath and leaned in a little closer, close enough for Gladdy to smell the bacon and eggs he'd had for breakfast on his breath. Then he whispered, "Marberry is a fool, too. He don't know what he's dealin' with. He knew Dawson as a boy, not the man he is. He's underestimating him. Doesn't realize the skills he acquired bein' an Army scout and a marshal. There's a reason why Dawson is still alive and there's a slew of graves in his shadow."

"Why's that?" Gladdy asked, suddenly cold, suddenly feeling a draft wrap around his ankles like a snake who ate snow for dinner.

"Because he's smarter than Marberry thinks he is. We're on a fool's errand is what we are, and if we don't watch ourselves, we'll end up just like the rest of those men who jumped up on Trusty Dawson and tried to take him down."

"We'll be dead."

"That's right," Red Jack Lewis said. "We'll be dead. So think about that and your Merry Christmas as we roll along. It might be all that you have left."

Chapter 26

Trusty cinched up the saddle on Horse's back, adjusted it for the last time, then went around and made sure his paniers were as secure as the saddle. The barn was cold, but not frigid; his breath mingled with Horse's, making little clouds that vanished almost as quickly as they formed. Horse had recovered from the long ride to the fort, and Trusty was relieved that the roan didn't have any frostbite to contend with. He patted Horse's strong neck as he eased along the side of him, appreciative of his mount in a way that he had never been before. The landscape and weather in the Dakota Territory had been the most severe and trying bit of traveling that Trusty had ever experienced. His time in Fort Robinson in Nebraska had shown him struggles, some demanding winter weather, and losing Jasper, but nothing like the Dakota Territory. Maybe it was the barrenness of the land, the whiteness, and the loneliness that had made the ride seem so unforgiving. Or maybe it was just cold as hell, and that was it. Any way he looked at it, Horse had never staggered, never given up, never complained too much, just kept his head down and marched forward like any good soldier would. Trusty had lost a good horse before because of his own ignorance. He wasn't about to do it again. Not a horse who had as much spirit and drive as Horse.

Trusty stopped and patted the beast on the withers. "What do you think, buddy? You ready to ride again?"

Horse scraped the frosty straw-covered floor with his right hoof and snorted. A narrow cloud of his breath lingered a little longer before it disappeared.

"You like that idea, huh?" Trusty didn't think for a second that the gelding had understood a word he'd said, or the intent of it, but he liked to think that maybe there was some kind of understanding between the two of them that maybe hadn't been there before. "How about," Trusty said, thinking out loud, "I call you Buddy from here on out? Would you like that, Buddy?"

Horse did the same thing, scraped his right hoof. Trusty smiled and had a flicker of a memory; of the dream that had turned into a nightmare. He remembered Buddy, the brown-haired dog, and the feeling he'd had when he saw him: the dog had loved him, and he had loved the dog. "All right, Buddy it is." He tapped Buddy's shoulder again, then set about pulling on his buffalo coat, readying to leave.

"Hey, there, Dawson." It was Jonah Farley, walking up on him. Trusty figured he had come to say goodbye—but on closer inspection, it looked like Farley was getting ready to travel himself.

"I didn't expect to see you here, Farley," Trusty said, stepping away from Buddy.

"Well, I figured I would ride along with you. I'm glad I caught you before you left so I wouldn't have to run roughshod catching up with you."

"You have business in Bismarck?"

"I suppose I do."

Trusty let a wall of silence settle between the two of them before he said anything, looking Farley up and down all over again. "Did Townsend send you along to ride with me?"

"In a way. Your Marshal requested a rider through Townsend."

"And you volunteered."

"I did."

Trusty fell silent again, trying to find a way to tell Farley that he preferred to ride alone, and figure out why Marshal Delaney had asked for an escort for him. He was unsettled. "You have any idea what this is all about?" Trusty said.

"All I know is Delaney is concerned about a new threat against you. Wants to make sure you arrive back in Bismarck in one piece. I'm already broke in, so I was the obvious choice. Besides, it'll quiet down here for a few days with Christmas settin' down on the world. I'd rather be out on a ride, if you don't mind, instead of sittin' around waitin' for the days to pass into the new year. Besides, I ain't been to Bismarck in a coon's age."

"You sure you're willin' to take that risk?"

"Would I be here if I weren't?"

"I suppose not. Thank you, I guess."

"You guess?"

"You think I like the idea of another man lookin' after me? That's my job. I'm not sure you'd like the idea of havin' a guardian."

"Don't you worry about it. They're payin' me well." Farley smacked Trusty on the back and laughed. "My horse is packed and ready, outside."

"Looks like there's no time like the present," Trusty said.

"Sounds about right." Farley nodded, then walked off, leaving Trusty there alone to mount his horse, and get on with it. But Trusty hesitated, wondered if his plan to ride back to Bismarck was worth it. He could resign right then and there. Send Delaney a wire, and ride to Saint Louis without looking back. But that was a risk, too. He didn't know whether Marberry was in Saint Louis or not. He didn't know where Marberry was. Maybe Delaney did. The Marshal had a lot of men looking for Marberry. Farley didn't say what the new threat was, and Trusty hadn't asked. Part of him didn't want to know what the Marshal knew.

Farley had stopped at the barn door. "You comin' or what?"

"Yeah, I'm comin'. I just needed to digest all of this." He jumped up into the saddle, grabbed the reins, and said, "Come on, Buddy, let's go. It looks like we're gonna have company on the ride home."

Saint Louis, Missouri, June 1886

Sam stood in front of Madame Duchamp's house, surprised, in a way, that it was still there. Sometimes his entire life felt like part dream, part nightmare. A lot had happened since he had left Saint Louis to join the army, then started to ride with the U.S. Marshals after. Everybody called him Trusty—whether he liked it or not. But nobody in Saint Louis knew him by that name. At least as far as he knew.

The wrought-iron fence that had been made by Sam and his father, still stood, freshly painted black, shining in the early afternoon summer sun. The house, too, had a fresh coat of paint on it. Katherine Duchamp had always liked to keep things up. All of the houses up and down the street reflected the same level of care. There had always been something contagious about the way the woman did business and lived her life. There were only two buggies parked in front of the house. It must have been a slow day. No boats had come in yet. Maybe later in the night, the place would be swinging like it did in the past.

If there was a homecoming long overdue, it was this one.

Sam walked up to the kitchen door and knocked. The smell of rice and beans cooking on the stove greeted his nose, and a smile rose on his face. Voices came from inside the kitchen, low and steady, an order here and there, but nothing urgent. One of the voices was familiar, broadening Sam's smile.

A young Negro girl came to the door, and said, "Who are you? We ain't expectin' no deliveries today."

Sam was tempted to open the door and rush inside the kitchen like he used to, but he restrained himself. There was no use upsetting anyone. "I'm here to see Miss Kabbie Mae Brown, if you please?"

"Kabbie Mae? And who should I tell her is here to see her?"

Sam didn't have to say another word. A shadow lumbered behind the girl, and when she saw that it was Sam standing on the stoop, she about knocked the girl over getting to the door. "You scat, silly girl. That be Sam Dawson, finally come home to see me." A piano row of white teeth gleamed into a broad smile against Kabbie Mae's dark skin.

The girl stood aside with a perplexed look on her face, then rolled her eyes and went back to doing whatever she had been doing before he knocked on the door. She didn't know who Sam Dawson was any more than she knew who Trusty Dawson was.

Kabbie Mae was at the door in a blink. Sam rushed into her waiting arms. "I swear," she said, "if I wasn't lookin' at you with my own set of God-given eyes, I wouldn't believe it." Her face looked the same, no wrinkles on her soft brown skin, but her hair had gone white, like someone had replaced everything atop her head with cotton. She was stooped over, holding herself up with a hand-carved cane made of oak, with a female lion's head carved onto the top knob.

Kabbie Mae had always been a big woman, but now, she looked smaller, more compact. Maybe it was Sam's age, and the way he saw things through eyes that had grown up a bit. But there was no denying that Kabbie Mae had gotten old on him. He was just glad she was still alive.

"You get in here and sits your tail down at the table and tell me all about what you's doin' now. The Madame done told us you was a Marshal. Boy, oh boy, look at you. All growed up and wearin' a badge. Who would have thunk it?"

"I suppose none of us," Sam said.

Kabbie Mae led him by the hand to the table. "We gots lemonade. Fresh-squeezed. Get us some lemonade, Fanny. We gonna sit a spell." She sat down and pulled Sam down with her, refusing to let go of him.

The girl, Fanny, stopped and looked at Kabbie Mae with an expression that suggested a sass was about to come out of her mouth, but she thought better of it, and set about preparing two glasses for the company that had arrived unannounced.

Before Sam or Kabbie Mae could say another word,

Katherine Duchamp appeared at the door. She looked Sam up and down without any kind of readable expression on her face at all. "So, you're the cause of all of this turmoil in my kitchen. I should have guessed it was you, Sam Dawson. Or should I call you Trusty like everyone else?"

Sam, stood up, prying his hand from Kabbie Mae's. "Sam would be just fine, ma'am."

"Ma'am. I've moved up in the world." A crook of a smile started to grow on her face. Like Kabbie Mae, Katherine Duchamp had aged. Sam was twenty-seven and he had always figured that the madame was twelve or thirteen years older than him, making her around forty if his guess was right. It was hard to tell with a woman like Katherine Duchamp. Her curves were still in the right places, nothing sagging, and her face and hair hadn't changed much. She might have been a little heavier, but not in a way that hurt her none. Her beauty still took Sam's breath away. She was wearing an afternoon robe, light for the summer, made of a thin yellow linen, and her brunette hair was piled atop her head. Sam had always been glad that she wasn't blond. There was nothing about Katherine that reminded him of Jessica Marberry, other than the location of her house in Saint Louis. "Are you just going to stand there and gawk at me like a silly schoolboy, or are you going to come and give me a hug?" Katherine Duchamp said.

The next thing Sam knew he was wrapped up in her arms, fighting the temptation to kiss her. No kissing allowed. Not even when they had been naked together. She smelled of comfort and sandalwood. "Come on, tell me why you're here." Katherine pulled Sam away from the kitchen leaving a disappointed Kabbie Mae behind. He made a note not to leave without sitting with the Negro woman for a bit before he did.

They sat in the turret on a new divan, next to each other, their knees touching. "It's good to see you," Sam said. "How'd you know about my nickname, Trusty?"

"The whole world passes through these doors, Sam. You know that. People always coming and going." Her French New Orleans accent was as strong as it ever was. Time in Saint Louis hadn't tainted her native tongue a bit. "I have kept up with you when I could. I have my fair share of Army regulars. You know I have a penchant for men in uniform. Especially officers. They relax here, are more themselves."

Sam nodded, though that was a detail he hadn't remembered about her. He wondered which officers he knew had been in the house. He knew better than to ask. An admonishment from a long time ago reminded him to mind his own business when it came to her business.

"What brings you to Saint Louis," Katherine asked.

"Business," Sam answered. "I have to escort a new judge to Indian Territory. He's coming in on the train from New York City. Gordon Hadesworth. Do you know him?"

"Can't say that I've ever had the pleasure. You should bring him by before you head out."

Sam didn't respond, just smiled. "It's nice to be back here."

Katherine studied Sam's face, tried to judge his mood by the looks of it. "I thought maybe your girl was back in town?"

"Jessica?"

"The one and only."

"She is still in England. I get a letter every once in a while. No, she's not here that I know of."

"That is a good thing. She needs to stop writing you, torturing you with the hope that she will return to you. You need to get on with your life."

"I have."

"Sure, you have." Katherine paused, then said, "Are you going to see your father while you're here?"

"No," Sam said, surprised by the question. "Why do you ask?"

"You need to make peace with him as much as you need to leave Jessica Marberry in the past where she belongs."

"Maybe he needs to make peace with me."

"Maybe. But you are the one with the heart, the romantic. I think you will find your life is less angry if you go see him."

"He still comes here?"

Katherine hesitated, looked away then back to Sam. "From time to time. Not so much anymore. He is getting old, you know."

"I suppose he is."

"I won't beg you. It's a suggestion is all."

Sam sat rigid, doing his best not to look at Katherine Duchamp. He had almost asked not to be the new judge's escort because it brought him to Saint Louis. Conflict had ridden next to him like a seasick dog all the way home. "I can't stay long." He turned back to her and met her eyes. For a minute he hoped they could spend some time together for old time's sake. But he knew better. That had been a one-time event. She was right, some things were better off left in the past.

Sam stood up. "I couldn't come to Saint Louis without

seeing you and Kabbie Mae. This place was more my home than anyplace else."

"I'm happy that you are not embarrassed about that." Katherine Duchamp stood up and kept her eyes locked to his. "You are always welcome here. You know that, Sam. You're not as alone in the world as you think you are."

Sam smiled, reached in and hugged the madame, took an extra-long whiff of her sweet toilet water, then headed for the door.

"Your father won't be here forever," Katherine said.

Sam stopped, faced her, with Kabbie Mae standing behind him in the kitchen. "You told me once that a man's business is his own. You were right about that. What's between me and my father is my business, and that's how it's going to be," he said, then hugged Kabbie Mae on the way out and got on with his assignment, promising to talk with her the next time he was in town.

North of Fort Yates, Dakota Territory, December 1888

Farley had already proven to be a reliable traveling companion. If there was going to be anyone escorting Trusty back to Bismarck, offering another set of eyes and a trigger finger, he was glad that Jonah Farley had been the one to accept the ride—and the danger that came along with it. Farley was more knowledgeable about the Dakota Territory than Trusty was. He had spent years in the confines in and around Fort Yates. He had originally hailed from Minnesota. Cold temperatures and severe weather had been seared into Farley's blood since birth. So had hunting and providing sustenance for himself and the horse he rode.

THE BROKEN BOW 291

Farley showed Trusty how to find green blades at the root of Indiangrass, Blue Stem grass, and timothy to collect and serve to their horses. While the land was covered in snow and ice, there were still plenty of animals to provide a meal; mule deer, white-tailed deer, jackrabbits—the trail favorite—or weasels, if worse came to worse. Farley promised Trusty that he could cook up a weasel stew that would leave him wanting more. Trusty doubted that to be true but didn't say so. The best thing about riding with Jonah Farley, on top of all of his survival knowledge, was he knew how to be silent. The two of them could go for hours without saying a word, and that was just fine with Trusty. It took enough effort staying warm and focused on the trail.

"How you doin', Buddy," Trusty said after a while, as they rode north into the blind white world.

"I thought you called that animal Horse and nothing more. I haven't heard you call him that once since we've been out here." Farley was side-by-side Trusty at an easy pace.

"I've always hesitated to give an animal a name is all," Trusty said.

"Afraid you'd get too close?"

"Something like that, I suppose."

"Makes sense for a man like you without roots. You ever think about settlin' down, farming a little patch of ground, growin' a family instead of chasin' after warrants all of the time?"

Trusty looked at Farley but didn't answer straight away. The sky was clear as far as the eye could see. The sun hung burning bright in a white sky; the cold had long since shattered the blue out of it. Clouds skittered along, thin and white, too, without any visible threat showing. What wind that flared up was tolerable and the air was as dry as it was cold. Trusty was almost too warm inside the buffalo coat. "I think about that sometimes, but I'm not much of a farmer. Wouldn't know where to start. I figure a man who lives like that had to start on the land when he was a boy, acquire skills from his father, and his father before him, know how to read the ground and the sky, know when to plant and when to harvest. But most of all, how to get through the disappointments and failures that the weather and life are sure to bring. I don't know nothin' about any of that. I'd be startin' from scratch. I've never planted one seed of anything in my life."

"You've got time," Farley said.

"Do I?" Trusty asked, looking out in front of him, seeing nothing but flat, blank land that went for miles and miles beyond his vision. "Maybe one of these days I'll set the badge aside, live a little less dangerously. There's something out there that might make me reconsider the risk I take with the way I live my life. But there's things out of your control, isn't there? Men like Marberry who want to settle a grudge and a hate with death instead of talkin' things out, learnin' the truth of the matter, or acceptin' it. That would be too much to ask.

"For a long time, I didn't think there was evil in the world. Just good luck and bad luck. Good men and bad men for whatever the reason, but now I think there really is evil out there. Evil spawned by greed and hate and maybe some other things I don't understand. I ain't never claimed to be the smartest man in the room. I'm not sure I'll ever be able to outrun all that's happened and find a place that's safe. A place where I can love something enough to name it and keep it."

"Like your horse?" Farley said.

"Yes," Trusty said, "like Buddy. He's a start, but I got a long way to go."

Chapter 27

Cannonball, Dakota Territory, December 1888

Brazos Joe was standing outside the door of the trading post when Trusty and Farley rode up. "Well, if I hadn't seen it with my own damn eyes, I wouldn't have believed it," the trader said, stroking his scraggly beard. Like the last time that Trusty had been through Cannonball, the only show of a weapon on Brazos Joe's buckskin outfit was the ever-present thirteen-inch Bowie knife that hung sheathed on his hip. At the moment, even that looked unneeded with the big smile he wore on his face.

Trusty returned the smile as he rode up to the trading post, dismounted, tied Buddy to the hitching post, then made his way to Brazos Joe and gave him a hearty shake of the hand. "It's good to see you, too, old man," Trusty said.

"I figured you'd be dead by now, but I underestimated you." Brazos Joe looked around Trusty and eyed Jonah Farley with a little more suspicion than Trusty might have expected. "I see you're not travelin' alone these days."

Farley tied up his horse and joined the two. "Jonah Farley," he said, extending his hand for a shake. "Nice to make your acquaintance."

Brazos Joe shook Farley's hand then pulled it back. "You sure we ain't never met before? You look familiar."

The comment didn't seem to bother Farley. He didn't miss a beat with his reply. "A lot of folks tell me that. Must be my round belly and round face. Seems pretty common in these parts."

"I suppose so," Brazos Joe said. "Well, it's nice to meet you Mister Farley."

"Farley'll do."

"Well, come on inside both of you and warm up by the stove." Brazos Joe spun around and headed inside the trading post without another word. Both men followed.

The place was exactly the same as it had been the first time Trusty had walked in the door. Goods and supplies packed from the floor to the ceiling. Brazos Joe navigated the narrow aisles like he could do it with his eyes closed and headed behind the counter where he planted himself in his usual spot.

Trusty and Farley were like loyal dogs, following, doing what they were told.

"Either of you in need of a shot of whiskey?" Joe said.

Trusty shook his head, while Farley nodded his.

"I'll pass," Trusty said.

Brazos Joe reached under the counter and pulled up a bottle of amber liquid filled halfway. "You sure?" he said with an unconscious lick of the lips.

"Positive," Trusty said.

"Well, I guess it's just me and my new friend here." Brazos Joe set about pouring two glasses of whiskey, a finger each to start, then shoved one toward Farley. "Where do you hail from?"

Farley had the glass almost to his lips and went ahead and tipped the whiskey back before answering. He shook off the burn in his throat. "I was reared in Minnesota, but like most men out this way, I've been here and there and back again. Fort Yates has been my domicile for a number of years now, before that I trapped out Yellowstone way, spent some time in California lookin' for my treasure. One adventure after another until now."

Brazos Joe digested every word Farley said, turning them over in his mind to see if there was any untruth underneath them. Trusty knew the look on the old man's face because that's exactly what he had done with him the first time they'd met.

"I got something for you, Trusty," Brazos Joe said. He swigged down the whiskey without one ounce of discomfort then disappeared into the room behind the counter.

"You'd think a man who sells goods for a livin' might be a little more friendly," Farley said. "He looked at me like I'd robbed a bank he owned."

"I wouldn't think nothin' of it," Trusty said, even though he found Brazos Joe's reception of Farley a little odd himself.

Joe came back carrying a quilted blanket made of rags and cut up clothes all sewed together. "Here you go," he said, handing the blanket to Trusty. "That's the first one of those my wife made with that Singer sewing machine that you left behind for her. She said it took her a quarter of the time and she sure is grateful. All the women in Cannonball are jealous and have lined up to learn how to use the darned thing."

Trusty accepted the blanket with half a smile. "Thanks, I'm glad she could use it. What did you do with the rest?"

"Like you said would happen, some men from the Singer company came along asking for the inventory and took off down the road. They was salesmen, too, so I'd imagine they'd been knockin' on one soddie door after the other pushing their wares. Good for them. I'd rather stand under a roof."

"Your wife does fine work," Trusty said.

"You can tell her yourself at supper. You are stayin' aren't you?"

Trusty nodded again. "For the night, if you don't mind. We'll head out first thing in the mornin' for Bismarck. The sooner I get there, the sooner I can get on with my life."

Farley stood back and listened but stayed out of the conversation. He was comfortable after the shot of whiskey.

"I don't get your meanin', Trusty," Brazos Joe said.

"I'm givin' up the badge," he said, surprised as both men that he'd said it. If he was ever going to have a life like him and Farley talked about, he knew he had to go and find Theodore Marberry and the baby girl and put an end to the bounty once and for all. He wasn't going to ride side saddle with a guardian for the rest of his life. "I got a life out there somewhere and I aim to go get it. I figure I owe Marshal Delaney and the service an explanation face to face. Then after that, I'm on my own. No offense to you, Farley, but I've ridden alone most all of my life, and I ain't lookin' to change that now."

"No offense taken," Farley said.

All Brazos Joe could do was nod. "Well, I heard tell there's more trouble comin' your way. I could tell you're the type of man who meets things like that head on, so I'm not surprised."

"What kind of trouble?" Trusty asked.

Brazos Joe poured another whiskey in a clean glass and pushed it toward Trusty. "That bounty that's on your head has been tripled. Your life's worth three thousand silvers now."

Brazos Joe insisted that Trusty and Farley sleep inside the living quarters of the trading post. And, Joe, being married to a Sioux woman, was more than a gracious host, knowing the ways of treating guests in the Indian world, offering Trusty his own bed—which Trusty declined. He was more comfortable in the stable alone with Buddy, next to a stove, on a bed of straw, his buffalo blanket, and the new quilt that had been gifted to him. Farley chose to stay under a roof and sleep in a real bed. The truth of the matter was, Trusty wanted to spend some time alone and chew on the decision he had made. He didn't want anyone put to threat because of his presence, either, not with the bounty being raised like it had been.

The barn was just as warm as a house, and it wasn't long before he was comfortable and asleep. But the sleep, no matter how deep, didn't last long. It felt like he had been asleep for only a minute when he heard the slow cock of a hammer on a gun and felt a cold steel barrel pressed against his temple.

"You move an inch, Dawson, and I'll pull the trigger right now."

Trusty opened his eyes, though he didn't need to see the man to know who was doing the talking. It was Farley.

"Now, I want you to stand up, and walk out of the barn. I'm gonna keep my gun in your back, so don't get any stupid ideas like callin' out for help from your friend in there. You'll be dead before his feet hit the ground out of the bed. You and me are gonna take us a long walk, and when we're far enough out, that'll be the end of you."

Trusty didn't move. "Why now, Farley?"

"I didn't know you was worth three thousand silvers is why. You have to ask? That kind of money can change any man's life. I've killed men for a lot less, and so have you. Don't be so surprised. It ain't nothin' personal. I liked you well enough, but I like the idea of that money more."

"I didn't have you pegged for that kind of man."

"Most men don't get the opportunity to find out if they're made that way, now do they? Faced with government wages for the rest of their life, or a life in poverty of one type or another, most men just accept their lot in life and live in misery. Life don't offer too many second chances, so when one comes along a man like me has to take it and see how far it'll go. Your life is a chance at a new life for me, Trusty Dawson."

Trusty saw a shadow move behind Farley and he hoped like hell it was Brazos Joe come to back him up. "All right, I'm gonna stand up slow and easy. Don't get itchy."

"Make it slow and keep your hands where I can see them."

Trusty had hung his gun belt next to the stable gate along with his knife. He didn't have any kind of weapons on him. "I have to take this blanket off me, then I'm gonna put my hands out to the side and bring my knees to my chest then I'll stand up. I don't want you to misunderstand a simple move I make. My weapons are over there." Trusty nodded to the post with his gun belt.

Farley glanced at the Colt in its holster, then said, "I ain't going to kill you here, Dawson, don't you fret none about that. Last thing I want to do is tangle with that Brazos Joe fella and bring down half of the reservation on my tail. I can't outrun a hundred Indians and I ain't going to try."

"You've got this all thought out, don't you?"

"I do." Farley was proud of himself.

Trusty moved from under the blanket, then put his arms out and pulled his knees up under his belly just like he said he was going to. Instead of standing up, though, he swiveled his hips, came up on his side, and swept his right leg out, catching Farley unaware behind the knees with all of the effort he could muster. The blow popped Farley's feet out from under him and he fell backward. He hit the ground with a thud and his gun, a Colt, too, went flying into the darkness beyond the stall.

Trusty didn't take time to ponder his next move. He jumped up like a maniacal frog and landed on Farley's ample chest with his knee, knocking the air out of the man's lungs. A crack of bone, most likely a rib, came before a groan, distant but the damage assured. Restraining the man was going to be a feat, so Trusty punched Farley in the face with both fists, pummeling him into submission.

In the throes of his attack, Trusty got lost in his own rage, in the anger created by the existence of the bounty and the cause of it. He was tired of paying the price over and over again for one mistake. But he had forgot one simple thing. It was foolish to underestimate an injured and angry bull.

Farley used all his might to push himself up off the floor, sending Trusty flying across the stall. He hit the post hard with the back of his head, sending a new kind of pain through every inch of his body. There was no stopping Farley. His face was bloodied, his nose angled sideways from its normal place, and his breathing was labored, a struggle. His ears were red with rage and blood, and he spit out teeth as he lumbered toward Trusty, pulling his knife from its sheath on his waist.

Trusty was no match for the man, half in and half out of consciousness. He saw two of Farley and couldn't get his legs to move fast enough to scurry out of the way. There was nowhere to go.

"Stop right there, Farley, if that be your real name." It was Brazos Joe. The command was followed by a twin cock of a ten-gauge Wm. Moore & Co. double-barreled shotgun.

Farley was no fool. He stopped, allowing Trusty to skitter to the corner of the stall.

"This ain't got nothin' to do with you, old man. You'd be wise to mind your own business."

"Your business is done here," Brazos Joe said. "I ain't in no mood to see a man killed in my barn, especially considerin' I've been as hospitable as I've been. Drop the knife and you and I will have no problem. Once you do that, then you're gonna get on your horse and ride out of here. Head south and not stop until you're off Indian land. You try to double back, and you'll wear an arrow in your shirt where your heart is. You understand what I'm sayin' to you?"

"My gear's inside," Farley said.

Brazos Joe didn't flinch, didn't move a muscle, kept Farley in his sights. "Your gear is my gear now. Consider it payment for my troubles. Now drop the knife and go before I change my mind and shoot you."

"My coat . . ." Farley protested.

"You should have thought about that before allowin' your stupidity and greed to get the best of you."

"I'll freeze to death," Farley said as he dropped the knife to the floor. It clanged, then went silent. All of the horses and other animals in the barn were quiet as the mice watching.

"There are worse ways to die. Now go." Brazos Joe tipped the barrels, encouraging Farley not to linger any longer.

Trusty watched Farley go as his vision settled into singular focus. He wanted to tell the man that if he ever saw him again, he'd arrest him on the spot. But as he thought about it, Farley probably wasn't going to make it off the reservation alive.

Chapter 28

Cannonball, Dakota Territory, December 1888

"There's no way I can get you to change your mind, Dawson?" Brazos Joe said, standing outside of the trading post. The weather had turned gray, windy, with the promise of a fierce cold pushing down from the north. "It'll be Christmas on the morrow."

Trusty shook his head no, glanced over to the Catholic mission with nary a candle burning in the window, then looked up to the troubled sky. At least the sun wouldn't be so bright that it would sting his eyes; his head was still throbbing from the hit on the post he'd taken the night before. He was lucky that post hadn't killed him. The only sign of Farley was a set of horse tracks heading south off the reservation, just like they were supposed to. Something told him that Jonah Farley was a dead man. He hoped he would never know what happened to the greedy man. The betrayal still stung. There was no getting used to such a thing, but the regularity of it had made him suspicious of every man's heart and motives.

"It's time I put an end to this bounty business," Trusty

said to Brazos Joe. "My luck's gonna run out one of these days. I can't count on men like you to come to my rescue every time I'm in a lurch, every time a trusted man turns on me."

"Ain't no such thing as a trusted man in the world you're livin' in, is there, Trusty Dawson?"

"I gave you a fair amount of leeway with my life," Trusty said. "I wouldn't be standin' here if it wasn't for you."

"You're a fool then." Brazos Joe let a serious look settle on his face. "You don't think I considered takin' a turn at the bounty, 'specially when I heard it was tripled? Money can bring a man a lot of comfort, change the scenery from cold to warm, set him on a fresh start, give him security of not starvin' to death. But you're lucky. A man like me has already had the bad luck of more fresh starts than he can count, and I learned the price of comfort and change is higher in the end than it looks at the outset. I have everything I want right here and now. It might not look like much, but I know what to expect, where my head's gonna lay at night and who it's gonna lay with. I sleep easy, but that ain't always been the case. I know what it's like to sleep with one eye open, waitin' for someone to come along and take everything you've got. I don't need change to make me feel alive. But I thought about that bounty, I sure did. It's a lot of money for a second's worth of work pullin' a trigger. Don't kid yourself, Dawson, every man and woman is human and has to bat down greed when the opportunity to dance with it comes along. You're a nice feller, but that don't mean on a bad day I might have come to a different conclusion and killed you when I had the chance."

"That's not much of an argument to keep me here."

"I suppose it's not. You're right. If you think you know

how to end this thing, then you best get on with it, no matter whether it's Christmas or not."

Trusty went over and shook Brazo Joe's hand. "Thanks for everything and tell your wife I appreciate that blanket. You know if I was more of a curious sort, I would question if you really had a wife. I haven't seen hide nor hair of a woman either time I've been in Cannonball. Now that I think about it, you're the only man I've seen, too."

Brazos Joe finished shaking Trusty's hand, then said, "She's shy. All of them Sioux are around the likes of you. They got eyes on you, though. And they will have until you leave the reservation. The gift of the sewing machine earned you their respect and the way you treated Charlie Littlefoot guaranteed you their protection. They'll do their best to keep you alive while you're on Indian land, but you're on your own after that."

Trusty stayed the course on the known trail, went north the same way he had come south. Buddy, who he still called Horse every once in a while, walked head-long into the wind that the troubled clouds promised to bring. The temperature jumped up and down, and the precipitation danced between rain, snow, and sleet, making the way to his resignation harder than he had hoped it would be.

It didn't take long with darkness threatening to come even earlier than it usually did for Trusty to find a spot to pitch camp. The riverbank offered thin patches of spindly trees, and enough dried sticks and branches on the ground to build both a fire and a lean-to. Brazos Joe had sent some fresh jerky along for the ride, if Trusty couldn't rustle up a dinner of jackrabbit stew. Luck had favored him, though, when it had come to dinner. Not with a rabbit but a weasel.

The meat was tough, but it was fresh. Farley had promised him that he could make a weasel taste good. Farley turned out to be a weasel himself, and Trusty still had a bad taste in his mouth from the encounter.

Halfway through the night, the weather and wind calmed, and Trusty woke up with the need to relieve himself. The sky above him was free of clouds, and the stars and half-moon shined brightly overhead. The snow on the ground reflected the light, making it easy to see where he was going, and beyond, out in the world, white in the middle of the night, calm and peaceful. If what Brazos Joe had told him was true, then there were eyes on him from somewhere, watching over him, allowing for a rare night's sleep alone without worry—for once. That seemed like the best Christmas present he could have asked for.

Bismarck, Dakota Territory, December 1888

Marshal Michael Delaney sat behind his desk, planted there like he had roots growing out of the soles of his boots. His desk was piled high with books, ledgers, and mileage sheets to sign and approve. His face was as gray as the office. Light had been shunted by the pull of a blind, blocking out the view of downtown Bismarck. Trusty walked in with his buffalo hat in his hand, his coat left outside on a coat tree. He was going to get a new Stetson before leaving town. His old Cavalry hat told too many stories. It was one of the ways Trusty hoped to start fresh.

Delaney looked up and let the paperwork stress fall from his face. "It's good to see you, Dawson."

"Same to you, Marshal. I hope you and your family had a warm Christmas."

"We did, thank you. My wife's a little cross with me for leavin' out and coming into the office. But I have stacks to get through and reports to write that are due at the end of the year."

Bureaucracy had never appealed to Trusty. He could read and write well enough. His high school teacher had encouraged him to go to college, but his father wouldn't hear of it. *Better you than me,* he thought.

Delaney leaned forward with a pencil still in his hand. "I'm glad you were able to get Charlie Littlefoot back to Fort Yates. The trial is set for after the first of the year."

Trusty nodded. "It wasn't without its casualties."

"Did you expect it to be?"

"I suppose not. Do you mind if I sit down, sir, there are some things I'd like to talk to you about," Trusty said.

A concerned look passed across Delaney's weathered face. He nodded and watched Trusty sit down. "Is everything all right, Dawson. I know of the troubles you had out in the field. I called off the Mounties. Bisset was disappointed that you didn't make it to Canada. He was looking forward to working with you. Maybe some other time?"

"About that." Trusty slid to the edge of the chair so he was as close to being eye-to-eye with the Marshal as he could get. "Is there any word on Marberry."

"Yes, actually there is. He's here in Bismarck. There's a two-story place off Main Street, The Drewery House. You know it?" Delaney said.

"I've stayed there," Trusty answered. "Please tell me he is there."

"He is. Along with two thugs working as protection. Deputy Morrison is following the men when they leave.

Only one leaves at a time for food and other needs. Marberry went in but hasn't left once as far as I know."

"What's he doin' here?" The words came out of Trusty's mouth without thinking. There could only be one reason why Theodore Marberry and two thugs were in Bismarck. He was the reason. Either that, or a big coincidence, but that didn't seem likely. He didn't give Delaney time to answer the question. "It's just him and his protection?"

Delaney shook his head no. "There's a woman with him. His wife we presume."

Trusty's mouth went dry, and his heart started to race. Normally he was calm, unable to be riled too much, even in a shoot-out. "His wife," he said.

"Yes, caring for a baby, which we find a little strange." Delaney was watching Trusty closely.

"It's not strange." It was all Trusty could do not to jump up and rush out of the office. But he restrained himself. "I believe that child is my daughter."

It took a second for what Trusty said to sink in, but the Marshal finally nodded. "The reason for the bounty. You crossed a line that you shouldn't have."

"Something like that."

"The presence of the baby complicates things."

"She has since I learned of her existence."

"And when was that?"

"I'm sorry, I should have told you. It's just that I'm not sure. I've only had a glimpse of the baby. I was too far away to tell anything, if that's possible anyway. All I have to go on is what Vance Calhoun told me, and the fact that I was there. She could be my child, is what I'm sayin', but Jessica died after the baby was born. She never got word to me that she was pregnant, that the baby might have been mine."

"She was Vance Calhoun's wife, correct?" Delaney said.

"I think that was a business deal between Marberry and Calhoun. They both had assets that each man would have envied. Marberry, a railroad. Calhoun, a ranch. But I don't know for sure. The timing is right. I encountered Jessica in Muskogee not long before she met and married Vance Calhoun."

"Sounds like a whirlwind romance."

"I suppose so," Trusty said. He stood up and took his badge off and put it on Delaney's desk. "I fulfilled my duty, brought in Charlie Littlefoot like I said I would, but now I have to resign and go attend to my personal affairs. If Marberry is here, then I have to end this for everyone, especially that baby girl."

Delaney's face flushed red, and he snapped a pencil in two. "Put that badge on and sit your ass back down, Dawson. That's the most ridiculous thing I have ever heard come out of your mouth. If you walk out that door without the aid and protection of the U.S. Marshal Service, you're a dead man. You know that? A dead man. One of the men riding for Marberry is Red Jack Lewis. He's killed seven men and never been caught and tried for any of their deaths. Think about that. He knows what the heck he's doing."

"He left his riding buddy with a bullet in him." Trusty hadn't moved. He wasn't taking orders from Delaney anymore.

"What happens to that baby if you're dead?" Delaney said. "She's an orphan then. No mother, no father. In the care of a man on the run, protected by thugs. What kind of life is that?"

"I'll kill Lewis if I have to. It'll be self-defense."

"You just admitted that you're premeditating murder.

Now do what I told you to do and put that badge back on and sit down. I have a plan."

Trusty lowered his head and exhaled. He knew the Marshal could have booted his ass out of the office and left him to face Marberry on his own. But he didn't. Trusty wasn't on his own, and he didn't know what to say about that or how to feel. He withered back into the chair and put his badge back on his chest. "If anybody faces Marberry's thugs, I want it to be me. Enough blood has been spilled because of my actions, and it has to end here."

"I couldn't agree more," Marshal Delaney said. "I'm glad you've come to your senses. But you have to agree to do exactly what I tell you to do."

"Haven't I always?"

"Yes, Dawson, you have, but there's never been a child involved in my orders before. Your child, if you're right. That changes everything, doesn't it?"

Chapter 29

Bismarck, Dakota Territory, December 1888

Gladdy O'Connor sat staring out the second-floor window, thinking about nothing in particular, when he saw Red Jack Lewis make his way across the street and duck into an alley that separated the milliner's shop and a Chinese laundry. The windows cranked from the left to right and were sealed shut at the moment. A Model 1886 Winchester sat at Gladdy's side. The '86 belonged to Lewis, by way of Theodore Marberry. It was a fine weapon, and Gladdy ached to fire the rifle. The '86 was able to chamber heavy rounds, government .45 or .50-110 express buffalo cartridges. This Winchester was far more diverse than the '73, the model a lot of men still swore by, including Gladdy. Lewis had .45 cartridges loaded and ready to go in the rifle—which sat in the hold, the bird's eye view of the street from the room, picked by Marberry for that very reason. *Hmm, what are you doin', Lewis?* Gladdy thought but didn't say aloud.

The baby was sleepin'. The last thing he wanted to do was set the fuse that woke the little screamer up. His ears were still ringin' from her last cryin' bout. Gladdy knew one thing. Bein' around the baby girl had cured him of ever wantin' children of his own. Not that he thought too much about that kind of thing. That would mean bein' respectable, holdin' down an income payin' job of some kind, and findin' a girl who wanted the same such thing. He wasn't gonna be no boot licker, no sirree, especially to no girl. The last three people he'd taken orders from were dead.

It was midafternoon, almost time for Lewis to relieve Gladdy at the window. The duty was simple: Watch for Dawson or a Marshal. Marberry figured they would see one or the other sooner or later. And they would be ready when that happened. It was a simple idea, and one that seemed fraught to Gladdy, but Marberry had faith in Red Jack Lewis, considered him a sure thing. Gladdy wanted to tell Marberry there wasn't a sure thing against Trusty Dawson. He wanted to point out to the Boss that through everything that he had thrown at Dawson, the Marshal was still alive. He hadn't tucked tail like Lewis had after confronting Dawson with the deceased Glo Timmons and *run* back to find the safety of Marberry and his fancy hotel. Gladdy had made his way there on his own with no one to tell him how or what to do. He sat up straighter at the thought—but he was still concerned about Lewis. *Where had he gone?*

There were more weapons in the room than Gladdy had ever seen in one place outside of the war. Six Winchester '73s, four more '86 models, five Peacemakers; Colt single-action revolvers with the ability to use the same cartridges as the Winchester '73 Model. Three more crates sat unopened, and Gladdy had assumed they held more rifles and handguns. A small gun sat next to the Peacemakers, a .22 caliber Rupertus Derringer. Gladdy liked the look of the gun and stuffed it in his deep pants pocket—just in case he needed it.

What Marberry really needed was more men, but that didn't seem to be a concern. Killing Trusty Dawson was up to Gladdy and Red Jack Lewis—which Gladdy still didn't favor too much. Somehow, he had to figure how to reinstate and revise the plan he'd concocted for Clovis: Get Lewis to kill Dawson and then he could kill Lewis and collect all of the bounty money from Marberry for himself. Killing Lewis would get him in a lot less trouble than killing a U.S. Deputy Marshal.

Gladdy watched for Lewis to come back out of the alley, but he didn't.

Something was wrong. Gladdy could feel it. He didn't like it; Lewis had been as reliable as a clock until that moment. A quick glance over his shoulder toward the closed door of Marberry's room warned Gladdy off knocking on it, disturbing the old man and waking the baby. He didn't know what to do. Lewis was supposed to stay at his post downstairs, stay in sight all of the time, and point to the sky if he saw a marshal or Trusty Dawson himself. Gladdy didn't figure he'd see hide nor hair of Trusty Dawson in Bismarck, but he was wrong about that.

Trusty Dawson walked out from the alley that Red Jack Lewis had disappeared into.

Gladdy sat up even straighter now.

Trusty Dawson was square in the middle of the street, looked right up at the window where Gladdy was sitting and waved for him to come down.

Gladdy got a big lump in his throat, and his heart started to race like a rabbit tryin' to outrun a coyote. He grabbed up the '86 as he stood and started to point it at Dawson but thought better of shooting out the window. "Dang it!"

He was exasperated as he set down the rifle and cranked open the window as fast as he could. When he grabbed up the Winchester and re-aimed it, Dawson was gone, and the street was oddly empty. There were no horses trotting by or any wagons going one way or the other. It was like Christmas had come all over again and no one was out and about.

Marberry must have heard Gladdy fumbling with the window. He eased out of the bedroom like he was walking on thin ice, creeping on his toes, doing his best not to wake the baby. "What are you doing, you fool?" Marberry said in a gravely, demanding whisper.

Cold air invaded the room with the window open, and Gladdy stood with the '86 pointed down at the street. "Lewis disappeared into the alley across the street. Then Trusty Dawson appeared, walked right out in the street like he didn't have a fear in the world. He looked right up to me and waved me down."

"He's here." It wasn't a question. It was a full-throated, full-voiced realization. "You're sure it was him?" The doubt came, if only for a second.

"I told you, I saw Dawson before. I'd know him anywhere. He's a big man, but he ain't wearin' his normal hat is all. I'm sure it's him."

"They knew we were here," Marberry said. "How did they know we were here?"

"I don't know, but somebody must have figured it out."

"You're a bright one, aren't you?" Marberry rolled his eyes as he made his way to the window. He peered out standing at the edge of the glass so no one could see him. "There's no one there."

"I done told you that."

"No. No one. It's like they have the street closed off."

"Sure, looks that way, don't it?"

"How about you keep your mouth shut until you're spoken to." Marberry stomped off, no longer worried about falling through the ice or the ear-splitting screams of a child woken from a deep sleep. He opened the bedroom door, and said, "Grab the baby, Matilda, we have to go."

Gladdy was still glued to the window, watching for Dawson. The street remained eerily empty. He suddenly felt like a target and pulled back from the window.

Gladdy heard the first whimper of the baby girl. "Come on, now," Marberry demanded from the door. "Hurry. We have to go *now*!"

"What about my things?" Matilda said from inside the room. Her voice was cold, unmoved by her husband's demands. Any other time, Gladdy would have wondered who was really in charge.

"I'll buy you more things. Don't I always buy you more things?" Marberry was as purple in the face as a ripe plum. He turned his attention to Gladdy. "Go make sure the hallway is clear. If it's not, shoot anything that moves."

Gladdy stared at the man for a long moment. He didn't like that plan. Even if he could figure out whether or not Trusty Dawson was outside, there had to be more marshals than just him waitin' for them. He didn't move an inch. "When Calhoun got captured by the marshals, it was by the Three Guardsmen. You ever heard of them fellas?"

"Why aren't you doing what I told you to do?" Marberry was halfway across the room before Gladdy could take a breath. When he took another breath, Marberry was in front of him and backhanded him without warning. The loud crack startled the baby, who was at the door, covered in a white blanket, cradled in Matilda's trembling arms. The baby screamed at the top of her lungs.

Gladdy staggered backward, stunned by the surprise hit. He almost fell to his knees, the '86 still in his right hand. He rubbed his cheek with his left hand and said, "Why'd you go and do that for, Mister Marberry. I'm just tryin' to tell you that there's more men out there than just Trusty Dawson."

"I know that you damned fool. We have to run now. I don't need an idiot to tell me that we're outmanned."

"Maybe you ought to just give up then."

"I'm not telling you one more time to go and clear the hallway." Marberry picked up the closest gun, a Peacemaker that was laying on a table, cocked it and pointed it at Gladdy. "Now do as you're told!"

"Theodore," Matilda gasped. "What are you doing?"

"I am saving us." He waved the revolver at Gladdy, urging him to the door.

Gladdy didn't stumble or retreat. He went to the door, opened it, then looked up and down the hallway. He didn't see anybody. But even if he had, he was gonna say he hadn't and lead Marberry right to whoever was there. The son of a bitch had hit the wrong person. Money or no money. "It's clear."

"Are you sure?"

"I don't see no one."

"Okay, lead the way."

Before Gladdy knew it, the three of them were in the hall heading for the staircase, with Matilda and the crying baby behind him with Marberry bringing up the rear.

They made it to the staircase without issue. Gladdy stopped and peered down without seeing anything.

"Go down and make sure there is no one there," Marberry ordered.

The baby had stopped crying. It must have been the

movement or the shake of Matilda's arms that calmed her down.

Gladdy didn't hesitate. *Please be there, Dawson,* he begged inside his head, but didn't say. There was no one at the door. When he looked outside, he didn't see anything but an empty street. "It's clear," he said to Marberry.

Gladdy watched the old man and old woman carrying the baby hurry down the stairs, rich, wealthy people fleeing like thieves escaping a bank robbery. Everyone was alike, he decided right then and there. Out for themselves and no one else. Money was just a suit of nice clothes and a reason to order people around. Or feel like you had the right to hit them in the face when you didn't.

When Gladdy turned around to make his way out the door, he came face to face with the barrel of Trusty Dawson's pearl-handled Colt .45. "So, we meet again, Gladdy O'Connor. You best stop right there and drop your weapon," Dawson said.

Gladdy panicked, turned and looked back up the stairs to Marberry who had stopped midway down at the sight of Dawson. His purple face had turned white. There was another marshal at the top of the stairs, aiming a rifle down at the three of them.

The baby whimpered and squirmed under the blanket.

"You, too, Marberry. Drop your gun and call off your man. This is over," Trusty Dawson said, still holding Gladdy O'Connor in his aim.

Chapter 30

There was no tremble in Trusty's hands. His finger was on the trigger. If O'Connor moved an inch, he was prepared to pull it. "Come on, outside," he ordered the man before him. "You rode with Vance Calhoun. Turned on him at the end if I remember right. You walked free because of that squeal. Now here you are, Gladdy O'Connor, in my gunsights again. Drop the gun."

"Happily," Gladdy said, staring at Dawson with a surprised look on his face. He dropped the gun, stepped over it, then walked into the sunlight of the day.

"You, too," Trusty heard Marshal Delaney say to Marberry. The clunk of iron hitting wood echoed out from the enclosed staircase. "Go on move it downstairs and outside." The baby whimpered.

Trusty was focused on Gladdy. They stood in the middle of the empty street a foot apart. "You gave up one man to ride with a worse one," he said to O'Connor. The Irishman looked skinnier, his hair longer than the last time he had seen him. The desperation in his eyes was the same.

"It ain't what it looks like, Dawson," O'Connor said.

"I think it's exactly what it looks like. You came here to collect the bounty on me, is what you did."

O'Connor shook his head, was about to say something else, but Marberry and his wife walked out of the hotel with Delaney close behind, holding them in check with the point of a rifle.

"Shut up!" Marberry screamed at O'Connor.

Marshal Delaney poked Marberry in the back, and said, "You keep quiet, you understand."

Marberry gasped and his face changed color again, back to enraged purple. He bit his lip.

Now that they had the three of them under control, Trusty knew the next move was theirs. Red Jack Lewis was in custody, confined and could offer Marberry no help. Lewis, in the end, had been much like O'Connor when it came time to turn on his boss, only easier. Once approached—which had been part of Delaney's plan—he turned on Marberry quickly and agreed to come in from the cold. Lewis had also informed them of O'Connor's presence and no others, but Delaney had closed down the street in case trouble rang out. Neither of them knew what O'Connor or Marberry would do once they were put in a corner. As it turned out, they had run, which had been a mistake.

Trusty couldn't take his eyes off the bundle in Marberry's wife's arms. Jessica's mother. Trusty had never met her. They needed to be cautious in the presence of the baby.

Delaney joined Trusty, and they both held the three of them at bay with the points of their guns. Cold swirled around them, pushed down the street from the north, bringing with it a spit of snow. "We need to get moving," Trusty said, concerned about standing out in the open any longer.

The baby started to cry, and the woman eyed Trusty like

he was the lowest thing on earth she had ever seen. "This is all your fault," she hissed.

"Shut up, Matilda. This is over with. Don't say a thing." Marberry's shoulders sagged in defeat. His face drained what anger had remained as he came to realize the situation they were in. "We will not say another word until we have spoken to our lawyers."

"What about me?" Gladdy O'Connor said.

"You're going to jail for a long time to come," Marshal Delaney said. "We have a small cell reserved just for you."

O'Connor drew back like he had been struck, then a look of fear landed on his face and stayed there.

Neither Trusty nor Delaney expected O'Connor to run. But he did more than that. He reached over and yanked the baby away from Marberry's wife and sprinted away from them as fast as he could. Stunned for a long second, Trusty reacted as quick as he could, and fired a shot into the air. "Stop!" he demanded, but O'Connor kept running.

Trusty didn't think twice about what to do next. He took out after O'Connor and the baby.

O'Connor swerved into the first alley he could find, hustled through it, and came out the other side where life was going on as normal. The street was full of people, horses, and wagons, carrying on the business of the day, maybe a little more packed because of the closure of one street.

Trusty almost lost the two of them, but the screaming baby was like a beacon, drawing him closer and closer to her.

O'Connor was a fast runner, but Trusty was faster. He had more of a reason to run. If anybody would know who the father of their daughter's baby was, it was her mother. "This is all your fault" was all he needed to hear, to know, that the baby was his. "Stop that man!" Trusty shouted as he went.

O'Connor turned down another alley, but like Trusty he didn't know the layout of Bismarck at all. The alley was a dead-end.

"You're trapped, O'Connor," Trusty said, panting, coming to a stop, realizing that O'Connor had nowhere else to run. He kept his Colt leveled at the man's head, aware of the bundle that was still screaming and wrestling around against O'Connor's tight hold. "Give me the baby, and you won't get hurt. This is over, you hear. Whatever you thought you were gonna do to get out of this ain't gonna come to you, you understand."

"Maybe me and you can make a deal," Gladdy said as loud as he could, over the baby's screams.

"The only deal is you give me the baby and you're going to jail."

"I'm not goin' to jail, Dawson. I'll do anything not to go to jail."

"You should have lived a different kind of life then."

The baby wailed louder if that were possible.

"I was all right as long as I was with Haden," O'Connor yelled. Tears started to roll down his cheeks.

Trusty took a step closer to O'Connor. "I don't care about your past. Hand over the baby." The sound of a crowd gathering behind Trusty met his ears in between the baby's screams.

"I can't go to no small jail cell," O'Connor said.

Trusty took another step forward, calculating where to shoot the man if he had to and miss the baby. But if he dropped O'Connor, he would drop the baby.

O'Connor nodded. "Here take her." He reached the baby out to Trusty.

Trusty opened his left arm and held the gun on O'Connor as he scooped the wiggling blanket into his grasp. Once she was fully in his arms, he stepped back a couple of feet.

The steps gave O'Connor time to pull a derringer out of his pants pocket. Without saying another word, he pointed the .22 at his temple and pulled the trigger. The pop made the baby jump, and Trusty instinctively pulled her closer to him as he watched Gladdy O'Connor crumble to the ground, dead before he hit it, the .22 bullet still rattling inside his head, destroying his brain and any hope for life as it went.

Trusty exhaled, loosened his grip on the baby, and holstered his Colt.

She stopped crying as Trusty pulled the blanket away from her face. A mix of his blood and Jessica's stared back at him, her face red, tear-stained, and afraid. Blond hair, blue eyes, and round cheeks that looked like her mother's.

Now what the hell am I going to do? Trusty thought but didn't say. He pulled the baby closer to him and hugged her as tight as he could. "Hello," he said. It was then that he realized he didn't know the girl's name.

The girl stared back at Trusty, then touched his face with her thick little fingers, then smiled.

Trusty shook his head, then turned to go find Marshal Delaney. He pushed through the crowd, holding the baby, leaving Gladdy O'Connor's dead body behind, and headed back to the hotel.

He met Delaney halfway there, running until he saw Trusty, with a panicked look on his face. "There you are," he said, coming to a stop in front of Trusty. "You found the baby. Good."

"O'Connor's dead. Shot himself as I took the baby. I think the threat of jail terrified him. Where's Marberry?"

Delaney sucked in a deep breath and said, "He's locked up in the hotel."

"He?"

"Yes. She's gone. His wife is gone."

"What do you mean she's gone?"

"When you took off after the baby I joined you for a few steps, then I realized I couldn't help. He took the baby for Christ's sake. I have children. It was my instinct to go after him, too. When I turned back around, the missus Marberry, she was gone. The mister was easy to catch. He's not much of a runner. I've lost her. She was gone."

"There's still a bounty on my head as long as there is a Marberry free and able to see it through."

"I know. I'm sorry. You can't be sure that she's that kind of woman. That she wants you dead like her husband did."

"I hope not."

"I'll make this right. We'll find her. I promise. If it's the last thing I do." Delaney looked stricken. He sighed and looked at the baby. "What are you going to do with her?"

"I don't know," Trusty said. "I don't even know her name." He pulled the baby's head closer to his chest, then looked out into the crowd, searching for a familiar face, but he didn't see anyone he recognized. Delaney didn't know the Marberrys like he did. Something told him that Matilda Marberry was just as vengeful as her husband. Maybe more.

St. Louis, Missouri, January 1889

Trusty tied Buddy to the hitching post, then walked up to the kitchen door and knocked. The screen door was locked, and the door was closed. Cold wind howled around him, but he was warmed by the thickness of his buffalo coat and the baby girl pulled tight to him, wrapped in the blanket Brazos Joe's wife had made for him. Footsteps approached, and Fanny, the kitchen girl he'd met the last time he had been at Madame Duchamp's house, opened the door and stared at him. It took her a second to recognize Trusty. Once she did, her eyes fell to the baby. "Well, ain't you a sight, Sam Dawson. What you got there?"

"Can I come in?" Trusty asked.

"Of course, you can." Fanny opened the door and urged him inside, out of the cold.

Trusty stopped and Fanny closed the door behind him. The warmth of the kitchen greeted him, as did the smell of baking bread and Kabbie Mae's yellowed eyes. The old Negro woman sat next to the oven staring blankly at the door.

"I know that's our Sam," Kabbie Mae said, with a smile growing on her face. She made no attempt to stand up.

"She blind now." Fanny stood in front of Trusty and peeled the blanket away so she could see the baby girl's face. "What have you got here, Sam Dawson? Somethin' I never expected of you."

"Me, either," he said.

"What's her name?" Fanny asked.

Trusty hesitated. "I didn't know. My mother's name was Meredith even though everybody called her Maimie. I call the baby Merry. Seemed like the only thing to do. I loved my mother. She seems to like it, don't you, Merry?"

The baby cooed and squirmed in his arms.

Kabbie Mae was up, making her way to him when Katherine Duchamp walked into the kitchen. "What on earth is going on in here. I thought I heard . . . a baby. Sam," she said with a surprised pause. "Oh, Sam . . ."

Trusty looked at Katherine Duchamp, held her gaze, and said, "I didn't know what else to do. Where else to go. Can you help me?"

Katherine sighed, took in the sight of him and the baby, then smiled. "Of course, I can. We can. This is her home as much as it is yours."

Trusty smiled, relieved. "It's good to see you all," he said, holding on to Merry as tight as he could. "I suppose you'll be wantin' to hear my side of the story?"

"I'll put the coffee on," Fanny said.

"Let's see that baby, now," Kabbie Mae said, peeling off the blanket as gently as she could, expecting Trusty to put the child into her arms. Which he did. Merry settled into Kabbie Mae's arms like she belonged there, not afraid, or bothered by the strange new woman at all.

"Coffee sounds good," Trusty said, staring at Merry in Kabbie Mae's arms. "It sure is good to be here."

Trusty didn't have the heart to tell them, at that moment, he wasn't sure that the baby was safe. And neither was he. Not as long as there was a Marberry that was still alive and free.

Author's Note

There are several historical characters and events portrayed throughout this book, along with locations in the Dakota Territory that existed in 1888 and continue to exist. Please note that some timelines, locations, and characters have been altered in service to the story. While it is always my intention to be as historically accurate as possible when I write a novel, one of the joys of writing and reading fiction is delving into a reality that might be a little different from what really exists. Any research mistakes are my own.

TURN THE PAGE FOR AN EXCITING PREVIEW!

**First in a brand-new series from Spur Award–
winning author Larry D. Sweazy,
a lawman's grave mistake sends him gunning for
justice against a gang of badmen whose violent trail
of bloodshed ends at *Lost Mountain Pass* . . .**

Kosoma, Indian Territory. The outlaw Darby brothers have
been sentenced to hang until dead. Witnessing the
execution are Amelia Darby, sister of the condemned men,
as well as Deputy U.S. Marshal Sam "Trusty" Dawson
and Judge Gordon Hadesworth. After justice is served,
Trusty hits the trail, escorting the judge—and
begrudgingly, Amelia—back to Oklahoma.
Ambushed en route, the judge is murdered
and Amelia vanishes, leaving Trusty to believe she
led them into a trap for revenge.

To find Amelia, Trusty will have to put his faith in
Father Michael Darby, a fourth brother who gave up his
criminal ways to take up the cloth and collar.
Unwilling to let his sister continue to fall to the wicked
evil that claimed the rest of his family,
Michael joins the hunt for Amelia. But as their journey
turns deadlier by the day, Trusty starts to doubt that
Michael is truly on the righteous path . . .

**LOST MOUNTAIN PASS
A Trusty Dawson Deputy U.S. Marshal Western**

**BY
LARRY D. SWEAZY
Spur Award–Winning Author**

On sale now, wherever Pinnacle Books are sold.

Chapter 1

Three pair of boots burst through the gallows, toes aimed straight to the ground. The simultaneous snap of necks echoed on the wind like someone had stepped on a thick collection of brittle tree branches. In a quick last breath and the final blink of the eye, three Darby brothers swung from the gallows, two of them wet from the waist down, one staring sideways in a state of shock like he never thought he was going to die. Embarrassment and pride belonged to another world. This one was cold and harsh, awash in black-and-white judgment, law and order, and relief from the violence of angry men—if only for a moment.

Nothing moved beyond the lifeless bodies, not even a crow. Two of the shiny black birds stood atop the pitch of a nearby roof staring down at the crowd, hankering for something to steal. A few clouds lingered overhead, white, puffy, pausing to see if the truth of the human drama would finally be revealed. A baby started to cry in the distance. The piercing, uncomfortable sound of discomfort and need was quickly hushed. The townsfolk who had stood witness to the hanging needed a little time to digest the end of one life and the start of another. Madness and rage had been silenced. Peace and prosperity were at hand in Kosoma—if only for a moment. The baby wailed again, then was shushed by a solid, embarrassed hand clamping over the suckling mouth. New life could never be silenced for long, even in the shade of death, deserved or otherwise.

Murmurs started to grow in unison like an amen at the end of a long prayer. The entire town stood still, too nervous to leave, eyes shaded, directed toward the three dead Darby men, making sure the twitching and struggling was finally done and over with before they felt free to move, to breathe, to say a silent thank-you to the judge who had passed the execution order on the deserving gang of three. Regardless of what they saw, the crowd found it hard to believe that the Darby brothers, Cleatus, Horace, and Rascal—evil bullies, overbearing toughs, and unpredictable gunmen—were really dead, no longer a bother, no longer a threat to their daily comforts. The Darbys' terror had reigned for too many years to count. No one in Kosoma ever thought this day would truly come.

"Looks like my job here is done, Trusty," Eastern District of Arkansas Judge Gordon Hadesworth said. The judge held jurisdiction in Indian Territory along with Isaac Parker in the Western District. Hadesworth was a stately-looking gentleman with a well-trimmed goatee, bleached white by age, and wore a fancy dark blue suit that, like all of his suits, had been shipped to him directly from New York City by the tailors of his favor, Brooks Brothers. A lifetime spent poring over law books had left the elderly man stiff, arthritic, and hunched over; straight and upright he would have been as tall as an October cornstalk. A walking cane, carved from oak with a highly polished brass lion's head that served as the handle, helped keep the judge vertical and moving forward. The educated man's icy gray eyes stared forward at the gallows and bore no concern for the dead; their souls and their legacy were no longer his worry. The law had executed its judgment and it had been carried out to the fullest extent. Some scoundrels deserved to die because of the foul deeds they had committed. Judge Hadesworth made it clear to anyone within earshot that he was not in the salvation business.

"I suppose you'll be wantin' a bite of dinner before we start out toward Muskogee?" Deputy U.S. Marshal Sam Dawson—often referred to as "Trusty," by judges and outlaws alike—said.

Trusty didn't much care for the moniker folks called him by, but there wasn't much he could do about it. He couldn't argue against the reputation that he was reliable and trustworthy. Those were born traits, along with good eyesight when it came to pulling a trigger, and had got him out of more jams and scrapes than he cared to admit. Besides, he'd been called worse things than Trusty by men far more powerful than Judge Hadesworth. There were worse things that he'd had to force himself to live with.

Trusty stood stiff next to the judge, a good three inches taller and straighter in physical form than the jurist. The extra height gave Trusty the advantage of wide sight, allowing him to survey a crowd for any apparent or rising threat. The Darbys had their fair share of supporters in

Kosoma. A gang like them had deep roots in the town and in Indian Territory, even though the majority of townsfolk looked to be relieved by their deaths.

The Darbys' demise had been a long time coming. The blood and carnage they'd left behind in their wake was the stuff made of fireside stories, some true, some not, but real enough and valid enough to give Trusty reason to be suspicious of every man who itched the back of his neck or reached inside of his coat for a toothpick. The last straw had come when the three brothers had killed a beloved storekeeper in cold blood on a sunny day, in the middle of the town square—with no regard to the law or the man's right to live peacefully. No one claimed to know what had started the ill-fated confrontation, but even the most silent of citizens spoke up and demanded that something finally be done about the Darbys' lack of respect for life once and for all. Judge Hadesworth's appearance was called for a day later after a reluctant sheriff overpowered the trio and locked them up. The wounds were still raw, but Trusty hoped that the dangle of toes would put an end to the Darby troubles in Kosoma once and for all.

"Between you and me, Trusty, I'd just as soon get out of this stinking town as quick as possible," the judge said, lowering his voice so no one could hear, or take offense, to his comment.

Trusty nodded in agreement. The spring day was cool, and he wore a long coat over his utilitarian canvas pants and blue cotton shirt, concealing an 1880 Colt Single-Action, outfitted with custom-carved ivory handle grips that had come as a gift from his captain when he'd separated from the U.S. Army. His military days were well behind him, but he still wore the dark blue felt Cavalry

Stetson, only without the customary ropes, braids, and accoutrements that came from being active-duty army. Trusty had missed out on the War Between the States, being a child when that war had been waged. A Winchester '73 was loosely strapped to his left side, also hidden by the coat but always close to his touch. He was confident that the two weapons, along with his skills with them, could get him and the judge out of any trouble that might show itself.

"Suits me," he said to Judge Hadesworth. "Let's wait until the crowd starts moving out before we head to the hotel to get your things."

"If I never have to come back to Kosoma again it will be too soon," the judge said. "But something tells me that I will have to return sooner rather than later. It takes weeks to rid myself of the smell."

Kosoma meant "place of stinking water" in the Choctaw language. There were myriad bubbling, steaming springs fingering off the Kiamichi River, and they were all thick with putrid sulfur. Not even the smell of opportunity provided by the railroad, one of the first to get a land grant through Indian Territory more than ten years prior, could vanquish the residue of the springs from the senses or threads of the cleanest man's clothes. The St. Louis–San Francisco Railroad, referred to as the "Frisco," had built a rail line, completed in 1887, running from the north to the south, straight through the Choctaw Nation, connecting Fort Smith with Paris, Texas. Kosoma was perfectly located to capitalize on the rail line, smell or no smell, or the fact that it sat in the middle of Choctaw land. The future had been arriving every day with trainloads of Easterners, opportunity hunters, thieves, and speculators all hedging for a spot at the opening of Indian Territory land a year off, now that the Springer Amendment had passed through Congress. New ideas, the promise of change, and redskin conflict hung in the air alongside the pungent air. Most folks who had lived in Kosoma for any length of time were opposed to any kind of change—with the exception of exterminating toughs like the Darby brothers.

Trusty figured he hadn't been in town long enough to reach the point of immunity to the smell by any of his senses and had no intention of staying any longer than necessary. He was relieved to hear that the judge wanted to leave town immediately. "Not one of the nicer places I've ever been either."

The judge smiled, waiting for Trusty to lead him out of the crowd. "Not from the stories I've heard tell. There's a line of whorehouses and saloons from San Antonio to Abilene that tell of your exploits."

They had stood far enough from the gallows to make a quick escape if the need arose, but there was still a gathering of people milling about around them. More in front than behind. Main Street and arranged safety were just around the corner in an empty bank vault. Trusty didn't like that plan, but he was pretty certain that any threat would come from up close, or the rooftops overlooking the execution square. For now, everything was clear, but that didn't stop him from scanning the crowd like a scout expecting to find an ambush. His army training was never far away.

"You'd think a judge would be immune to embellishments and hearsay," Trusty said.

"We like rumor and gossip as much as any other man. Besides, you've a reputation to uphold. I am only endorsing your résumé and contributing to the myth that you are in the process of building, as well as living vicariously through your exploits. I am a bit jealous." The judge nudged Trusty with his elbow, then offered a smile to prove he was serious.

Trusty's face flushed red. There was no question that he had always liked the company of women and had a taste for good whiskey, but there was more to his past adventures than the judge knew or that Trusty wanted to share. He had only loved one woman in all of his life, and that ill-fated love had left him broken and bothered, in need of a salve that could never heal the wound—if he ever found it. He avoided touching that hurt, or thinking about that lost love, as much as possible. "Ain't nothin' but tales about me anyways, Judge. The past is the past. I've become a reformed man."

"You mean you've found Jesus?"

"Not in any of the places I've been lately. 'Course I ain't been lookin' much for Him neither. I was still an energetic boy after I left the army, before I took up the law as my calling. Besides, a woman tends to complicate a man's life, at least *this* man's life. I've always got some place to go, a judge to protect, a scoundrel to round up; you know, chasin' trouble is what I like to do best. It's been my experience that a fine woman likes to settle, live in a nice house, tie a man down, and extend roots into hard ground. I like to ride, see the country, have an adventure or two, while I still can. I'm not the marrying kind, Judge, simple as that." Trusty tapped the Deputy U.S. Marshal's badge on his chest with his stubby trigger finger and smiled. "This is all of the commitment I need these days."

"You just keep thinking that, Trusty, and we'll all have

plenty to talk about for a long time to come. But I'll offer you some advice if you'll have it."

"I'm always open to listening to a man of your stature and education about the nature of life."

"Well," Judge Hadesworth said, "look at me standing here next to you without Mrs. Hadesworth in sight. She's most likely back in Muskogee on another shopping excursion of one kind or another, keeping the fire lit for my return. It's been that way for nigh on forty-one years. I ride the circuit and she is waiting at home keeping things nice and warm. Distance does a marriage good, Trusty. It always has mine. The return is a sweet and welcoming adventure worth traversing the drudgeries of humanity for. Even at my age, if you're wondering."

"I wasn't. But I'll take your advice under advisement, Judge. Not that I'll heed to it, mind you. My duties on the trail are longer and less predictable than yours, and I do enjoy a dose of variety in my life."

"Me too," the gray-haired man said with a wink and another elbow nudge. "Me too."

Trusty laughed uncomfortably. "Let's get your belongin's from the hotel and dust our way out of here before the sun starts to dive west too fast. I'd like to get to Lost Mountain Pass before night settles in."

"Expecting trouble, Trusty?" the judge asked with a raised eyebrow.

"I'm always expectin' trouble, Judge. 'Specially after a hangin' as well-deserved as this one. I know a spot on the pass that's about as safe as I can get us for tonight," he said, looking past the judge at a flush of movement that had caught his eye.

Two men were pushing through the crowd toward them,

one as big as a bull, the other short and bulky as a boxer, reaching inside his duster for something that Trusty could only imagine to be a gun of some kind. "Anybody plottin' trouble for us will be waiting for us on the road south. I aim to head north, take a night in the pass to wait them out, then circle around south Kosoma from the west, and get you home as soon as possible."

Judge Hadesworth nodded with approval. "I like how you think, Trusty." He started to walk toward Main Street, back to the hotel.

The sight of the men heading toward them caused Trusty to plant his feet and extend a hand to impede Judge Hadesworth's forward motion. "Stop," Trusty said in a low, "don't argue with me" command.

The hunched man ceased to move immediately, silencing the click of his cane; even the old man's breath restrained itself, hidden, pulled inside himself. A serious look fell over both men's faces. Trusty had been responsible for the judge's life on more than one occasion—ten, as a matter of count—and the two men were past developing a shorthand and wordless manner in sight of a threat. The judge, always happy and accustomed to being in the lead, submitted to Trusty's instinct and drew back without question.

Trusty reached inside his coat to grip the Colt. The holster was unhinged and a cartridge sat in the chamber, ready to be called into action with a quick pull of the trigger. One yank and the pistol would be let loose into the world to prove its purpose: protect and kill.

The two unknown men continued their hard walk toward the judge and the deputy in step, on a mission, anger hanging on their faces as apparent as an OPEN sign at a barbershop. The crowd parted, pushed aside by the apparent suggestion of confrontation. Murmurs of acceptance and relief from the hanging quickly turned to fearful chirps, gasps, followed by an uneasy silence. All eyes were on the four men.

Trusty edged around the judge so the adjudicator was shielded from the coming threat as completely as possible, then he reformulated his escape plan. This one called for the swift death of the two approaching men. Wounding them would not do. Any threat to a federal judge's life had to be dealt with in the most severe terms. Trusty pictured two shots to the heart, if possible. If those shots weren't clear, then the target would shift to just above the bridge of the nose, square between the eyes—a head shot meant to stop both men in their tracks. Trusty and the judge would flee to safety before both bodies hit the ground. Refuge would then be taken in the bank vault in case there were more than two men—because there were always more than two. Always.

The Colt felt cold and ready as all of the sound drained from Trusty's ears. No distractions. No focus on anything but the approaching threat. His heart beat as steadily as if he were napping. Sweat retreated and no force of blood rushed through his veins. He was as calm and ready as the judge had been when he'd read the Darby brothers' verdict. Killing and protecting came as easily to Trusty as it did to the Colt in his grip. The army had given him license to do deeds untoward and inhumane that came natural to him but shouldn't have. Men that deserved to die did not haunt his dreams.

The boxer and most serious looking of the two men— the one who had reached inside his duster—made eye contact with Trusty, then glanced away and let his hands fall clear, out into the open so it was possible to see that they were empty. That did not give Trusty cause or a reason to relax his stance. Both men were heavily armed with two six-shooters, and probably more by the sound of the iron *clank* accompanying their strides and the determined look in their eyes. Revenge never wore a mask.

The crowd remained frozen in place. No one said anything out loud, or called the men by name, but there was wonder in the air. Wonder if these men had come to settle a score for the hanging of the Darby gang. Such a thing had been as expected as the sun arching across the perfect blue spring sky.

The other man—the bull—eyed Trusty, too, and kept walking forward, not wavering his route one inch. If the bull kept moving, one or two of the men would have to step out of the way. Trusty was firmly planted, and Judge Hadesworth stood as erect as an ancient oak could, refusing to sway in the wind, leaning forward on the cane instead of backward in retreat. Intimidation was something the judge reacted to. Gordon Hadesworth didn't have the capability to show fear. That had been lost a long time ago.

The two men veered at the last second, cutting past Trusty and the judge, pushing a bookish-looking man out of the way like angry rats sweeping past a meek mouse. They said nothing, but kept walking, determined in one way or the other to be done with the hanging.

All Trusty could do was watch the men disappear and hope that this would be the last time he ever saw them. "Come on, Judge," he said. "It's past time we put this dot on the map behind us." He didn't relax his grip on the Colt until the two men had vanished around the corner and the crowd sighed in relief.

Trusty took a last look at the three dead Darby brothers, stiff as planks now, swaying in the wind, starting to attract blowflies. Hangings and their aftermath had always unsettled Trusty, and this one was no exception.

Chapter 2

There were two hotels in Kosoma with the promise of a third on the horizon. One, the Margate, was little more than a flophouse across the street from the train depot. The other, the Hobart House Hotel, was a three-story building with a fancy redbrick façade that aspired to be grand, but failed in the attempt from a lack of imagination, materials, or enough investors to see the original vision brought to fruition. The building looked hastily thrown together because it had been. The inside was as bland and disappointing as the outside, offering little in atmosphere or comfort. All of the carpets were drab, the walls bare of original paintings, and the sour eggy smell from the outside had taken up residence inside the fabric of everything that graced the inside of the hotel. It was rare that Trusty spent time on a soft feather bed, but he had come to enjoy his stays in hotels around Indian Territory and out of it. But the beds in the Hobart House Hotel were as hard and bumpy as the jagged rocks in the Osage lands and just as barren. One more reason to get out of town. Sleeping on the ground offered more comfort and relief than the Hobart House mattresses.

The judge's room was on the first floor. He had opted for a single bed instead of what surely would be a disappointing presidential suite on the third floor at Trusty's urging. Upper rooms offered fewer escape routes. Judge Hadesworth wasn't a fussy man, and Trusty was glad about that. He shared the adjoining room, which allowed him access to the judge at all hours of the night; it turned out that was as much a mistake as staying in the Hobart House in the first place. Gordon Hadesworth was a world-class snorer. Mrs. Hadesworth probably looked forward to the nights the judge was out of town. She was probably catching up on sleep instead of the shopping excursion the judge had imagined.

"I've already packed most everything," the judge said. "Why don't you go on and get the horses ready, and I'll meet you at the livery."

"Not going to happen, Judge. I'll wait."

Hadesworth took a deep breath, puffed up his chest the best he could, and started to protest, but suddenly retreated with a shake of his head. "Do you ever relax?"

"Of course, I relax. We talked about blowin' off steam earlier. I'll get to that when the time is right. But that's not a concern at the moment. We need to get on the trail. I don't like the feeling in this town. The voice in the back of my head says I need to get you out of here as soon as possible. Those two toughs made a big show of themselves for a reason. I don't know what that reason was, or is, but I think if we stick around here long enough, we'll find out."

"Those two men in the crowd really set off your alarms, didn't they? They looked like typical troublemakers to me."

"They *did* set me off."

"You know them?"

"Nope. Never seen either one of them before, but I know their type. They looked like hired men to me."

"It's a little brazen for assassins to show themselves in broad daylight, don't you think?"

"Maybe. But I'd rather overreact than not react at all. You're not leaving my sight unless you make a demand of it. I'm not going to rest comfortably until I deposit you on your doorstep to Mrs. Hadesworth. Then she can look after your every move, and I'll go about relaxin' the best I can. There's a fine blonde in Muskogee I plan on callin' on when I get there. Does that strategy suit your myth-making?"

"It does, though I'd require a little more detail."

"You'll have to use that imagination of yours while we travel."

"Well, in that case, I do require use of the toilet."

"You can have all of the privacy you need. I'll wait."

The judge stood at the entrance of the livery, well within Trusty's sight, regaling a Mexican groomer with a long, drawn-out story while Trusty cinched the saddle on his horse. He rode a roan gelding that he'd never got around to naming. He called the horse *Horse*, and the easygoing beast didn't seem to mind the name at all. The two of them had traveled a lot of miles together, knew each other pretty well, but Trusty wasn't one to hold a high affection for any animal on a long-term basis. There was a job to do and that was that. Attachments were a danger to the job. The escapade with his object of lost love had taught him that.

The past held a stink to it that could outlive the current smell in Kosoma.

He kept one ear cocked toward the front of the livery, and looked toward the judge every second or two, like a wary bird, hoping the judge was doing the same thing. But at the moment, almost like every other moment, Gordon Hadesworth didn't seem ruffled or threatened at all. He acted normal, invincible, unconcerned about any enemies that might be lurking around the corner.

"I was hoping I would find you here."

The voice was a young female. She startled Trusty. He jumped and reached for his sidearm at the same time. The Winchester had already been packed into the scabbard. Trusty hadn't heard anyone come up behind him, which concerned him. Letting your guard down for one second on a hanging day could get you and your charge killed, and he knew it.

"I'm sorry, ma'am, do I know you?" he said, letting his hand fall away from the Colt.

She shook her head. "No, sir, you do not." She looked more like a girl than a woman. Lucky to be twenty years old at best, but probably younger, truth be told. Dressed in a black Bolero coat closed up tight at the neck, and a long skirt, deep black, too, parts of it matte, other parts shiny, sewn in a tight horizontal pattern, along with traveling boots and a fancy black bonnet with dangling chin straps. Her face was hard set and she bore a crow-like nose, eyes the color of granite, and dark brunette hair pulled back and swept up under the bonnet—all of which were stacked up on a skinny, unfulfilled body. There was nothing about the girl that Trusty found attractive at all. She instantly annoyed him, considering her stealthy skills and the darkness she carried with her.

The livery was quiet, not much going on. It was just the two of them inside as far as Trusty knew. A few stalls over, a horse snorted, then took a healthy piss. The judge was fully engaged with the groomer and hadn't noticed the woman talking to Trusty or didn't care.

"I understand that you are on your way to Muskogee?" the girl said.

"Yes, ma'am, that would be correct. How did you come upon that knowledge?"

"There are few secrets in this town, though there should be."

"That didn't answer my question," he said. This bit of information confirmed that his plan to exit Kosoma to the north and make his way through Lost Mountain Pass was necessary.

"I would like to secure passage in your company."

Trusty wiped his hands. "I'm sorry, ma'am, I'm a Deputy U.S. Marshal, not an escort. You'll need to make other arrangements. I don't hire out."

"Are you not Trusty Dawson?"

He flinched at the nickname. "I am. Sure as it's daylight, I am." He thought about telling the woman that his real name was Samuel but let that thought slide away. Something told him not to get too familiar with this one. She looked like she could peck his eyes out.

"Most folks call you Trusty, and that is the only reason why I have sought you out. Your reputation as a drinker and a womanizer is overridden by the fact that your gun skills are rumored to be superb, the best in the Territory from what I understand. You have never lost a charge under your care, and a man to be reckoned with by the worst of the worst. It is a fine reputation you carry, and I need protection, Deputy, or I will surely not make it out of Kosoma alive."

"Your life's in danger? How is that, ma'am?" He stepped away from Horse, his attention fully on the woman now.

She stared at Trusty like he had just asked the stupidest question in the world. "Fine. This was a waste of my time, just as I suspected it would be," she said, spinning in perfect balance on the heels of her polished black boots with the intention of stalking off. "My blood is on your hands, Deputy. Remember I said that."

By the time Trusty caught up with the girl, she had hurried off twenty feet away from him, nearly to the barn's rear double doors that stood wide open. A slight breeze pushed stinky air through the barn, mixing with the smell of animal excrements and sour straw. He really wanted to get the hell out of Kosoma.

"Wait," Trusty said, catching up to the girl. He grabbed her arm and brought her to an unexpected stop. "There's no need to go gettin' all haughty. Just tell me what's going on. If you're in trouble, that's another thing entirely. I'll help you if I can."

With a glare that cut through her tear-filled eyes, she said, "It's too late. I might as well succumb to my fate. You were my last hope. I will approach this journey on my own and take my chances, thank you very much."

Maybe it was the tears in her once rock-hard eyes, the vulnerability now apparent, but her features had softened. There was a beauty to her that Trusty had failed to initially notice, had overlooked at first glance. She was not the kind of woman he'd consider pursuing, but she wasn't such an ugly little bird either. Wearing a black coat and skirt didn't help her none. Her skin was white as paste, and it looked like it would crack if anyone dared to touch it.

"Let's start over," Trusty said. "What's your name, ma'am?" he asked in the softest, kindest voice he could muster.

"Amelia. Amelia Darby." She watched Trusty's reaction closely, surely accustomed to a negative response. "Cleatus was my brother. Horace and Rascal too. And just because I'm of the same blood as those three, people think I'm a killer, a thief, and a liar too. Folks around town think all us Darbys are meaner than snakes and not fit to walk on this earth. That I'm just like them. I guess I can't blame them. The three boys robbed anyone with a nickel in their pocket, and when they finally took to killing, they did it like it was fun and games with no consequences. Old Man Robinson, the one they hanged for, was target practice. They emptied their guns on him long after he was dead. Why should I be surprised, then, that everyone, and probably you, think I'm no better than them? I'll never get a fair chance in this town, and most likely this Territory. If I had the money to get myself to California, that's exactly what I'd do."

Trusty let his hand slide away from Amelia's arm. "I'm sorry, I had no idea who you were."

"How could you; you're not from these parts."

"I'll talk to the sheriff, see about gettin' you some protection. Maybe it'd be best to just let things settle down a bit before you go makin' a rash decision like leavin' town."

"I have had pig's blood thrown on my porch. Service refused me at the mercantile. No one will extend credit to me or hire out my skills as a milliner. I am nearly broke, sir, left with no kin to fall back on or any prospects for the future in this town other than the certainty of my death.

Just this morning, someone fired a gunshot through my front window. It was only a matter of luck that I was not walking through the front room, or I would be soon lying in a coffin in Poor Man's Hill alongside my brothers. I fear for my life, Deputy, surely you must understand that."

"There's no family left to help you out?"

"None that can help me. My brothers made sure that all of our ties within a hundred miles were broken beyond repair. I am alone in this world, sir, with no one to help me but you."

Trusty shifted uncomfortably. "How do I know that this isn't some kind of ploy to exact revenge on the judge for renderin' a well-deserved death sentence on your brothers, ma'am? How do I know that you don't have a plot to kill him? I'm sorry to say so, ma'am, but I have to consider such a thing. The judge is my responsibility. I've taken an oath to give my life for his if it comes to that. You sure don't look like no killer to me, but I've seen some real sweet ones, let me tell you, in my line of work."

Amelia Darby stared at Trusty with her deep gray eyes, unflinching. She had wiped away her tears and it was like they had never existed in the first place. "I would expect that you would think such a thing. Three things should be reason enough to believe me, Deputy. One. I have never hurt a fly. Never. You can ask anyone in this town. I, too, have worked at maintaining my character, for all of the good it's done me. Two. I am the last of the Darbys in Kosoma. When I am gone, there will be no legacy for anyone to shoulder, and all of my family's debts will be paid in full. I have made sure of that, which is why I have little money left. The Darbys will be a bad memory, quickly forgotten, and unknown to the greedy hordes that are filling the town and the territory in search of their fortunes. Three. I hated my brothers and what they stood for. They deserved to hang. They were cold-blooded killers and earned their punishments. They deserved what they got in the end. I have no mind for revenge, no need to set the record straight by bringing any harm to Judge Hadesworth. My only desire is to start a new life as far away from Kosoma as possible. It's that simple, Deputy. I long to open a milliner's shop in Muskogee or thereabouts. It is my dream, and I aim to fulfill it while I can still breathe and have the wherewithal to accomplish such a thing. That is my story and there is nothing I can add, other than the guarantee of my word that I mean no one any harm, especially the judge. You can take it or leave it. My fate is in your hands."

Trusty took a deep breath and stared up at the rafters. "I'll have to clear it with the judge, you understand."

"No need," Amelia said, "I already have."

St. Louis, Missouri, Summer 1865

Iron clanked against iron as regular as the tick of a clock. Only the sound was no tick. It was a hard slam fueled by demand, necessity, and an underlying rage that always seemed to exist in the palms of seven-year-old Sam Dawson's father's massive hands. The hard hit of a cross-peen hammer against soft red iron was powered by muscles developed from years of blacksmith work and the determination to bend the ore into something useful, tools or weapons, never decorations. Markum Dawson saw little difference between a boy and a piece of metal that needed transformed into something useful. It didn't matter by what method—heating, holding, hitting, or shaping. Flesh or steel bent the same way as far as Markum was concerned.

Once the blacksmith decided on the creation of something, he persisted until whatever it was came into being on his American wrought anvil. Sam wondered sometimes if his father wanted to set his head on the bench, take his hammer to it, and fashion a completely new person out of his skull and the brain inside it.

The shop was the place of his boyhood. The dim sooty cave of a worn slat barn where he had been forced to apprentice as a blacksmith whether he wanted to or not. That had been his plight as an only child. The last thing that Sam wanted to be when he grew up was a blacksmith. He didn't want to be anything like his father. But he had no choice. Sam was trapped in his father's world. He couldn't escape if he wanted to. Not at seven, or seventy, if he could even consider such a thing.

"What are you doin' just standing there, boy? Go fetch a bucket of cold water. We got rods to cool and more work to get to before the sun starts to set. Did you get your ma her breakfast before you left her this morning?"

His father had a booming voice that echoed inside Sam's head like a bullet looking for a place to exit. Markum Dawson was a towering behemoth of a man, wide in the shoulders, thick arms rippled from his daily work, his belly round from his nightly consumption of beer and food. "Big as an ox" didn't suffice as a description, but that was always what came to Sam's thinking when he pictured his father in his mind or had to face him. Sam had always thought his father looked like a giant beast of burden built of iron muscles and a heart made of steel. There was nothing small about Sam's father. His hands were as big as black skillets, and his eyes were always wide open, making them seem larger than normal. Even now, there was no way to know what color his father's eyes were; blue was the assumption, but everything in the shop was tinged with soot. Markum's face was always smudged black, mixed with sweat; even with a good bath it was hard to get off. He always looked overbaked, nearly burnt to a crisp, as dark as the footman on a fancy coach. Blacksmithing had left Markum Dawson stained in more ways than one.

"Yes, sir," Sam said. He lowered his head. His mother had suffered from consumption from the time Sam could remember. She was Mamie to everyone who knew her, but Meredith to her parents and the church. A bony woman, short in stature but tall in spirit, she was exactly the opposite of her husband: soft, pliable, comforting. She fought her way through every day, in the shadow of the blacksmith shop and the life it provided, doing her best to obey and serve her husband, even though she could barely stand to breathe the smoky fumes left in the big man's wake. As much as Sam was a bag of failure made of flesh and bones according to his father, Sam was a rare jewel in his mother's eyes. He was her one great contribution to the world, even though birthing him had nearly killed her. "She said she wasn't hungry, so I left the bowl of porridge on the table next to her bed," he said.

Markum Dawson stopped hammering and shot the boy an angry look. "Can't you do anything right?" He shook his head, then turned away from Sam. "I told you to make sure she ate something. She's never hungry."

"Sorry," Sam mumbled. He moved toward the door, saw his failure as a way to escape the shop.

"You best get to work and start turning those hanger eyes. I need a dozen of them."

Sam stopped, knew it was useless to go any farther,

nodded, and said, "Yes, sir," then grabbed up an iron rod with a pair of oversized pliers out of a crate next to the blazing forge. He was angry, upset at being yelled at one more time, and didn't measure the rod. He jammed the rod into the fire until it glowed red, then hurried it to the anvil and started hammering the bend.

"You've got a long heat," Markum yelled. "You're making more work for yourself and weakening the iron. Sizzle that damn rod and do another one like I've showed you a thousand times over."

Sam kept on hammering, bending the rod until it snapped, ruining it, at least for the hanger it was intended for, and said to himself: *I'll show you. One of these days, I'll show you that I can do everything right. I won't give up until I do. You wait and see.*

Kosoma, Indian Territory, May 1888

They rode toward the end of town, three horses abreast, Amelia Darby in the middle between Trusty and Judge Hadesworth. A few white people stopped on the boardwalks and glared at the trio. Indians, mostly Choctaws, dressed from the same shops that had denied Amelia credit, kept on walking without notice or care about the three riders. Some of those that took notice turned their backs, shunning Amelia Darby purposefully, leaving no question to what their hateful intention was. The sight of such disregard for the woman fortified Amelia's story and made it seem true. Trusty was relieved more than he was appalled by the shuns even though he didn't say so. He remained quiet, still uneasy about the new alliance and responsibility for the woman. There hadn't been a chance to ask the judge when he had given Amelia Darby permission to ride with them, but that would come at the first chance. The two of them, the old man and young woman, seemed to have an easy, warm rapport and that concerned Trusty. Something he'd have to keep an eye on. He still wasn't completely convinced that the Darby girl wasn't up to something.

Amelia stared straight ahead, her eyes set on the horizon, not allowing one gaze that fell across her face to dent her attitude or touch her heart. At least that was what she showed on the outside from her reaction to the folks on the boardwalk. Trusty knew her insides were another matter from the conversation they'd had inside the livery. The shunning would be another wound, a final nail in her reasoning to flee the town. *Good riddance*, Trusty imagined her saying inside her head. Good riddance. All the while her eyes remained cold as January icicles.

Trusty shifted the Winchester rifle that lay comfortably across his lap, and one hand dangled inches from his Colt, signaling to those who stood in watch that Amelia was under his protection. Horse had his ears erect, alert, sensing the tension in the air. One ear was white, the other red, or strawberry roan, depending on who was doing the describing. Trusty liked to think Horse's ear was red. Like a sunset falling behind a snow-covered mountain. Strawberry sounded sissified, and there was nothing about Horse that suggested he *was* sissified in any way.

Just as they were about to cross the last street before leaving Kosoma, a wagon passed in front of them, causing all three horses to come to a stop and wait. Trusty surveyed the crowd on both sides of the street, searching for the two men—the bulldog and the boxer—that he had seen earlier, but there was no sign of them or any other outward-looking toughs. Just normal folks in town for the hanging, making a trip out of it, a reason to shop and stock up before heading home.

The wagon was loaded with the Darby brothers' coffins, heading toward a cemetery on the opposite end of town, the place Amelia had called Poor Man's Hill. There was no parade of mourners following along with the wagon. The preacher sat shotgun, next to a glum Teamster, both of them stiff and on tenterhooks as if they expected something to happen at any second. They weren't alone. Trusty had an itch in his trigger finger, a sure sign that trouble was lurking about.

Judge Hadesworth leaned toward Amelia in his comfortable, well-worn saddle. "You sure you don't want to attend the funeral of your brothers, Miss Darby?"

"No, sir. I have no more tears left to shed for those three. Rascal held the greatest amount of promise and I will miss him the most. But in the end, his deeds were influenced by the other two, competing to be noticed and accepted, so they wouldn't treat him as a dunce or a punching bag. It never happened. Rascal died trying to impress Cleatus and Horace. Whatever awaits them on the other side of this life will be no different, I imagine. If there is such a thing."

"You are not a believer, then?" the judge asked.

Amelia turned her attention away from the coffins and stared Judge Hadesworth directly in the eye. "Let's just say I have questions. And you, Judge?"

Trusty stayed out of the conversation, his eyes darting to the rooftops and to the shadows of the alleyway that cut alongside a mercantile and an empty storefront with a FOR RENT sign in the front window. He felt the same tension in the air Horse did. The air smelled faintly of gunpowder and lead, but that could have been his imagination playing tricks on him, all things considered.

"My father was a Methodist minister," the judge continued. "I was raised in the ways of the Lord. But I am not one to proselytize, so you have no need to worry of my pestering you for a conversion or deep conversation based on verses put to memory as a child."

Trusty remained stiff in his saddle, listening to a story he'd heard from the judge about ten times over. One way or the other the Lord always worked His way into a conversation with the judge—whether He was welcome or not.

"Being pestered by you is the least of my worries on this journey, Judge Hadesworth," Amelia said. "I'm just grateful to be in your company and have the protection of Trusty Dawson. I fear I wouldn't have made it out of this town alive." She turned her attention to the wagon and the coffins as it moved on and cleared her throat. Trusty thought her eyes were glazed with a tear or two, but he couldn't be sure. It could have been the dust raised by the wagon and team of bored horses that were pulling it.

A wavering cloud of flies chased after the makeshift hearse, drawn by the smell of death and the opportunity that three rotting human bodies provided. The dead brothers were a jackpot of food and a virgin breeding ground. Flies obviously knew a boomtown when they saw it, too.

"Your decision is final then, ma'am?" Trusty asked. "You're sure you want to leave today and not pay your respects to your brothers?"

"Yes, Trusty, my decision is final. The sooner I'm out of this town, the sooner my new life begins." Amelia started to nicker her horse, a skinny chestnut mare that needed a good brushing, but the judge reached over and grabbed her by the arm in a gentle, but forceful way to stop her from moving on.

"I understand your reluctance, Miss Darby," Judge Hadesworth said, "but I would implore you to reconsider your decision. Regret adds to the venom of bitterness at unknown and unwelcome times. Those men are your brothers. Blood kin. No matter their vile actions on this good earth, you need to pay your respects. It is not our burden to open or close St. Peter's Gates, and I would suggest that not making a condemnation might lighten your ride, and the rest of your own journey going forward. Leave your anger and grief in Kosoma where it belongs instead of carrying it with you wherever you go."

Something flickered across Amelia's face that Trusty couldn't read. At first he thought she was angry, enraged by the judge's touch and suggestion, but the harsh look in her eyes melted away into something else. Surrender or admiration, he wasn't sure which it was. A confusing mix, at least to Trusty, if there was one.

"Your years as a litigator have served you well, Judge Hadesworth," Amelia said. "I suppose you are right. I owe it to my brothers and my parents, may they rest in peace, to attend their funeral. Especially Rascal's. We were friends once, along with being brother and sister. He looked out for me when he could, when he still had a pinch of goodness on the surface of his heart." With that she gently urged her skinny horse forward, taking lead of the trio, following after the wagon full of coffins with her face void of any further emotion and her head down, in shame or prayer, it was hard to tell.

Trusty had no choice but to follow after Amelia Darby,

even though he was concerned about the delay in leaving town. It still stank, and something told him that the threat he'd felt earlier in the day hadn't been left behind at the hanging. The back of his neck tingled with eyes on it, even though no one seemed to be paying him any mind at all. Everyone's attention was on Amelia Darby.

Visit us online at
KensingtonBooks.com
to read more from your favorite authors,
see books by series, view reading group guides, and more.

BOOK **CLUB**
BETWEEN THE **CHAPTERS**

Visit us online for sneak peeks, exclusive giveaways,
special discounts, author content, and engaging
discussions with your fellow readers.

Betweenthechapters.net

Sign up for our newsletters and be the first to get exciting news
and announcements about your favorite authors!
Kensingtonbooks.com/newsletter